Praise for
The Daughter of Highland Hall

"In *The Daughter of Highland Hall,* Carrie Turansky sweeps readers back into the early nineteen hundreds, to the glamour of London society as well as the desperate world of those struggling to survive in London's East End. This beautiful story is filled with endearing characters who will steal your heart and surprises that will keep you engrossed until the very end."
    —MELANIE DOBSON, award-winning author of *Chateau of Secrets* and *The Courier of Caswell Hall*

"From London's East End to the royal presentation court, Carrie Turansky pulls back the curtain on Edwardian England in this sweeping new drama. *The Daughter of Highland Hall* will delight romance fans as well as those who like a peek behind the scenes into the lives of the elite and the people who serve them. A delight from the first page to the last."
    —CARLA STEWART, award-winning author of *Stardust* and *The Hatmaker's Heart*

"Giving vivid entry into an Edwardian England setting, from genteel ballrooms to the gritty streets of London's East End, author Carrie Turansky has created a cast of multilayered, delightfully written characters I found engaging from beginning to end. *The Daughter of Highland Hall* is at its heart a story of personal courage, one sure to please fans of Turansky's *The Governess of Highland Hall,* as well as readers coming fresh to the series with this book."
    —LORI BENTON, author of *Burning Sky* and *The Pursuit of Tamsen Littlejohn*

"From first line to last, *The Daughter of Highland Hall* is a sumptuous Edwardian feast, brimming with romance, history, and spiritual truths. Society and its glitter fade away as what truly matters comes into play. A delightful addition to the Edwardian Brides series!"
    —LAURA FRANTZ, author of *Love's Fortune*

"*The Daughter of Highland Hall* sweeps readers back to historic London where a cast of endearing characters work toward a heart-stirring cause. With excitement happening both upstairs and down, this charming romance is a beautiful addition to Carrie Turansky's Edwardian Brides series and a reminder that the greatest joys can arrive in the unlikeliest of ways."

> —JOANNE BISCHOF, award-winning author of the Cadence of Grace series

"A debutante. A medical missionary. Two disparate worlds. *The Daughter of Highland Hall* celebrates God's ability to open eyes and soften hearts."

> —MONA HODGSON, author of nearly forty books for adults and children, including the Sinclair Sisters of Cripple Creek series, the Quilted Heart novellas, and *Prairie Song*

"*The Daughter of Highland Hall* is a compelling Edwardian love story that crosses class divides, where characters learn that snagging a titled and wealthy spouse is not the first concern of life. Carrie Turansky's meticulously researched and beautifully written novel lifts the heart, drawing the reader closer to Christ and reminding her of the possibilities of a faith-driven marriage. Characters that inspire readers to rekindle their romance with the Lord of life as well as with their own husband… How many books can do that?"

> —CATHY GOHLKE, Christy Award–winning author of *Promise Me This* and *Band of Sisters*

The
DAUGHTER
of
HIGHLAND
HALL

The
DAUGHTER
of
HIGHLAND HALL

EDWARDIAN BRIDES
BOOK TWO

CARRIE TURANSKY

MULTNOMAH
BOOKS

THE DAUGHTER OF HIGHLAND HALL
PUBLISHED BY MULTNOMAH BOOKS
12265 Oracle Boulevard, Suite 200
Colorado Springs, Colorado 80921

All Scripture quotations are taken from the King James Version.

The characters and events in this book are fictional, and any resemblance to actual persons or events is coincidental.

Trade Paperback ISBN 978-1-60142-498-3
eBook ISBN 978-1-60142-499-0

Copyright © 2014 by Carrie Turansky

Cover design by Kristopher K. Orr; cover photography by Mike Heath, Magnus Creative

Published in the United States by WaterBrook Multnomah, an imprint of the Crown Publishing Group, a division of Random House LLC, New York, a Penguin Random House Company.

MULTNOMAH and its mountain colophon are registered trademarks of Random House LLC.

Library of Congress Cataloging-in-Publication Data
Turansky, Carrie.
    The daughter of Highland Hall : a novel / Carrie Turansky. — First edition.
        pages cm — (Edwardian brides)
    ISBN 978-1-60142-498-3 (paperback) — ISBN 978-1-60142-499-0 (electronic) 1. Aristocracy (Social class)—Fiction. 2. Young women—Fiction. 3. Great Britain—History—Edward VII, 1901–1910—Fiction. 4. London (England)—History—20th century—Fiction. I. Title.
    PS3620.U7457D38 2014
    813'.6—dc23
                                            2014023631

Printed in the United States of America
2014—First Edition

10 9 8 7 6 5 4 3 2 1

• • •

*This book is dedicated to my daughter and son-in-law,
Melissa and Peter Morrison. Their love for each other and their
hearts to serve those who are in need is a wonderful inspiration
to me and to everyone who meets them!*

But seek ye first the kingdom of God, and his righteousness; and all these things shall be added unto you.

—MATTHEW 6:33

ONE

───•─•────────•─•───

London, England
April 1912

I f she lived to be one hundred and five, Katherine Evangeline Ramsey would never understand why every debutante must begin the London social season by curtsying to the king and queen. Of course, she was excited to be presented at court and to take part in her first season. She had looked forward to it for years, however, mastering the required skills had proven more challenging than she'd expected.

But her aunt, Lady Louisa Gatewood, insisted that was how every well-bred young lady made her debut into English society and announced she was ready for marriage. Kate certainly hoped her aunt was right. Because marriage to the right man was the only way she would gain control of her life and create a future for herself.

Pulling in a deep breath, she straightened her shoulders and prepared to practice her curtsy once more.

Mr. Philippe Rounpear, her gray-haired dancing master, lowered his bushy, silver eyebrows and pointed his white-gloved finger at Kate. "You must float over the floor like a swan gliding across a lake." He gave a firm nod. "Try again, please."

How many times was he going to make her do this? Kate stuffed down her frustration and cast a heated glance at her aunt Louisa, who sat on a high-backed chair by the piano, taking on the role of King George V.

Her aunt stiffened. "Katherine, the only way you will gain a position in society is to take your training seriously."

"I *am* taking it seriously!" The words flew from Kate's mouth before she could stop them.

"Then you must conquer these presentation formalities and do them perfectly."

Kate swallowed the sharp reply rising in her throat, tugged her skirt aside, and stepped into her next curtsy.

Mr. Rounpear's voice rang out. "No, no! You look as stiff as a broom." He crossed the oriental carpet of her cousin William Ramsey's London drawing room and tapped her left shoulder. "You must relax your posture. Think grace, think poise."

Heat flushed her face. She looked past the dancing master at her younger sister, Penny, who sat next to their aunt, pretending to be Queen Mary. Penny's eyes danced as she waited for Kate to attempt her next curtsy.

Kate narrowed her gaze at her sister. *Just wait. In two years you will be eighteen, and you'll have to prepare for your own presentation. You won't be laughing then!*

Mr. Rounpear clapped his hands. "Miss Katherine, our hour is almost over. One more time, please."

"All right." Katherine blew out a breath and tried to relax her shoulders. She would get this right or expire in the process. She had to. Her future depended on it.

Lifting her chin, she stepped to the side, then crossed one leg behind the other, and slowly sank down in front of her Aunt Louisa.

"Better." Mr. Rounpear nodded. "Not perfect, but better. Now lower your head, count to three, then rise slowly."

Katherine's legs burned as she waited and then rose.

"Now take two steps to the right, and curtsy to the queen."

Katherine glanced at Penny and took the first step, but when she took the second, her foot tangled in her skirt. She gasped and her hand shot out.

Penny smirked and covered her mouth.

Katherine swayed, struggling to recover her balance.

Mr. Rounpear scowled. "Is that how you will conduct yourself at your presentation?"

"Of course not." Kate untangled her skirt and turned toward the windows, frustration bubbling up within. This man was impossible! She would like to see him curtsy fifty times and never lose his balance.

"Face this way!"

Kate clenched her jaw and turned around.

"You must never turn your back on the royal family." He motioned toward Penny and her aunt.

"They are not the royal family, and neither are you!"

His eyes flashed, and he lifted his hand. "Very well. That will be all for today."

"Mr. Rounpear, please!" Aunt Louisa rose from her chair. "There's no need to cut the lesson short."

"It appears your niece is tired, and that has made her irritable."

"But Katherine's presentation is Friday."

"Yes, the time is short." The dancing instructor lowered his eyebrows and studied Kate. "I suppose I could come again on Wednesday at three o'clock."

"Yes. Thank you. We'll look forward to it." Aunt Louisa sent Kate a pointed glance and waited for her response.

Kate thanked Mr. Rounpear for the lesson, though it nearly killed her.

Louisa crossed the room and pulled the cord to summon the footman. He arrived and escorted the dancing instructor out. When the door closed, she swung around and glared at Kate. "There is no excuse for your rude behavior toward Mr. Rounpear."

Kate lifted her chin. "I don't see why he has to come back. I know how to curtsy."

"There is more to court presentation than learning how to curtsy."

"Of course, but he's so superior and demanding."

Louisa's nostrils flared, sending a warning. "You will have one more lesson with Mr. Rounpear, and I don't want to hear any more about it."

Kate's face burned. She clenched her hands, barely able to keep herself under control. But her aunt was her presentation sponsor, and if Kate didn't hold her tongue, she might lose her opportunity to be presented.

Louisa didn't seem to notice Kate's response, or perhaps she didn't care. She turned to Penny. "Have you tried on those two new dresses?"

"Yes, but the hem of the green silk is terribly uneven. Should we send it back to the dressmaker, or should I ask Lydia to fix it?"

"Goodness, you would think with the price I'm paying that dressmaker, she could at least hem a dress properly." Louisa motioned toward the open doorway. "I'm going to the Tremblys' for tea at four, and I need to change, but I suppose I have time to look at it."

"Splendid." Penny turned and dashed out of the drawing room.

"Penelope, slow down!" Louisa raised her hand to her chest and hurried after her. "This is not a racetrack!"

Kate shook her head as she watched them go, then turned toward the window. Sunlight poured through the tall panes, drawing her gaze up to the blue sky.

It would be a perfect afternoon for a ride. Of course, a tame promenade down Rotten Row in Hyde Park wouldn't be nearly as exciting as a high-speed race across the beautiful rolling hills at Highland Hall, her country estate in Berkshire.

That thought stopped her cold, and pain pierced her heart.

It wasn't *her* estate anymore.

It had been almost a year since her father's death, and when she lost him, she lost control of Highland as well. It wasn't right, but it was the law.

She had no brothers, and daughters could not inherit their father's title or the estate that was tied to it. So even though they barely knew him, William Ramsey—her second cousin once removed—had taken her father's title as baronet and become master of Highland Hall. Even worse, her father had named Cousin William to be her guardian until she married, and that had made her life very difficult these last few months.

Of course, her father had not left her penniless. Money had been put aside for her marriage settlement. But if she wanted freedom from her cousin's control and a home of her own, she would have to find a husband this season.

Which was exactly what she intended to do.

She crossed to the center of the room to practice her curtsy a few more times before tea. Perhaps without everyone hovering over her and criticizing her every move, she could relax and master the graceful movements she needed to impress the king and queen. And everyone else who would be watching.

Closing her eyes, she pictured the motions. Then she lifted her hand, stepped to the left, and sank down once more. Lowering her head, she counted to three, then slowly rose. There, that was better. She smiled at the imaginary queen. "Thank you, Your Majesty. I'm very pleased to meet you."

A giggle drifted in through the open doorway.

Kate glanced to the right, following the sound.

Six-year-old Millie, Cousin William's daughter, peeked around the edge of the doorway. Her ginger curls spilled over her shoulder as she leaned in.

A smile broke across Kate's face. "Millie, are you spying on me?"

"No, I'm just watching. What are you doing?"

"I'm practicing for my presentation to the king and queen."

Millie's blue-green eyes glowed. "You're going to the palace to see the king and queen?"

"Yes, I am. There will be two hundred other young women presented that day, but I'll have my turn to meet them, and you'll do the same when you're my age."

Millie's impish smile spread wider. "Really?"

"Of course." Kate's spirit lifted. Millie was right. Presentation at court was an exciting opportunity that would open the door to Kate's future. She shouldn't let her overbearing aunt or her gloomy dancing instructor squelch her happiness.

It was time to make the most of the day. She focused on her young cousin again. "Would you like to learn how to curtsy?"

"Yes!" Millie hurried across the room toward Kate.

"All right. Stand like this." Kate showed her young cousin the first position.

The little girl watched Kate with eager expectation, then lifted her skirt and followed along.

• • •

Jonathan Foster hopped down from the London omnibus and set off across Hathaway Court, a broad, tree-lined street in the heart of Kensington. The late April sunshine warmed his shoulders, and the fresh spring breeze carried a faint floral scent. What a perfect day.

The pleasant spring weather wasn't the only reason for his cheerful mood. In less than two weeks, he would finish his fifth term at medical school, and he could enjoy a bit more freedom and a lot more sleep for the next few months.

Jon glanced at his watch. He didn't need to be back at St. George's Hospital until seven this evening. That gave him plenty of time to call on his sister, Julia, and her future husband, Sir William Ramsey, and welcome them to London.

Although their parents were in favor of his sister's upcoming marriage, Jon wanted to become better acquainted with William and be sure he was the right man for Julia. Ramsey might be a baronet and master of a large country estate, but it was Julia's recent inheritance from their grandfather that had saved Highland Hall from financial ruin just two months earlier.

Did William truly love Julia, or had he pursued her for the inheritance? With their father still recovering from a prolonged illness and living miles away in Fulton, Jon wanted to make sure his sister was protected and her future secure.

He rounded the corner, and Ramsey House came into view. He studied the impressive three-story Queen Anne–style home built of red brick. It had white trim, an intricate dutch gable with a scrolled roofline on the left, and a large round turret at the corner on the right. Another arched gable sheltered the front entrance.

He stopped at the wrought-iron gate and surveyed the property. Two well-kept flower gardens and neat boxwood hedges lined the walkway leading to the front door. They added a warm welcome and softened the formal appearance of the house. He was sure his sister appreciated that.

William Ramsey's London home was certainly different from Jon and Julia's simple childhood home at the mission station in India—and the thatched cottage where their parents now stayed in Fulton. His sister would lead a very different life here. But he imagined she would accept those changes with the same grace and goodwill she had always shown.

Still…was this marriage what was best for her? Would she be happy here? That's what he needed to discover.

He pushed open the gate, mounted the steps, and rang the bell.

A few moments later, a stout butler in a neatly pressed black suit answered the door and ushered him in. "Please wait here, sir." The butler motioned toward a chair in the entrance hall.

"Thank you." Jon removed his hat and glanced around as the butler passed through a doorway at the end of the hall.

The interior of the house was even more impressive than the facade, with beautiful hardwood floors, thick carpets, and an elaborately carved wooden staircase leading up to the next floor. A large mirror in a gilded frame hung on the wall to his right between two large family portraits. He stepped closer and examined one of the paintings.

Could that be William Ramsey when he was a boy? The young lad had the same features as the man he'd met at his sister's engagement dinner at Highland Hall in February. Two boys stood with him. Jon guessed they were his brothers. A younger sister and their parents sat in front of them in a garden setting. If that boy in the middle was William, he looked rather somber, even as a child.

A soft female voice followed by a little girl's giggle drifted from the partially open doorway down the hall.

Jonathan tipped his head and listened. Was that Julia with Sir William's daughter, Millie? Julia had grown very fond of Sir William's two young children since she'd become their governess at Highland Hall six months ago. And in a few months she would become their stepmother.

"Very nice, Millie. Let's try it again."

No, that wasn't Julia's voice. Perhaps it was Katherine Ramsey or her sister, Penelope. Jon had met William's cousins at Julia's engagement dinner at Highland, and he had seen them again at William's sister's wedding earlier this month.

"Show me again." Millie's young voice carried a smile.

"All right. Follow me."

Jonathan moved closer and looked into the drawing room. The plush furniture had been pushed back. Katherine Ramsey stood in the center of the room wearing a sky-blue dress, with Millie standing beside her. Katherine's back was to the entrance hall, so she didn't see him step into the doorway.

Katherine lifted her skirt a few inches and exposed a bit of ruffle around her slim ankles. "Step to the left and place your right foot behind. Then slowly sink down until your knee almost touches the floor, but not quite."

Millie copied each movement, though hers were not as smooth as Katherine's.

"Now, lower your head." Katherine demonstrated and Millie followed. "Hold perfectly still while you slowly count to three before you rise."

Millie wavered, then gasped and tipped to the side.

Katherine lunged to catch her, but Millie crashed onto the carpet, and Katherine landed in a heap beside her.

Jonathan dashed across the room. "Miss Ramsey, are you all right?"

She looked up at him, and her cheeks flushed bright pink. "Mr. Foster... Yes, of course, I'm fine."

Millie giggled as she pushed herself to her hands and knees and then stood. "I guess I need more practice."

"I suppose I do as well." Katherine started to rise.

Jon extended his hand to her. "Please, allow me."

She glanced up at him, her eyebrows slightly arched. "I promise you I've curtsied dozens of times today, and this is the only time I've fallen."

"Of course. I'm sure it was only because you were trying to help Millie. Now, please, let me be a gentleman and help you." He smiled and continued to hold out his hand.

She hesitated a moment, then reached out and clasped his fingers. He helped her to her feet, then she slipped her hand from his.

"Thank you." As she looked down and brushed off her skirt, Jon had a moment to observe her more carefully. Her long, golden-brown hair was tied back with a blue ribbon that matched the color of her eyes. One wavy strand of hair had come loose when she fell. She reached up and tucked it behind her ear, her hand grazing her flushed cheek.

His gaze drifted from her cheek to her full, pink lips.

She looked up. "Mr. Foster?"

He swallowed and looked into her eyes. "Yes?"

"Have you come to see your sister?"

"Yes."

She glanced over her shoulder and then back at him. "Does she know you've arrived?"

He blinked, struggling to find an answer. "Yes."

She searched his face with a slight frown. "Mr. Foster, are you quite all right?"

"Yes." He shook his head and looked away. What was the matter with him? "The butler asked me to wait in the entrance hall, but I heard your voice and thought you were Julia, so I looked in. Of course then I realized you weren't Julia... You were you." His neck warmed. He was rambling on like an idiot.

A hint of amusement lit her eyes. "Well, we're very grateful you came to our aid, aren't we, Millie?"

The little girl nodded, her curls bobbing on her shoulders. "Are you staying for tea?" Millie looked up at him with a friendly smile and wide, innocent eyes.

He glanced at Katherine.

"Yes, of course. You're welcome to join us for tea. I'm sure Cousin William and Julia will be down soon." She placed her hand on Millie's shoulder. "Why don't you go tell them Mr. Foster is here?"

Millie nodded and turned to go just as William and Julia walked into the drawing room with Andrew, William's eleven-year-old son.

"Jonathan, what a wonderful surprise." Julia crossed the room and greeted him with a kiss on his cheek. "I'm so happy to see you."

"Thank you. I'm very glad to see you as well. Welcome to London." He shook hands with William and turned to Andrew. "How are you, young sir?"

"Very well, thank you." The sturdy little fellow's face was covered with freckles, and his red hair was an even brighter shade than his sister's.

"We hope you're still coming to dinner on Thursday," Julia said.

"Yes, I'm looking forward to it. But my classes were canceled this afternoon, so I thought I'd stop in and say hello."

"That's wonderful." Julia turned to Katherine. "Thank you for entertaining Jonathan while he waited for us."

Katherine shot him a questioning glance, and he returned a reassuring smile. Her secret was safe with him. He would not mention her fall.

"Yes, Katherine and Millie were very kind and…quite entertaining."

"We invited him to stay for tea," Millie added with a proud smile.

William touched his daughter's shoulder. "That was very thoughtful, Millie."

Millie looked up at her father, soaking up his praise.

"Yes, please stay for tea and tell us all your news." Julia took his arm and led him out of the drawing room.

As they crossed the threshold, he glanced over his shoulder at Katherine. Her gaze connected with his for a split second, then she looked away, a hint of a smile on her lips.

• • •

Kate took a sip of steaming hot tea and glanced across at Jonathan, who sat opposite her in the library. He stirred sugar into his tea, his movement smooth and relaxed. The discomfort he'd shown earlier in the drawing room seemed to have disappeared, leaving Kate wondering, *What was that about?*

Julia poured a cup of tea and passed it to William. The children were gathered around a small table near the library fireplace.

William helped himself to a scone and glanced at Julia. "Won't Penny and Louisa be joining us?"

"They've gone to call on the Tremblys, and then they plan to stop at the dressmaker's on the way home."

William lifted his dark eyebrows. "More dress fittings?"

"An adjustment was needed on the hem of one of Penny's gowns."

Kate nibbled on a lemon tart and glanced at Jonathan again. His blue eyes looked very similar to his sister's. But his hair was light brown with a touch of gold rather than dark brown like Julia's. He had pleasant features with a high forehead, straight nose, and a strong, square chin. With his broad shoulders and athletic build, he would be considered quite handsome by most women.

That certainly didn't matter to Kate. She knew what she was looking for in a husband. She and her aunt had discussed it at length. If Kate hoped to gain a place in society, she must marry a wealthy man from an aristocratic family, preferably one in line to inherit a title and estate. Of course, he would also be handsome, with pleasant manners and fine character, but that went without saying.

Jonathan looked up and smiled at her, with an invitation to friendship in his eyes.

Was it right to judge a man so quickly because of his lack of fortune and family connections? She looked away, dismissing the slight wave of guilt that pricked her conscience.

William set his plate aside and settled back in his chair. "The stories in the newspaper about the *Titanic* have certainly been tragic."

Julia glanced at the children, concern in her expression. But Andrew and Millie were enjoying their fruit tarts and sandwiches and didn't appear to be listening.

"Did you know anyone on board?" Jonathan asked.

"I went to school with Kirby Brumfield. We belonged to the same club." William lowered his voice. "His wife and two children were rescued, but he was not."

Sorrow flooded Julia's expression. "It's such a tragedy. We must pray for them all."

Jonathan nodded and looked across at Kate. "Have you read the articles about the *Titanic,* Miss Ramsey?"

The temptation to say she had rose in her mind, and her face warmed. A few months ago she would've easily lied to give a better impression, but since Julia's arrival Kate had been learning the value of telling the truth, even when it reflected poorly on her.

She lifted her eyes and met Jonathan's gaze. "No, I haven't."

He studied her for a moment with a hint of disappointment in his eyes, then glanced down at his teacup.

Regret washed over her. Of course she'd heard about the *Titanic* sinking a week earlier, but with their move to London, the dress fittings, and her preparations for the season, she hadn't thought much about it. But now, hearing how William's friend had lost his life, the tragedy seemed more real—and her lack of concern, more shameful.

Julia shifted in her seat and glanced at Andrew and Millie again. "Perhaps we should talk about something else. I don't want to upset the children."

"You're right, dear. That's a topic for another time." William turned to Jonathan. "How is your training coming along at the hospital?"

"Very well. Making rounds with the doctors and observing surgeries is much more helpful than sitting in a classroom or pouring over textbooks."

Julia nodded looking pleased. "You always have liked learning from practical experience."

"That's true." Jonathan helped himself to a small sandwich. "How are your plans coming for the season?"

"Katherine's presentation is Friday." Julia smiled at Kate. "I'm sure she'll receive several invitations after that. We expect to have a very full calendar."

Jonathan turned to Kate. "This Friday?"

A bite of lemon tart stuck in her throat. She nodded and forced a slight smile.

"And her ball is planned for the eleventh of May," Julia said. "We hope you'll be able to come."

"Of course. I'd be honored to." Jonathan glanced around the room. "Will you be holding the ball here?"

"We planned to." William frowned and shook his head. "But Lady Gatewood, Katherine's aunt, insists there's not enough room. We have over one hundred and fifty guests on the list."

A thrill ran through Kate, and she couldn't hold back her smile. "Aunt Louisa helped us make arrangements to hold it at Sheffield House. They have a large ballroom with a lovely terrace and gardens."

"Katherine's aunt is friends with the Tremonts, who own Sheffield," Julia added. "They've been very kind to allow us to host the ball there."

Jonathan focused on Kate with a slight smile. "I've never been to a debutante ball."

"It should be wonderful."

"I'm sure it will be." Julia turned to Jonathan. "So, when will you finish your classes?"

"Just two more weeks. Then I'll start two mornings a week at the hospital for the rest of the summer."

"That should be a nice change for you," Julia said.

"Yes, I'm looking forward to it, although I'll have to hunt for a new flat right away."

Julia tipped her head. "You're moving?"

"I must. The owner of our building is selling the property. I have to be out by the fifteenth of May at the latest."

William frowned. "That's certainly short notice."

"Yes, it is. Theo Anderson, one of my fellow students, invited me to stay with him, but I'm afraid his flat is even smaller than mine. I'm not sure how well that would work."

"Why don't you stay here?" William set his plate aside and continued. "We have four guest rooms, and we're not expecting to fill them all."

Kate darted a glance at Jonathan. She supposed having him stay with them wouldn't be too awkward, but what would people think? Of course, with her aunt, cousin, and Julia as her chaperones, even London's scandal-loving society shouldn't object.

"Sarah and Clark will be coming to town for Katherine's ball," William added, "but they're only staying for a few days. We don't return to Highland until early August. You're welcome to stay with us as long as you'd like."

"Thank you. That will give me plenty of time to look for a new flat before classes start again in the fall."

"How soon would you like to bring your things over?" William asked.

"I could come tomorrow, if that fits in with your plans."

"Excellent. We'll send the car around. Just name the time."

"Would three o'clock be convenient? I have a trunk and a few boxes of books, so it would be very helpful."

William nodded and set his teacup on the table. "I'll ask Lawrence to arrange it."

Julia's expression brightened as she looked from William to Jonathan. "It will be wonderful to have you here with us."

Jonathan offered them both a grateful smile. "It will be a pleasure, and it should give me a chance to get to know William and the rest of the family." His gaze shifted from William and Julia to Kate.

Kate looked down at her plate. She doubted she would see much of Jonathan Foster after her presentation. Once the season moved into full swing, invitations would pour in, and her days and nights would be filled with parties, dinners, balls, and outings. She glanced at Jonathan once more, and a twinge of regret traveled through her.

• • •

Lydia Chambers hurried down the back stone stairs, carefully carrying Miss Katherine's large lavender hat. Perhaps Mrs. Adams, the housekeeper, would know how to reattach the ostrich feathers that had somehow come loose on the trip from Berkshire to town.

Lydia heaved a sigh as she passed the main floor landing and continued downstairs. She'd been so happy with her promotion from Highland housemaid to lady's maid for Miss Katherine and Miss Penelope. The idea of traveling with the Ramsey family to London had been thrilling for a simple farm girl, but now she had a whole new set of responsibilities: fixing the young ladies' hair, caring for their clothing, and even sewing their undergarments.

There was much to learn! And if she didn't do it well, she'd be demoted back to housemaid and find herself on the next train back to Berkshire.

Had she been a fool to accept the promotion?

She bit her lip and knocked on Mrs. Adams's door.

"Come in."

Lydia opened the door and stepped into the housekeeper's cozy parlor. "Good afternoon, ma'am."

Mrs. Adams turned in her chair. "What can I do for you, Lydia?"

"Miss Katherine wants to wear this tomorrow." She held out the hat and pulled out the three ostrich plumes. "And I've no idea how to get these blessed feathers back in place."

A hint of a smile touched Mrs. Adams's lips, and her eyes crinkled at the corners. "Let me see it." Lydia handed her the hat, and Mrs. Adams turned it in her hands, inspecting the flowers, feathers, and netting. "My goodness there's quite a garden here, isn't there?"

A smile tugged at Lydia's lips. "Yes, ma'am."

"Well, you've come to the right place." Mrs. Adams looked up, her soft gray eyes shining. "My mother was a milliner, and I grew up making hats. I'll show you how to fix it."

Lydia clasped her hands. "Oh, thank you. I thought I was going to be sacked before I finished my first week in London."

"Don't worry, my dear. By the time we're finished, Miss Katherine could wear this hat in the worst windstorm and never lose a feather."

"I'm ever so grateful. I really do want to learn to be a proper lady's maid."

"Of course you do, and I'm happy to help. Now let me find what we need, and then we'll take it to the servants' hall. It's almost time for tea." Mrs. Adams handed Lydia the hat, then took her sewing basket from the shelf in the corner. She motioned toward the door. "After you, my dear."

Lydia's tense shoulders relaxed as she walked into the servants' hall and took a seat at the long wooden table. Most of the other servants had already gathered there and were enjoying their tea and a short break from their busy day.

Ann Norton, the nursery maid, looked up and smiled as Lydia settled in next to her. "You better watch out for that hat. You don't want to get jam or tea on it."

"You're right about that." Lydia carefully laid the hat in her lap. "I wouldn't have brought it in, but Mrs. Adams is going to show me how to fix the feathers." Lydia glanced across the room at the housekeeper.

Mrs. Adams stood at the head of the long table, speaking in a low voice to Mr. Lawrence, the butler. Together they oversaw the staff. Mr. Lawrence took charge of the male servants, including the two footmen, the chauffeur, and a groom. Mrs. Adams watched over the female servants, two housemaids, Ann, and herself.

Mrs. Murdock, the cook, bustled in and set a tray of sandwiches on the table. She frowned at Nelson, the footman, who was already eating. "You're certainly in a hurry. Couldn't you wait for the rest of us?"

"Sorry." Nelson glanced at Mr. Lawrence.

The butler turned to Mrs. Murdock. "I told them to go ahead. We have quite a bit to do, and I saw no need to wait."

Mrs. Murdock rolled her eyes. "Oh well, that explains it."

Lydia and Ann exchanged a smile. Since their arrival in London, Mrs. Murdock and Mr. Lawrence seemed to be testing each other, trying to determine who was truly in charge at the meals. Although Mrs. Murdock oversaw two kitchen maids and all the meal preparations, she still answered to Mrs. Adams and Mr. Lawrence.

Each one had their place and knew they needed to keep to it and show the proper respect to those above them.

Ann glanced at the housekeeper. "That's nice of Mrs. Adams to help you with the hat."

"Yes, she's kind." Lydia leaned closer. "Ever so much nicer than Mrs. Emmitt."

Ann's lips puckered as though she'd tasted something bitter. "I'm glad we won't be taking orders from her when we go back to Highland."

"So am I."

Mrs. Emmitt, the previous housekeeper at Highland, had tried to sack Ann last winter when she'd been caught alone with Peter Gates, a former groom. But Miss Foster had spoken up for Ann and convinced Sir William to overrule the housekeeper and keep Ann on.

Ann brushed a breadcrumb from her apron. "It's good the truth about Mrs. Emmitt finally came out. Imagine, her trying to get rid of Miss Foster."

Lydia shook her head. "She ought not to have done that."

"Especially since Miss Foster and Sir William had feelings for each other."

"It's quite romantic, isn't it—a fine gentleman like Sir William falling in love with a governess?"

Ann shrugged one shoulder. "I suppose. I'm just glad Mrs. Emmitt was the one who was sacked instead of Miss Foster or me."

The staff had been told Mrs. Emmitt had resigned and gone to live with her sister in Bristol, but the truth had been whispered from one servant to the next, and few were sorry to see the old housekeeper go.

Lydia carefully poured herself a cup of tea, making sure not to splash any on Miss Katherine's hat. "Do you think Mrs. Adams will be coming back to Highland, to replace Mrs. Emmitt?"

Ann shook her head. "I heard she has two daughters and a grandchild here in town. I doubt she'd want to take a job so far from her family."

"Well, they'll have to find someone to run the house."

Ann spread butter on a slice of bread. "I wish I could apply, but they probably want someone with more experience."

Lydia nodded. "It's a big job to manage a house like Highland."

Patrick, the second footman, walked into the servants' hall. His light brown hair was neatly combed, and he wore a smart livery. "The afternoon post, sir." He handed Mr. Lawrence a stack of envelopes.

"Thank you." Mr. Lawrence quickly sorted through the pile and set most of the letters aside. He looked down the table. "Lydia, you have a letter."

Lydia hopped up to accept the envelope from the butler. "Thank you, sir."

He nodded and passed out two more pieces of mail.

Lydia glanced at the envelope and her spirit lifted. Letters from home were a rare treat, and she eagerly tore open the envelope. She unfolded the one sheet of paper and scanned the first few lines. Her breath caught in her throat as she quickly read the rest.

Your sister Helen has run off, and we are heartsick and so worried. We have no idea who she is with or where she's gone. Have you heard from her?

Your father has spoken to some of the young people in the village and nearby farms. He even offered a reward. No one has come forward yet, but we hope someone will speak up soon. I feel certain one of them knows where she's gone.

Please pray for her and for us. Your father is beside himself, and my heart is breaking. If you hear from her, please send word right away.

I hope you are well and you are able to learn all that's needed in your new position. There are many temptations in London. I hope you will avoid them all and stay on the straight and narrow path.

Your loving Mother

Lydia's hand trembled as she stared at her mother's script. Why would Helen run away? Of course, life on the farm was not easy, but how could she just up and disappear without telling their parents? Where would she go? How would she live?

If she longed to leave home that much, why didn't she take a respectable job in service with a good family, rather than running off and causing so much trouble for their family? But Helen had always been a romantic soul and longed for the day when a young man would woo her and whisk her away to a charmed life.

Foolish girl!

Lydia folded the letter and slipped it back in the torn envelope.

"Lydia? What's wrong?" Ann leaned toward her. "Is it bad news?"

Lydia swallowed and looked around. She couldn't speak of her sister's troubles here in the servants' hall, not with everyone listening.

Ann reached for her arm. "Goodness, your face has gone as white as a sheet."

Lydia pulled away and stood, but her legs felt shaky. "I'm all right. I just need…some fresh air." She turned and strode out of the servants' hall.

"But what about Miss Katherine's hat?"

"I'll come back for it." Lydia hurried down the hall, then pushed open the back door. Stepping out to the rear courtyard, she squinted against the late afternoon sunlight. The smell of horses and hay drifted from the open stable door past the carriage house.

She leaned against a stack of wooden crates and tried to still her racing thoughts.

Oh Helen, what have you done?

TWO

———————•———

Jonathan walked down the hospital corridor with Theo Anderson, his friend and fellow medical student. The scent of antiseptic hung in the air, and a few small puddles from a recent mopping left a sheen on the edges of the smooth tile floor. Jon lifted a hand to his mouth and stifled a yawn.

Theo chuckled. "Don't start that. It's only nine o'clock."

"Sorry. I didn't get to bed until after one last night."

"Studying for exams?"

"That's what I should've been doing, but I was packing up my flat."

Theo glanced at Jon. "You're going to take me up on my offer?"

"I appreciate the invitation, but I've decided to stay with Sir William Ramsey, my sister's fiancé, in Kensington. At least through July."

Theo grinned. "Well, you're certainly moving up in the world."

Jon returned a slight smile. "Yes, I suppose I am."

"That should be nice, having your own staff of maids and footmen."

Jon's smile faded. "I'll take care of myself."

"Maybe at first, but I think you'll get used to having someone clean your shoes and press your suits."

Discomfort tightened Jon's chest. "I'm not staying with them because they have servants. William has a large house with plenty of room, and it's only a ten-minute ride to the hospital."

"That's an advantage."

"It will give me more time with my sister and William...or to do any number of things."

A fleeting vision of Katherine Ramsey passed through his mind, but he quickly banished the thought. She might be beautiful, but she seemed to be self-absorbed and wrapped up in her preparations for the season. She'd rebuffed his smiles and avoided looking him in the eye yesterday. And he knew why. Julia had told him Katherine's goal was to receive a marriage proposal this season from a titled peer with a family estate. He could never compete with someone like that—

He shook his head at himself. He had no desire to compete, whether he could or not. When he married, *if* he married, it would be to someone who shared his values and goals.

"Moving to Kensington makes sense," Theo said, "especially since you've received that inheritance from your grandfather."

"I won't see any of it until I turn twenty-five in August, but what does that have to do with it?" Jon glanced around, hoping none of the other hospital staff or students had heard. He was still getting used to the idea of the unexpected inheritance from his late grandfather, and he didn't want others to know about it and treat him differently.

"It could open the door for you to be accepted in the better circles of society."

"I suppose, especially if my aunt Beatrice and Grandmother Shelburne have anything to say about it."

Theo's grin returned. "They're still trying to introduce you to all their friends?"

Jon stopped at the end of the hallway, and a smile tugged at his lips. "Yes, it's part of their not-so-subtle campaign to try and convince me to stay in England."

"Really?" Theo lifted his eyebrows, humor reflected in his eyes.

"They're hoping I'll find a wife, sign on for a position at the hospital, and settle down in London."

Theo cocked his head. "Would you consider that?"

Jon shifted his gaze to the windows, a hundred conflicting thoughts running through his mind. "I don't know."

"I thought you were going back to India."

"That was the plan, but I always imagined my father and I would work together."

Theo sobered. "He's not going back?"

Jon shook his head. "It doesn't look like it. His health has improved, but not enough for him to make such a long sea voyage or work in India's climate. His doctor says it would be too hard on him, and I have to agree."

Theo placed his hand on Jon's shoulder. "Why not strike out on your own? With your experience and training, you'd do well wherever you go."

"Thanks. I appreciate your vote of confidence." Jon rubbed the bridge of his nose as another wave of tiredness washed over him. If he was going back to India next year, he should have already started the application process with the London Missionary Society. But each time he pulled out the paperwork, heaviness came over him.

Did he want to spend the rest of his life serving as a medical missionary? Was that the best use of his gifts, talents, and training? Had the Lord provided the inheritance so he could return to India independently, without the support of the missionary society? Or did He have some other plan in mind for Jon?

If he went overseas as an unmarried man, he would most likely be giving up the possibility of marriage and children—or at least postponing it for a good many years. Was he willing to make that kind of sacrifice?

But how could he stay in England and enjoy the life his inheritance would provide when there was such great need overseas? How could he walk away from all his parents had taught him about living a life focused on serving others and sharing the love of Christ with those who had never heard of Him?

What was his responsibility? What did God want him to do?

Theo thumped Jon's shoulder and stirred him from his reverie.

"One thing is certain—at least you won't have to spend your summer working at Hargrove's like you did last year."

Jon pushed his questions aside to consider later. "Yes, that's a relief." Loading crates of fruit and vegetables onto trucks had provided the funds he needed for his medical training, but it had been backbreaking work.

"Cheer up, Jon. You're the envy of all our friends now."

"You mean because I won't be sweating my summer away on the docks?"

Theo grinned. "Yes, and because of your inheritance."

"I thought I asked you not to say anything about that."

"I haven't said a word to anyone, but George Maddox asked me about it, and I heard Mrs. Worthington mention it to one of the other nurses."

Jon narrowed his eyes. This was not good news. "It must be my aunt then. She seems determined to spread the news as far and wide as possible."

Theo sent him a questioning glance.

"She hopes it will reach the ears of the social matrons, and I'll be invited to some of the events this season."

"That doesn't sound so bad. I wouldn't mind attending a few dinner parties or the races at Ascot."

Jon rubbed his chin. It would be interesting to see how aristocrats entertained and enjoyed themselves. This might be his last chance to take part in events like that if he planned to return to India. But even considering it made him feel a bit guilty. How could he enjoy a lavish lifestyle when so many didn't have the basic necessities?

He shook his head. He might be uncertain about taking part in the season, but one thing was clear: he did not want to become the focus of gossip. He turned to Theo. "If you hear anyone else discussing my inheritance, I hope you'll put a stop to it."

"I will. You have my word."

"Thank you."

Dr. Alfred Pittsford strode down the hall toward them. He wore a white physician's coat, and a stethoscope hung around his neck. In his arms he carried a stack of bulging file folders. Dr. Pittsford taught two classes for the medical students, but he spent most of his time working at a free clinic he had opened on the East End.

"Good morning, gentlemen." Dr. Pittsford's close-clipped red beard and moustache partially hid his smile.

"Morning, sir," they both replied.

"Mr. Anderson, it was good to have you at the Daystar Clinic last Saturday. Will you be joining us again this week?"

"Yes sir. I have a commitment in the morning, but I plan to come for the afternoon."

"Very good. We'll be open until seven. With the warmer weather there has been a rise in the number of patients. We'll be glad to have your help." Dr. Pittsford shifted his gaze to Jon. "And what about you, Mr. Foster? Have you made a decision about volunteering at Daystar?"

Jon looked up and met the doctor's gaze. "I'm still considering it, sir."

"Why not come along with Mr. Anderson on Saturday and see the work for yourself? It would be a great opportunity to gain more practical experience. And I think you'll find it very gratifying to help those in the East End who have no other access to medical care."

"I'd like to, but I have an engagement on Saturday."

A shadow of disappointment crossed the doctor's features, then disappeared. He gave a slight smile. "Well then, maybe next week." Dr. Pittsford bid them good day and continued down the hallway.

Theo watched him go, then turned to Jon. "Are you sure you can't come on Saturday?"

"Positive." Jon started down the hall toward their next class.

"I thought you'd be one of the first to sign up to help at Daystar. The work sounds very similar to what you did in India."

"Our focus there was rescuing young girls from a terrible life in the temples and caring for children who were abandoned."

"But you provided medical care for the poor, didn't you?"

"Yes, my father and I worked side by side at our clinic in Kanakapura."

"That's what we're doing in the East End, and every patient who comes through is offered prayer and spiritual counsel as well as a physician's care."

"I have no doubt it's worthy work. But I can't come this week. Dr. Gleason and his wife invited me to a garden party at their home. And you can't very well say no to the president of the hospital."

A smile formed on Theo's lips. "Ah, now I see what's happening."

"What?"

"Dr. Gleason has three unmarried daughters, and he'd like nothing better than to marry one of them off to a promising young medical student like you."

Jon shook his head. "I'm sure that's not why he invited me."

"Sorry, Jon, but that's the most likely reason. That, and he's probably a good friend of your aunt's."

"Now I wish I'd sent my regrets."

"Don't worry. I hear the older two daughters are a bit long in the face, but the youngest is quite pretty. She's just coming out this season."

Jon stifled a groan as he pulled open the door to the lecture hall. "Wonderful."

"I expect a full report on Monday." Theo chuckled and followed Jon through the doorway.

• • •

Kate stared at her reflection in the bedroom mirror and pulled in a slow, deep breath. She hardly recognized the woman looking back at her. Dressed in her white satin presentation gown, with an abundance of petticoats, lace, and beading, she looked like a princess. In three hours she would face the king and queen and step into her future as a debutante.

Her hand trembled as she reached up and adjusted one of her pearl earrings.

"Oh, Kate, you look so beautiful. I can't imagine a lovelier dress." Penny gazed at her with a dreamy smile. "I'm going to wear one exactly like it for my debut."

Julia stood behind Kate, affection shining in her eyes. "You do look lovely, Kate."

"Thank you," Kate murmured. She glanced over her shoulder at the yards of white fabric, edged with lace, swirled on the floor behind her. "I hope I can manage this long train."

Her aunt's brow creased as she stepped closer to examine the train. "Mr. Rounpear should've had you wear it for your final practice session."

Kate wished he had, but there was nothing to be done about it now. She glanced at her aunt's stern expression and decided it was best not to reply.

Louisa would accompany Kate to the palace as her sponsor, and she was dressed for the occasion in an elegant dark-green brocade gown. A diamond tiara had been tucked into her upswept hairstyle, and around her neck she wore an elaborate emerald-and-diamond necklace.

"I'm sure Kate will do well." Julia reached out and gently ran her hand over the satin-covered buttons that attached Kate's train to the back of her dress at her shoulders. "She has natural grace and poise." She caught Kate's gaze in the mirror once more and sent her a reassuring smile.

But Louisa's lips tightened to a firm line. "When you enter the palace, you'll carry the train over your left arm until you reach the throne room, then you gently ease it down to the floor. The pages will spread it out behind you before you approach the king and queen."

Kate nodded, though it seemed her mind was swimming through a thick fog.

"Remember to carry your bouquet in your right hand, and your presentation card in your left. You won't be allowed to take anything else into the palace with you."

Kate nodded again. She had gone over each step in her mind countless times. But what if she dropped her bouquet or her mind went blank and she forgot how to curtsy? There was so much to remember, and she had only one opportunity to do it well.

Louisa narrowed her eyes as she looked into the mirror. "Her hair is fuller on the left than it is on the right. That will never do." She turned toward Lydia with an impatient huff. "Chambers, fix her hair."

"Yes, m'lady." Lydia picked up the comb, stepped around to the right, and carefully fluffed out Kate's hair a bit, checking her handiwork in the mirror.

"That looks perfect," Julia said. "Thank you, Lydia."

Louisa motioned toward the gauzy veil on the bed. "Attach the headpiece, and we'll see if her hair still looks balanced."

Lydia placed the comb on the dressing table and carefully lifted the veil with the two white ostrich plumes attached at the top. The feathers trembled slightly as she placed them at the back of Kate's head, poking the comb and hard tip of the feathers into Kate's hair.

"Oh, for heaven's sake, girl, that is not the right angle!" Louisa slapped Lydia's hands away. "Do you want her to look like a peacock?"

The maid gasped. "No, m'lady. I'm sorry. I've never seen one of these before."

"Don't make excuses. You are a lady's maid. You should know how to arrange hair and attach a headpiece."

"Yes, m'lady." Lydia blinked several times as she stepped back.

"It's all right, Lydia." Julia laid her hand on the maid's arm. "This is new to all of us."

"Except Aunt Louisa," Penny added. "She was presented to Queen Victoria."

"That's right." Louisa's frown faded and a faint smile lifted her lips. "I was only seventeen, and I kissed her hand."

Kate shuddered at the thought. "I'm glad they've dropped that part of the presentation."

Louisa turned her attention back to attaching Kate's headpiece. "It must be lower, so the plumes rise just a few inches above her head." Her aunt jammed the feathers in deeper.

"Ouch!" Kate winced and pulled away. "That's my scalp!"

Her aunt ignored her cry and wiggled the feathers into place. "We don't want them to come loose or flop about."

Penny laughed and shook her head. "No, we wouldn't want that."

Louisa glared at Penny. "This is not a laughing matter, Penelope. Katherine's every move will be judged and reported in the newspaper tomorrow. And all the society matrons who have eligible sons will be reading the article and taking notes."

Julia glanced at Louisa. "Surely with so many young women being presented, they won't all be mentioned in the paper, will they?"

"No, they won't, but Katherine will. I've made sure of it."

Kate swung around and faced her aunt. "What do you mean?"

"My brother-in-law is acquainted with the owner of the *Daily Sketch*. And your uncle Albert paid a generous sum to assure that you will be one of the debutantes who is mentioned."

A bolt of panic shot through Kate. "Oh, Aunt Louisa! Now I'm going to be even more nervous."

Her aunt's cheeks flushed, but she waved away Kate's words. "You should be grateful. Only six girls will be featured in the article."

Kate stood and tried to take a deep breath, but it was impossible. "Can we please loosen this corset? I can hardly breathe."

"We don't have time for that now." Louisa fussed with Kate's train.

"I have to catch my breath, or I'm sure I'll faint dead away before I even reach the throne room!"

Louisa gripped Kate's shoulder. "Look at me, Katherine."

Kate stilled and focused on her aunt.

"Your uncle and I have invested a great deal of money in your gowns and lessons, and you've spent months preparing for today. Now you must pull yourself together and act like the gracious and confident young woman you've been trained to be. Do you understand?"

Making a good impression at her presentation would help her be accepted in London society, and that was her key to freedom…the only way she could have a life of her own. She swallowed and nodded.

Louisa stepped closer, and her heavy perfume enveloped Kate like a noxious cloud. "Promise me you'll do your best."

Kate straightened, holding her breath. "I will."

"All right." Her aunt's stern expression eased. "I need to collect a few things from my room before we go. I'll meet you downstairs in five minutes." She turned to Lydia. "Help Katherine manage the train."

"Yes, m'lady." Lydia bobbed a quick curtsy.

Louisa turned and sailed out the door with a swish of her emerald gown.

"I wish I was going." Penny released a wistful sigh.

Julia placed her hand on Penny's back as she guided her toward the door. "I'm sure you'll do just as well as Kate when it's your turn. Let's go find

Millie. She wants to help see Kate off." Julia turned to Kate with a smile. "We'll see you downstairs."

"All right." Kate turned and stared toward the mirror once more. She might not appreciate her aunt's tone, but what she said was true. Kate had dreamed about her presentation for months, and she must make the most of this opportunity, especially now that a reporter would be watching.

Being featured in the newspaper would practically guarantee that she would receive invitations right away—if everything went well.

She turned to Lydia. The maid stood by the bed, slump-shouldered, staring at the carpet. "I'm sorry my aunt was so harsh. I'm afraid she's not known for her patience, especially with the staff."

Lydia looked up. "It's all right, miss. I'm used to it." Her expression remained pained and somber.

"Is there something else?"

Lydia bit her lip, and her eyes filled. "I was thinking of my sister Helen."

"Your sister? What's wrong? Is she ill?"

"No, miss, she's run away from home, and we don't know where she is."

Kate pulled in a sharp breath. "I'm sorry."

"Thank you, miss."

Kate's mind spun. How could the girl just disappear? That didn't make sense. "Surely someone knows what's happened to her."

"My father has been searching for her and talking to the folks in the village. He's even offered a reward."

"That should prompt someone to come forward."

"I hope so, miss." Lydia sighed and shook her head. "Helen's a dear girl, but she's a dreamer."

"That's not always a negative quality."

"No, but it can leave a woman open to temptation, and I'm afraid that's what's happened to Helen." Tears glistened in Lydia's eyes. She sniffed and looked away. "I'm sorry, miss. I've no call to get all teary-eyed and put a damper on your happy day."

"It's all right. If anything happened to my sister, I know I'd be upset and want to do whatever I could to help her."

"That's just it, miss. There doesn't seem to be anything I can do."

If only she could give a practical suggestion to ease Lydia's distress. Julia would probably offer to pray for Lydia right then and there if she were with them. Kate wished she could do the same, but she wasn't comfortable praying aloud. She'd only been learning to say private prayers these last few months, since Julia had come to stay at Highland as her governess.

She reached for Lydia's hand. "I'll pray for Helen and for you."

Lydia's expression eased. "Thank you, miss. That's very kind."

Kate shook her head, wishing it were more. "It's the least I can do."

Lydia bent down to pick up the end of Kate's train. "We'd better go downstairs."

"Yes, I suppose you're right. We don't want to keep my aunt waiting too long."

A slight smile lifted the maid's lips. "No, miss. We most definitely do not."

THREE

J on slid his draught piece across the board and glanced at Andrew. The lad was a surprisingly skilled opponent, and he had already jumped several of Jon's pieces.

Andrew studied the board a few seconds, then a smile broke across his face. "I see what you're doing." He picked up one of his pieces and jumped over one of Jon's, and then jumped a second, landing in the corner space of the last row. "Crown me!"

Jon groaned and sat back. "How did I miss that?"

Andrew's eyes danced as Jon crowned the boy's piece.

William lowered his newspaper, glanced at his son, and then at the board. "Don't be too hard on him, Andrew."

Jon held up his hand. "No, play your best game, Andrew. Don't hold back on my account."

The boy grinned. "All right, I will. It's your move."

Jon rubbed his chin and studied the board.

Millie rushed into the drawing room. "It's time! Kate's ready. Come and see."

Andrew spun around and knocked into the draughts board, sending the pieces flying across the drawing-room carpet. He winced and looked at Jon. "Sorry."

"It's all right." Jon bent and scooped up a few pieces.

Andrew scrambled across the rug to help.

William stood and folded the newspaper. "Let's clean up the rest later. We don't want to miss seeing Kate off."

Andrew jumped up and dashed out to the entrance hall. William sighed with a weary smile. "I'm sorry. Andrew rarely slows down."

"It's all right. I enjoy his zest for life."

William chuckled, and he and Jon walked into the entrance hall together.

Julia met them at the bottom of the stairs along with Millie and Lady Gatewood. Lawrence and the two young footmen waited by the front door.

Penny appeared at the top of the staircase and leaned over the banister, her face glowing with a happy smile. "Are you ready?"

"Yes, we're all waiting," Lady Gatewood replied with an impatient sigh.

Penny moved to the side, and Kate stepped into view.

From where Jon stood, he could only see her head and shoulders, but that was enough to make him catch his breath.

Kate's golden brown hair was swept up in a most appealing fashion, and two white feathers fluttered softly overhead as she began her descent. Around her neck she wore a pearl choker with a diamond-and-pearl pendant. One look at her creamy white neck and shoulders above the beaded bodice of her dress was enough to make him swallow hard.

Kate's usually confident expression had been replaced by a guarded, searching look as she continued down the stairs. When she rounded the turn at the lower landing, the rest of her figure came into view. Her dress looked like a shimmering cloud of white, with its full skirt and the lacy veil and long train spreading out behind her on the stairs…just like a royal bride dressed to meet her noble groom.

All he could do was stare in stunned silence. He swallowed again and tried to take a breath, but his chest seemed locked tight.

"So, what do you think?" Kate directed her question to William.

"You look beautiful. I'm sure every head will turn when you walk into the throne room."

Millie stepped forward. "Here are your flowers." The little girl held out a large, fragrant bouquet fashioned of white roses and jasmine with a few trailing vines of variegated ivy.

Kate reached for the flowers. "Thank you, Millie." She lifted her gaze to meet Jon's, a question shimmering in her blue eyes.

He opened his mouth, wanting to say she looked breathtakingly beautiful, but somehow he couldn't form those words. Instead he forced a smile. "Good luck, Kate. I hope it goes well."

Her countenance faltered for a split second. "Thank you," she murmured, then turned away.

"Come along." Lady Gatewood swept toward the front door. "There will be a huge crowd of carriages, and we don't want to be last in line."

Julia stepped forward and kissed Kate's cheek. "We'll be praying for you."

"Thank you." Kate glanced at Jon once more.

He sent her what he hoped was an encouraging smile.

Lawrence opened the door, and Lady Gatewood led the procession outside. Millie scurried to help Kate with her train.

Lady Gatewood turned. "For goodness' sake, Katherine, pick up your train and place it over your arm. You don't want it to get dirty!"

Kate's face flushed as she bent to scoop up the train and carefully drape it over her left arm.

Everyone followed Kate out the door and down the front steps. The carriage waited on the drive, the door festooned with flowers and ribbons that matched Kate's bouquet. One of the footmen sprang forward, opened the carriage door, and offered Lady Gatewood his hand to help her climb in. Kate climbed in after, and the second footman tucked her long train around her feet before he carefully closed the door.

Julia slipped her arm through Jon's and leaned closer. "I hope she'll be all right."

"I'm sure she'll be fine," he answered in an equally low tone.

"Kate puts on a brave front, but I can tell she's nervous."

"Really? She always seems so confident."

"Didn't you see her hand shake when she took her flowers?"

He tensed and glanced her way. "No, I didn't notice."

The two footmen climbed up to their position standing at the back of the carriage. The smartly dressed driver slapped the reins, and the horses pulled forward. Kate looked out the carriage window, lifted her white-gloved hand, and waved as the carriage rolled down the drive.

"Good-bye!" Penny followed the carriage until it passed out the gate and into the street.

Jon waved with the others. Too bad they couldn't all go along to the palace and see how Kate fared. But that wasn't done. Her aunt would accompany her into the throne room, but Kate would be on her own, those last few steps, as she curtsied before the king and queen.

Be with her, Father. Give her courage and grace. Guide her through today and into the right path for her future.

Andrew tugged on his sleeve. "Can we finish our game?"

Jon watched the carriage disappear around the corner. He lowered his gaze to the lad. "I'm afraid we'll have to start over."

"That's all right. Maybe it will give you a chance to win."

Jon's teasing growl filled the air as he chased Andrew up the steps and back into the house.

• • •

Kate gripped the ribbon-wrapped stem of her bouquet and followed the long procession moving slowly down the high-ceilinged hallway of Buckingham Palace. The scent of roses and jasmine floated in the air.

She glanced at the women walking ahead of her. Each one who would be presented wore a white satin gown with a veil and carried her long train draped over her arm just like Kate. Their dresses were unique, though the rules of court dress made them share some common features.

The soft red carpet hushed their footsteps, and the only sounds were the rustle of satin and petticoats swishing around the women's ankles and an occasional hushed exchange between a debutante and her sponsor.

Aunt Louisa walked beside Kate, scanning the line and sizing up the other women. She leaned toward Kate. "There is Gertrude Hoffman," she whispered, "and I believe that is her new daughter-in-law, Priscilla."

Kate nodded, though she had no idea which women her aunt was talking about.

The procession slowed to a stop as the next group entered the throne room, and a decorative barricade was placed in front of the open doorway.

Kate shifted her weight from one foot to the other, feeling her shoes sink into the carpet. Her left shoe felt tighter than the right, and that foot was beginning to go numb. *Wonderful.* Soon she'd be hobbling her way into the throne room. She wiggled her toes trying to relieve the painful sensation, but it was useless. If only she could sit down, remove her shoe, and rub her toes back to life.

Hoping to distract herself from her painful foot, she glanced at the large painting on the wall to the left, but the rather gruesome battle scene didn't hold her interest. She scanned the line of women ahead, trying to tell how long it would be until she reached the throne room.

Why was it so warm and stuffy? The heavy train draped over her arm felt like a hot, sticky blanket. Moisture gathered between her shoulder blades and trickled down her back. She sighed and glanced toward the tall window to her right, wishing someone would push it open and let in a cool breeze. She smoothed her gloved hand over her skirt.

"For heaven sake, hold still and stop fussing," Aunt Louisa hissed.

"I'm not fussing. I'm simply trying to get comfortable." Kate straightened her posture and tried to look serene, but doubts stormed her heart.

She tried to recall the compliments William had given her before she left the house and Julia's encouraging words, but they faded as her aunt's critical comments flooded back. The entire ride to the palace Kate had listened to a litany of her shortcomings and warnings of what would happen if she failed to remember her training. Why, just once, couldn't her aunt say something encouraging or reassuring?

The memory of Jon watching her come down the stairs rose in her mind. He seemed impressed at first, but his bland comment left her feeling deflated and full of doubt. "Good luck"? What kind of send-off was that? It sounded like something you said to a pal heading off to school to take an exam. If only he had said she looked beautiful, then she might have believed it.

Up ahead, two pages dressed in black-and-gold uniforms removed the barricade and signaled the next group to enter the throne room. Kate's stomach tensed. It was almost time.

Her aunt gripped her forearm. "This is important, Katherine. Remember your training."

Kate clenched her jaw. How could she forget?

The page motioned them ahead. "This way, please. Have your card ready." He lowered his voice. "You will curtsy three times—to the king, the queen, and to Princess Mary."

Kate swallowed and nodded. Her aunt would accompany her through the doorway, but then she would step back and let Kate go ahead.

The page pointed at her arm. "Your train, miss."

"Oh, yes." She lowered her arm, and the fabric slid to the carpet. The page used his long wand to straighten out the material behind her. "Thank you," she murmured and started to step forward.

But he held out his hand. "One moment, please." He watched the young woman in line ahead of her approach the queen and begin her curtsy, then he turned and nodded to Kate.

She pulled in a deep breath and stepped forward. *"Think grace, think poise."* Mr. Rounpear's words floated through her mind as she followed the red carpet to the center of the room where the king, queen, and princess sat in elaborate chairs on a dais.

The Lord Chamberlain—a distinguished man with silver hair, who was dressed in white tights, black knee-length pants, and a black-and-gold jacket—stood to the right of the king. Kate's hand trembled as she handed him her card. The young woman in line in front of her made her final curtsy to Princess Mary.

The Lord Chamberlain nodded to her, and she crossed in front of King George.

"Miss Katherine Evangeline Ramsey, daughter of the late Sir Randolph Ramsey, Baronet of Highland Hall, and the late Lady Eden Ramsey. Presented by her aunt, Lady Louisa Gatewood of Wellsbury."

A dizzy wave swept through Kate, and all the air seemed to rush out of her lungs, but she had to keep moving. She focused on the king's shoulder as she stepped to the right and sank down for her first curtsy. Lowering her head, she counted to three. As she rose, the king offered a slight smile, which she returned. He was a small man, almost frail-looking, with large blue eyes and a neatly trimmed dark brown beard and moustache. He was not nearly as impressive as the paintings she had seen of him.

Her train swept along beside her as she crossed in front of Queen Mary and began her second curtsy. Her legs shook, but she managed to sink down and then rise without swaying. The queen wore a beautiful royal-blue gown, a pearl necklace with several strands, and a sparkling diamond-and-pearl tiara. Her blond, wavy hair was beautifully styled, and she acknowledged Kate with a brief nod, her delicate pearl earrings swaying as she did so.

Relief flowed through Kate. Just one more curtsy and she would be finished. She stepped to the right two paces and faced Princess Mary. The young woman's bored gaze drifted around the room.

Kate tensed and waited, but the princess did not look her way. *How rude!* Princess or not, she ought to at least acknowledge those who bowed before her. Perhaps she should just stand there until the princess met her gaze. Or what if she tossed her bouquet into the princess's lap? That might get her attention.

Kate dismissed those thoughts. It might give her a moment's pleasure to startle the princess, but it would probably give her aunt a heart attack and make Kate a social pariah.

She sank down before the princess and lowered her head, but she didn't bother to count to three. Why should she? The princess was obviously bored and eager for the event to conclude.

She rose, thankful to be finished, and turned to go. The whole room suddenly grew quiet. She glanced back. The princess's eyes flashed to life and drilled into her.

Kate froze. Mr. Rounpear's instructions flooded her mind. Turning her back on the royal family was a supreme insult. She was supposed to back out of the room and keep her face toward them at all times. Heat surged up Kate's neck and into her cheeks. Slowly, she turned and faced the royal family again.

The princess glared at her, then lifted her chin and looked away.

Kate lowered her gaze, took a step back and then another, but her shoe snagged her train. She tried to kick it gently to the side, but the heavy fabric tangled around her foot. Everyone watched her now. She had to keep backing up and make her way out of the throne room, but how could she get her feet free from the volumes of material now swirled around her? She glanced about, desperately wishing her aunt or a page would come to her aid, but no one moved toward her.

The next young woman in line approached the Lord Chamberlain, but then hesitated as she watched Kate.

Kate pulled in a deep breath. It seemed she would have to solve the problem herself, and that was precisely what she would do. "Excuse me, Your Highness." She gave a firm nod, lowered herself as gracefully as possible and untangled the train from around her feet.

The crowd gasped.

Kate's face flamed as she spread the train out to the side. Then she rose and backed across the carpet, and this time her train flowed along beside her. As she passed through the doorway, her legs turned to jelly, and she reached out toward the page.

He grabbed her arm. "Are you all right, Miss?"

"Yes, yes…I'm fine." But that was one of the biggest lies she had ever told.

He scooped up her train and waited. "Your arm, miss."

"Oh yes, thank you." She barely managed to choke out the words and accept the train before she fled down the hallway, her face on fire and her heart racing like a thoroughbred at Ascot.

● ● ●

Jon glanced at the clock on the library mantel, then lowered his gaze to his textbook. He thought Kate would be back by now, but there was a reception following the presentation, and he supposed that was what had kept her out so late.

The evening had turned cool, and a faint breeze from the partially open window drifted in, carrying the fresh rain-washed scent from the front garden. Jon sighed and settled back in his chair. Everyone else had gone to bed, content to wait until morning to hear Kate's report about the evening. But he had decided to stay up and use the time to review several chapters for his exams next week.

He wasn't really waiting up for Kate. He needed to study.

He turned the page, stifled a yawn, and focused on the description of the techniques for throat surgery. But the words faded, and the image of Kate descending the stairs rose in his mind. He didn't think he had ever seen anyone quite so beautiful.

He shook his head. He ought not to think of her that way. It would only make things uncomfortable between them.

The sound of a coach approaching broke through his thoughts. He rose from his chair and crossed to the window. Pushing aside the curtain, he glanced outside. The Ramsey family carriage rolled to a stop on the front drive. The footman sprang down from his perch on the back and opened the carriage door.

Lady Gatewood reached out, took the footman's hand, and stepped down. "I don't understand how you could forget something so important." Her harsh tone cut through the quiet evening air.

Katherine followed her aunt out of the coach. "How many times do I have to say I'm sorry?"

"Until I believe you truly mean it!"

"I made a mistake. It was a difficult situation. I did the best I could."

"The best you could? The best you could!" Lady Gatewood huffed, lifted her skirt, and marched up the front stairs. "After all the money your uncle and I have invested in your preparation, you could have at least made an effort to remember the most basic rules of etiquette."

Jon stepped back from the window and shook his head. After only a few days staying with the Ramseys, he had developed a strong dislike for Kate's overbearing aunt. The woman never had a kind word for anyone, especially Kate, though she usually managed to cover her disapproval with false smiles and thinly veiled sarcasm.

Nothing was veiled tonight.

He crossed to the library doorway and glanced across the entrance hall. Lawrence opened the front door. Lady Gatewood strode past the butler without a word and marched up the stairs, her face a fuming mask.

Kate walked in, her shoulders sagging as her gaze followed her aunt up the stairs.

Lawrence closed the front door. "Good evening, Miss Katherine."

"Good evening, Lawrence." She sighed and handed the butler, her wilted bouquet. "Could you take care of this?"

"Of course, miss." Sympathy filled the butler's eyes. "May I assist you in any other way?"

"No, thank you." She turned and saw Jon in the doorway, and her face blanched.

"If you don't require anything else, miss, I will bid you good night." Lawrence locked the front door, then walked down the servants' stairs.

Kate clasped her hands and looked up at Jon. "I'm sure you heard my aunt's comments."

"Yes. I'm sorry. I didn't mean to eavesdrop."

Kate sighed. "How could you help it? I'm afraid she's quite upset."

He nodded, then glanced over his shoulder, debating his next words. "I've been studying in the library. There's still a nice fire. Would you like to join me?"

Kate glanced up the stairs, then back at Jon. "I suppose it would be all right. It wouldn't do any good to go up to my room now. I'm sure I won't be able to fall asleep for quite some time."

Jon motioned for her to go ahead, and she walked past. The scent of jasmine floated around her. He inhaled, savoring the sweet aroma.

She crossed the room and sank down on the settee by the fireplace, her train pooled at her feet. "I know it would be terribly rude, but my foot is throbbing. Would you mind if I took off my shoe?"

Jon grinned. "Not at all. It's your home. Take them both off if you like."

She bent and slipped off her shoes, then proceeded to rub her left foot. "I'll probably be permanently crippled if I ever have to wear these shoes again."

"Too tight?"

"Yes. They felt fine when I first put them on, but after standing in them for several hours, I'm sure the left is a size smaller than the right. Either that or my feet are different sizes." She smiled, though there was still a trace of sadness in her eyes.

He returned her smile. "It sounds as though this evening didn't go as well as you'd hoped."

"That's putting it mildly."

"Care to tell me about it?"

"I might as well. I'd rather you hear my version before you read it in the newspaper tomorrow."

Jon cocked his head. "You think it will be in the paper?"

"Probably. My aunt and uncle arranged for a social columnist to attend specifically to report on my presentation, and I'm afraid I put on quite a show."

"What happened?"

"Well, I didn't fall, if that's what you're thinking."

He held up his hand. "Please, I'd never think such a thing."

She shifted on the settee. "I'm afraid my temper got the best of me."

"Really?" He struggled to suppress his grin. During the last few days, he'd seen a few examples of Kate's rather strong personality, but he didn't find it offensive. In fact, he rather liked her more for it. She didn't put on airs like other women he'd met. Instead, she said what she was thinking and took action rather than sitting back and waiting for someone else to solve a problem.

"It was all terribly nerve-racking. I had to wait in line at least two hours before I could walk into the throne room, and then everyone's eyes were on me." Kate stared toward the fire. "I did fine with my curtsies before the king and queen, but Princess Mary was so bored she wouldn't look my way."

"Not even a nod?"

"No, not even one. And that made me so flustered that as soon as I rose from my curtsy, I turned away to walk out." She closed her eyes and shook her head. "You must never turn your back on royalty."

"I didn't know that."

She opened her eyes, and he couldn't miss the dismay in them. "Well, I did. It's one of the first lessons they teach you when you're practicing for your presentation."

He sent her a sympathetic look, but he was surprised to hear such rules still existed.

"As soon as I realized my mistake, I faced them again, but when I backed up to leave, I stepped on my train, and I couldn't get it untangled from around my feet."

Jon grimaced.

"No one would help me, so I had to bend down and untangle it myself. I did it as gracefully as possible, but the whole room fell silent and stared as though I had crashed onto the carpet." She rubbed her forehead and sighed. "Now I'll be the laughingstock of London—the girl who insulted the royal family and destroyed her chances of being invited anywhere this season." She lowered her hand and looked at Jon again. "At least, that's my aunt's opinion."

"I wouldn't worry. I'm sure it wasn't as bad as you think."

Kate sent him a doubtful look. "I've heard of girls being scorned the entire season for much less than that."

Jon frowned and drummed his fingers on the arm of the chair. "I know you want to make a good impression, especially on potential suitors, but do you really think you'll be judged worthy or unworthy based on one small mistake?" He studied her for a moment. "A man choosing a bride is more interested in her character and personality than her ability to curtsy or remember the rules for a royal presentation."

She stilled, her gaze fixed on him.

Did she think he was talking about his own preferences? Heat rose up his neck. "I mean…I know every debutante hopes to receive a proposal her first season."

"Yes, of course." Her voice sounded soft and strained. "That's what's expected."

"Well, just remember you're a unique young woman with many fine qualities. I'm sure you'll handle yourself well at the next event, and the whole thing will soon be forgotten."

Her expression softened, and appreciation filled her eyes.

"Katherine?" Julia stepped through the doorway, wearing her dressing gown and slippers. "I thought I heard you come in." She noticed Jon and questions filled her eyes.

His back stiffened. "Kate was just telling me about her presentation."

Julia shifted her gaze back to Kate. "How did it go?"

"It was very long and stressful, but I only made one mistake, and Jon thinks it won't really matter in the long run."

"Good." Julia held out her hand to Kate. "Come upstairs. I'll help you get ready for bed, and you can tell me more."

Jon rose from his chair. He should have known better than to invite Kate into the library when no one else was present. It wasn't usually done, but they were almost like family...

Indeed? And is that how you see her? As family?

He brushed the disturbing thought aside, watching Kate scoop up her shoes and rise from the settee.

"Good night, Jon. Thank you for listening to my tale of woe." She offered him a fleeting smile, then walked out of the library with Julia.

As she disappeared from view, he blew out a slow, deep breath, sorry their conversation had been cut short. Truly, he could have enjoyed her honesty and humor all night...

His eyes widened. What was he thinking? Kate was young, self-focused, and caught up in the season. And yet...

He studied the empty doorway. She hadn't seemed self-focused tonight. In fact, she'd seemed charming and delightful.

That thought caught him by surprise, and a warning flashed through him. It was a good thing Julia had come in and interrupted their conversation when she did.

He needed to focus on his training and his plans for the future and not on Miss Katherine Ramsey—no matter how delightful she might be.

FOUR

W illiam walked into the entry hall and scanned the row of staff members lined up by the stairs. Lawrence nodded to him, indicating the staff were all present and ready for morning Scripture reading and prayer. The entry hall at Ramsey House was a good deal smaller than the great hall at Highland, but William believed it was important to bring everyone together and begin the day this way.

He opened his Bible. "Good morning, everyone."

"Good morning, sir," Lawrence replied for the staff.

William smiled at Julia, and she returned a loving look as she took her place beside him. Some days it still surprised William that this beautiful and caring woman had set aside her plans to return to India as a missionary and accepted his proposal. His affection and appreciation for her grew deeper every day, and he only wished the wedding would come more quickly, so they would never have to be parted again.

Kate, Penny, Andrew, Millie, and Jon joined them by the fireplace, neatly dressed and ready for the day. Lady Gatewood never graced them with her presence this early in the morning. As the only married woman among them, she followed the tradition of having her breakfast in bed and joining the family later.

Her decision not to come down had irritated William at first, but Julia reminded him Louisa's attitude and comments often made them all uncomfortable, and it was probably best that she did not to take part.

"This morning I'll be reading Psalm 46." William cleared his throat and lowered his gaze to the page. "'God is our refuge and strength, a very present help in trouble. Therefore will we not fear, though the earth be removed, and though the mountains be carried into the midst of the sea; though the waters thereof roar and be troubled, though the mountains shake with the swelling thereof.'"

He continued reading and then slowed as he came to his favorite part of the psalm. "'Be still, and know that I am God: I will be exalted among the heathen, I will be exalted in the earth. The LORD of hosts is with us; the God of Jacob is our refuge.'" He let those words sink in and bring him comfort. "Let us pray."

He bowed his head. "Father, You are a great and holy God, but You are also our personal place of safety and strength. We thank You for your faithfulness and generous provision for our staff and family. We ask for Your guidance and protection over our household today. May all we do and say bring honor and glory to Your name. In Christ's name we pray. Amen."

Lawrence lifted his head, a look of appreciation in his eyes.

William exchanged a nod with his butler. It had been only eight months since he inherited Highland Hall and took charge of the staff and estate that had belonged to his second cousin, Randolph Ramsey. There had been a bit of a struggle as everyone adjusted to the changes, but it seemed he had finally won the loyalty of his butler. No doubt bringing Lawrence and some of the other staff to London with him had helped that process.

Lawrence turned and dismissed the servants to continue with their duties.

Kate crossed the entrance hall toward the butler. "Lawrence, have the newspapers arrived?"

"Yes, miss. They're in the dining room."

"Thank you." Kate and Penny exchanged excited glances, then hurried into the dining room ahead of the rest of the family.

Julia leaned closer to William. "I hope the article is not too unkind toward Kate." Earlier that morning she had told him about Kate's struggle at her presentation. William could only hope it wouldn't make it more difficult for his young cousin to receive invitations for the season's events. They were already under a bit of social scrutiny since William's sister, Sarah, had married Clark Dalton, the head gardener at Highland, and William himself was now engaged to his children's governess.

He touched Julia's hand. "I think it's more likely they'll leave Katherine out of the article altogether, but we shall see."

They entered the dining room, and Julia led Andrew and Millie to the buffet where she helped them prepare their breakfast plates. William stood to the side and waited his turn with Jon. "I understand you're attending the garden party at Dr. Gleason's home this afternoon."

When Jon didn't answer, William turned toward him. Jon's gaze was fixed on Kate and Penny as they spread the newspaper out on the dining-room table. "Jon?"

Julia's brother blinked and turned toward him. "I'm sorry. What did you say?"

"I asked if you were going to Dr. and Mrs. Gleason's this afternoon."

Jon's eyebrows lifted. "Why, yes, I am."

William smiled. "I'm not a mind reader. Your aunt stopped by yesterday with an invitation for us, and she mentioned you might be attending."

"Dr. Gleason invited me last week, no doubt at my Aunt Beatrice's prompting. But he is the head of St. George's Hospital, so I thought I should accept."

William nodded. "Your aunt thought it might be a nice opportunity for Kate to meet a few people before the rush of the season begins."

"Look, there you are!" Penny pointed to a photo at the top of the page.

Kate gasped and lifted her hand to her mouth.

Jon's gaze swung toward her. "What does it say, Kate?"

"Just a moment." Kate bent closer and scanned the article, her expression growing brighter as she read. "It seems...all right."

"All right?" Penny sent Kate a questioning smile. "It's wonderful."

Julia turned from the buffet table. "Why don't you read it aloud?"

Kate hesitated, her cheeks flushing.

"I'll read it." Penny leaned over the newspaper. "'A very pretty girl among those who were presented at court last evening was Miss Katherine Ramsey, the elder daughter of the late Randolph Ramsey, Baronet of Highland Hall, and the late Lady Eden Ramsey. Miss Ramsey made her appearance in society under the wing of her aunt, Lady Louisa Gatewood of Wellsbury, who is well known in London society. Miss Ramsey's pleasing appearance as well as her grace and poise during her presentation won her the praise and admiration of all in attendance.'"

Penny grinned and gave her sister a one-armed hug. "See? I told you they wouldn't mention you turning your back on the royal family."

"Thank goodness."

Penny continued reading. "'Miss Ramsey much resembles Lady Gatewood, with the same golden-brown hair and blue eyes, although she is taller than her aunt. She is a fine horsewoman who enjoys country life. But she is also gifted with an exceptional voice and sings charmingly when she gathers with friends and family.'"

William scooped some eggs onto his plate. "That's an interesting bit to include since it has nothing to do with your presentation."

"I'm sure Aunt Louisa supplied that information," Kate added.

Penny bent over the newspaper again. "'Up to the moment of her appearance on the social scene, Miss Ramsey has been deeply engaged with her studies and has received an excellent education.'"

Julia placed Millie's plate on the table and smiled, looking pleased by that comment.

"And listen to this part." Penny beamed as she continued reading. "'Miss Ramsey has a younger sister, Miss Penelope Ramsey, who is sixteen and may be one of next year's most celebrated debutantes.'"

William shot Julia a questioning glance. He thought they had two more years before Penny would be presented. Was this Louisa's way of placing the idea of an early debut in Penny's mind? He certainly hoped not. He would have to speak to Louisa and make sure she understood his position.

Kate was eager to receive a proposal, but eighteen was awfully young to be thinking about getting married. Hopefully, if she did catch the eye of the right young man this season, they could put off the wedding for at least six months and hopefully a year.

"That all sounds very complimentary," Jon said.

Kate glanced down at the newspaper again. "I'm so relieved they didn't say anything about my feet getting tangled in my train."

"That's because the article was written and approved by your uncle and me well before the events of last night." Louisa crossed the dining room toward the table.

Kate's smile faded. "So they made up the part about my grace and poise at the presentation?"

"They wrote what we paid them to write."

The joy drained from Kate's face, and she lowered her gaze.

William clenched his jaw. Couldn't Louisa ever temper her words? Didn't she realize how these statements affected Kate?

Jon glared at Louisa as he set his plate on the table.

"There's no need to look so deflated, Katherine. You should consider yourself lucky," Louisa continued. "I was afraid your poor behavior would prompt the man to change what had already been written."

Kate looked up. "But the people who attended the presentation saw what happened."

"There is nothing we can do about that now." Louisa took a seat at the table. "Thankfully most of London was not there. They will believe what was reported in the newspaper, and you can thank your lucky stars for that."

William sent Louisa a stern glance. The woman was intolerable! "Let's fold up the newspaper and have breakfast."

Louisa returned William's look with equal strength and took the newspaper from Penny. "I've already eaten, and I want to read the rest of the article." She squinted toward the page.

Julia sent William a sympathetic glance, but it did little to remove the sting of Louisa's comments. His stomach burned as he sat at the head of the table and placed his napkin in his lap.

What had possessed him to agree that Louisa could stay with them for the next three months? Of course, Katherine needed a sponsor for her presentation, and that had to be a woman who had been presented when she was a debutante. When Louisa told them she had promised her late sister, Eden Ramsey, that she would take on that role for Katherine, he didn't feel he had a choice. Still, he wasn't sure it was worth the aggravation.

William glanced down the table at Jon. At least Julia's brother was an agreeable houseguest. His interest in the children was refreshing, and his kindness toward Kate and Penny was also welcome. Jon was an interesting young man with admirable goals, and William was glad he had this time to become better acquainted with him.

• • •

Lydia straightened her shoulders as she stood with Ann in the lower hallway and faced Mr. Lawrence and Mrs. Adams.

Mr. Lawrence clasped his hands behind his back. "I must urge you to be very careful and never let the children out of your sight. Do you understand?"

"Yes sir. We'll keep a good eye on them." Lydia tried to sound confident, but underneath she felt a bit uneasy about the outing. The park was only a few blocks away, but she'd never walked the streets of London alone. Of course, Ann and the children would be with her. Still, the responsibility of it all weighed down upon her.

"Sir William has entrusted the children into your care, and you must be sure to watch them well."

Ann nodded, her expression sober. "We will, sir."

Mrs. Adams turned to Mr. Lawrence. "I'm sure Lydia and Ann know how to take charge of two children and walk them to the park."

"But this is their first time to do so in London. And an outing to Wiltshire Park is not the same as a walk around the grounds at Highland."

A bit of amusement shone in Mrs. Adams's eyes. "I suppose you're right, but they're sensible young women."

"As long as they keep their minds on their duty and don't become distracted."

Mrs. Adams sent Mr. Lawrence an indulgent smile. "I'm sure they'll be fine."

He straightened his vest. "I hope so."

"All right, then." Mrs. Adams turned to Lydia and Ann. "Off you go, and enjoy the afternoon. But be sure to bring the children back by three-thirty so they have time to wash and change before tea."

"Yes ma'am." Lydia nodded to the housekeeper, then hurried up the stone stairs to collect the children. Ann followed close behind.

Ten minutes later the four of them walked out the front gate and set off toward Wiltshire Park. Hooves clattered on the cobblestones as two carriages rolled past. Lydia lifted her gaze to the white clouds scuttling across the bright blue sky. "My, it's a lovely day."

"The nicest we've had since we arrived in London."

A motorcar buzzed by at a frightening speed, spewing exhaust and honking at the carriages it passed. Lydia clasped Millie's hand more tightly.

Millie smiled up at Lydia. "I like London, but it's rather noisy."

"Yes, that's true. I hope the park will be a bit quieter."

As they rounded the corner, Andrew hurried on ahead.

"Please wait for us, Andrew." Ann quickened her steps.

The boy slowed and looked over his shoulder. "I hope you won't make me walk this slowly when we reach the park."

"Never mind about that. You'll have a good romp when we get there."

Andrew sighed, but he stayed with them as they passed through the open wrought-iron gateway. A broad, green lawn opened up before them, dotted with several tall shade trees. Birds twittered overhead, and a fresh breeze whisked away the pungent scent of the street. A curving pathway led through the park toward a small lake in the center. Gardens filled with red and yellow tulips lined one side of the walkway. For just a moment it reminded Lydia of the fields and pond at her family's farm.

Several women and a few men strolled along the pathway around the lake in groups of two or three. Most of the women wore large hats or carried parasols to shade their faces from the sun. Boys and girls ran across the grass, some pushing hoops with a stick and others playing a game of tag. A group of young boys knelt on the lakeside path, engaged in a game of marbles.

Andrew pointed to the boys. "May I join them?"

Ann studied the group, and turned back to Andrew. "All right, but remember, if you want to have friends, you must be friendly."

"I will!" With that, Andrew dashed off.

"Be sure to play fair," Ann called, but Andrew didn't look back.

Ann and Lydia took a seat on a wooden bench nearby with a clear view of Andrew. Millie followed them, but she didn't sit down. Three young girls played hopscotch on the path a few feet away, and Millie watched them.

Lydia touched her arm. "Would you like to play with those girls?"

Millie bit her lip. "I don't know them."

"It's all right. Just go up and say hello. That's how you make friends."

Millie twisted the toe of her shoe in the grass for a few seconds, then slowly walked toward the girls. The tallest girl with long blond curls looked up and invited Millie to join their game.

Ann sighed and sat back. "At last—a moment of peace."

"Yes, it will be nice to have a bit of a rest." Lydia gazed across the park, taking in the lovely view and enjoying the warmth of the sun on her shoulders.

"I don't know why, but I thought things would be easier here."

Lydia turned to Ann. "You're finding it harder here than at Highland?"

"Keeping Andrew out of mischief is never easy, but being cooped up inside every day…"

Sympathy rose in Lydia's heart. Her position as lady's maid to Katherine and Penelope might be difficult at times, but she didn't envy Ann, overseeing the children all day, every day. "I'm surprised they brought Andrew and Millie to London. Most families coming in for the season leave their younger children in the country with the governess."

"They couldn't very well do that since Miss Foster has come along as well."

"Yes, that's true."

Ann shifted on the bench. "It's a bit strange isn't it? She's the governess, but she's Sir William's intended, and in September they'll marry and she'll become mistress of Highland."

"I'm glad it's worked out that way. She's always been kind to me."

"Yes, to me as well. She knows what it's like to work for a living and take orders from those above her. I'm sure she'll be an understanding mistress."

Ann nodded, and her gaze drifted to the boys kneeling together on the path. "Even though Andrew gives me fits, I'm still glad I came. I've always wanted to see London."

"So have I." Lydia sat forward, her spirit lifting. "Why don't we do some sightseeing next time we have our half day?"

"That would be nice. What do you want to see?"

"Maybe the changing of the guard at the palace, or we could go to a picture show."

Ann smiled. "Yes. Let's check the newspaper and find out what's playing next week."

Lydia started to reply, but something caught her eye. About thirty yards away, a young woman in a dark coat crossed the park toward the lake. She wore no hat, and though her back was to Lydia, the tilt of her shoulders and the way she walked looked familiar.

Lydia took a sharp breath and squinted against the bright sunlight reflected off the lake. The woman looked like Helen! But that didn't make sense. What would her sister be doing in London…at Wiltshire Park?

"Lydia, what is it?" Ann followed Lydia's gaze.

A heavyset, broad-shouldered man walked with the woman. He wore a red plaid cap, faded brown jacket, and heavy work boots. Lydia's heartbeat sped up. It was hard to tell from the back, but he looked a bit like Charlie Gibbons, the farmhand who worked for their neighbors, the MacGregors.

The woman turned, bringing her profile in view.

Lydia gasped and jumped to her feet. "Helen!"

The woman slowed and looked over her shoulder, scanning the park. The man grabbed her arm and tugged her off at a quick pace through the trees at the side of the path.

Lydia lifted her skirt and ran after them.

"Lydia, wait!" Ann jumped up from the bench.

Lydia reached the spot where the woman had disappeared and skidded to a stop. Panting, she bent and peered through the trees, but there was no sign of them now.

Ann caught up with her. "Lydia, what are you doing?"

"I thought…I thought I saw Helen."

Ann's eyes widened. "Your sister? The one who ran away?"

"Yes." Lydia lifted her hand to her chest, trying to catch her breath.

"Are you sure?"

"I don't know. It looked like her." Lydia rubbed her eyes and glanced around, trying to make sense of it.

A shout rang out behind them. Lydia and Ann spun to find that the marble game had turned into a wrestling match. Andrew grabbed hold of a pudgy blond lad's jacket. The other boys circled around, clapping and shouting, urging them on.

"Oh no!" Ann ran toward the tussling pair.

Lydia hiked up her skirt and hurried after her.

"That's enough!" Ann grabbed hold of Andrew's shoulder and pushed the other boy away.

Andrew's face glowed red beneath his freckles, as he squirmed and tried to break free. "Let me *go*!"

"Not until you settle down." Ann gave Andrew a slight shake and a stern look. "What's going on here?"

The other boy thrust his finger toward Andrew. "He cheated!"

"I did not!" Andrew's eyes blazed.

"I saw you move the marble with your foot."

"That's not true!" Andrew glared at the other boy. "You called me a liar!"

The blond boy's mouth twisted into an angry grimace.

"All right." Ann looked back and forth between them. "Misunderstandings happen in games and in life, but it's better to talk them out or walk away rather than trying to settle them with your fists." She turned to Andrew. "Why don't you say you're sorry and offer to shake hands?"

Andrew crossed his arms and turned away, his jaw set.

Ann stepped closer to Andrew and lowered her voice. "You better do as I say, or I'll tell your father what happened. And if he finds out you've been fighting, I won't be bringing you back to the park anytime soon."

The battle raged across Andrew's face for a few seconds, but he finally turned around and extended his hand. "Sorry."

The blond boy continued to scowl.

"Go on, then." Ann tapped the blond boy's shoulder. "Shake hands like a gentleman."

"Oh, all right," he muttered and gave Andrew's hand a brief shake.

Millie ran up and joined them. "Andrew, why were you fighting with that boy?"

"Never mind." Andrew strode off toward the gate leading out of the park.

"Andrew, wait!" Ann took Millie's hand and turned back to Lydia. "We'd better go."

Lydia looked over her shoulder to where the man and woman had disappeared. Was it truly Helen, or had her longing to see her sister made her imagine the woman looked like her? But if it wasn't Helen, why had the man hustled the woman off when Lydia called to her?

"Maybe you can come back and look for your sister tomorrow." Ann slipped her free arm through Lydia's.

Lydia nodded. Her throat tightened, and she blinked away her tears.

"Come on." Ann patted Lydia's arm. "We better catch up with Andrew before he gets out of sight."

Lydia stuffed her hands in her pockets and trudged down the path toward the park gate.

FIVE

Kate collapsed her parasol and stepped into the shade beneath the large white tent set up in the side garden of the Gleasons' stately home in Chelsea. About forty guests had been invited to the garden party. Some stood in small groups around the edge of the tent engaged in conversations. Others were seated in white wicker chairs at round tables. Small bouquets of bright spring flowers decorated the center of each table.

If only she felt as fresh and pretty as those bouquets, but with her corset tied so tight, and the stiff fabric of her new blue dress prickling her skin, she found it nearly impossible to relax and enjoy the party.

She plucked at her high collar, wishing a breeze would blow through the tent, but the air felt warm and damp. A trickle of perspiration gathered on the side of her forehead, just below her broad-brimmed hat. She lifted her gloved finger and discreetly wiped it away.

Her aunt scanned the tent, perusing the guests. "Come along, Katherine. There are people we need to meet." She took Kate's arm and led her away from William, Julia, and Jon.

Kate glanced over her shoulder. Jon gave her a half smile as he watched her go, then turned and followed William and Julia in the other direction.

A footman walked past, dressed in formal livery and carrying a silver tray filled with tempting-looking sandwiches. He stopped at a nearby table and offered them to the women seated there. A maid in a neat black uniform, white ruffled apron, and starched white cap circulated around the tent, offering cups of tea and fruit punch to the guests.

Louisa tightened her hold on Kate's arm and lowered her voice. "There's Agatha Harcourt with her daughter, Laurel. She was presented just after Easter." She narrowed her eyes. "Goodness, look at that girl's hair. What a sight. I'd never allow you out of the house with hair looking like that."

Laurel's hair was a bit overdone, with ribbons circling her head in the Grecian style and a large, pink silk rose clipped on at the side, but her hair-style was no more elaborate than some of the other women's. Of course many wore large hats covered with feathers and flowers so you couldn't see their hair at all.

Kate glanced across the tent and saw Jon talking to Dr. and Mrs. Glea-son and their three daughters. She'd met the Gleasons at a dinner at her aunt and uncle's home last fall, and her aunt had told her they were impor-tant people. Kate searched her memory for the girls' names. Ethel, Erma, and…Evelyn? Yes, that was it. Evelyn was the same age as Kate and was also coming out this season.

Jon smiled at something Evelyn said. Kate frowned, then turned away. Why should she care if Jon found Evelyn amusing? She hoped he would make some good connections this afternoon. Perhaps they would be helpful to him in the future.

"Louisa, I was hoping to see you today." A tall, regal woman in a cream-colored suit approached and extended her hand to Kate's aunt. She wore a beautiful cream hat with a wide brim decorated with several black ostrich feathers. Walking by her side was a handsome young man with wavy blond hair and deep-set gray eyes.

"Lady Wellington—Eleanor—how lovely to see you again." Louisa took the woman's hand. Her smile spread wider as her gaze traveled to the young man.

"You remember my eldest son, Edward?"

"Yes, of course." Louisa beamed at Edward and then smiled Kate's way.

Her aunt had told her to expect an introduction to Lord and Lady Wel-lington's oldest son. His father was the Earl of Dunaway, and they owned a large country estate in Somerset.

Eleanor motioned toward Louisa. "Edward, this is Lady Louisa Gate-wood of Wellsbury and her charming niece, Miss Katherine Ramsey of Highland Hall."

Edward waited and watched Kate with a slight smile.

Kate's training flashed into her mind. She must be the first to speak to him. With a practiced smile, she offered him her hand. "Mr. Wellington, it's so nice to meet you."

His expression warmed. "Miss Ramsey, the pleasure is all mine." He bowed over their clasped hands. "Since my mother and your aunt are such good friends, I hope you'll call me Edward."

Kate's heart fluttered. That was a positive sign.

He turned to Louisa, still holding Kate's hand. "That would be all right, wouldn't it?"

Her aunt could barely contain her pleasure. "Why, of course, Edward. That would be fine. The bond of friendship between our families goes back many years."

Kate slipped her hand from his, but she sent him her brightest smile.

For the next few minutes they discussed the warm weather, the number of guests attending the party, and the fine menu being served. Edward asked her several questions about her interests and life at Highland Hall, then listened attentively to her answers.

"My, you two certainly seem to have a lot in common." Good heavens. Louisa was practically gushing!

Kate's cheeks warmed and she looked away. Edward Wellington was charming, but with her aunt and his mother hanging on every word they spoke, the conversation felt a bit…strained.

Louisa turned to Eleanor. "Elizabeth Gleason and I are on the committee planning the St. George's Hospital bazaar, and I know she wanted to speak to you about joining us." She smiled at Edward. "I hope you'll excuse us for a few minutes."

"Of course." He smiled. "I'm sure Katherine and I can keep each other company."

Relief coursed through Kate. Thank heaven they were willing to leave her and Edward alone.

"We'll be back in a few minutes." Louisa's eyes flashed from Kate to Edward, then she whisked Eleanor Wellington away.

Edward turned to Kate. "Would you like some punch?"

"Yes, thank you." She actually was very thirsty, and a glass of punch sounded wonderful.

He signaled a maid, and she approached with a tray. He took two glasses, and offered one to Kate. "I understand you were presented at court last evening."

Kate's hand stilled, her punch glass halfway to her mouth. Had he read it in the paper or talked to someone who had been present? Kate swallowed and forced a smile. "Yes, I was."

"My sister MaryAnn is making her debut this season as well, so presentations are one of the main topics of conversation at our house," he said, gray eyes twinkling. "I read about your debut in the *Sketch* this morning. That was quite a feat, being one of the debs mentioned in that article."

Kate's sip of punch turned into a gulp, which sent her into a fit of coughing.

Edward reached for her arm. "Are you all right?"

She nodded, though she couldn't push out a word past her burning throat.

"Shall I get you a glass of water?"

"No, I'll be fine," she managed to croak and then coughed again, covering her mouth with her gloved hand.

Lines crinkled around his eyes as he tried to suppress his smile. "I'm sorry. This punch is chokingly sweet."

Kate shook her head. "It's not that." She glanced around the tent at the refined, well-dressed guests, feeling out of place. Was it because this was her first social event of the season—or because she was more used to country life than London society? Either way, the urge to throw off the rules was too hard to resist.

She looked back at Edward. "You know, that article didn't really tell what happened last night."

He cocked his head. "It didn't?"

"No. It was written days ago, and my aunt and uncle paid a hefty sum to be sure I was painted in a positive light."

Curiosity flickered in his eyes.

She drained her punch cup and set it aside. "The truth is, I made the three curtsies without too much trouble, but then I forgot you should never turn your back on the royal family."

A ripple of surprise passed across his face. "You didn't."

"I did." She sent him a firm nod. "I didn't realize my mistake until the room hushed and Princess Mary shot me the most terrible glare. Then my feet tangled in my train, and I had to bend down and try to sort it out before I could back out of the room."

Edward's grin spread wider. "My goodness. I would've loved to see that."

Kate smiled and then laughed. He joined her, and relief poured through her. She fanned her face, trying to regain her composure. "It was quite a spectacle, I can assure you."

He lifted his punch cup toward her as if in a toast. "Katherine Ramsey, I find your honesty quite refreshing."

"Thank you. But, please, my friends call me Kate."

"All right, if that's an invitation to be considered your friend, then I would be delighted to call you Kate."

Her heart lifted. Edward's warmth and humor made her glad to welcome him as a friend…and perhaps in time something more.

They continued their conversation for a few minutes, then he set his empty punch cup on a nearby table and turned back toward her. "The Ballet Russes is performing at Covent Garden this week. Our family has box seats for the season. Would you like to join us on Tuesday night? Of course your aunt or whomever you like would be welcome to come along as your chaperone."

Kate's eyes widened. "The Ballet Russes?" She'd read about their performances in the newspaper and had hoped to see them while they were in town.

He took a step closer and placed his hand on her arm. "They're quite modern. I hear they astounded Parisian society with their primitive costumes and exotic music."

A thrill raced along Kate's arm. "Thank you, Edward. I'd love to attend the ballet with you. And I'm sure my aunt or Julia would be happy to go with us."

"Is Julia your sister?"

"No, she's…" Kate hesitated. How should she explain her relationship to Julia? She didn't want to add to the gossip that was surely circulating about her governess and her cousin. "Julia is engaged to marry my cousin William. He's my guardian. She sometimes accompanies me as my chaperone."

"Of course." Edward's expression gave no hint that he had heard anything about William and Julia. "I'd be delighted to meet her and your cousin."

"They're here today." Kate glanced around, but she didn't see them.

"It's all right. I'll call on you tomorrow afternoon to meet them properly, and then we can make arrangements for Tuesday evening."

How thoughtful he was. "That sounds wonderful. I'll look forward to it."

Glancing past Edward's shoulder, she noticed Jon standing with Evelyn Gleason just outside the tent. The bright sunlight reflected off his hair, shooting it with threads of gold and highlighting the strong contours of his face. He looked her way. Then he glanced at Edward and his forehead creased.

What was that about? Did he know Edward? That didn't seem likely.

Evelyn said something to him, and he focused on her again. She was quite a beauty, with a petite figure and creamy complexion. Her father was not titled, but he was president of St. George's Hospital, and the family had good standing in society. She would be a fine match for Jon.

Kate quickly dismissed the idea. Evelyn Gleason didn't seem like the type of girl who would be eager to give up her life in London and become the wife of a missionary headed for India. Why was she even thinking about who Jon would marry? His future plans were none of her concern.

Kate focused on Edward again, listening as he spoke about his love for riding and hunting.

Edward Wellington was exactly the type of young man she had hoped to meet. Her aunt would be thrilled when she heard he had invited her to the ballet. How exciting it would be to walk into Covent Garden on the arm of such a handsome man from a well-respected family.

What a stroke of luck to be introduced to him at her very first event of the season!

• • •

"You lived in India? My goodness, that sounds terribly exciting. How long were you there?" Evelyn Gleason's large, dark-brown eyes sparkled as she looked up at Jon. Her fair complexion and upturned nose made her look younger than eighteen, though he knew that was her age. Her mother had announced it when they had been introduced, along with the fact Evelyn had been presented at court just two weeks earlier.

Evelyn's rose-colored hat matched her silky dress and seemed to give her cheeks a pink tint. Was she truly interested in Jon's missionary work in India, or was she simply hoping to capture a potential beau?

He chose to believe the best about her, though he couldn't help remembering Theo's comment about Dr. Gleason wanting his daughters to meet and marry medical students. "I lived in India from the time I was twelve until I returned to London two years ago to continue my medical training."

"How interesting. I've never traveled more than a day's journey from London, but I hope to see more of the world someday."

"Traveling and living overseas can be a wonderful experience. It opened my eyes to what God is doing around the world."

She nodded, her expression eager. "I imagine actually living in a country and serving as a missionary would give you a much better understanding of the people and culture than simply traveling through on holiday."

"Yes, it does." His gaze drifted past Evelyn to the other side of the tent, where Kate stood with a tall man about Jon's age. He wore a well-cut, cream-colored suit with a red rose pinned to his lapel. His intent focus on Kate and pleased expression made it clear he was enjoying their conversation.

"Jon?"

He blinked and shifted his gaze back to Evelyn. "I'm sorry, what did you say?"

She tipped her head. "Who are you watching?"

His neck warmed. "Forgive me. I was distracted for a moment."

"It's all right. That's why we young people do the season—to see and be seen and hopefully find our future life's companion." She lifted her finger to her lips. "But I'm sure my mother would not approve of that comment." A teasing smile tipped up the corners of her mouth. "Who do you have your eye on?"

"I was just checking on a friend."

"Come now, tell me who she is." She waited, her face upturned. Obviously she would not be satisfied until he answered.

He looked across the tent. "Katherine Ramsey. My sister is engaged to her guardian, William Ramsey."

Evelyn casually glanced over her shoulder. "Oh yes. I met her last fall." She watched Kate for a moment, then turned back. "I believe she was one of the debutantes mentioned in this morning's paper."

"Yes, that was Kate." A surge of something close to pride rose in his chest as he recalled the comments in the article. Lady Gatewood may have paid the columnist to write it, but the facts were true. Kate was a beautiful and accomplished young woman, and he was sure she'd soon have a long line of suitors. He pushed that unpleasant thought away.

Evelyn looked back at Jon. "She's very pretty. I can see why you have your eye on her."

He let those words roll past and kept his focus on Evelyn. It wouldn't do to have Evelyn spread gossip about him and Kate, especially when there was no truth to it. "This is Kate's first event of the season. I thought it might be a bit intimidating for her."

Evelyn glanced Kate's way again. "I'd say she's doing quite well. That's Edward Wellington she's speaking to now. He's the son of Lord Wellington, the Earl of Dunaway. They own a very large estate in Somerset." She lowered her voice. "He's the eldest, and he's in line to inherit it all."

"What else do you know about him?"

"Only that he recently ended a long courtship with a young woman and left her with a broken heart."

Jon tensed and glanced at Kate. She and Edward Wellington were laughing about something. Then Edward took a step closer, laid his hand on Kate's arm, and whispered something in her ear.

Irritation coursed through Jon. It seemed very forward for Edward to take such liberties with a young woman he had just met.

"It's kind of you to watch out for her, but it looks as though Edward is taking very good care of Miss Ramsey."

He watched them a moment more, then turned away just as his Aunt Beatrice, Julia, and William crossed the tent toward him.

"Jonathan." Beatrice leaned in and kissed his cheek, then she turned to Evelyn with a bright smile. "Please introduce us to your lovely friend."

"This is Evelyn Gleason, Dr. and Mrs. Gleason's youngest daughter. Evelyn, this is my aunt, Lady Beatrice Danforth, my sister, Julia Foster, and her fiancé, Sir William Ramsey, Baronet of Highland Hall."

Beatrice took Evelyn's hand. "Why Evelyn, I didn't recognize you. You've grown into a beautiful young woman.

"Thank you, Lady Danforth. It's a pleasure to see you again. I'm so happy you could join us today." Their conversation continued as Beatrice asked Evelyn about her family, and then Evelyn questioned Lady Danforth, Julia, and William about their plans for the season.

Aunt Beatrice turned to him. "So, Jon, are you enjoying the party?"

"It was kind of the Gleasons to invite me. It's always a pleasure to meet new friends." He hoped that answer would suffice. He couldn't very well confess he was rather bored and wished he had agreed to volunteer at the Daystar Clinic rather than come to the party. Perhaps it wasn't too late to change his mind. If he could slip away soon, he might be able to spend a few hours with Theo and Dr. Pittsford and see why they were so eager to be involved in the work on the East End.

He focused his attention on Julia. "Have you seen the Gleasons' flower gardens?"

Julia hesitated. "No, I haven't."

"Why don't we go take a look?" He offered her his arm. "William, I promise I'll bring her back in a few minutes."

William sent him a quizzical look, but nodded. "Of course. Take your time. Enjoy the flowers."

Jon led her away.

"Touring the gardens to see the flowers?" Julia asked in a hushed tone. "What is this all about?"

"I wanted to speak to you in private."

"All right." They followed the pathway around the side of the house and into the gardens.

"I don't want to be rude, but I think I'm going to slip away."

"I don't suppose anyone will mind. You've put in an appearance and made Aunt Beatrice happy." Julia smiled up at him, affection filling her eyes.

His gaze traveled from the tent to the formal garden. "It's strange, isn't it?"

"What do you mean?"

"Trying to make our way in London society when we're much more used to village life in India."

Her smile faded. "Yes, it is a bit of an adjustment, I'll grant you that. I often feel I'm pulled in different directions."

He knew exactly what she meant. Even after two years in London, he sometimes still felt like an outsider.

"I want to please William and fit in with his family and circle of friends," Julia continued, "but I don't quite feel at ease, at least not yet."

He studied his sister. She had only returned to England last autumn after twelve years in India, almost half her life. It couldn't be easy, adjusting to her changing role and preparing to become William's wife, as well as the mistress of his London home and Highland Hall.

He laid his hand on her arm. "You're doing a splendid job. I can tell William is very happy to have you by his side, and he will be even happier when you become his bride."

Julia's smile returned. "You are a dear. I'm so glad we have this time together."

"I'm thankful for it as well." Jon glanced toward the tent.

Julia followed his gaze. "I wonder who that is talking to Kate."

"I believe his name is Edward Wellington."

"Have you met him?"

"No, Evelyn Gleason mentioned him to me. He's the eldest son of the earl of…something, and he's in line to inherit his father's title and property." He thought about mentioning the rest of what Evelyn had said, but he wasn't sure if it was true, so he held his peace.

"I suppose Louisa must have introduced them." Julia released a soft sigh. "He sounds like the type of man she hopes to find for Kate."

"Surely you and William will be the ones to make that decision. With Kate, of course."

She sent him a doubtful glance. "Louisa is very determined to lead the way and see that Kate is engaged by the end of summer."

"I don't mean to be rude, but I don't understand why William allows her to have any say in it."

"Apparently Louisa promised Kate's mother that she would bring Kate and Penny into society and make sure they married well, and deathbed promises are not easily forgotten."

"That may be true… Still, I don't know how any of you put up with her."

"She can be difficult."

"Surely there must be some other reason for all the pressure she is putting on Kate."

"Louisa has no children of her own, and I suppose there's a sense of power and influence that comes with being a debutante's sponsor."

Jon huffed and shook his head. "She's certainly seems to relish that, and the season's only begun."

Julia sighed. "Don't remind me."

Jon shifted his gaze back toward the tent and studied Edward Wellington once more. Even from a distance he looked self-assured, like a man who knew what he wanted, but what about his character? He turned to Julia. "Is Edward Wellington the kind of man you want Kate to marry?"

"I don't know anything about him, except what you've told me. But I'm not worried. If he is interested in Kate, he'll have to meet William and get his permission to call on her. If that happens, we can make discreet inquiries about him and his family."

"Good." Jon nodded. "Someone ought to look into his background and be sure of his reputation."

Julia laughed softly. "You're sounding very much like a protective older brother."

Jon straightened. He was feeling protective…but not particularly brotherly. "I'm just watching out for her." He pushed his concern aside and checked his watch. "I think I'll take my leave. Will you make my excuses to the Gleasons and thank them for me?"

"All right, but why are you leaving so soon?"

"My friends from the hospital are working at a free clinic in the East End, and I'd like to join them for a few hours."

A faint line creased Julia's brow. "I've heard there is quite a bit of crime in that area."

He leaned in and kissed her cheek. "Don't worry. I've walked the streets of Bombay and tramped through the villages around Kanakapura. I can certainly handle a few hours in the East End."

• • •

Kate walked in the front door and stepped into the cool and quiet entrance hall at Ramsey House. Aunt Louisa, William, and Julia followed her inside.

Late afternoon sunshine slanted through the front windows as William took off his hat and handed it to Lawrence with a weary sigh. He turned to Julia. "I'll be in the library if you need me."

Understanding flickered in her eyes, and she squeezed his hand. "I'll go up and check on the children."

He headed to the library, while Julia climbed the stairs.

"Kate, you're home!" Penny looked over the upper banister, and then came bounding down the steps. "How was the garden party? Who did you meet? Were the men all terrifically charming and dashingly handsome?"

Louisa handed her parasol to Lawrence. "Penelope, please don't run down the stairs."

"Sorry, Aunt Louisa." Penny barely acknowledged her aunt before she turned back to Kate. "What did people say about your hat and dress?"

"Which question shall I answer first?" Kate smiled, thinking of Edward as she unpinned her hat.

"Tell me who was there."

"There were about forty or fifty people, most of them were new acquaintances, and several were...very interesting."

Her sister's eyes widened. "Oh, I want to hear all about it."

Lawrence lifted a silver tray from the side table and held it out toward Kate. "These came for you, miss."

Kate stared at the stack of envelopes. "Those are all for me?"

His mouth pulled up at one corner, hinting at a smile. "Yes, miss."

Louisa reached past Kate and scooped up the envelopes and silver letter opener. "Come along, Katherine. We'll open these in the drawing room."

Penny frowned at her aunt and sent a questioning glance at Kate.

Kate shook her head, then followed Louisa through the double doors. She had already endured a lecture on the ride home for telling Edward about the mishap at her presentation, and she wasn't eager for another. Her aunt had seen her and Edward laughing, then had demanded to know what had been said.

Her aunt's scolding words rang through Kate's mind as she entered the drawing room. *You should never have discussed your presentation with Edward. We don't want that story circulating! His mother knows everyone, and she is not one to keep a secret.*

Louisa pursed her lips and quickly sorted through the envelopes. "Most of these are replies to our invitation to your ball." She set several small cream-colored envelopes aside, then scanned the writing on a square, white envelope. "But this one is from the Hoffmans." She lifted it with a gleeful smile.

"Who are the Hoffmans?" Kate moved to her aunt's side.

Louisa sent Kate a scornful glance. "Gertrude Hoffman is one of the most influential women in London. I pointed her out to you last night at the palace. She was with her daughter-in-law, Priscilla. Don't you remember?"

Kate shrugged.

"For heaven's sake, Katherine, how many times have I told you shrugging is not ladylike?"

Kate released an exasperated sigh. "I don't see why it matters. There's no one here to see me but you and Penny."

"Good manners should be practiced at home so they come naturally when you're in public."

Kate rolled her eyes.

"Never mind. Receiving an invitation from Gertrude Hoffman is a good sign, a very good sign in deed." She slit the envelope and pulled out the card.

Penny stood on tiptoe and leaned closer. "Is it a ball?"

"No...it's a dinner on the third of May. That's only a week before your ball. I wish it were sooner, so there was time for word to spread, but it will do."

Kate frowned. "What do you mean?"

Louisa looked at Kate as though she were a simpleton. "When people hear Gertrude Hoffman has invited you to dinner, those who haven't responded to our invitation will reconsider." Louisa continued opening the invitations. "You met some important people today at the Gleasons', but making an appearance at a dinner given by the Hoffmans will be even more helpful. Now if we could only secure an invitation from the Taylor-Mumfords, that would be a real coup. Then all the doors of London society would swing open for you."

Kate lowered herself into a chair, her mind spinning. The season had just started, and she was already struggling to remember the names and faces of everyone she'd met. How was she supposed to keep them all sorted out and know who was who? Would all these invitations and connections really help her meet her future husband?

Edward Wellington's face rose in her mind, and pleasant warmth flowed through her.

Perhaps she already had.

SIX

J on reined in his mount and slowed his pace to stay even with Kate. She rode sidesaddle next to him down Rotten Row, the wide, sandy path leading through Hyde Park. Several other riders dressed in impressive outfits and tall black hats trotted along the pathway.

Jon would've preferred riding in the country, but Kate's aunt had insisted this was the place to be seen by those in town for the season. A girl's father or brother usually escorted a young woman on a ride like this, but Kate had neither, so William had asked Jon to accompany her. Lady Gatewood had not been pleased with that prospect and tried to persuade William to escort Kate. But William would not be swayed. He and Julia had promised the children a trip to the London Zoological Gardens, and he did not intend to change his plans if Jon was willing to ride with Kate.

Lady Gatewood had huffed and strode out of the dining room as though she had been insulted, but Kate was eager to ride and willing to be escorted by Jon, so they'd set off.

The morning was cool and slightly overcast, making it a pleasant day for a ride. Kate glanced his way. "Do you know why they call it Rotten Row?"

"Because of all the cleanup needed?" He grinned and glanced at the sandy path.

She smiled, a teasing light in her eyes. "No. It was originally called the *Route de Roi,* the Royal Route or the King's Road, but those who didn't speak French thought it sounded like Rotten Row."

"Ah, that makes sense. Where did you learn that bit of history?"

"From my excellent governess, of course."

He was glad to see Kate smile about his sister. According to Julia, Kate had given her quite a difficult time when she first arrived at Highland as the new governess. But Kate slowly adjusted to the changes following her father's death, and it seemed she finally accepted and appreciated Julia's help with finishing her education and preparing for the season.

Since they'd come to London, Kate's aunt had taken a more dominant role in Kate's life as her sponsor and chaperone, and Julia had stepped back a bit to allow it. Jon wasn't sure that was wise, but it seemed that was what they had all agreed to.

A stout young man with a dark moustache nodded to Kate and gave her a lingering smile as he rode past on a large bay.

Jon bristled and brought his horse closer to Kate's. "Do you know that man?"

Kate glanced over her shoulder with a slight smile. "I don't believe so." She turned back to Jon. "Perhaps we met at the Gleasons' garden party. But it's hard to tell with everyone dressed so differently today than they were on Saturday."

The breeze teased the netting on Kate's black hat, and she lifted her gloved hand to adjust it. Her cheeks were flushed a pretty pink, and she looked very smart in her black riding outfit with the fitted jacket and long full skirt. She was an expert rider, and her posture and the tilt of her chin made a very fetching picture. He could see why the man took a lingering look.

Kate glanced his way again. "Why did you leave the garden party early?"

A ripple of surprise traveled through Jon. He didn't think she would notice his departure. "I wanted to join some friends who were volunteering at a clinic in the East End."

"Isn't that quite a dangerous place?"

"I suppose it can be if you don't know how to take care of yourself."

She lifted one eyebrow. "But you do?"

A smile tugged at the corners of his mouth, and he nodded. "I like to think so."

The humor faded from her expression. "What was it like?"

"The East End or the clinic?"

"Both."

He shifted in the saddle, images flowing through his mind. "It's a very poor area. Many of the buildings look as though they're ready to fall down. Conditions are cramped and dirty, and there's little light or fresh air. I can see why there is so much disease and discouragement. On many of the streets, I saw destitute young women and children in ragged and dirty clothes."

He thought she might be disgusted by his description, but sympathy shone in her eyes. "Why are the children on the streets? Are there no schools?"

"There are some, but many children appear to be on their own without any parents to watch over them."

"They're just out on the streets?"

"I'm afraid so, and unfortunately some turn to a life of crime to get by." Dr. Pittsford had shared a few sad stories with him on Saturday.

Kate sent him a skeptical glance. "What kind of crimes could children commit?"

"Some become pickpockets or steal from vendors. And the young women turn to..." He shook his head, unwilling to finish that sentence, but he could tell she understood his meaning. "Dr. Pittsford, one of my teachers at St. George's, opened Daystar Clinic to provide free medical care, but there is so much more that needs to be done."

Kate pressed her lips together and looked down the path. "It doesn't seem right that children and young women should suffer so. Perhaps William's church here in London could take up the cause."

"I was thinking of bringing the need to my church. They support many foreign missionaries, but there is a great need right here in our own city."

Kate nodded and her expression eased. "Do you miss your life in India?"

He looked at her, surprised by her shift in the conversation. "In some ways, yes."

She returned his gaze, genuine interest in her eyes. "What did you like best?"

"Working with my family, especially my father. I've learned so much from him, medically, and about life in general. I miss seeing him and my mother every day and sharing so many experiences together." He thought for a few more seconds. "And I miss the girls we cared for there. They became like our extended family."

"Has the work continued since your parents left?"

"Yes. My father insisted nationals be trained to carry on, in case we had to leave, and it's a good thing he did. The girls are well cared for. Their schooling continues, and nurses at the clinic serve the basic medical needs of those in the village."

"I'm glad to hear it." Kate fingered the reins. "I've enjoyed the stories Julia told us about your work there. It must have been very rewarding to see the girls who had been rescued growing up safe and happy."

"Yes." But that pleasant thought was soon replaced by a painful memory. He clenched his jaw and look toward the trees. "I'm afraid not all of the girls are safe and happy."

Kate tipped her head. "What do you mean?"

He shifted his reins to the other hand, debating if he should tell her the story. Would she understand the struggle he still wrestled with even though so much time had passed? He looked across at Kate, and her open expression encouraged him to continue.

"I was just remembering Lalita, one of the girls we rescued from an abusive home when she was twelve. We kept her safely hidden away with us until shortly after she turned sixteen." His throat tightened, and he looked down.

"What happened then?"

"After her family learned she was living with us, they hired men to break into our compound and take her away one night."

Kate stared at him, her face growing pale.

"The next morning, after we discovered she'd been taken, my father and I set off to search for her. The local authorities even agreed to help us when we explained the circumstances. Three days later we learned she had been taken to a neighboring village and married off to a wretched man older than her father. Her new husband had a terrible reputation as a thief and drunkard. Her parents told the authorities they did it to protect her from us and our *heathen* God, but I believe they did it for the money."

"The money?"

"Yes, a beautiful young girl like Lalita would bring a very high price."

Kate's eyes flashed. "That's terrible!"

"Yes. It is. Her life with him is probably no better than the worst kind of slavery." He gripped the reins, his throat burning with the injustice of the situation and his powerlessness to do anything about it.

"It's not right, Jon. Things like that shouldn't happen." Conviction filled Kate's voice.

"No, it shouldn't, but our hands were tied. They were married. The law was on his side." He blew out a deep breath, trying to release the guilt and regret pressing down on him.

"What happened to her?"

"I don't know. They wouldn't allow us to see her." He stared down the sandy path, remembering all the times he had prayed and asked God to sustain her through her trials. But was that enough? Should he have done more? His father said they had no recourse. But for a boy of eighteen who cared deeply for Lalita, it had not been enough.

She had trusted him to keep her safe, and he had failed her.

"Kate!"

Jon and Kate reined in their horses and looked to see who was calling to her.

Edward Wellington rode toward them, a young woman on a white horse at his side. He tipped his hat to Kate. "Good morning. What a pleasure to see you again."

Kate's pink cheeks signaled her pleasure at the encounter. "Hello, Edward."

He shifted his gaze to Jon and nodded, though he did not look as happy to see him. "Foster."

Jon nodded. "Wellington." He had met Edward at the house the day before, when Edward called on Kate. William and Julia had invited Edward to stay for tea, which had given Jon time to observe him and determine he was a decent fellow. Nevertheless, he planned to keep his eye on him.

"Have you met my sister, Lady MaryAnn?" Edward made the introductions, then brought his horse around, alongside Kate's. "Why don't we join you?"

Jon frowned slightly. "Aren't you going the other way?"

Edward looked over his shoulder. "We were, but we have to head back in this direction to meet our groom. I'm sure MaryAnn won't mind." He glanced at his sister.

"It's fine with me." MaryAnn stretched in the saddle. "This is my first time riding in a few weeks, and I am a bit tired already."

"Very well." Kate smiled at Edward. "We'd be happy to have you join us." They rode off together, and Jon and MaryAnn set off after them.

MaryAnn's gaze followed each male rider who passed by, and she nodded to a few with a self-assured smile. Jon made an attempt at polite conversation, but MaryAnn's replies were brief, and it was obvious she did not consider him of any interest.

He shifted his attention to Kate and Edward. They seemed to be enjoying a lively conversation comparing riding in Berkshire to riding in Somerset.

Jon gave his head a slight shake. He certainly had nothing to contribute to the conversation. He might as well keep his mind on his own affairs and the decisions he needed to make about his future.

He had enjoyed his first visit to Daystar Clinic. Theo had volunteered to go again on Thursday. Perhaps Jon would join him and make it a regular commitment. The needs there were certainly great.

Kate's idea of mentioning the clinic to William and Julia was a good one. His sister would definitely be interested in the work being done there, and he hoped William would as well. Perhaps he could arrange for Julia and William to visit the clinic with him and see the conditions on the East End. If they did, he had no doubt they would find a way to help.

. . .

Lydia draped Miss Foster's freshly ironed lavender dress over her arm and left the laundry room. She'd better keep moving. Both Miss Katherine and Miss Foster would need her help dressing for the evening.

Ann walked down the steps, carrying a tray with the remains of the children's tea. She glanced at the dress in Lydia's arms. "My, that's a pretty color."

"Yes, Miss Foster is wearing it tonight when she goes to the ballet with Miss Katherine and Mr. Wellington."

Ann's eyebrows took on a sarcastic slant. "Wouldn't that be nice?"

Lydia glanced at the dress again with a sense of longing. Little silver beads trimmed the neckline and the royal blue sash. She'd never worn anything this pretty, and she probably never would. Sometimes mistresses passed on dresses they no longer wanted to wear to their maids, but she couldn't imagine Miss Foster doing that anytime soon. All her dresses were new, made especially for her since she became engaged to Sir William. Miss Katherine's were mostly all new as well.

Ann leaned closer, a teasing light in her eyes. "Did you see Mr. Wellington when he came calling on Miss Katherine the other day?"

"No. What's he like?"

Ann's expression turned dreamy. "Tall, with blond hair and blue eyes and plenty o' muscles to fill out that suit of his."

Lydia sighed. "He's probably rich too."

"Sure he is."

"I'm thinking Miss Katherine will have her pick of gentlemen callers this season."

Ann looked around then lowered her voice. "I don't see why we can't have callers. It's not fair."

"Fair or not, that's the rule."

"Some rules are meant to be broken." The stubborn tilt of Ann's chin sent a warning through Lydia.

"You better not let Mrs. Adams hear you saying that."

Ann looked up the stairs. "She won't hear. She's in the dining room, sorting out the table linens."

"Well, if you want to hold on to your job, you'll remember the rules and stick to them."

Ann huffed. "I won't be staying in service forever. I want to get married and have a family."

"So do I, but that's a long way off for both of us." Lydia pushed that cherished dream away, deep in her heart. "I had better go up. Miss Foster and Miss Katherine are waiting."

Ann started toward the kitchen, then looked back. "Say, did you hear any more from your parents about your sister?"

Lydia bit her lip, worry weaving through her thoughts again. "No, not yet."

"Did you tell them about seeing her at the park?"

Lydia shook her head. "I didn't want to raise their hopes, especially when I'm not even sure it was Helen."

"You seemed certain of it that day."

Lydia replayed the scene in her mind. "It looked like Helen, but it was quite a distance." She sighed. "Oh, I just wish my parents would write and tell me she's come home."

Sympathy filled Ann's eyes. "Don't worry. I'm sure you'll hear something soon."

Lydia nodded. If only she could believe that were true.

• • •

Kate leaned forward in her plush balcony seat in the Wellingtons' private box and looked down on the main floor at Covent Garden, which her aunt had urged Kate to call by its proper name, the Royal Opera House.

Whatever you called it, it was simply lovely.

Their curtained-off section of the first balcony had a good view of the stage and the audience below. Above were two more balcony levels and a beautiful ceiling decorated with an elaborate gold-and-white, star-shaped design and glowing lights.

Stylish women dressed in exquisite evening gowns and distinguished men in white tie and tails made their way down the aisle to the few remaining seats. A soft murmur of voices rose from those seated below while everyone waited for the curtain to rise on the Ballet Russes.

Edward leaned toward Kate, and his shoulder touched hers. "I'm glad you were able to join us tonight." He smiled at her and then shifted his gaze to Julia, who sat on Kate's left as her chaperone.

Julia smiled. "Thank you, Edward. I've never been to a ballet, so this is very special."

"Yes, thank you for inviting us. It's quite thrilling." Kate's gaze traveled around the hall again.

He laughed softly. "The program hasn't even begun. Wait until you see the ballet."

She gently waved her carved ivory fan to cool her warm cheeks. "Just being here and seeing everyone is an experience."

Edward's sister, Lady MaryAnn, sat on his right, and his parents, Lord and Lady Wellington, were seated in the row behind them with two of his mother's friends.

Kate looked across at the boxes on the other side of the great hall and scanned the faces. Had she met any of them at the Gleasons' garden party? There were a few young faces among the crowd, but most of them seemed to be about the age of Edward's parents, and none looked familiar. She released a soft sigh and sat back.

An elegant woman wearing a purple gown and a sparkling diamond tiara nestled in the blond hair piled high on her head stepped into the box directly across the hall from the Wellington's. A tall man with dark hair and trim moustache followed her in.

Kate pulled in a sharp breath. David Ramsey, William's younger brother and her second cousin once removed, took a seat next to the woman in purple. He handed the woman a program, and then looked across the hall, his gaze traveling over the crowd.

Kate snapped open her fan and turned her head to the side, shielding her face. She knew David Ramsey lived in London and that she might see him this season—but she hadn't expected it would be tonight.

Memories of his visit to Highland Hall last December flooded her mind, and her cheeks burned. He had flirted with her the entire week, and she had been flattered and attentive. Finally one evening, they'd shared a secret kiss in a darkened hallway. She sank lower in her seat, remembering how the thrill of her first kiss had been quickly washed away by guilt, leaving her feeling foolish and ashamed for allowing it. She didn't truly care for David Ramsey, and she doubted she was more than a passing fancy for him.

Kate couldn't resist the urge to peek around the side of her fan and catch one more glimpse of David. He leaned toward the woman in purple, and they exchanged an intimate smile.

Kate pulled in a sharp breath and looked away. The woman seemed a few years older than David, but they definitely appeared to have a romantic interest in each other.

She was just about to mention his arrival to Julia when the lights lowered and the conductor walked forward and took his position. Kate lowered her fan, thankful the dim lights prevented David from seeing her.

The crowd hushed. The conductor raised his baton, and the music rose from the orchestra pit in front of the stage. The deep red-and-gold curtain slid back, and the dancers leaped onto the stage.

Kate clutched her fan to her chest, her gaze fixed on the ballet. She'd never seen such colorful costumes or expressive dancing. The music rose and fell and seemed to vibrate through her as the story played out across the stage. She was so captivated she almost forgot about David Ramsey and the woman in purple...but not quite.

The program continued for nearly an hour, then the curtain came down and applause filled the auditorium.

Kate turned to Edward. "Is it over?"

He smiled. "No, this is the intermission. Come, let's take a walk and see who we can see."

Kate rose from her chair, and she and Julia followed Edward and his family into the upper foyer. People gathered in small circles for polite conversation, while others strolled past, greeting those they knew and watching those they did not.

Edward turned to Kate. "Excuse me for a moment." He walked away toward the men's lounge.

Julia took Kate's arm. "Let's visit the ladies' lounge."

They excused themselves and strolled across the foyer. Inside the lounge, several women sat in front of tall mirrors adjusting their jewelry or fixing their hair. Kate stood to the side, waiting for Julia and admiring the lovely gowns of the ladies who passed by.

A middle-aged woman in a pale green dress with a plunging neckline sat in front of the closest mirror just a few feet away. Her red hair had been put up in an elaborate style with a strand of pearls woven through the curls. She removed one of her pearl earrings and rubbed her earlobe. "Did you see Dorothea Martindale in her box?" She glanced around and leaned toward the older woman seated next to her. "She's with that young Ramsey fellow again."

Kate froze and stared at the woman's reflection in the mirror.

The older woman laid her black-beaded purse on the counter. "He hovers around Dorothea, like a bee near a rosebush."

The redhead's eyebrows rose. "I'd say he's more like a fox by the henhouse."

Both women chuckled and exchanged knowing looks.

The older woman adjusted the black ostrich feather in her silver hair. "I saw them together at the theater last week, and the way they were carrying on, it's obvious they're more than friends."

"She's at least ten years older than he. It's deplorable!"

"I couldn't agree more. No respectable woman would flaunt her paramour like that."

The redhead gazed into the mirror. "Where is her husband?"

Kate stifled a gasp. David's companion was married?

"Off in Spain on some diplomatic mission, I suppose."

"Well, *he* certainly won't be happy when he returns home and hears what his wife has been up to."

"I'm sure he will not."

Kate clenched her hands and glanced toward the door. She should slip away before someone recognized her or greeted her by name, but the desire to hear the rest of the conversation kept her glued to the spot.

The redhead reattached her earring. "Who is this Ramsey fellow? Do we know his family?"

"I heard they own an import business. Dorothea's *friend*, David, is in charge since his older brother, William, inherited a baronetcy and moved to Berkshire." She looked away and thought for a moment. "I believe the estate is Highland Hall."

A cold chill traveled up Kate's back, and she bit her lip.

The redhead's eyes narrowed. "Isn't William Ramsey the one who recently became engaged to his children's *governess*?"

"Yes, I believe so." The silver-haired woman lifted her finger. "And I heard his sister married the estate gardener last month." She sent her friend a superior look. "They're not the kind of people Dorothea usually chooses as friends…but then, *friendship* may not be what Dorothea has in mind."

Both women chuckled again.

How could they laugh about David's indiscretion?

"Are the Ramseys in town for the season?"

The older woman turned to her companion. "Yes, I believe one of the girls is making her debut."

Kate shrunk back against the wall, wishing she could disappear.

"Oh, that's right. What's her name?"

"I'm not sure, but I heard she made quite an impression at her presentation."

"Well, she won't get very far with her family's name being dragged through the mud. I doubt she'll receive a proposal this season, even if she is pretty and clever."

"You're right about that. She might as well pack her trunks and go back to Berkshire."

Tears burned Kate's eyes, but she blinked them away with an angry toss of her head and pushed herself away from the wall.

How could those women be so cruel? Did they even consider who might overhear their conversation?

She pulled open the lounge door and shot a glance across the foyer. Lord and Lady Wellington and MaryAnn stood near the entrance to the balcony boxes, but Edward was not with them. MaryAnn turned and looked Kate's way.

Kate pulled in a sharp breath and ducked behind a pillar. She could not face the Wellingtons right now, not with her cheeks flaming and her eyes burning. She slipped out of her hiding place and strode in the opposite direction. A short walk would give her time to collect herself before she returned to her seat. Julia might be worried, but she would make up some kind of explanation.

She lowered her head, hurried around the corner, and ran straight into someone. "Oh, I'm sorry!" She lifted her head and gasped. "You!"

"Katherine." David Ramsey reached out to steady her. "What a surprise to run into you here." He grinned, looking pleased at his play on words.

She clamped her lips together.

"It's a pleasure to see you…but you look upset."

"Yes, I am upset, and I have a very good reason to be."

His brow creased. "Why is that?"

She pointed her white-gloved finger at him. "You and your…*philandering* have put me in a very awkward position."

His pulled back. "What do you mean?"

"Don't try to pretend with me. I just overheard two women talking about you and Dorothea Martindale."

David's face flushed and he looked around. "Lower your voice, please."

"As if that would make any difference. It seems the whole town is talking about it."

David stepped toward her, his expression growing steely. "Dorothea Martindale and I are friends. I sometimes accompany her to a concert or the theater. There is nothing wrong with that."

Kate lifted her chin. "You can't fool me. I know what's going on, and so does everyone else who sees you together."

"You should not believe everything you hear, Katherine. Those stories are made up by people who have nothing better to do than slander someone else's good name."

"Ha! Do you think I'm a child, that I'll believe everything you say?"

"No, not at all." He sent her a false smile. "I think you're a very beautiful young woman who is smart enough to make up her own mind and not be swayed by others."

Kate shook her head. "Flattery won't work this time, David. I saw you and Dorothea come in together. It's obvious how you feel about her."

He tipped his head and studied her with a mocking grin. "Why, Katherine, you sound jealous."

Bile rose in her throat. "That's ridiculous. I'm not jealous."

"Are you sure?"

Fire flashed through her. "Your choice to be seen around town with your mistress is tarnishing our family's name."

He stepped forward and gripped her upper arm. "Don't call her that."

"It's the truth, isn't it?"

He tightened his hold. "Listen to me, Katherine. This is none of your business. And I won't stand for you insulting Dorothea or making—"

"I say, what's the meaning of this?" Edward walked toward them, a scowl lining his face.

David loosened his hold, but he did not let go. "Who are you?"

"Edward Wellington the Third, and Miss Ramsey's escort this evening." His uncertain gaze shifted from Kate to David. "If you don't drop your hand, I'll be forced to…contact the management."

David huffed. "That's quite a serious threat." But he let go of Kate's arm. "There's no need to be upset. I'm Katherine's cousin. We've finished our conversation." His eyebrows rose and took on a haughty slant. "Haven't we?"

She returned his look. "Yes, we have."

Edward held out his arm to Kate. "Let's return to our seats. I believe the program has already started."

Heat radiated from her face as she slipped her hand through Edward's arm and walked away.

Edward leaned toward her. "What a ghastly fellow. Are you all right?"

"Yes, I'm fine. "

"What was that all about?"

"It was nothing…just a misunderstanding." She couldn't very well explain the conversation. It would ruin Edward's opinion of her and her family. Dread washed over her, stealing away all the joy she had felt earlier that evening as one horrible question flooded her mind…

How long could she keep her family's secrets from Edward?

SEVEN

"Please don't say anything to Aunt Louisa. She's going to be so upset if she hears this." Kate sank down on the settee facing the library fireplace.

Julia sat beside her. "I could tell something was wrong after intermission, but I had no idea you'd overheard such unkind remarks or seen David."

"I wanted to tell you right away, but I couldn't let Edward or his family overhear."

"Of course, I understand. But I'm glad you've told us now."

William paced across the library, a brooding frown lining his face. "How could David do this? It's unconscionable." He shook his head, still looking dazed by the news. "I knew his moral compass was off the mark, but I had no idea he had strayed this far. Our parents would be appalled if they had lived to see it."

Kate wished she hadn't been the one to tell him about David's involvement with Dorothea Martindale. But William needed to know the truth, especially since it could impact the whole family.

"I'm so sorry, William," Julia said softly.

"So am I." He turned and faced them. "I'll have to speak to David, though I doubt it will do any good."

"He is your brother—surely he'll listen to you."

William's expression softened as he looked at Julia, but doubt still shadowed his eyes. "You saw what it was like last Christmas. There's a gulf between us, and every attempt I've made to cross it has only pushed us farther apart."

"But if you come alongside, perhaps you can appeal to his conscience."

William grimaced. "I'm not sure David has one."

"Of course he does, but sin is very deceptive, and he has obviously been pulled into a trap."

William gave a slight nod. "I must try, for his sake and for ours." He turned to Kate. "I'm sorry you had to hear about this first and face David on your own. That must have been difficult for you."

Kate's nose tingled, and she pressed her lips together. She was not used to receiving such kindness and concern from the adults in her life.

"But even more than that," William continued, "I regret the way this may put a damper on your hopes for the season."

Jon strolled into the library. "Good evening, everyone. I'm surprised to see you're all still awake." Jon's smile faded as he looked around. "What's wrong?"

Julia glanced at William, and he gave a slight nod. "I'm afraid Katherine had an upsetting encounter tonight."

Jon's expression darkened. "Was it Wellington?" He shifted his gaze to Kate. "Did he treat you in a dishonorable way?" He looked ready to hunt the man down and exact revenge if he had.

"No, it wasn't Edward." Kate glanced at William, uncertain if he wanted her to share the details.

William released a deep sigh. "You might as well know. It was my brother, David." He gave Jon a brief explanation of what had happened at Covent Garden that evening.

Jon listened, his expression taut and somber. "What an upsetting turn of events. I'm sorry to hear it." Jon's gaze settled on Kate, unspoken questions flickering in his eyes.

The clock struck eleven and William sighed. "Well, there's nothing more to be done about it tonight. Let's get some rest, then we can address it in the morning."

Julie rose and joined William by the fireplace. She looked up at him, affection warming her gaze. "We all need some rest. Hopefully, everything will look clearer tomorrow." She took his arm, and they walked out of the library.

Kate rose and followed Jon through the doorway. But as she crossed the entrance hall, she remembered she'd left her fan in the library. When she returned to the entrance hall, she found that Jon had waited for her at the bottom of the stairs.

"I'm sorry, Kate. I'm sure this is upsetting." He searched her face, his golden-brown eyebrows shadowing his eyes.

She rested her hand on the banister. "Yes, I feel like someone has taken a sharp pin and popped the balloon of my hopes for the season."

A smile tipped up one corner of his mouth. "I wouldn't count yourself out yet."

"You didn't hear those dreadful women gossiping about our family or laughing about my poor prospects."

The sympathy returned to his eyes. "They don't know what they're talking about."

"But most of what they said is true, and after that news spreads around town, no one is going to invite me anywhere. I'm finished."

Jon shook his head. "They don't control your future."

"But they have the power to destroy my reputation and our family's."

His glaze remained steady. "They may spread their gossip, and that may close some doors for you, but I believe God is in control, and He is the One who holds your future in His hands."

She released a soft sigh. "I wish I could believe that."

"You can." He straightened, confidence filling his eyes. "He has a purpose and plan for your life, one that's full of hope and meaning."

Those words stirred a pleasant memory. "I think Julia read a verse like that to me before we left Highland."

Jon's smile warmed. "Here's another that we memorized when we were young. 'And we know that all things work together for good to them that love God, to them who are the called according to his purpose.'"

Those words were not familiar, and for some reason they made her feel a bit uneasy, like she had somehow missed the mark. She pushed that uncomfortable feeling aside and looked up at Jon again. "That's an interesting thought, but do you truly believe verses written hundreds of years ago apply to my life today?"

"I believe they apply to everyone who loves God and is called to serve and follow Him." His sincere gaze seemed to look straight into her troubled heart.

Kate's face warmed, and she lowered her eyes. Of course she believed in God, but she wasn't sure she could honestly say she loved Him. And the idea that she ought to serve and follow Him had never really entered her mind. Wasn't that level of commitment reserved for those called to be ministers or missionaries? She was just an ordinary girl, and she had no plans to sail off for darkest Africa to live a life of sacrifice and service. But she didn't want Jon to think she was a heathen.

She looked up. "I was baptized when I was an infant, and I've attended church with my family since then."

He watched her, as though waiting for her to say more. When she didn't, he glanced away. Was that disappointment in his eyes?

Why would he be bothered by her reply? She said her prayers and was at least as faithful as most of the people she knew...but she wasn't as dedicated as Jon and Julia. "You and your sister seem very serious about the practice of your faith."

He sent her a questioning glance.

"I mean...I haven't met many people who place such importance on their faith and actually bring it into the fabric of their everyday lives."

Jon thought for a moment. "Faith isn't just a matter of what you believe; it should be seen in the way you live and the way you treat others."

"I suppose that's part of your upbringing as a missionary."

"My parents' faith has been a great example to me."

"And the path you've chosen, to go back to India, that's part of it too, isn't it?"

His jaw tightened and he shifted his gaze away, "I'm not certain where I'm headed when I finish my medical training, but wherever I go, I'll be serving God in some way."

Surprise rippled through Kate. "You're not going back to India?"

"That was my plan, but I've been reconsidering it lately."

"What would you do? I mean, I know you're training to be a doctor, but where would you practice?"

"Dr. Gleason has offered me a position at St. George's."

Kate's heart lifted. "Really? That's wonderful! Did you tell Julia and William?"

"Not yet. I'm not sure if I'll accept. My Aunt Beatrice and my grandmother are both encouraging me to stay."

"What about your parents? What do they say?"

"I haven't discussed it with them. But they expect me to return to India and continue our work in Kanakapura."

Kate sat on the third step and looked up at him. "When must you decide?"

Jon sat beside her. "If I hope to go out with the London Missionary Society next year, then my paperwork must be turned in by the first of August."

"What about Dr. Gleason? Has he set a deadline for your decision?"

"No, but he won't wait forever. There are plenty of promising candidates who would be happy to accept his offer if I turn it down."

Kate tensed and focused on him again. "Oh, Jon, how are you going to decide?"

He drew in a breath and leaned back against the stair. "I'm not sure."

The urge to comfort him flooded her. She wanted to say she would pray for him, but she felt terribly inadequate, especially considering she would be praying for someone who was so deeply committed. But he had confided in her, and he needed her encouragement. She pushed her discomfort aside and laid her hand on his arm. "I promise I'll pray for you."

He turned and she could see the faint smile in his blue eyes as he laid his hand over hers. "Thank you, Kate. That means more than you know."

Her stomach fluttered, but a warning flashed through her mind. She must not encourage Jon. It wouldn't be right. She slipped her hand away from his and stood. "I should go up. It's late."

He rose beside her, so close she could feel his warm breath on her cheek.

Kate swallowed, determined not to look up at him. "Good night, Jon." She turned away and climbed the stairs.

"Good night, Kate." His voice was low and seemed to carry a wistful note.

A shiver traveled down her arms as she hurried up the stairs.

• • •

Lydia rolled the final section of Katherine's hair around her finger and then carefully pinned it in place. She glanced in the mirror, hoping Katherine would be pleased. She'd been working for almost an hour, trying to copy the style from a photo Lady Gatewood had cut from a magazine.

Lydia stepped back. "How is that, miss?"

Katherine turned her head to the right and left. "I'm not sure about the way it swoops down across my forehead."

"I think it looks very nice. It draws attention to your eyes, and they're one of your prettiest features."

Katherine's brow creased as she studied her reflection in the mirror.

Her confidence had certainly come down a few notches since she'd arrived in London. And it was no wonder, with the way Lady Gatewood was always finding fault with everything Katherine said and did. Lydia offered a reassuring smile. "With that ribbon matching your dress, it will be perfect."

Katherine glanced at the pink silk gown hanging from the front of the tall wooden wardrobe. "I wish Julia was going with me tonight rather than my aunt. I have no idea who I'll be seated next to at dinner."

Lydia took the dress down. "I'm sure you'll do well, miss." A smile lifted the corners of her mouth. "You don't usually have trouble carrying on a conversation."

"Yes, but I don't usually attend a dinner at the Hoffmans' either."

A knock sounded at the door.

"Who is it?" Katherine called.

"It's Ann, miss."

"Come in."

Ann slipped through and closed the door. In her hand she held a slim, white envelope. "I'm sorry to interrupt, miss, but the post arrived and there's a letter for Lydia."

Lydia's heartbeat quickened. "Is it from my parents?"

"Yes." Ann glanced at Katherine, waiting for permission to hand over the letter.

"Please, go ahead. I know you're anxious for word about your sister."

"Thank you, miss." Lydia hurried to meet Ann, then took the letter and tore it open. Her hand trembled as she unfolded the single sheet of paper. She skimmed the short greeting from her mother, then focused on the second paragraph.

One of the young men who works for the MacGregors finally told us he saw Charlie Gibbons and Helen together a few times before they disappeared. Your father spoke to Charlie's sister in Fulton, and she said he's gone to London to look for work.

Lydia stifled a gasp. So that must have been Helen and Charlie she'd seen in Wiltshire Park. She focused on the letter again.

Charlie's sister says he never mentioned Helen, but she finally showed your father a letter Charlie had written, and it had his London address. We hope you'll go there and see Helen. If you find her, try to get her to come home. But don't go alone. Take a friend with you, someone who knows their way around town. Please be careful. Charlie is known for drinking and stirring up trouble, and I don't want anything to happen to you. We'll be praying and waiting to hear from you. The address is:

Charlie Gibbons
2118 Marlton Street, Number 3B
The East End, London, England

Your loving Mother

Katherine watched her closely. "Have they heard from your sister?"

"No, but they think she's here in London."

Ann gasped. "Then it was Helen you saw at the park."

Katherine looked from Ann to Lydia. "You saw your sister?"

"Yes, I believe so, miss...last week, when Ann and I took the children to Wiltshire Park."

"Did you speak to her?"

"No, I called out, but the man she was with hustled her off before I could reach them."

"Do you think she lives somewhere around here?"

Lydia shook her head. "My mother says she's staying at this address in the East End." She held out the letter.

Katherine took it and quickly scanned down the page.

"They want me to go there and try to get her to come home."

Katherine looked up. "Jon knows his way around the East End. He's been volunteering at a clinic there. Maybe he could help you find this address."

Lydia shrunk back. "Oh no, miss. I couldn't ask Mr. Foster."

"Why not?"

"It wouldn't be right for me to go with him, not by myself."

"Perhaps Ann could go with you."

The nursery maid's eyes widened, and she shook her head. "That's a rough area. I'd be afraid to go."

Katherine thought for a moment, then looked up. "I'm not afraid. I'll go with you."

Lydia stifled a gasp. "Oh no, miss, you can't go there. The East End is no place for a lady like you."

"I don't see why not. I'm sure if I speak to Jon, and he agrees to go with us, we'd be safe enough."

The door opened, and Lady Gatewood sailed in, then pulled up short. "Katherine, why are you still in your dressing gown? It's almost time to leave." Her expression darkened. She turned to Lydia and pinched her arm. "Chambers, stop fiddling and help Miss Katherine finish dressing!"

Lydia stifled a cry and snatched the pink gown off its hanger. *Wicked woman! I'll be sportin' a bruise in the morning.*

"There's no need for that." Katherine sent her aunt a heated glance. "Lydia has been fixing my hair, and I think she's done quite well."

Lady Gatewood surveyed Katherine's hair. "That pink ribbon looks ridiculous. Take it out."

Lydia laid the dress on the bed, hurried to Katherine's side, and carefully removed the ribbon.

"Ribbons are only worn in the day. A tiara or jeweled hair ornament is the proper adornment for a dinner party like this." Lady Gatewood peered into the mirror. "Your hair doesn't look like the picture, but there's no time to change it now."

Katherine stood, and Lydia slipped the gown carefully over Katherine's head. "I don't understand why we're in such a hurry. The dinner isn't until eight o'clock."

Lady Gatewood sighed and looked at Katherine as though she were a foolish child. "It will take at least thirty minutes to travel to the Hoffmans', and it would be rude to arrive any later than that."

With Lady Gatewood glaring over her shoulder, Lydia quickly did up the buttons on the back of Katherine's dress, but her fingers fumbled.

Lady Gatewood opened Katherine's jewelry case, then took out a comb covered with sparkling gems. "Here, put this in her hair."

Katherine sat on the dressing table bench again.

Lydia's hands shook as she took the comb and looked in the mirror, trying to decide where to place it.

"Oh, for heaven's sake, girl!" Lady Gatewood snatched the comb from Lydia and shoved it into Katherine's hair. Katherine gasped.

"There. That will do." Lady Gatewood released a huff, then strode toward the door. "Collect your things, Katherine, and meet me downstairs in five minutes." She walked out without waiting for a reply, and the door closed behind her.

Katherine rose and turned to Lydia. "I'm sorry. I don't know why she has to be so abrupt."

Lydia lifted one shoulder. "It's all right, miss."

"No, it's not. She shouldn't treat you that way, but I doubt either one of us can do anything about it." Katherine glanced at her reflection, and a slight frown creased her forehead.

Lydia met her gaze in the mirror. "You look very nice, miss."

Katherine ran a hand down her skirt. "The dress is lovely, though pink has never been my favorite color."

Lydia handed Katherine her shawl and beaded handbag. "Don't forget these."

"Yes, thank you." She draped the shawl over her arm. "I hope the letter from your parents will ease your mind about your sister."

Lydia pondered that a moment. "I'm glad to know she's here in town, but I'm still worried about her. Charlie Gibbons is not a man to be trusted."

The look of concern in Katherine's eyes deepened. "I'll speak to Jon the first chance I have. I'm sure he'll help us."

"Thank you, miss. I'd be ever so grateful."

Would Mr. Foster be willing to help them search for Helen? Miss Katherine seemed certain he would, but what if that was only wishful thinking? How would she find her sister and convince her to go home?

• • •

Jon opened the front door and stepped outside, his thoughts on what his duties might be at the hospital that day. A misty fog hung in the morning air, limiting his vision to a few feet in front of him. He checked his watch, placed his hat on his head, and started down the steps.

"Jon, wait!"

He turned as Kate hurried out the front door. Her light-green dress swished around her ankles as she descended the steps and met him at the bottom.

"Good morning, Kate."

"Good morning." She glanced over her shoulder, then came closer, her blue eyes bright. "I have an important favor to ask."

She smelled faintly of jasmine, and his heartbeat picked up speed at her nearness. He set his jaw and squelched his response. "Of course. What can I do for you?"

"My maid, Lydia, needs to go to the East End to find her sister Helen."

Jon's brow creased. "*Find her?* What do you mean?"

"A few weeks ago Lydia's sister disappeared from home. Her father made some inquiries. They believe she ran away with a man who worked on a neighboring farm, and the two of them have come to London. Lydia's parents wrote and asked her to go to Helen and try to convince her to return to her family."

"Do you know where she's staying?"

Kate nodded. "Lydia received a letter from her parents with the address." She took a folded sheet of paper from her skirt pocket and handed it to him.

He opened it, skimmed down the page, and focused on the address in the last paragraph. He wasn't familiar with Marlton Street, but he was certain he could locate it without too much trouble. The situation sounded serious and should be addressed as soon as possible. He lifted his gaze to meet Kate's. "I'll go there today when I finish my shift at the hospital."

Kate pulled back. "Oh, you can't go without us."

"*Us?* Surely you're not thinking of going."

"Of course. Lydia and I must go. Her sister doesn't know you. And I doubt you could convince her to leave the man she's with and return to her parents. Lydia must speak to her, and she won't go without me."

Jon took in a deep breath, considering Kate's request. He and his father had traveled through the night many times to rescue girls who were kept as slaves or abused in the temples in India, but they always scouted out the situation first and spent time praying and preparing. The Lord had gone before them in India—surely Jon could count on His help here on a similar mission. A wave of assurance rose and filled his mind. With the Lord's help and guidance, he would find Lydia's sister and bring her safely back to her family.

But taking Kate along was another matter.

He straightened. "It's not wise for you to go along. Your aunt would never approve, and I doubt William or Julia would either."

Kate clicked her tongue and waved away his concerns. "If we all go together, I'm sure they'll agree to the plan."

Jon wasn't so sure. He glanced back at the house, doubts pressing in. He didn't want to put Kate in danger or upset Julia and William. But convincing Helen to leave the fellow she had run away with could be a challenge. Lydia and Kate would have a stronger influence on the woman than Jon ever could.

"Please, Jon." Misty fog swirled around Kate, and drops of moisture clung to her hair. "We don't know how long they'll stay at this address. We have to go reason with Helen while we have the chance."

His resistance eased, but he would not make any promises. "I'll locate the address and check out the area. But I won't take you or Lydia unless it seems safe. And you must speak to William and Julia and gain their permission."

She crossed her arms, looking slightly perturbed. "If you insist."

"I do."

A hint of a smile lifted the corners of her mouth. "My, you certainly are cautious. Don't you think you're being a little overprotective?"

"The East End can be a dangerous area."

"That's what I've heard, but I thought you said you know how to take care of yourself."

"I do. But you're asking me to be responsible for you and Lydia and to convince her sister to leave a man who is known for drinking and fighting." He looked at Kate, hoping his words would sink in. "That man had no qualms about stealing Helen away from her family. We have no idea what he might do to keep her. That's nothing to joke about."

She shook her head, a teasing light still flickering in her eyes. "I think you're just trying to frighten me into staying home."

He reached for her arm. "I'm not joking, Kate. It's serious business to confront the darkness and pull someone back from the edge. I don't take that lightly, and neither should you."

The humor faded from Kate's eyes. "I understand. It's not a game."

He nodded, but he doubted she knew what awaited her in the East End.

EIGHT

William stood with his hat in his hand and glanced around the front office of Ramsey Imports. It had been almost a year since he had sold his half interest in the family business to his brother, David, and moved to Highland Hall. The office reception area looked much the same, though a new clerk had greeted him when he arrived.

What had happened to Lionel Mortensen? He had been his father's clerk for almost twenty years, and after William's father died, he assisted William for four more years. Lionel was getting up in age, but he had always been faithful and hardworking.

Had David sacked the man? William certainly hoped not.

The new clerk, a young man in his twenties with unkempt dark hair and rumpled suit, returned to the front office. "Mr. Ramsey will see you now."

William thanked the clerk and walked through the doorway into his old office. David looked up from behind the large oak desk. Stacks of ledgers, folders, and miscellaneous papers were spread around him in disarray. A trunk and several open boxes sat on the floor beside his desk. The curtains where closed, and the only light in the room came from the twin lamps on each side of the desk. "William, what brings you here?"

"Good afternoon, David. How are you?" William held out his hand.

David grimaced and rose. "Sorry." They shook hands briefly, and David sat in the large black leather chair again. "I don't mean to be rude, but I have a stack of paperwork to go through and a meeting with one of our ship captains at three."

"I understand, but there's an important matter we need to discuss."

David's frown returned, but he motioned William to take a seat. "What is it?"

William lowered himself into the chair. "I understand you saw Katherine at the ballet on Tuesday evening."

David stilled and met William's gaze. "Yes. We saw each other at intermission."

"Katherine told us she overheard two women discussing you and… Dorothea Martindale."

David's face flushed and he looked away. "I don't listen to gossip, and neither should you."

William eyebrows rose. "Is it true? Are you involved with her?"

David huffed. "I don't believe that's any of your business."

William's irritation stirred, but he determined not to allow his emotions to overrule his good judgment. "I am your brother, and I'm concerned for you."

"Well, that would be quite unusual."

William clenched his jaw. "I don't want to make assumptions, David. I'd like to know the truth."

David fixed his stony gaze on William for several seconds. "Very well. Dorothea and I met a few months ago. She's a beautiful woman with a large circle of friends, and we have a great deal in common."

"But she's married to the Earl of Stratford and has two young children."

David's face turned ruddy, and he shifted in his chair. "Her marriage is not a happy one. Reginald Martindale does not treat her as he should. They only married to please their families, and now he spends most of his time out of the country on diplomatic missions in Spain and Portugal. He cares nothing for Dorothea."

"Even if that's true, it doesn't justify becoming involved with her in an affair."

David leaned forward, his gaze intense. "This is not a passing fancy, William. I care deeply about Dorothea, and she feels the same way about me."

His brother seemed sincere, but that didn't make it right. "If you truly care for her, then you'll end it before you hurt her any more than you already have."

David's eyes flashed. "You don't know what you're talking about. I'm not hurting Dorothea. I'm the one bright spot in her very painful life."

William shook his head. "I'm sorry, David, but there can be no happy ending to this story. You're damaging your reputation, and that is going to reflect poorly on everyone connected with you."

"Ha!" David slapped his hand on the desk. "Now we see what really brought you here. You don't care what happens to Dorothea or me. You're concerned about the damage this might do to the family's reputation."

"Protecting our family is my responsibility, and I take that very seriously."

"Well, you should've thought about that before you proposed marriage to your children's governess."

Heat surged into William's face. "That's enough! Do not say another word about Julia!"

David held up his hand. "All right. Calm down. I suppose that was out of line."

William straightened his jacket. "I came here because you are my brother, and I feel a responsibility toward you. And in spite of our disagreements in the past, I want what's best for you."

"I have a hard time believing that's your true motivation."

Regret burned William's throat. No matter what his brother thought, he did care, and he didn't want to see him throw his life away. "Please, David, consider the consequences for everyone involved. End this affair and make a clean break from Dorothea before it's too late."

David rose, his mouth set in a firm line. "I've heard your concerns, but I disagree with you. There's nothing more to say."

William studied his brother, his anger fading to sorrow. The path David had chosen could only lead to loss and misery. "I'm sorry, David." He rose from his chair and softened his tone. "I pray someday you'll see things clearly and have a change of heart."

A muscle in David's jaw flickered, but he gave no reply.

William turned away, placed his hat on his head, and walked out of the office.

• • •

Kate noted the luncheon at the Carmichaels' on her calendar and then set aside their invitation. She had no idea who they were, but her aunt said they were important members of society, so they should accept.

"Read the next invitation." Her aunt lay on the couch with a damp cloth covering her eyes and forehead, nursing a headache.

Kate opened the cream-colored envelope. "Mr. and Mrs. Virgil Poindexter-Hollander request your presence at a tea dance on Friday, the seventeenth of May, at four o'clock." Kate sighed. "Who are the Poindexter-Hollanders?"

"No one of importance." Her aunt huffed. "A tea dance. For goodness' sake. What is the world coming to? Send our regrets."

Kate rolled her eyes and set the invitation on the regret pile.

Louisa adjusted the cloth. "Are there any more?"

"Just one." Kate slit open the large, light-blue envelope and pulled out the card. "Lord Matthew Harcourt and Lady Agatha Harcourt request your presence at a ball given in honor of their daughter Laurel Marie Harcourt on Saturday, the eighteenth of May." Kate scanned the rest of the information. "Didn't we meet them at the Gleasons' garden party?"

"Yes, Laurel was the one with the outlandish hair style."

Kate smiled. "Oh yes, I remember." She thought Laurel's hair actually looked quite nice, but she didn't want to argue the point with her aunt, especially when Louisa had a headache.

"Agatha Harcourt is a high-minded prig, but they're well connected. Send our acceptance." Louisa slowly sat up and rubbed her temple. "Oh dear, it's almost time to change for dinner. I don't know how I can manage it with this headache."

"Perhaps Julia should come with me, and you can stay home and rest."

Louisa's eyes widened. "And miss dinner with the Wellingtons? I'd have to be on my deathbed before I'd let that happen." Her aunt dropped the cloth into the bowl on the end table. "This is the first time Edward's parents have invited you to their home. We must both be there. And you must be on your best behavior."

What would it be like to spend the evening with Edward's family? Of course she'd met his parents when she attended the ballet with Edward, but being invited to dinner at their home was a quite different matter. "Do you think it will be a large dinner party or small?"

"I don't know. We should be prepared for either."

Kate sent her aunt a quizzical look. How did one prepare to attend a dinner?

Louisa stood, her hand on her forehead. "I'm going to ask Mrs. Adams if she has any headache powders, then I'll go up to dress."

"All right." Kate turned back to the desk. "I'll just finish these responses and then go up."

"Do them quickly. You'll need to redo your hair." Louisa stopped by the library door and looked back at Kate. "Wear the violet silk gown with the silver beading. That one shows off your figure to the best advantage."

Heat infused Kate's cheeks. She loved the color, but that particular dress had a rather low-cut neckline. "Are you sure? That one seems a bit risqué for dinner with the Wellingtons."

"Nonsense! You want to catch Edward's eye, don't you?"

"Yes, but I'd like him to look at my face and not my neckline."

"For goodness' sake, Katherine. Don't exaggerate! That dress is perfectly respectable." Louisa strode out of the library.

Kate sighed and turned back to the pile of invitations on the desk. She took a note card from the box and penned their acceptance to the Harcourts. Then she jotted a quick note of regret to the Poindexter-Hollanders.

"Ah, Kate, there you are." Jon entered the library. "I hoped I'd see you,"

Kate turned and greeted Jon with a smile. "How was your day at the hospital?"

"Not too bad. I went to the East End after I finished my shift. I found the address for Lydia's sister."

"Oh, Jon, that's wonderful. What's it like?"

"The building is a bit run-down. There's a butcher shop on the ground floor, and several flats above that. It's not a very pleasant place, but I believe I could take you and Lydia there without putting you in too much danger."

"Thank you. Lydia will be so grateful. When can we go?"

"Tomorrow, if you like."

Kate turned back to the desk and studied her calendar. "I'm going riding with Edward in the morning, and I have a tea and a dinner tomorrow."

He crossed to the desk and looked over her shoulder.

She glanced at the events as he read them and her face warmed. None of them seemed important enough to delay their search for Helen. She scanned the coming week, looking for a few free hours. "If we went on Thursday morning, could we be back by one o'clock?"

Jon rubbed his jaw. "I'm supposed to work at the hospital that day, but Theo might cover for me."

"Theo?"

"Yes, I worked his shift last Friday, so he might take Thursday for me."

Kate studied him, wishing she knew more about Jon's friends and his work at the hospital. The few things he had told her made it sound quite interesting. "It must be wonderful to train for an actual occupation."

He cocked his head and studied her, a question in his eyes.

"I mean, I know it must take a great deal of hard work and sacrifice to become a doctor, but you'll be saving lives every day."

"It probably won't be that dramatic, but it should be a rewarding career."

She glanced at her calendar, a wave of uneasiness rising within. "My future doesn't seem nearly as inspiring as yours."

"Women may not always have the same opportunities as men, but marrying and raising a family can be just as rewarding."

"Yes, of course… Still, I admire your dedication and commitment to—"

"Kate!" Louisa stepped through the doorway and glared at Jon. "Look at the time. You have to change. We're leaving in twenty minutes."

Kate sent her aunt a pointed glance. "I'm aware of the time. I'll be along in just a moment."

"See that you are." Her aunt turned and stalked away.

Jon stepped back. "I'm sorry. I don't mean to delay you."

"No. It's all right. I have more than enough time to change. She's just in a dither because we're going to the Wellingtons' for dinner."

Jon stilled and met her gaze. "Edward Wellington's?"

"Yes."

He studied her for a moment, some undefined emotion shimmering in his eyes. "I hope you have a pleasant evening." He started toward the door.

"Jon…"

He stopped and looked over his shoulder, his mouth set in a firm line.

"I appreciate you searching out that address. I do want to go with you on Thursday. I'm sure Lydia will as well."

A muscle in his jaw flickered. "I'll check and see if I can make the arrangements."

"So…you'll let me know?"

He hesitated a moment. "Yes. I will. Good night, Kate."

She watched him go, her spirit deflating. For some reason she had disappointed him. Was it because they had to postpone their search for Helen until her social calendar cleared, or was it something else?

If only Louisa hadn't come in and cut off their conversation…but she wasn't sure that would've solved the problem. She had the unpleasant feeling she'd let Jon down, and she didn't like that feeling at all.

• • •

"Good night, Papa." Millie offered William a sleepy smile and kissed his cheek.

"Good night, Millie. Rest well, my dear, and we'll see you in the morning."

She yawned and took Ann's hand. "All right."

Andrew hugged Julia, then stood before William. "Are we going to see the changing of the guard tomorrow?"

William glanced at Julia, and she returned the question with her eyes. "I'm not sure, son. It depends on the weather and Kate's schedule."

Andrew clasped his hands. "Oh, please. You promised we'd go."

"I know, but we'll have to wait and see." He gave the boy's shoulder a pat. "Good night, son."

Andrew blew out a deep breath. "All right. Good night, Papa."

Ann led Millie and Andrew out the doorway and upstairs to their bedroom.

William eased back on the settee next to Julia, stretched out his long legs, and released a contented sigh. Raindrops drummed softly on the drawing room windows, and flames leaped and crackled in the fireplace, spreading welcoming warmth.

He leaned closer to Julia, enjoying her nearness and savoring the faint trace of lavender in the air around her. What a treat to have a few moments alone together. How much he was looking forward to their wedding day, their trip to Cornwall, and then returning to Highland to build their future together.

She looked up and smiled, the firelight glowing in her eyes. "How was your visit with David?"

William's happy thoughts of his future with Julia faded as the issues with his brother rose to fill his mind. "Not well, I'm afraid."

Julia's smile dimmed. "What did he say?"

"The whole conversation lasted less than ten minutes, and none of it was pleasant."

"So it's true? He's involved with Dorothea Martindale?"

"Yes, I'm afraid so, and he didn't want to listen to anything I had to say about it."

"How did you leave it?"

"I told him he should put an end to it. But he insists he cares for her deeply, and he won't give her up."

Julia took his hand. "I'm sorry. I know that puts you in a difficult position."

"Yes, it seems my brother and I are always at odds about something, but this— It cuts so much deeper." Thoughts of his late wife washed over him in a sorrowful wave. He lifted his hand to rub his eyes, wishing he could wipe away the memories of her unfaithfulness and banish the stain it had left on him and his family, but that was impossible.

Julia's hand tightened around his. "I know this brings up painful memories from the past."

William lowered his hand and looked her way. How could she read him so well? "I wish I could say it didn't, but I'm afraid Amelia's actions still cast a shadow over our lives, and to see my brother choosing the same destructive path makes it even more painful."

Julia sat quietly for a few moments, her hand still in his. "There is nothing we can do about the past except forgive Amelia and release those burdens to the Lord, but it's not too late for David to change course. God can still draw him back to his faith and his family as He did the prodigal son."

William sighed. "I don't know. He seems far away from us and from God right now."

Julia acknowledged that with a nod. "David has chosen a difficult path, and it may take some time eating from the pig's trough before he wakes up and sees where those choices have taken him."

"Yes, I suppose that's true." William ran his thumb over the top of her hand, thankful to have someone so wise and caring willing to listen to his concerns. He didn't deserve the love of a woman like Julia Foster. She was a saint compared to him, but he was learning to live out his faith day by day with her encouragement.

When he thought how he had almost let the painful issues from his past and her lack of social standing keep them apart, it shook him deeply. What a terrible mistake that would have been.

But the Lord had used his sister, Sarah, and her husband, Clark, to help him see the truth. And Julia had been gracious enough to forgive him, sacrifice her plans to return to India as a missionary, and accept his proposal. It was nothing short of a miracle in his mind, and he would never cease to be grateful.

He looked across at her and squeezed her hand. "Thank you."

She tipped her head and smiled. "For listening?"

"Yes, and for encouraging me not to give up hope."

"God has been so faithful to us. That helps me believe He can do the same for David."

William nodded, his burden easing. Julia was right. God was bigger than all these problems. He could touch David's heart and turn the situation around for good. Their job was to keep praying and trusting Him. He shifted and focused on Julia. "So, tell me about your day."

"We received a letter from Sarah this afternoon. She and Clark are back from their honeymoon, and she sounds very happy."

"I'm glad to hear it." His sister had married Clark Dalton, the head gardener at Highland, in early April, and the couple had traveled in Scotland following the wedding. Knowing she and Dalton were safely home at Highland eased his mind.

"Sarah interviewed two women for the position of housekeeper, but she hasn't found a replacement for Mrs. Emmitt…so she is proposing another idea."

"What's that?"

"Clark's mother, Mrs. Irene Dalton, would like to be considered for the position."

William frowned. "Wouldn't that be a bit awkward?"

"Perhaps, but Sarah believes it will work. Apparently Mrs. Dalton was a housekeeper for Dr. Laidlaw in Fulton for a few years. But when her daughter and son-in-law passed away, she left and took on the care of her granddaughter, Abigail." Julia slipped her hand from his and turned to face him. "Mrs. Dalton lives with Clark in his cottage on the estate, but she could move into the main house if we would allow her to bring her granddaughter along."

William frowned and shifted in his seat. "What about Clark and Sarah? Have they decided where they will live?" He had invited them to live in the main house with him and Julia, but they had not told him their decision yet.

"If Mrs. Dalton were given the position of housekeeper, I think it might make Clark and Sarah more inclined to accept our invitation and stay with us."

William glanced toward the fire, turning the situation over in his mind. "I like the idea of Sarah staying close by, but it would be a bit of an adjustment, having the gardener eating in the dining room with us each evening."

"It would be a challenge for Clark as well...but it would keep the family together, and that's what's most important."

That was true. He loved his sister and had always looked out for her. Even though she was married now, he wanted to be sure she was happy and had everything she needed. If Dalton was willing to stay with them, then he would have to be agreeable.

He laid his hand over Julia's. "I'm glad Sarah asked us before she hired Mrs. Dalton, but I'm not sure we can make that decision while we're here in London. I've only met her once at the wedding."

"I believe you also met her at the staff Christmas party."

"Yes, but that was just in passing. I have no idea if she has the skills or character to manage the house and staff."

"Housekeeper is an important position." Julia thought for a moment. "Perhaps we could invite Mrs. Dalton to come to London with Sarah and Clark next week. Then we'd have a chance to get to know her."

William mulled that over for a moment. "That sounds reasonable. But won't it be awkward if Mrs. Dalton comes to London, then we decide not to bring her on?"

"It would be more awkward to hire her without the interview, then have to let her go. That would cause hurt feelings for sure." Julia turned to him. "But if she is as skilled and experienced as Sarah says, then she may be just the person we're looking for."

"Very well. Why don't you write to Sarah and ask her to make the arrangements with Mrs. Dalton? It will be a busy time with Katherine's ball and the extra houseguests, but it's important, and it will hopefully build a stronger connection between us and Dalton."

"You mean Clark." Julia smiled and took his hand again.

"Yes, I must get used to calling him Clark."

"I know that would make Sarah happy."

"Calling him by his given name, or hiring his mother as our new housekeeper?"

"Both." She leaned in and kissed his cheek. "Inviting her here is a wise decision. Thank you."

William's chest expanded, and gratitude flowed through him. Managing a large estate like Highland was going to be much easier now that he and Julia could truly team up to make plans and decisions together.

He stared into the flickering flames. Finding a new housekeeper and accepting Clark Dalton as his brother-in-law seemed like minor issues compared to dealing with his brother's situation.

How long would it take David to see the light and end this foolishness… and how much would it cost the family in the meantime?

If word of David's indiscretions continued to spread, Kate's hopes for the season might all come to nothing.

———◆———————◆———

NINE

K ate lifted her skirt and stepped out of the car in front of the Wellingtons' impressive Berkeley Square home. Tall columns supported an
arched entryway, and wide stone steps led to the double front door.

"Remember, this is a very important night." Aunt Louisa glanced across
at Kate as she moved toward the steps. "Lord and Lady Wellington will be
watching, and you must make a good impression."

Kate followed her aunt, irritation prickling through her. "You've already
made that very clear."

"And I will repeat it as many times as it takes. You must do all you can
to encourage Edward. He is your most promising prospect and the one who
has shown the most interest."

There was no need to remind Kate of that fact. Though she'd met several young men, Edward was the only one who had called on her at home
and invited her to attend an event with him.

Louisa mounted the steps. "Don't spoil your chances by forgetting your
manners or getting carried away with idle chatter as you did at the garden
party."

"Edward appreciates my honesty. That's why he invited me to the
ballet."

"He might have been amused by your comments, but it will take more
than amusement to secure a proposal." She stopped by the front door and
lifted her finger. "It's not enough to please Edward. You must please his
parents as well."

Kate's stomach tensed at that thought. "Of course."

"They're eager for him to choose a bride this season, but he won't do
anything without their approval."

Was that really true, or was her aunt exaggerating again? She opened her mouth to protest, but the door swung open, and a tall footman in black-and-gold livery greeted them.

"I am Lady Louisa Gatewood, and this is my niece, Miss Katherine Ramsey."

"Good evening, m'lady, Miss Ramsey. This way, please." He ushered them inside and took their wraps.

Kate glanced around the large entry hall. Gold brocade draperies hung at the tall windows, and a thick oriental carpet covered most of the dark hardwood floor. An antique chest containing a display of blue-and-white Chinese pottery sat against one wall, and an elegant marble fireplace took center stage on the opposite wall.

A low murmur of voices drifted out from one of the adjoining rooms.

Lady Wellington stepped into the entry hall and crossed to meet them. "Louisa, I'm so glad you could join us this evening." She kissed the air near Louisa's cheek, then turned to Kate. "Welcome to our home, Katherine." She smiled, but her voice held a touch of cool reserve.

A ripple of unease passed through Kate, but she forced a smile. "Thank you. I'm pleased to be here."

"The other guests are in the drawing room. Shall we join them?" Lady Wellington motioned toward the open doorway on the left.

Louisa walked into the drawing room with Lady Wellington, and Kate followed behind. It was a lovely room with pale-green silk wall coverings and a sparking chandelier overhead. Several large family portraits from centuries back hung on the walls.

Kate scanned the guests, but she didn't see Edward or anyone she knew. The men were dressed formally, in tails and white ties. The women wore beautiful evening gowns and sparkling jewels. Though Kate didn't like the way her aunt had scolded Lydia, she was right—a hair ribbon would not have been the right choice for this evening. Most of the women wore tiaras or some type of jewels in their hair. She reached up and touched her jeweled comb to make sure it was still in place.

Someone tapped her on the shoulder, and she turned.

Edward smiled and gave a brief bow. "Good evening, Kate. I'm so glad you're here."

She returned his smile, relieved by his warm welcome. "Thank you, Edward. It's good to see you again. Your home is lovely."

He glanced around, his smile fading a bit. "It's not really very comfortable, not like our home in the country. But my parents had it decorated with entertaining in mind."

"So your family entertains often?"

"Yes, they host several parties throughout the season—even more this year since MaryAnn has come out. But most of the guests are my parents' friends. I'm afraid the conversation can be terribly dull." He leaned toward her and lowered his voice. "There is a full moon tonight. Would you like to step outside and see the garden?"

She stilled and looked up at him. "Before dinner?"

He glanced toward the windows and back at her with a twinkle in his eyes. "It will be a few minutes before everyone arrives. I think we have time."

Kate glanced around, wishing she could say yes, but her aunt's words rose in her mind. "I don't think we can just disappear."

"Are you sure?" He sent her a pleading look. "I'd really love to show it to you."

"I'm afraid I'm under strict orders from my aunt to be on my best behavior tonight." She smiled, hoping he would understand.

His chuckled. "All right. We wouldn't want to upset your aunt." He cocked his eyebrows. "Perhaps we can take a stroll after dinner?"

Taking a moonlit walk in the garden with Edward sounded very romantic, but before she could answer, Lord Wellington approached with another man and introduced him to Edward and Kate. The two older men launched into a conversation about the upcoming session of Parliament. Edward seemed quite interested and joined in. Kate listened for a few minutes, but did not really understand much of it. Her gaze drifted across the room and connected with a young woman standing by the piano.

Recognition brought a smile to Kate's face. Margaret Covington, one of her oldest friends from Berkshire, returned her smile and subtly motioned

Kate to join her. Kate excused herself from the men and crossed the room to meet her friend.

"What a wonderful surprise." Margaret reached for her hand and gave it a squeeze. "I didn't know you were acquainted with the Wellingtons."

"My aunt is a good friend of Lady Wellington's. She introduced me to them at a garden party. How do you know them?"

"My father and Lord Wellington have been friends since they were boys. Our families have visited each other several times in the past few years."

"How nice. Then you must be good friends with MaryAnn and Edward."

"Oh yes. MaryAnn is a dear girl. We enjoy riding together in the country and here in town." Margaret's gaze shifted across the room. "Edward is a very clever young man, isn't he?"

"Yes, he is."

"I saw you talking to him. He seemed quite interested in what you were saying." Margaret cocked her head. "Is there a romance blossoming between you two?"

Kate blushed. "I really couldn't say. We've only just met."

Margaret's green eyes sparkled. "Not according to MaryAnn."

Kate's heartbeat sped up. "What did she say?"

"That you and Edward have gone riding three times, and he took you to the ballet with his family."

"Yes, that's true. We saw the Ballet Russes at Covent Garden. It was amazing. Have you seen them?"

Margaret smiled. "Not yet, but don't try to change the subject. MaryAnn thinks he's quite taken with you."

Kate glanced at Edward. "We have enjoyed our time together."

"Well, his parents are pleased." Margaret leaned closer. "I'm sure they're very happy to see him finally interested in someone from the right kind of family."

"Why do you say that?"

Margaret looked around and leaned closer. "Two years ago he fell helplessly in love with Florence Piedmont, but she is the illegitimate daughter of

Felix de Rothschild, and of course that made her an unsuitable match, even though Rothschild is a very wealthy banker."

Kate glanced past Margaret's shoulder at Edward. She shouldn't listen to gossip, especially about Edward, but she couldn't deny she wanted to hear the rest of the story. "I don't believe I've met Florence Piedmont."

"I doubt you ever will. Since Edward broke things off, she rarely goes out. It's quite sad. I feel sorry for them, but Edward had no choice."

"What do you mean?"

"As the oldest son, he'll inherit the title and the estate after his father's death, but until then he is dependent on his parents for an income. He could never marry without their consent...that is unless he wants to live as a pauper, and I doubt Edward would do that."

"No, I wouldn't think so, but how sad for them to be kept apart because of matters out of their control."

"Yes...it's a shame for Florence. But perhaps it's a stroke of luck for you."

Kate bit her lip, pondering the story and what it might mean for her.

"Your aunt's connection with the Wellingtons gives you a great advantage. And MaryAnn says they wouldn't have any objection to you and Edward developing a friendship that could lead to something more."

Kate's hopes rose, but questions rushed in. Edward and his family approved of her now, but what would they say when they learned her cousin Sarah had married Highland's head gardener? Did they know her cousin William's fiancée was the former governess? And what if the news of David's affair with a married woman continued to circulate? What would they think of her and her family then?

A wave of dizziness passed through Kate, and she leaned against the piano to steady herself. Would the choices her family had made destroy her hopes for marriage? Would anyone look past those issues, consider her as an individual, and choose her as his wife?

The butler approached and announced that dinner was ready to be served. Lady Wellington circulated around the room, arranging the guests in order of precedence to enter the dining room.

She motioned to her son. "Edward, will you escort Katherine, please?"

"I'd be delighted." He offered Kate his arm.

She slipped her hand into place, and a nervous flutter passed through her stomach. The guests stepped back so they could pass through the room, but their eyes followed her. She lifted her chin and tried to ignore their questioning glances. It wasn't easy, especially with the knowledge of her family's secrets weighing her down each step of the way.

• • •

Jon closed his mouth and held his breath as he stepped over a large pile of horse droppings in the middle of the street. Kate lifted the skirt of her navy-blue suit and sidestepped the offending mess.

"Sorry." He glanced her way. "They don't clean the streets in the East End as often as they do in Kensington."

"It's all right. I'm familiar with horses and what they leave behind. It doesn't bother me." But the firm set of her mouth made him question her words.

Lydia scanned the darkening sky and moved closer to Kate's side. "It looks like we're in for a downpour, miss."

Kate looked up with a slight frown. "I wish I'd thought to bring my umbrella."

Jon grimaced. He should have suggested that. A cold wind whipped past, sending torn pieces of newspaper and bits of trash swirling down the cobblestone street. He tugged his hat lower on his head. The cool temperatures made it feel more like March than May.

"Is it much farther?"

"We turn left at the next corner, and then it's just a short distance." He should have insisted they take a cab, but Kate said she didn't mind riding the bus.

"My mother was right." Lydia clutched her pocketbook close as two rather shady-looking characters crossed the street toward them. "This is not the best area of town."

Jon kept a close eye on the men until they passed.

Kate lifted her chin and took Lydia's arm. "It certainly isn't, but we have to find your sister."

"Of course, miss, and I'm ever so grateful to you and Mr. Foster for your help."

"We're glad to do it." Jon sent Kate a quick smile. In spite of the threatening storm, the dirty streets, and the unsavory characters, she seemed determined to press on.

They rounded the corner, and Kate slowed and touched his arm. "Look, Jon." She nodded toward two little girls huddled in a shop doorway. Both wore ragged, stained dresses. The older girl looked to be nine or ten, and she held the other, just a toddler, on her lap. The little one coughed, and a wheezing sound followed.

He noted her flushed face, damp hair, and glassy eyes. She was obviously ill, and it looked as though she had a fever. Was it bronchitis? pneumonia?

The older girl looked up at them with dirt-smudged cheeks. "Please, sir, you want to buy some matches?" She reached in her sweater pocket and pulled out a small, dented paper box.

Jon's heart clenched, but he hesitated. If he gave her money, would it be used to buy food and medicine, or would a desperate parent use the funds to buy drink or something worse? And where were their parents? How could they leave such young children alone on the street?

He glanced at the flushed toddler and pushed aside his questions. It would be better to err on the side of compassion. "Yes, I would. Thank you." He reached in his pocket, then bent down and held out the folded note to the older girl.

Her eyes widened, and she shook her head. "That's too much, sir."

"No, it's all right." He held his hand steady.

She bit her lip, and her wide brown eyes darted from Jon to Kate and Lydia.

Kate stepped forward. "Please, we want you to have it."

The girl slowly extended her hand with the box of matches and exchanged it for the one-pound note.

Jon crouched before her. "Is this your sister?"

"Yes," she whispered and ran her hand gently over the younger girl's dark-brown, tangled hair.

Jon touched the toddler's forehead, and heat radiated into his hand. "I'm afraid she's unwell. She should see a doctor."

The older girl's eyes widened, and she bit her lip.

"There's a free clinic not too far from here, on the corner of Fourth and Conover Street. Do you know where that is?"

She hesitated, then nodded, though it was unconvincing. The toddler shifted on her lap and coughed again.

Kate touched his arm. "Perhaps we should take them there."

The older girl clutched her sister and pulled back. "No, our brother can take us. He'll be back soon. He just went to get us something to eat."

Kate glanced at Jon, doubt shadowing her eyes.

Was the girl telling the truth? How could he walk away without knowing if she would take her little sister to Daystar?

Lydia reached in her pocketbook. "Why don't you enjoy these peppermints until your brother comes back?" She handed the older girl two candies.

The girl took them and whispered her thanks. She unwrapped the first one and gave it to her sister. The little one slipped it in her mouth and turned her head away.

Jon stood, a plan forming in his mind. They would come back this way after they spoke to Helen, and if the girls were still here, he would take them to Daystar Clinic himself, though he wasn't sure how he would convince them to go along.

"Hey! What's going on here?" A scruffy lad who looked about twelve or thirteen pushed past Kate and stood in front of the little girls. He raised his pointed chin and glared at Jon. "Don't be bothering my sisters."

Before Jon could answer, the older sister tugged on her brother's shirttail. "They just stopped to buy some matches." She held out the folded note to him.

The boy's expression eased. "Oh, well, it's all right then."

Jon placed his hand on the boy's shoulder and took him aside. "Your younger sister has a fever. You should take her to the Daystar Clinic on Fourth and Conover."

Suspicion shadowed the boy's eyes. "Why should I listen to you?"

"I'm a doctor in training at St. George's Hospital. I can see she's ill."

The lad's stubborn stance eased. "We don't have money for a doctor."

"It's a free clinic. Ask for Dr. Alfred Pittsford. He'll take care of your sister." Jon gave him directions. The boy took it in with a confident nod. He seemed to be an intelligent lad and was certainly protective of his sisters.

"Come on, Rose. Let's go." The lad reached out a hand to help his sister up.

Rose grimaced and struggled to rise and lift the toddler.

Jon's heart lurched in his chest. Was Rose unwell herself?

"Here, I'll take her." The lad stepped forward and lifted his younger sister into his arms. He straightened and shifted her weight, but it was obvious it would be a long and difficult walk for them to reach the clinic.

Kate moved to Jon's side. "Let's hail a cab for them." She reached in her purse and pulled out three folded notes.

He glanced down the street. There weren't many cabs in this part of town. How long would they have to wait for one to pass by?

Lydia pointed toward the corner. "Look, there's one now."

Jon lifted his fingers to his mouth and gave a loud whistle, then waved his arm in the air.

"My, that's certainly a loud whistle." Kate's eyes glowed as she looked up at him.

He grinned. "It's come in handy a few times."

The horse-drawn cab rolled to a stop at the curb. Jon stepped forward and spoke to the driver. Kate joined him and held out the money.

Jon covered her hand. "I'll take care of it."

"No, I want to help." She held his gaze until he nodded.

The driver took the notes from Kate. Lydia helped the children into the cab while Jon gave instructions to the driver.

He touched his cap. "Don't worry. I'll look after the young ones."

"Thank you," Kate called as the cab rolled away.

Jon's gaze traveled from the cab to Kate, warmth spreading through his chest. She truly cared about those children and wanted to do what she could to help them. This was a side of her he hadn't seen before...one that connected them in a new way and made him appreciate her even more.

• • •

Kate watched the cab as it disappeared around the corner, then she glanced at Jon. He had been so gentle with those little girls, and he'd shown just the right balance of firmness and kindness with the young boy. She hadn't seen those qualities displayed very often by the men in her life. Her father had been aloof and brusque, more interested in his horses and hunting dogs than his daughters. She had longed for his approval when she was young, and she'd taken up riding in the hope of winning it, but it hadn't helped. She wasn't the son he had always wanted, and there was no way she could win his love.

Thank goodness Jon was nothing like him.

"That was quite wonderful." She smiled up at him, and an unexpected lump lodged in her throat.

He returned her smile as they started down the street again. "I'm glad they're safely on their way. I'm sure Dr. Pittsford will take good care of them."

Kate swallowed and blinked away the moisture in her eyes. "I don't know why helping them touched me so."

Jon glanced her way. "Some of the best moments of my life have been when I'm helping someone in need. And when it's a child, that brings even greater joy."

Jon's words resonated in her heart, and she nodded. "All my life I've been surrounded by wealth and comfort. I've rarely seen anyone truly in need, let alone reached out to help them. Of course I've heard about the poor in sermons and taken gifts to the retired servants on Boxing Day, but they weren't really needy."

"It's quite different to see the poor face to face—to realize each one is an individual with their own story and needs similar to our own." His voice was soft, but filled with conviction.

"Yes, it is."

"Helping someone like that always makes me feel as though I'm part-nering with the Lord in a special way."

Was that why it moved her so, that connection with God, that feeling of being used by Him?

A few raindrops splashed on the pavement in front of them. Jon lifted his hand to his hat. "We'd better hurry."

Lydia took Kate's arm again, and they hustled down the street. An old woman, hunched over and burdened with shopping bags, walked past. A delivery truck honked and swerved around a slow-moving, horse-drawn cart carrying crates of vegetables.

"There it is." Jon motioned across the street to a butcher shop with an entrance at the side. "That door leads to the flats upstairs."

They waited for the traffic to clear, then crossed the street. Jon opened the side door.

Stale air, ripe with rotting food, greeted Kate as she stepped inside. She covered her mouth and nose against the foul odor. Jon closed the outside door, and the light in the hallway became so dim she could barely see.

"Helen's flat is number 3B." Lydia squinted and looked up the narrow stairs. "It must be up there."

"I'll go first." Jon led the way up the rickety staircase. Kate followed, and Lydia brought up the rear.

The stairs creaked underfoot, and a shiver raced down Kate's back. What a horrid place. She couldn't imagine living in this stench and darkness. They reached the first floor, and Jon stopped and looked down the hallway.

An eerie squeak and scratching sound came from the corner. Kate stepped closer to Jon. "What was that?"

Before Jon could answer, a rat ran out of the dark corner toward them.

Kate yelped and grabbed Jon's arm.

"Go on!" Jon stamped his foot and frightened the rodent away.

Kate lifted her hand to her chest. "My goodness. I've never seen a rat before, except in a book."

Lydia chuckled. "I've seen plenty of them on the farm, but not as large as that one."

"Come on." Jon placed his hand over Kate's, keeping her close to his side as they continued down the hall. The number 3B was scratched into the door at the end.

"This is it." Lydia lifted her hand and knocked gently three times.

They waited, and when no one answered, Jon stepped forward and rapped on the door again, louder this time. Still no one came.

Lydia's shoulders sagged. "All this way, and no one's home."

Kate scanned the hallway. "Perhaps one of the neighbors can tell us when they might return."

Lydia walked to the door marked 3A and knocked.

Seconds later, the door squeaked open a few inches. An old woman with frizzy gray hair peered out. She wore a faded brown dress covered by a stained apron. Her eyes narrowed as she looked them up and down. "What do you want?"

"Good day, ma'am. My name is Lydia Chambers. I'm looking for my sister, Helen Chambers. I believe she's staying in 3B." Lydia pointed to her sister's door. "She's not home. Do you know when she's coming back?"

The old woman hesitated. "Maybe I do"—she looked past Lydia at Jon, and suspicion clouded her eyes—"and maybe I don't."

"Please, ma'am, she's only eighteen, and my parents are worried about her. We think she's with a man named Charlie Gibbons. He's a big, tall man, about twenty-five, with reddish-brown hair."

The old woman's gray eyebrows rose. "Your parents have a reason to worry about that one! He spends more time in the pub than he does looking for work."

Lydia flashed a concerned glance at Kate. "Do you know where they've gone or when they'll return?"

"They won't be coming 'round here anytime soon. Butcher Nelson sent them packing when Gibbons didn't pay the rent." The old woman shook her head. "I hope they found somewhere to stay, her being with child and all."

Lydia gasped. "She's pregnant?"

The old woman cocked her head. "You didn't know?"

"I haven't seen my sister since December."

"Well, I'm sorry, but it's true. She tried to keep it a secret, but I heard her crying in the hallway one night, and I called her in. She told me the whole sorry story."

Kate stepped forward. "Why was she crying in the hallway?"

"Gibbons is a tough fellow, especially when he's in his cups. His shouting and cursing scared that poor girl half to death. Too bad she didn't have the good sense to get away that night." She clicked her tongue. "She should've gone home to her family before it was too late."

Lydia leaned toward her door. "Too late? What do you mean?"

"He has a powerful hold on her, never lets her out of his sight—when he's sober that is."

"Do you have any idea where they might go?"

The old woman shook her head. "They never said where they were going. I suppose Gibbons didn't want to leave a trail for Butcher Nelson to follow."

Tears filled Lydia's eyes, and Kate reached out to steady her.

Jon nodded to the old woman. "Thank you. We appreciate your time."

Kate reached in her purse and took out her calling card. "If you do hear from Helen, would you give her this card? Please tell her that her sister Lydia works here, and she is looking for her and wants to help her."

The woman accepted the card and squinted at the writing. "I don't think she'll come around, but I'll pass it along if she does."

"Thank you." Lydia's voice came out in a choked whisper.

Jon touched Lydia's elbow and steered her away from the door. "There's nothing more we can do here."

Lydia released a soft moan. "Oh, Helen, what have you done?"

"Come on, let's go home." Kate wrapped her arm around Lydia's shoulder, but her heart felt like a stone in her chest as she guided Lydia down the stairs and back out to the street.

TEN

J on took a lemon drop from the small glass jar on the Daystar Clinic counter and handed it to the five-year-old boy who waited with his young mother. "Here you go, Peter."

The little boy smiled and slipped the candy in his mouth with his good hand. The other arm was wrapped in a thick bandage and held close to his chest in a sling. He had broken his arm when he'd taken a fall at home that morning. "Thank you," he mumbled around the lemon drop and wiped his lip with his sleeve.

Jon shifted his gaze to the boy's mother. She had scraped her mousy-brown hair back in a careless bun, and gray smudges shaded the area beneath her dull brown eyes.

"He must wear the sling and keep his arm immobile as much as possible for the next month. Then bring him back to the clinic, and we will re-check and see how it's healing."

Weary lines creased the mother's face as she looked at her son. "I'll try to keep him still, but Peter is a busy boy."

"The discomfort should discourage him from being too active at first." But doubt rose in Jon's mind as he watched young Peter shift from one foot to the other, then reach out and fiddle with the window latch.

His mother tucked the clinic appointment card in her pocket. "I'm not sure how I'll keep him from using that arm."

"I understand it will be hard, but if you want him to have full use of it when it heals, then you must do what you can to keep him calm and the arm immobile."

She raised a shaky hand to her mouth, and shook her head. "I have six children, and two are younger than Peter. I can't be watching him all day."

Jon clenched his jaw. Six children was a lot to handle for anyone, let alone a woman who looked so tired and beaten down. "Just do the best you can."

She released a shuddering sigh. "I'll try, Doctor."

"May I pray for you?"

She gave a slight shrug. "If you think it will help."

"I'm sure it will."

She gave a resigned nod and bowed her head.

He placed one hand on the woman's shoulder and the other on the boy's and closed his eyes. "Father, I come to You on behalf of Mrs. Cummings and her young son Peter. You see their situation, and You know exactly what they need. I ask You to watch over them and provide for them. Please help Peter's arm heal properly and quickly. And please give Mrs. Cummings the strength she needs to care for her family. We ask You to show Your great love and power in their lives. Thank You for hearing our prayer. We'll be watching and waiting for Your answer. We ask these things in the name of Jesus. Amen."

"Amen," the young mother whispered. She looked up and blinked, a trembling smile on her lips. "Thank you. I'm grateful for your kindness and care, and so is Peter. Aren't you, son?"

The boy nodded.

"You're welcome. I hope I'll see you next month." He squeezed Peter's shoulder. "Be a good lad, and listen to your mother."

Peter bobbed his head and smiled. "I will."

"Very good. Take care now." He ushered them out of the waiting room, and they left by the front door.

Theo walked in from one of the other examining rooms. "Was that our last patient?"

"Yes." A warm sense of satisfaction filled him as he slipped off his white medical jacket and hung it on the hook behind the door.

"Dr. Pittsford left about ten minutes ago. He asked us to lock up."

"All right." Jon took his suit coat off the hook.

"Would you like to stop for something to eat before you head home?"

"Not tonight. I promised Julia I would join her and William for dinner."

Theo's eyes lit up. "Will Kate be there?"

Jon frowned and looked away. "No, she's been invited to dinner at… I'm not sure where, but she's going with her aunt."

"I see." Theo's tone held a hint of amusement.

Jon looked up. "You see what?"

"I see you're not too happy she won't be home for dinner."

Jon huffed. "Don't start."

"All right." Theo grinned. "I'll leave it alone for now, but I can tell you've grown quite fond of her." He slipped off his white jacket and hung it next to Jon's.

Jon sighed. So much for Theo leaving it alone. "Kate's a fine young woman, but there can be nothing more than friendship between us."

"And why is that?"

"Her aunt is intent on matching her up with a wealthy aristocrat in line for a title and estate." Those words tasted bitter in his mouth, and he was afraid it was revealed in his tone.

"And Kate agrees?"

His spirit deflated. "Yes, I'm afraid she does."

"Well, then perhaps she's not the girl for you."

Jon shoved his arms into his suit coat. "I suppose not."

"Say, I've been meaning to ask if you found that young woman you were searching for… What was her name?"

Jon took his hat from the shelf, glad to leave the topic of Kate and her future plans behind them. "Helen Chambers."

"Yes, that's the one."

"I found the address where she was living, but when I took Kate and Lydia there, Helen had moved on."

"Hmm, that's too bad."

"Yes, Lydia was certainly disappointed, especially when we learned more about the situation and her sister's condition."

Theo cocked his head. "What do you mean?"

"Helen's expecting a child, and the man she is with, apparently the baby's father, is an irresponsible lout."

Theo's brow knit. "So you've no idea where she's gone?"

"None. We spoke to a neighbor, but they left no forwarding address. In fact it seems they slipped away to avoid paying the last month's rent."

"Perhaps her pregnancy will bring her to the clinic."

"I suppose that's a possibility." Jon placed his hat on his head, then reached for the door handle. "But I doubt it. I don't think there's much hope of finding her now."

"The Lord knows where she is."

Jon checked the lock and pulled the front door closed as he pondered those words. "Yes, I'm sure He does."

"Then we must pray He reveals it to us."

Jon slapped his friend on the shoulder, his spirit lifting. "Yes, you're right. We must."

• • •

Penny's usual sunny expression clouded as she looked across the dining-room table at Julia and William. "I don't understand. Why must I stay home? Who would be offended?"

Julia glanced at William. She didn't want to disagree with him, especially in front of the rest of the family, but was it fair to exclude Penny from Kate's ball simply because she wasn't quite old enough to be out in society?

William frowned and looked down at his breakfast plate. "Your aunt Louisa feels it would not be appropriate because you've not been presented."

"But I thought all the family would attend." Penny shifted her gaze to those seated across the table. "Clark and Sarah are going, and so is Jon. Why should I be the only one to miss out?"

"They're all adults." William's voice was firm. "You are not."

Sarah and Clark, along with Mrs. Dalton, had arrived last night. Julia had invited Clark's mother to eat breakfast with them, but she said she'd be more comfortable eating with the staff. Julia understood from her own experience how it felt to be uncertain whether you fit in with the staff or the family, and she wanted to make sure Mrs. Dalton felt welcome with both.

She and William would meet with Mrs. Dalton at ten o'clock to discuss her taking on the role of housekeeper at Highland. Hopefully the interview would go well, and Mrs. Dalton could begin working for them as soon as she returned to Berkshire.

Julia glanced around the table, trying to judge the others' thoughts about Penny attending the ball. Jon sat beside William, quietly observing the conversation, but Julia could tell by his expression that he agreed Penny should attend. Millie watched the conversation with wide-eyed interest from her seat next to Penny, while Andrew focused on eating his eggs and toast, oblivious to it all.

Julia offered William a slight smile. "I understand the desire to follow tradition, but couldn't we make an exception for Penny this one time?"

"I'd be happy to act as Penny's chaperone if that would ease the situation." Sarah glanced at Penny, then shifted her gaze to William. "I know you and Julia will be busy greeting guests and hosting the event, but Clark and I could watch over her."

Penny's expression brightened. "Yes, that's a wonderful idea. Thank you, Cousin Sarah." Penny turned to William again. "Please, just this once?"

Kate laid her napkin on the table. "I don't mind if Penny comes. I'd be happy to have her there."

William rubbed the bridge of his nose. "Your aunt was quite insistent when we discussed it last night. I'm sure she'll be upset if we go against her wishes on this."

Julia pressed her lips together. Following the rules of London society was important and so was keeping the peace with Louisa, but they were not more important than a young girl's heart. "You are the host of the party, William. Surely you should have the final say."

William's expression eased. "That's true."

Penny looked back and forth between Julia and William, her expression brightening. "So it's all right? I can go to Kate's ball?"

William held up his hand. "I haven't made my decision yet, but I'll speak to your aunt and see if we can bring her around."

Penny sighed and sat back. "All right. I'll wait. But I want you to know I'd be perfectly happy for the rest of my life if you'd just say yes this one time."

Jon grinned. "I'd help keep an eye on Penny as well." He glanced at William. "That is, if you decided she may attend."

"Thank you, Jon." Julia glanced across at her brother, grateful to have him with them. The conversations they'd shared around the table and in the evening had been a great comfort to her.

She looked down the table at William's sister, Sarah. Seeing her happy smile and the affection in Clark's eyes as he looked at his wife warmed Julia's heart. It was wonderful to have them here to celebrate Kate's coming out. Surely when William spoke to Louisa he could convince her to grant Penny's request.

After breakfast, Jon approached Julia. "I was wondering if I might bring my friend Theo along to the ball tonight. He seemed very keen on the idea when I mentioned it yesterday."

"All right. Another single, well-mannered young man is always welcome at a ball."

Jon grinned. "Theo's a fine fellow. I'm sure you'll like him."

"If he is a friend of yours, then I'm sure I will." Julia took her brother's arm, and they walked out of the dining room together.

• • •

"This way, please." The tall, silver-haired butler led Kate down the marble-floored hallway at Sheffield House, while she tried to calm the fluttering in her stomach. The night of her ball had finally arrived. Louisa, William, Julia, Penny, Sarah, and Clark followed Kate through the doorway and into the large ballroom.

Kate's steps stalled, and her eyes widened. She had only been to Sheffield in the daytime, but seeing it in the evening was completely different. Three large, glittering chandeliers sent sparkling light dancing across the highly polished wooden floor and bouncing back from several tall mirrors around the room.

A smile rose from Kate's heart to her lips. "Oh, it's beautiful."

Penny took Kate's arm. "Yes, it's perfectly lovely."

Potted pink-and-white azaleas sat in front of each window, and gold-cushioned chairs ringed the room, leaving most of the floor open for dancing. Off to the left side, double doors had been pushed open, and a long buffet table was spread with an elaborate display of candles, flowers, and delicious-looking food.

"I've never seen anything like it," Penny added in a hushed voice.

"It's much more than I expected." Kate turned to Julia and William. "Thank you so much."

Julia leaned in and kissed her cheek. "We're happy for you, Kate. We hope you have a lovely evening."

Kate's gaze traveled around the room again. "I'm sure I will."

William nodded. "They've done a splendid job preparing everything. We must be sure to thank the Tremonts."

Louisa sniffed as she regarded the empty room and overflowing buffet table. "It's a shame Elizabeth Harrington's ball is being held the same night as Katherine's."

Julia turned to Louisa. "I don't think we should worry about that."

"Well, I won't be surprised if our number of guests is much lower than we expected."

Kate's stomach tensed. Was her aunt right? Would she receive only a handful of guests this evening? That could be disastrous.

Julia took Kate's hand. "Everything is going to be just fine."

"Of course." Kate straightened her shoulders. She would not allow her aunt to spoil the evening before it had even begun.

"Here come Lord and Lady Tremont." William glanced toward the elegant couple entering the ballroom. Julia and William crossed to meet them.

Kate started to follow, but Louisa reached for her arm and stopped her. She took a small card from her beaded purse and handed it to Kate. "These are the names of the young men you must be sure to pay attention to this evening."

Kate studied the list, and her brow creased. "I don't recognize any of these names."

Louisa sighed and clicked her tongue. "You met Charles Felton at the Howards' dinner last week. He's quite tall, with red hair."

Kate's eyes widened as the memory rushed back. The rude, puffy-faced young man had ogled her as though she were a dessert on display in a pastry shop. He had crooked teeth, bad breath, and was completely lacking in conversational skills. She did not look forward to seeing him again, and heaven forbid she would have to dance with him.

Louisa pointed to the card. "Each one is a possible prospect. You must make an effort to encourage them all."

Kate stiffened. "I thought you wanted me to encourage Edward."

"Of course. That goes without saying. But we don't want to limit our options this early in the season."

Kate glared at the card and then at her aunt, but Louisa didn't seem to notice.

"Edward needs to see he is not the only one pursuing you. Men like a bit of competition. They want to feel as though they are in a race to win the prize."

Kate did not like the sound of that. She was a young woman in need of a husband, not a piece of real estate up for auction. Her future happiness depended on finding the right man to marry, but how was she to know which one she ought to encourage when she barely had time to talk to them?

Was it enough to see their names on a list provided by her aunt? Should she trust her future to a woman who believed a man's worth depended on his bank account, family connections, and social standing? What about her feelings for the man, or even more important, what about the way he treated her? Shouldn't those factors be considered too?

Louisa frowned at Kate and reached up to adjust the feathered-and-jeweled fascinator pinned in her hair. "Study that list until the guests begin to arrive. Memorize the names. And when you meet them, ask them questions. Men love to talk about themselves."

"That's true, especially most of the men I've met this season."

Her aunt lowered her chin, her expression stern. "Don't be impudent, Kate. It's not fitting for a well-bred young lady."

Kate huffed.

"And for heaven's sake, mind your manners and watch what you say!" She strode off to speak to the Tremonts.

Kate lowered her gaze to the list and read the names once more.

Charles Felton. Well, that was one name she could cross off the list right now. The thought of encouraging him turned her stomach. *Patrick Hamilton. Neil Lawson. Henry Fletcher Harding. Archibald Spalding. Leonard Radcliff.* To her knowledge she'd never met any of these men, or if she had, they'd made no impression on her. How would she recognize them? Was she supposed to flirt with and flatter every man introduced to her?

Kate's eyes began to burn. She blinked several times and lifted her gaze to the beautifully painted ceiling.

Dear God, I know I haven't prayed as often as I should. I'm sorry for that, but I need Your help, so I hope You're still listening. I want to make a good impression tonight and please my family, but most of all I want to find the right path for my future. Would You please help me?

• • •

The cheerful hum of conversation filled the air as Jon entered the large ballroom at Sheffield House. Two hours earlier he'd hurried home from the hospital to change, then caught a cab and picked up Theo on the way. But a snarl of traffic, caused by an accident, had delayed them for at least thirty minutes.

Scanning the ballroom, he estimated the number of guests to be at least one hundred. He smiled, remembering how Kate had told him one of her greatest fears was that only a few people would come. Happily, that was not the case.

Ladies and gentlemen dressed in their finest evening wear stood around the edges of the room clustered in small groups. A few matrons and their young debutantes were seated in chairs awaiting the next invitation to dance. At the far end of the room, a quartet of musicians with stringed instruments appeared to be taking a break between songs.

Theo straightened his white tie and smiled at Jon. "So, this is how society celebrates a young woman's coming out." He surveyed the room. "Not bad. Not bad at all."

Jon nodded, then scanned the crowd again, searching for Kate and the rest of the family. He spotted William and Julia, engaged in conversation with two other couples.

"Come with me. I want to introduce you to Julia and Sir William." Jon wove through the guests, and Theo followed. Jon had only gone a few steps when someone called his name.

He stopped and turned as his Aunt Beatrice approached.

"Hello, Jonathan dear." Her gold dress with black beads and lace seemed rather bright for a woman her age, but her smile was warm and welcoming. The black ostrich plume in her hair fluttered as she held her hand out to him.

"Hello, Aunt Beatrice." He took her hand and kissed her cheek.

"I'm so glad you're here. This is a wonderful opportunity for you to meet some lovely young people." She smiled at Theo. "And who is this?"

"My good friend, Theo Anderson. He is a fellow medical student at St. George's." He turned to Theo. "This is my mother's sister, Lady Beatrice Danforth."

Theo smiled and nodded. "Lady Danforth, it's a pleasure to meet you."

"Thank you. I'm pleased to meet you as well. Jonathan seems so busy with his training, I didn't know he made time for friends."

Jon shot a surprised glance at his aunt. "Of course I do."

"I'm glad to hear it." She smiled. "Applying yourself to your studies is admirable, but you must make time for social events if you want to be a well-rounded person and be included in the best society."

"My responsibilities are much lighter this summer. I'm sure I'll have a bit more time for leisure."

"You should bring Mr. Anderson with you the next time you visit your grandmother." She turned to Theo. "Her health doesn't allow her to go out often, but she loves to receive visitors, and she especially enjoys seeing her grandchildren." She sent Jon a pointed look.

He glanced away. He ought to visit his grandmother more often, but they had only met for the first time a few months ago, following his grandfather's death. He still felt a bit awkward around his mother's relatives and uncertain what to say about the strained relationship between his parents and his late grandfather. But he must put that all aside and visit her soon.

Theo sent his aunt a gracious smile. "Thank you, Lady Danforth. I'd enjoy that very much."

Jon looked across the ballroom. "I should let William and Julia know we've arrived. You'll excuse us, won't you, Aunt Beatrice?"

"Of course, dear." Her expression grew more serious, and she laid her hand on his arm. "But I do hope you will take advantage of the evening and dance with several partners. You never know, you might meet the young lady you've been looking for."

Jon stifled a groan, but gave her a brief smile before he turned away.

Theo chuckled. "She certainly hopes you'll meet someone special tonight."

"Could she be any more obvious?"

"I suppose she believes it's her duty to steer you toward marriage."

"I'm not here to find a wife. I've come to support Kate and keep an eye on Penny."

"Kate's younger sister?"

"Yes. She's not officially out yet, and I promised I'd help watch over her."

Theo smiled. "Sounds like a pleasant duty. Perhaps I can assist you."

Jon lifted his eyebrows. "We'll see."

"Come on, Jon. You can't have all the fun."

"If I allow it, you must promise to be on your best behavior. Penny is only sixteen, and this is her first ball."

"Of course. You can count on me. I'm always a gentleman, and knowing Miss Ramsey's age and family connections, I'll be even more careful."

"All right. I'll introduce you." He smiled at his friend. "But remember, I'll be watching your every move." He might jest with Theo, but he knew he could trust him. They'd been fast friends for the past two years through all the trials of medical training, and they shared an equally strong commitment to their faith.

The music began, and couples took to the dance floor in a swirl of color in motion. Jon turned toward the edge of the room to stay out of the way.

Two young women seated with their chaperones looked up and smiled as Jon and Theo approached. The petite blonde waved her fan, her amber eyes issuing a hopeful invitation. He gave a slight smile, then looked away. Perhaps he should take his aunt's advice and meet some of the eligible young women...but there was only one girl he was searching for this evening, and she seemed hopelessly out of reach.

Jon pushed that discomforting thought aside. He must not think of Kate that way. He was her friend and protector. Those were the only roles he could claim in her life, even if it was becoming harder to be satisfied with that.

They joined William and Julia, and he introduced Theo. "It looks like you have a good number of guests."

"Yes. That's quite a relief. Lady Gatewood was predicting disaster." Julia smiled as she looked around. "But it seems the Lord has smiled down on Katherine tonight."

"And where is Kate?" Jon asked.

Julia's smile faded. "I'm afraid Lady Gatewood has taken her around to introduce her to all the guests."

William grimaced. "I hope she will ease up and allow Katherine to enjoy the evening. It is her ball. She should be allowed to dance."

Jon couldn't agree more. Lady Gatewood's overbearing ways could suck the joy out of any event.

"Ah, there's Kate, by the potted palms." Julia motioned toward the far corner of the room.

Even from this distance, Jon could read Kate's discomfort in her tense posture and guarded expression. That wasn't right. This was her special night. She shouldn't be trapped in uncomfortable conversations with people she hardly knew. "Perhaps I should ask her to dance and give her a break from all those introductions."

"That's a splendid idea," Julia said. "I know she'd appreciate it."

He started across the room, but as he reached the buffet table, Edward Wellington appeared at Kate's side, and a look of relief washed over her face.

Jon's steps stalled. He picked up a plate and pretended to be surveying the desserts while he watched Edward and Kate.

Edward extended his hand. Kate took it and excused herself from her aunt and the others with them. A smug expression filled Edward's face as he guided her onto the dance floor and took her in his arms. They swung easily into the waltz.

A sinking realization washed over Jon. He was too late to rescue Kate.

Someone else had stepped in and swept her away, and he did not like that at all.

ELEVEN

W illiam tapped his foot in time to the music as he watched couples circle the dance floor. He checked the main doorway for newcomers, but saw none. As soon as he was certain most of their guests had arrived, he planned to take Julia out on the floor and join the dancers. The thought brought a smile to his face.

Julia looked especially lovely tonight in her cream and powder-blue silk dress. Her dark brown hair was swept up, revealing silver earrings with little blue gems. A few wispy curls dangled down the back of her neck, teasing him to come closer.

He cleared his throat and looked away. It was still four months until the wedding, and for the life of him he couldn't imagine why he had agreed to wait that long. But she was worth waiting for, no matter how long it would be.

Sarah, Penny, and Clark returned, carrying small plates filled with delicious-looking desserts. His sister appeared to be very happy tonight. Leaning on Clark's arm, her limp was hardly noticeable. She might not be able to join Clark on the dance floor, but he didn't seem to mind. In fact, he seemed quite pleased to have his wife close by his side.

William had not been in favor of their union when he'd first discovered his sister was carrying on a secret romance with his head gardener at Highland, but as he got to know Clark, he had changed his mind. And now he was glad he'd reconsidered and admitted Clark into the family.

William turned to Penny. "So, are you enjoying the ball?"

She looked up at him, her cheeks flushed and eyes glowing. "Oh yes, it's lovely." She looked quite grown up in her light-green dress with ivory lace at the neck and sleeves. Penelope had begged her aunt to allow her to wear her hair up like Katherine, but Louisa had put her foot down and would not be swayed.

Penny lowered her gaze, then smiled up at Theo through her eyelashes.

William supposed he ought to introduce them. "Penelope, I'd like you to meet Mr. Theo Anderson. He is a medical student at St. George's and Jon's good friend."

She held out her hand. "Mr. Anderson, I'm happy to meet you."

Theo took her hand and bowed. "Miss Ramsey, it's a pleasure." He asked her about her time in London, and she asked him about his studies at St. George's. He commented on the number of guests attending the ball, and she asked if he'd had any refreshments yet.

William watched it all closely. Penelope seemed to be handling herself well, and Theo appeared to be respectful and courteous.

Theo turned to William. "I understand this is Miss Ramsey's first ball."

"Yes, that's true."

"Would it be all right if I asked her to dance?"

William's eyebrows rose. He glanced at Penelope. She smiled, signaling her positive reply. He turned back to Theo. "Yes, I believe that would be fine, and thank you for asking me first."

"Of course, sir." Theo held out his hand to Penelope. "May I have this dance?"

Her cheeks flushed a deeper pink, and her eyes sparkled. "Yes, you may." She handed her plate to Julia, then took Theo's hand. He guided her onto the dance floor.

Julia leaned toward William, lowering her voice. "That was kind of him to ask her to dance."

"I'm not sure kindness is his only motivation."

"William." She sent him a playful smile.

"I simply mean Penelope is a lovely young woman, and I'm not surprised he wants to dance with her."

"I'm sure he'll treat her well."

"Yes, I suppose he will." William watched them for a few moments, then looked for Katherine. Had Jon been able to steal her away from Louisa, or was she still tied to her aunt, making an endless round of introductions?

He located Jon, standing alone by the buffet table, his gaze focused on the dance floor. William looked in that same direction and saw Katherine and Edward dancing near the center of the room.

He bent toward Julia. "Katherine is dancing with Edward Wellington."

"Yes, I see them."

"I thought Jon was going to ask her to dance."

"I suppose Edward asked first."

"Do you think he's serious about her?"

"You mean Edward?"

"Yes, of course."

A faint line creased the space between Julia's eyebrows. "He has paid her a great deal of attention."

"What is Louisa's opinion of him?"

"She's very fond of his mother. I'm sure she'd be in favor of them becoming more serious."

"Do we know anything else about him or his family?"

"Not really."

William narrowed his eyes. "Then perhaps it's time we found out."

• • •

The music ended, and Kate stepped back. Edward smiled as they turned and clapped for the musicians. She'd enjoyed their waltz, especially since Edward's invitation had given her an exit from the conversation with that awful Charles Felton. But Edward hadn't said more than two sentences to her during their dance. She must remember her training and make more of an effort to engage him in conversation.

The next song started, and he moved to her side. "Shall we take a walk? It's a bit warm, and I could do with some fresh air."

Kate glanced toward the open window. "That would be lovely. Perhaps my cousin Sarah and her husband Clark would like to join us, or my sister Penelope."

A smile lifted one corner of his mouth. "I'd rather it be just the two of us."

Kate's heartbeat sped up. She wanted to say yes, but should she go outside with him without a chaperone?

He tipped his head. "There's no need to worry. I'll take good care of you."

"I'm sure you would, but my aunt might not approve of me leaving my other guests."

"I don't think she'd mind. Why don't you ask her?" A hint of a challenge appeared in his gray eyes.

"All right. I'll just be a moment." She crossed the ballroom toward her aunt.

Louisa narrowed her gaze as Kate approached. "What's wrong? Why did you leave Edward standing there by himself?"

Kate leaned toward her aunt and lowered her voice. "He asked me to go outside for a walk…alone."

Louisa's expression brightened. "That sounds promising."

"Yes, but shouldn't someone go with us? I thought you said I must always have a chaperone."

"If you stay on the terrace in the light, no one should object."

Kate glanced back at Edward.

"Well, don't just stand there! Hurry along before Edward becomes distracted and asks someone else to dance." Louisa huffed and turned away, apparently certain Kate would follow her instructions without any more questions.

Kate blew out a hot breath. She was just trying to do the right thing. Why did her aunt have to scold her for asking?

A waiter approached, carrying a tray of glasses filled with punch. Kate suddenly realized she was terribly thirsty and helped herself to a glass. The cool punch soothed her dry throat. She finished her drink, set her cup aside, and rejoined Edward.

He cocked his eyebrow. "So, do we have your aunt's permission?"

"Yes, she suggested the terrace just outside those doors." Kate motioned toward the open double doors at the end of the ballroom.

He offered her his arm. "That sounds perfect."

She slipped her hand through the crook of his elbow, and they set off. Several people turned and watched them as they crossed the ballroom and walked out onto the terrace.

The gentle splashing of a fountain could be heard in the distance, and overhead, stars sparkled down from a blue velvet sky.

"Ah, this is better." Edward led her to the edge of the terrace overlooking the gardens. Torches had been lit on the balustrade and along the pathways below. A light breeze ruffled the leaves of a nearby tree, and the quiet hum of insects filled the air.

Kate pulled in a slow deep breath of the cool evening air. "This is lovely."

"Yes, lovely."

She glanced at him and realized he was focused on her, not the garden or the night sky. She looked away, and pleasant warmth filled her face.

"Kate." He waited until she looked at him again. "I've enjoyed getting to know you these last few weeks, and I'd like to know you more. Would you be open to that?"

Kate hesitated. "To…what?"

"Please, Kate, it's not easy for a man to be open about his feelings."

"I'm sorry. I'm just trying to understand what you mean."

"I think we could make a good match, and I'd like to know if you're open to…exploring that possibility."

She blinked at him. What should she say?

He took her hand. "So what do you think, Kate?"

She looked down at their clasped hands. Edward had many of the qualities she was looking for in a husband, but they'd only spent a few hours together. Was that enough time to make such an important decision?

She slowly raised her gaze to meet his. "I'm flattered by your…interest, but don't you think it's a bit early in the season for you to focus on just one person?"

He laughed softly. "Kate, your honesty always surprises me."

"I'm sorry. I suppose that wasn't the right thing to say."

"Don't apologize. I want to know what you're thinking, and I want to be honest with you as well." His expression grew more serious. "My parents are eager for me to marry. They've encouraged me to choose a wife this season. My mother and your aunt both seem in favor of it. I think they'd be pleased."

She searched his face. He seemed sincere, but he hadn't said anything about his feelings for her. Were family connections and a common background enough of a basis on which to build a happy marriage? Would love grow if she gave it time?

She'd seen the way William looked at Julia, and how Clark Dalton could not take his eyes off Sarah. She'd always hoped the man she married would feel that way about her, and she about him. Was that too much to hope for?

"Please Kate, don't keep me in suspense. I'm not asking for a commitment now—just your willingness to consider it."

Once again she read the sincerity in his eyes, and there only seemed one answer she could give. "Yes, I'm open to it."

His smile spread wider. He took her hand, lifted it to his lips, and kissed her fingers.

• • •

A couple danced past, blocking Jon's view of the terrace. He leaned to the side, trying to keep Edward and Kate in sight. Since they'd left the ballroom, he'd stationed himself a few feet from the door, and he didn't intend to shift his gaze away until Edward brought Kate back inside. So far, Edward had kept a respectable distance, but Jon was ready to intervene the moment Edward did anything the least bit questionable.

Jon tapped his fingers in a steady rhythm against the side of his punch glass, his eyes fixed on Kate. It was hard to read her expression in the torchlight. If only he could hear their conversation, but the distance was too great.

Edward turned toward Kate with a warm smile, then lifted her hand and kissed her fingers.

Jon tensed. What did that mean? None of the possibilities he considered eased his mind.

As Kate and Edward entered the ballroom, light flooded her face. A slight crease between her eyebrows seemed to indicate uncertainty. She glanced around the room as though searching for someone.

Jon's hopes rose. Perhaps Edward's kiss on Kate's hand was simply his way of ending their conversation and nothing more. At least he could hope that was all it meant.

Edward excused himself and left Kate by the punch table.

Jon straightened. This was his chance, and he did not intend to delay another moment. He crossed the room and came up behind her. "Hello, Kate."

She turned, and her face brightened. "Jon, I wondered where you were."

"You were looking for me?" He couldn't hold back his smile.

Her cheeks flushed. "I didn't see you come in, and I thought you might have been delayed at the hospital."

"We were delayed on our way because of an accident." As if on cue the next song began. "Would you like to dance?"

She nodded, her smile warm and genuine. "I'd like that very much."

He guided her onto the dance floor and took her hand.

After a few steps she said, "I didn't know you danced."

"My mother taught me, much to the chagrin of my father."

"He doesn't approve of dancing?"

"I wouldn't say that, but his upbringing was rather strict, and his family didn't dance. My mother was raised here in London. In fact, she was a debutante in '84."

"Really, I didn't know your mother took part in the season."

Jon smiled down at her. "There are many things you don't know about me and my family."

She returned a smile, her eyes sparkling. "I suppose that's true."

She looked especially lovely tonight with her hair up in an elaborate style. Diamond earrings dangled from her ears, and a sparkling tiara crowned her head. "I like the tiara. It makes you look quite regal."

"Oh…thank you." Her expression faltered and she looked away. "It was my mother's." He almost didn't hear her soft reply.

"I'm sorry. I didn't realize…"

"No. It's all right. I just wish she could be here with me tonight. I think she would be pleased."

"Yes, I'm sure your parents would be very happy for you."

"My mother would, though I doubt my father would've arranged anything this lovely for me."

"Why do you say that?"

"My father didn't like coming to town, especially for the season."

"Why was that?"

"He was an outdoorsman who loved country life—hunting, riding, fishing. Those were his passions. But he was a hard man to please, and he never got over the fact he didn't have a son to inherit his title and estate. That was a constant source of contention between my parents."

"Really?"

"Yes. He blamed my mother for not producing an heir."

"Then he'd be very surprised to hear he was the one who determined whether his children would be male or female."

She looked up at him. "Are you quite sure?"

"Yes. It's a new theory, but it makes sense scientifically."

"Well, it's a good thing he didn't live long enough to hear that. It would have tilted his world off its axis."

Jon chuckled. "Either way, whether we are male or female, God says we are all fearfully and wonderfully made. And I don't think He's simply referring to the amazing way our bodies are designed, though my medical studies have shown me that is definitely true. I believe men and women reflect His glory in unique ways. Each of us is valuable and loved by Him."

She sent him a doubtful glance. "You really believe that?"

"Of course. Men and women are equally chosen to inherit God's likeness and able to receive the blessings of salvation."

"So if you had only daughters, you wouldn't be disappointed?"

He thought for a moment, picturing a little blue-eyed girl who looked very much like Kate, then smiled. "No, I would not, not in the least."

Her expression brightened, and she shook her head. "Jonathan Foster, you are a very modern and forward-thinking man."

"Forward thinking, perhaps, but those ideas aren't modern—they're taken from Scripture."

"I've never heard a sermon like that."

"I'm sorry. I don't mean to be preaching, especially while we're dancing."

"Don't apologize. It's a message I'm glad to hear, and someone I'm very glad to hear it from." When she looked up at him, her smile was so endearing, his breath caught in his chest.

Was that affection reflected in her eyes? Could it be true? Did she also sense the growing attraction between them?

He couldn't deny his feelings for Kate any longer. She was special, so very special, and every day he found himself more drawn toward her. The differences between them flooded his mind, sending him a warning, but he pushed those thoughts away.

Those differences were not as important as all they shared in common. And somehow he must find a way to convince her that was true and win her heart.

• • •

Julia's mother had taught her how to dance when she was a young girl. Her brother had been her partner then, but that was nothing like dancing with William. He led her through the steps with confidence and ease, and in his arms she felt treasured. She looked up at him, and joy bubbled up from her heart.

He returned a loving gaze, and they swirled around the dance floor until the waltz came to an end. Then they stepped apart and clapped for the musicians.

"That was lovely," she said. "Thank you."

"Truly, it was my pleasure. You are a charming dancer."

She took his arm, and they returned to the side of the room where Sarah and Clark waited.

Sarah reached for Julia's hand. "You and William dance beautifully together."

"Thank you." Julia glanced around. "Where is Penny?"

Sarah looked toward the dance floor. "She is dancing with Theo Anderson again."

Julia turned and searched through the crowd. She soon spotted Penny and Theo near the far end of the ballroom. Just to the left of them, Kate danced with Jon. Kate gazed up at Jon with a delighted expression. Was it the rush of excitement on this special evening...or something more?

Julia's thoughts flashed back to the past few weeks. Jon did seem to have a particular interest in Kate. He was always eager to go riding with her, or to spend time with her in the evenings. And he seemed especially intent about watching out for her.

He had been cautious and protective when they were growing up. She had teased him about it then, but she'd felt safe with him wherever they went. Her father trusted Jon as well, often sending him along as a guide for other missionaries traveling through their area.

She observed Jon for a few more seconds, and his focus on Kate hinted at deeper feelings. Did Kate see it? How did she feel about him?

Perhaps she should speak to Jon and see if she was reading the situation correctly. She wasn't sure how she felt about the possibility of Jon and Kate developing a closer friendship, but one thing was clear: Louisa would not be happy about it. And that was only one issue. What about Jon's future plans? Would Kate want to travel to India as the wife of a missionary doctor?

The small spark of faith she had observed in Kate seemed to be growing, but had she truly made a commitment to Christ? Julia would never encourage her brother to seriously pursue Kate unless that was true. He needed a wife who not only loved him but was also committed to serving God. Marriage was challenging enough. Without a common faith, it could be painful and difficult.

A movement to her right caught her eye. A man in a dark cape approached William through the crowd. David Ramsey came into full view, and a tremor traveled through Julia. He had not responded to their invitation, and she had not expected to see him tonight.

"William, I must speak to you." David's taut expression and serious tone put Julia on alert. What did he want?

William nodded to David. "Good evening, David. I'm glad you decided to join us."

"I've no time for pleasantries. This is urgent." Anxious lines creased his forehead as he looked around the room. "Where can we speak in private?"

William's posture became rigid. "We can step out on the terrace."

David nodded and set off without waiting for William.

William shook his head and turned to Julia. "I'm sorry. I don't know what has put David in such a mood, but it's best I deal with it now before he disrupts the evening."

Julia watched David cross the ballroom. "Yes, I understand."

Appreciation flashed in his eyes. He squeezed her hand, then he turned and strode after his brother.

• • •

William stepped onto the terrace and crossed to meet David. "Now…what is so urgent?"

The torchlight cast deep shadows across David's face. "I'm in serious trouble, William."

"What do you mean? What kind of trouble?"

"Reginald Martindale has been shot."

William pulled in a sharp breath. "David, you didn't—"

"No, I didn't shoot him, but everyone will assume I did." David gripped the terrace balustrade and stared across the gardens.

"Tell me what happened."

"Dorothea and I were…in the drawing room at her house when Reginald arrived quite unexpectedly."

William clenched his jaw and suppressed a groan. "David."

He lifted his hand. "I know, I know. We should never have been there alone together."

"Or anywhere else, for that matter."

David faced William, his eyes wide. "Reginald was irate, ranting, threatening to kill us both. Then he stormed out of the room. Dorothea was terrified. She said he kept a gun in his desk in his study. She urged me to go, but I couldn't run away and leave her there with him." He closed his eyes and raised his hand to his forehead. "Only a few seconds passed, and we heard a shot."

William gasped. "Did he shoot himself?"

"No. We ran into the entrance hall and saw Reginald on the floor, and another man dashing out the front door."

"Who was it?"

"I don't know. He wore a hat and dark coat. We didn't see his face."

"He shot Martindale?"

"Yes! It had to be him!"

"Is Martindale...dead?"

"I don't know." David shook his head, his face pale. "Dorothea sent a servant to fetch a doctor who lives nearby, but she urged me to leave before the doctor or the police arrived."

"So you just left?"

"Yes! What else could I do?"

"You could've stayed and told the truth about what happened."

David rubbed his hand across his jaw and chin, looking dazed.

"Do you think Dorothea will tell them you were there?"

"I don't know."

"Did any of the servants see you?"

David looked up and met William's gaze. "Yes, the butler and a footman."

William gripped the balustrade. "Then you'll be questioned. There's no way you can hope to escape."

TWELVE

K ate left her packages in the entrance hall and reluctantly followed
her aunt into the library. An explosion was coming, and there was
nothing Kate could do to stop it.

Louisa strode across the room. "William, I must speak to you."

Jon and Julia turned toward Louisa. William looked up, his expression
wary.

Her aunt slapped the newspaper down on William's desk and jabbed
her finger at the bold headline. "Do you know this man…this Reginald
Martindale?" Her accusing tone made her suspicions clear.

Jon shot Kate a questioning glance. She sensed his concern and support, and it bolstered her courage.

That morning at breakfast William had told the family about his conversation with David at Kate's ball, but Louisa had not been present, and no
one wanted to tell her. An hour later, Kate and her aunt went shopping on
Bond Street, and a newspaper boy shouted the headline, "Reginald Martindale Shot in His Berkeley Square Home." Kate bought a copy to take back
to William and Julia, since she knew they were anxious for news about the
events surrounding the shooting.

Louisa questioned her all the way to Ramsey House as to why she had
bought the paper, and Kate finally told her that William knew the man. That
wasn't a complete explanation, but it was all she could bring herself to say.

William rose from his desk and faced Louisa. "I don't know Reginald
Martindale personally. I only know of him."

"Don't be vague. What is your connection to this man who has been
murdered in cold blood in his own home?"

Julia gasped and lifted her hand to her mouth. "He's dead?"

Louisa pointed to the article again. "Apparently, if this newspaper can
be relied upon to tell the truth."

William picked up the paper and scanned the article. His shoulders sagged as he laid it on the desk again. "We may not know Reginald Martindale, but I'm afraid there is a connection between us."

"Well, what is it?" her aunt demanded.

"My brother David has been romantically involved with his wife, Dorothea, for a few months."

Louisa's hand flew to her chest. "Good heavens… Your brother had an affair with the wife of a diplomat?" Her eyes widened. "Is he responsible for this?"

"If you're asking did he shoot Reginald Martindale, then no, I don't believe he did. But his connection with Dorothea and his presence at the house last night will make him a suspect in the case."

"He was there…when the man was murdered?" Louisa sank down in the chair and lifted her hand to her forehead. "Oh dear, this is terrible! I feel quite faint."

Sick dread washed over Kate. A man had been murdered, and though David had not fired the shot, he had played a role in it.

Julia rose and crossed to Louisa's side. She laid her hand on the older woman's shoulder. "I know this is upsetting, but perhaps when you know the facts it will help you come to terms with what's happened."

"I doubt hearing the details will sooth my nerves." Her aunt looked up at William. "But I suppose you should tell me the rest."

William relayed what had happened at the Martindale home the night before.

Louisa's face flushed, and she grimaced as the story progressed. "If your brother is interviewed as a witness, his involvement with Dorothea Martindale will come to light, and nothing can stop the spread of that kind of poisonous gossip once it starts."

William's eyes clouded. "Yes, I'm afraid that's true. There is no turning back the tide on a story like this, even if David is never arrested."

Louisa paced across the room, intent in thought. When she reached the piano, she spun around and glared at William as though he were the one who shot Reginald Martindale. "Of course you know this could ruin all our hopes for Katherine. No one will want their son to marry into a family rife with scandal!"

Kate's thoughts flashed back to her ball. She had been the star of the evening, with a line of young men eager to dance with her. What would they say now?

William lowered his dark eyebrows. "We all care about Kate and want the best for her, but a man's life has been lost, a family destroyed, and my brother may be accused of a murder he did not commit. Certainly those are the most important things to consider right now."

"Of course, but there's nothing we can do about those matters." Louisa shifted her unhappy gaze to Kate. "Our focus should be on Katherine and containing the damage this will do to her reputation."

A dizzy feeling swept through Kate. Her eyes burned as she tried to blink away her tears. She would not cry—not in front of everyone. She swallowed hard and forced out her words. "Excuse me. I…have some things I need to do." She turned and hurried toward the library door.

"Oh, Katherine…" Julia's voice choked.

Rather than comforting her, Julia's sympathetic tone broke through her wall she'd raised to protect her emotions. A renegade tear slipped down her cheek as she strode out of the library and across the entrance hall. How foolish! She must get hold of herself.

"Kate, wait a minute." Jon stepped out of the library.

She quickly swiped her cheek before she turned to face him.

He pulled the library door closed behind him and crossed to meet her at the bottom of the stairs. Compassion filled his eyes as he took a handkerchief from his pocket and handed it to her. "I'm awfully sorry about all this."

She accepted the handkerchief and blotted away her tears. "I don't know why I'm crying. It's not going to change anything."

"There's nothing wrong with a few tears."

"I'm surprised to hear you say that. Most men hate to see a woman cry."

"I have a mother and a sister. I am used to it."

"I can't imagine Julia crying over something like this."

"Oh, she's shed plenty of tears over issues much less important."

"Do you think my aunt is right?"

Jon paused for a moment. "London society does seem to place a great deal of importance on a family's reputation."

"Yes, I suppose that's true, but if they find the person who murdered Mr. Martindale, then David's part might only be a small line at the bottom of a newspaper story."

Jon glanced away, looking doubtful.

She frowned. "Well, it could happen like that…if they find the man who did it."

"I'm sorry Kate, but your cousin's involvement with Mrs. Martindale and his presence at her home the night of the murder are facts that won't soon be forgotten. It's unfortunate, but people seem to relish a murder mystery, especially one that involves a romance."

Kate sank down on the steps. "You're probably right. This will make us all outcasts for the rest of the season. Perhaps we should just leave and go home to Highland."

"Give up just because the road has become rough?" He sat down beside her. "That doesn't sound like you."

She glanced at him. "It doesn't?"

He shook his head and watched her a moment more, kindness in his eyes. "I have an idea. Why don't you take a break from all this and come with me to the Daystar Clinic?"

She straightened and met his gaze. "What would I do there? I'm not a doctor or a nurse."

"You could lend a hand at the reception desk, or better yet, comfort a child who is ill or help a mother who is trying to manage two or three young children while she waits to see the doctor."

"Would they welcome an untrained volunteer?"

"You'd only be untrained for the first ten minutes." His smile warmed. "What do you think?"

The tension in Kate's shoulders eased. "It would be wonderful to get away for a few hours."

"I'm sure Dr. Pittsford and the rest of the staff would welcome your help." His voice softened. "I've often wished I had an assistant—not just another set of hands, but someone who was kind and caring—to help me with the patients."

She looked into his eyes, trying to read the emotion behind his words. Was that friendship reflected in his gaze...or affection? A shiver raced down her arms, and she pushed the question aside. Jon was a kind and caring person. Friendship was all he felt for her, and that was all she would allow herself to feel for him.

Louisa walked out of the library and spotted them sitting on the steps. Her eyes flashed. "Katherine, how many times have I told you ladies do not sit on the stairs?"

Katherine rose to her feet, but she refused to apologize.

Jon stood beside her.

Louisa glared at her. "Go upstairs and get your hat and gloves."

Kate frowned. "Why? Where are we going?"

"I want to make a few calls and see what we can do to squelch the gossip that is sure to be circulating."

Kate stared at her aunt. How could she even think of paying calls today?

"Well...don't just stand there. Hurry up. We've no time to waste."

"But Jon asked me to go with him to the Daystar Clinic this afternoon."

Louisa shot a disdainful glance at Jon. "A medical clinic on the East End is no place for a lady, especially a *free* clinic." Her lip curled. "Who knows what kind of diseases those people carry."

Kate stiffened. "I'm sure I'll be perfectly safe with Jon."

He gave a firm nod. "I wouldn't allow Kate to have contact with contagious patients."

Her aunt shook her head. "It's out of the question."

"I don't understand why you are making such a fuss." Kate clenched her hands. "I've done everything you asked and gone everywhere you wanted for the last month. I'm simply asking for one afternoon to do as I choose."

"I don't want to discuss it. Now go upstairs and get your things."

Kate locked gazes with her aunt, her face growing ever warmer. She hated to admit it, but she could not win this battle, and continuing the argument in front of Jon would only cause everyone more embarrassment. She turned and stalked up the stairs, but as she passed the lower landing she glanced back at Jon.

He stood by the bottom step, his stance unyielding.

When Kate reached the upper landing, she took one last look at Jon and her aunt.

He remained where she had left him, facing Louisa like a silent sentinel.

Her aunt lifted her chin. "Why are you still standing there? Do you have something to say?"

"If I were not a gentleman, I would tell you exactly what I think of your overbearing manner toward Kate, but since I am, I will keep my opinion to myself."

"Ha! A gentleman indeed." Louisa lowered her voice. "I've seen the way you look at my niece."

Kate froze, then leaned against the wall, just out of sight, and waited to hear what would be said next.

"There was nothing I could do to prevent William from becoming engaged to your sister"—Louisa's tone came harsh and cutting—"but I do not intend to stand by and let Katherine throw her life away on someone who would carry her off to India to suffer a martyr's death among the heathen!"

Jon huffed out a mocking laugh.

"You think this is a laughing matter?"

"No, it's just your perspective on missionary life is quite...unusual."

"You listen to me, young man." Louisa lowered her voice, but Kate could still hear her clearly. "You are not a suitable match for Katherine, and you will keep your distance. Do I make myself clear?"

Kate held her breath, waiting for Jon's answer.

"More than clear. But it's hard to believe you could be so presumptuous and cold hearted."

Louisa gasped.

Jon's footsteps crossed the entrance hall, the front door opened, and then it banged closed.

Kate's heart pounded as she slipped down the hall toward her room. Jonathan Foster was a brave man to stand up to her aunt like that. It made her admire him even more, and nothing her aunt said would change her opinion of him.

• • •

Lydia snipped the white thread with her sewing scissors and chose a needle from the felt packet. She only had a short time before tea, but if she hurried she might be able to repair the rip in Miss Katherine's petticoat before everyone else came to join her in the servants' hall. She spread the lacy ruffle across her lap and examined the torn section. Miss Katherine had stepped on it while dancing last night.

Miss Katherine had told her about the evening while Lydia helped her undress before bed. Miss Katherine had danced with at least a dozen different partners, twice with Mr. Jonathan Foster and four times with Mr. Edward Wellington, the future heir of some estate in Somerset.

It all sounded wonderful.

She was glad for Miss Katherine. She deserved some happiness after losing both her parents when she was so young. It wasn't always easy being her lady's maid—Miss Katherine knew what she wanted and she spoke her mind. But she'd tried to help Lydia find her sister, and though nothing had come of their search, Lydia would always be grateful for that.

The scent of bread baking drifted in from the kitchen, and Lydia's stomach grumbled. She shifted in her chair and focused on her sewing again. Thank goodness it was almost teatime.

Patrick, the second footman, walked in and sat next to her at the long wooden table. "What's that you're working on?"

"Never you mind, Patrick Sawyer."

His eyes widened and his face reddened as he glanced at the lacy garment. "Sorry, Lydia. I didn't mean anything improper."

A smile tugged at the corners of her mouth. "I know you didn't. You're just too easy to tease."

He smiled. "Say, I was wondering… I have my half day tomorrow, and I thought I might do a bit of sightseeing. Maybe go to the park for a band concert." He shifted on the bench and glanced her way. "Would you like to come with me?"

Lydia blinked and stared at him. "You and me…go off on our own?" She shook her head. "I don't think Mrs. Adams would like that."

Ann took a seat on the other side of Lydia. "You should go. This might be your last chance to get out and see the sights."

"Oh, we've plenty of time." Lydia pulled the needle through the next stitch.

Ann tipped her head. "That's not what I heard."

Lydia looked up. "What do you mean?"

"I think we may be headed back to Highland any day."

Patrick frowned. "Where'd you hear such a thing?"

Ann lowered her voice. "I just heard Lady Gatewood carrying on something awful. There's a scandal brewing, and she said it's going to ruin the family."

Patrick leaned forward. "What kind of scandal?"

"Sir William's brother, David Ramsey, was with a lady friend last night when her husband was shot."

Lydia gasped and poked her finger with the needle. "Oh my stars! Did he shoot him?"

"I don't know. I didn't hear the rest. Nelson walked into the hall, and I had to step away from the door—"

Someone cleared his throat.

Lydia's stomach dropped. Lydia, Ann, and Patrick jumped to their feet as Mr. Lawrence approached.

The butler narrowed his eyes. "Eavesdropping is not an acceptable practice for any member of this staff."

Lydia stood stone still and clenched her sewing to her chest. Gossiping about the family was not allowed, and many a servant had been dismissed for doing just that.

"Do you understand?" Mr. Lawrence's gaze raked them.

"Yes sir." Lydia looked down as Ann and Patrick echoed her reply.

"And if you happen to overhear a private conversation in the future, you are to keep it to yourself. Do I make myself clear?"

All three answered in unison: "Yes sir."

"Now I suggest you find something else to discuss or take your break in silence." Mr. Lawrence turned on his heel and strode out of the servants' hall.

Lydia sank down on the bench, her heart thumping. "Goodness gracious," she whispered.

"Sorry." Ann glanced at Lydia and Patrick. "I didn't mean to get us all in trouble."

"We'll live," Patrick said.

Lydia tried to still her trembling fingers. "Yes, but what's going to happen to Miss Katherine?"

Ann and Patrick looked at her with somber expressions, but none of them were willing to continue the conversation.

● ● ●

Kate picked up her skirt and followed her aunt up the front walk leading to the Wellington home. A movement in an upstairs window caught Kate's eye. A woman's face appeared for a split second, then the lace curtain swished back in place. Was that Edward's mother or a servant? Kate glanced at her aunt to see if she had noticed, but Louisa's determined gaze was focused on the front door.

"Now remember, don't say anything about that awful incident at the Martindales'. If they mention it, pretend you've heard nothing."

Kate lifted her chin. "You want me to lie?"

Her aunt shot a heated glance her way. "If they mention it, just let me handle it."

Kate frowned. Lying to Edward and his family was no way to build a stronger connection. What was her aunt thinking?

She mounted the steps and stood to the side as her aunt reached for the brass knocker and made their presence known.

"Just follow my lead."

Before Kate could answer, the door opened, and a tall, stern butler looked out. "May I help you?"

"Yes, I'm Lady Louisa Gatewood, and this is my niece, Miss Katherine Ramsey. We're here to see Lady Wellington."

The butler nodded and ushered them into the entrance hall. "Wait here, please."

Kate glanced around and rubbed her arms against the chill that seemed to be in the air.

The butler returned within two minutes, his expression even more solemn. "I'm sorry, Lady Wellington is not at home."

Louisa's nostrils flared. "Is Mr. Edward Wellington at home?"

The butler glanced toward the doorway at the end of the hall and back at her. "No, m'lady. Mr. Wellington is also not at home."

Louisa's expression hardened. "Very well. We'll leave our cards." She opened her bag and took out her small white calling card, and Kate did the same.

The butler took a silver tray from the side table and held it out toward them. They placed their cards on the tray, and he gave a slight nod.

"Good day." Louisa turned and strode toward the front door. The butler hurried to reach it first and pulled it open. Kate followed her aunt outside, and the door closed behind them.

"Not at home!" Louisa turned to Kate, her eyes blazing. "I don't believe a word of it. Eleanor must have heard about your cousin David. That's why she won't see us."

"She might be out shopping or paying calls herself."

"Ha! I don't think so!" Louisa descended the steps, her skirt swirling around her feet.

Kate hurried after her aunt. "If that news is already circulating, then we might as well go home." Perhaps if Jon hadn't left yet, she might still be able to go with him to Daystar Clinic.

"We are not going home. We must call on the Tremonts and thank them for hosting the ball, and then we'll stop by the Hamiltons' if we have time before tea."

Katherine sighed. "Must we?"

Her aunt turned and glared at her. "Katherine, I am trying to salvage your future. You could at least show a little gratitude and cooperate!"

Katherine clenched her jaw. "Very well. But we're going to receive the same kind of treatment wherever we go."

They exited the front garden. Their chauffeur sprang into action and opened the rear door of the motorcar. Louisa climbed in and Kate slid in after her. She looked up at the Wellingtons' lovely home, her spirits sinking. Had Edward and his family refused to see them because of the Martindale scandal? What about her conversation with Edward on the terrace last night? How could he ask her to consider a courtship one day and refuse to see her the next?

She didn't know if she was more heartbroken or angry, then decided she was a good measure of both. Yes, her cousin had been foolish and reckless.

But why should *she* suffer for it?

• • •

Jon straightened his tie and knocked on Dr. Gleason's door. He wasn't sure why he had been summoned to the office of the hospital president, but the note said to come as soon as possible.

"Come in," Dr. Gleason's deep voice called from beyond the door.

As Jon stepped inside, Dr. Gleason looked up. Piles of charts and folders covered one side of his large oak desktop. Bookshelves packed with medical texts lined the walls behind him.

"Good morning, sir."

Dr. Gleason rose from his chair, a weary expression lining his face.

"Good morning, Mr. Foster." He reached out, and the two men shook hands. "Please, have a seat."

"Thank you, sir." Jon sat in the wooden chair facing the desk.

Dr. Gleason returned to his chair. "I heard how you saved that young boy last Friday." Dr. Gleason studied him through narrowed eyes. "That was a very good call."

"Thank you, sir."

"The combination of symptoms was quite unusual. How did you make that diagnosis?"

"My father treated a young woman with similar symptoms a few years ago. The memory stayed with me since it was an unusual case."

Admiration shone in Dr. Gleason's eyes. "Well done."

Jon shifted in his seat, feeling a bit uncomfortable with the praise. All he'd done was recall his father's example and follow the training he had received.

Dr. Gleason sat back and folded his hands over his protruding stomach. "So...have you reached a decision about the position you've been offered here at St. George's?"

Jon straightened. So this was the reason for this summons. "I've been giving it a great deal of thought, sir."

"I know it would be a change in direction for you, but you could put your skills to good use here."

"I want to use my training where it's most needed."

Dr. Gleason's brow creased. "You've decided to return to India, then?"

"Actually, I'm considering another option."

"Has someone else made you an offer?"

"I've been volunteering on the East End at Daystar Clinic. Dr. Pittsford has suggested I join him there when I finish my training."

"Why would you want to practice on the East End, especially at a charity clinic?"

"People there have little access to good medical care. The caseload at Daystar is quite heavy. Dr. Pittsford needs another full-time doctor."

"Pittsford is a good man, but he's an idealist. His potential to make a difference is limited by his lack of connection and financial support. I doubt his clinic will last another year. I see no future in it, especially not for a promising young man like yourself."

Jon didn't want to insult Dr. Gleason, but he needed to make his position clear. "I'm sorry, sir, but I don't agree."

Dr. Gleason's eyebrows lowered. "Think very seriously about this, Mr. Foster. These two paths lead to two very different destinations."

"I'm aware of that, sir."

"Are you?" He tapped his finger on the desk for a moment, then focused on Jon. "If you stay on at St. George's, you'll rise to the top of your profession and have a long, successful career. You'll be able to support Dr. Pittsford's clinic and other causes like it. Perhaps one day you might even sit in this chair and have a fine home and family of your own. Do you really want to turn down a future like that?"

A vision of walking into the hospital's annual dinner with Kate on his arm rose in his mind and filled him with a powerful longing. If he accepted Dr. Gleason's offer and let the word spread about his inheritance, he would be accepted in the finest society. Then he might be able to give Kate the kind of life she wanted.

But was that the best path for him to choose?

Jon looked across the desk at Dr. Gleason, his desires pulling him two very different directions. "I need more time, sir."

Dr. Gleason rubbed his chin. "I can give you a little longer, but I must have your answer by the first of August. If you decline my offer, I'll have to ask someone else to fill that position." Dr. Gleason looked at Jon over the top of his silver-rimmed glasses. "Think long and hard, Mr. Foster. You won't receive another offer like this."

"I understand, sir."

"Good." Dr. Gleason rose, and Jon stood as well. "By the way, we're hosting a dinner at our home next Friday. My wife will be sending you an invitation."

"Thank you, sir," he replied, but an uneasy feeling rose in his chest.

"My daughter Evelyn enjoyed meeting you. She said you two had quite an enjoyable conversation."

"It was a pleasure to meet her, sir…and your other daughters as well."

Dr. Gleason's expression dimmed, and he released a sigh. "Yes, three daughters, all of marriageable age, and not one promising match for any of them—at least not yet."

Jon's stomach tensed, but he remained silent. He certainly hoped he hadn't given the doctor reason to believe he was interested in Evelyn.

Dr. Gleason studied him a moment more, then motioned toward the door. "You may go."

"Thank you, sir. Good day." He rose from his chair and strode out of the office.

He had an important decision to make and not long to make it.

• • •

"Mrs. Adams!" Lydia hurried down the backstairs.

The housekeeper stepped out of the kitchen doorway and looked up. "Yes, Lydia?"

"Lady Gatewood is not feeling well. She asked if you'd come up and see her."

"Oh dear." Mrs. Adams smoothed her hand down her navy-blue skirt, jingling the keys clipped at her waist. "What seems to be the problem?"

"She says her head is pounding and her stomach's upset. She wouldn't even let me open the drapes. I asked if she wanted tea or something else, but…" Lydia lifted her hands. There was no pleasing Lady Gatewood when she was feeling poorly.

"Very well, I best go up." Mrs. Adams turned toward the stairs, then looked back. "There was a letter for you in the morning post. I left it on the side table in the servants' hall."

Lydia's heart lifted. "Is it from my parents?"

"I'm not sure, but you can take a moment to read it, if you like."

"Thank you, ma'am." She hurried down the corridor and entered the servants' hall.

Her fingers trembled as she scanned the writing on the envelope. It was not her mother's script, but her sister's flowing style. Her heart leaped. She dashed down the hall and out the back door, then tore the envelope open.

Dear Lydia,

    I saw my old neighbor. She said you came looking for me. I was so happy I cried when she gave me the card with your address. I thought everyone in the family must hate me for running off with Charlie Gibbons.

    I'm sorry for it now, but when I learned I was going to have a baby, I was afraid Father would be so angry he might kill Charlie. I thought going away was best for us all, but I'm not sure now.

    Charlie has a hard time finding work, and when he does, he spends most of what he makes at the pub, drinking away his troubles. He has a darker side I didn't see back at home. And when he drinks too much, it comes out and torments us.

    I'm afraid of what will happen when the baby comes. I haven't seen a doctor, so I'm not sure when it will be, but I think sometime in July. I wish I had someone to help me, but we keep to ourselves. I know you're busy with your job, but I hope you'll write. I miss you and send my love,

    Helen

Lydia bit her lip and stared across the courtyard. Helen needed her, and somehow she must find a way to help.

THIRTEEN

J on laid his fork and knife across his breakfast plate and sat back in his chair. The day was overcast, and the mood at the breakfast table was much the same. Julia and Penny had carried on a bit of conversation with the children during the meal, but Kate wore a pensive expression and barely touched her food. Jon tried to draw her out by asking her a few questions, but her answers were brief, making him all the more concerned for her.

The children finished eating and were sent off in Ann's care. William sat at the head of the table, scanning the newspaper.

Julia looked up. "Is there any more news about the Martindale case?"

William's brooding expression eased as he glanced across at her. "Just a small article on page three."

"Does it mention David?"

"Not specifically. It only says the police are continuing their investigation."

Julia's tense expression eased. "I'm glad he wasn't named."

Kate flashed a heated glance at Julia. "He may not be mentioned, but the news is definitely circulating among our friends, or should I say our *former* friends."

William lowered the paper. "Aren't you're being a bit dramatic?"

Hurt filled Kate's eyes. "No one would receive us yesterday, not even the Tremonts. Everyone told their servants to say they were not at home, when we knew very well they just didn't want to speak to us."

Julia rested her hand on Kate's arm. "I'm sorry, Kate. I wish people were not so quick to judge."

"Aunt Louisa says none of us will be welcome anywhere until the case is solved and even then David's connection with Mrs. Martindale will cast a shadow over the family."

William sighed and folded the newspaper. "That may be true, but we're not turning tail and running back to the country. That would make people think we believe David is guilty and we're not standing with him."

Kate's eyes widened. "You intend to stand with him, even after what he's done?"

"He is my brother."

"But he's guilty of…infidelity."

"Yes, and that's a terrible sin that has set off a dreadful chain of events, but he is not a murderer. I'm praying that somehow this will make him see his need for repentance and a better direction in life."

"I hope it does, but in the meanwhile, what are we to do?"

William glanced at Julia and then at Kate. "There are many activities you can take part in that don't require an invitation."

"I have the day off," Jon said. "Would you like to go riding?"

"No, thank you." Kate looked down at her plate. "Not today."

Jon sat back, wishing there was some way to help. He hated to see Kate so discouraged.

"I have a suggestion." Julia looked around the table. "Catherine Bramwell-Booth is speaking this morning in Clapton."

Jon turned to Julia. "Isn't she the daughter of General Booth, the founder of the Salvation Army?"

"His granddaughter, actually. I understand she is a very gifted speaker with deep convictions about meeting the needs of the poor and how that ought to go hand in hand with preaching the gospel."

"That sounds very similar to Dr. Pittsford's philosophy," Jon added.

Julia nodded. "I thought we could all go and hear her speak."

Penny's expression brightened. "Even me?"

"Yes, even you," Julia said. "It should be an enlightening lecture. I don't think anyone would object to you attending."

"Aunt Louisa won't object," Penny said with an impish smile. "She isn't feeling well this morning. I heard her moaning and complaining to Mrs. Adams."

"I'm sorry she's unwell." Julia pushed back from the table. "Perhaps I should check on her."

Lawrence walked in carrying a silver tray. "Sir, this message was hand delivered for you by a young boy."

"Thank you." William took the envelope and letter opener from the tray. He studied the writing on the envelope with a slight frown while the butler left the room.

Julia leaned forward. "Who is it from?"

William slit open the envelope, pulled out the sheet of paper, and glanced at the bottom. "It's from David."

Everyone stilled and waited while William read the brief message.

William looked up. "The police have called him in for questioning this morning at eleven. He wants me to go with him."

Jon tensed and glanced around the table, then focused on William. Saying you supported your brother in the comfort of your own home was one thing, but accompanying him to police headquarters for questioning was something else altogether.

"Will you go?" Julia asked in a hushed tone.

William refolded the note and slipped it back in the envelope. "Yes. Of course." He scooted his chair back. "But that shouldn't affect your plans. Go to the lecture and see what Miss Bramwell-Booth has to say."

Jon watched William stride out of the room, his admiration for his soon-to-be brother-in-law growing even stronger. What a challenge to love your brother through difficult circumstances like these. He hoped if he was ever called upon to make a similar choice he would do the same for those he loved.

● ● ●

Kate checked her appearance in the large gilded mirror in the entrance hall while she and Lydia waited for the others to join them. She'd chosen a blue linen dress with a tunic style top, middy collar, and white crochet trim. Her simple straw hat had only a few flowers and a ribbon that matched her dress.

Lydia gazed at Kate's reflection in the mirror. "You look very nice, miss."

"Thank you. What do you think of the hat?" Kate's aunt usually chose her clothing for their outings, and though Kate liked choosing what to wear, she wasn't sure the hat was appropriate.

"Oh, the hat's lovely."

"I don't want to wear anything too elaborate since we're going to a lecture hall. Nothing is worse than being seated behind a woman in a large hat and not being able to see around her."

"It's a good choice, miss." Lydia's smile faded as she glanced up the stairs. "Do you think Mr. Foster will be able to take us to see Helen after the lecture?"

Lydia had told Kate about the letter she had received from her sister. Kate was elated to hear Helen had written, and she was determined to help Lydia see her as soon as possible.

"I'm sure he'll go with us if he doesn't have another commitment."

"Ever since I read her letter I've been so worried."

Kate turned to Lydia. "And you have good reason from the sound of things, but now that we have her address we can visit and hopefully convince her to go home or at least let us help her." Kate wasn't eager to navigate the East End with only Lydia as her companion, so she had invited Lydia to come along to the lecture with the hope that Jon would take them to see Helen after.

Jon descended the stairs followed by Julia and Penny. He smiled when he saw Kate waiting at the bottom of the steps.

Kate's heart fluttered, making her feel slightly off balance. Her sensible side told her she should not entertain romantic thoughts about Jon, but it was becoming harder every day to resist the strong pull she felt toward him.

She admired and respected him, and he had become her trusted friend.

He might not be able to offer her a place in society…but what about love? Could he give her that?

She looked up and met his warm gaze, and the look in his eyes seemed to say he could—that, and so much more, if she would let him.

She swallowed hard and tried to push those thoughts away, but her heart didn't want to listen.

He met her at the bottom of the stairs. "You look very nice, Kate."

"Thank you." Her voice came out hushed and strained.

He watched her carefully. "Is something the matter?"

"No. I'm fine." But her cheeks warmed, and she had the strangest feeling he could read her thoughts.

Julia checked the mirror and adjusted her hat. "Are we ready to go?"

Kate glanced around the group. "Yes, I believe so."

The footman opened the front door. Julia, Penny, and Lydia walked outside, then Jon started to follow.

Kate started after them. "Jon, may I speak to you for a moment?"

He turned. "Yes?"

"Are you free this afternoon, after the lecture?"

A slight smile lifted one corner of his mouth. "I thought I might go by the clinic, but I am available if you need me."

Kate tried to ignore the hint of teasing in his eyes, but it wasn't easy. "Lydia received a letter from her sister. She is still on the East End, and since we're going to be in Clapton, it wouldn't be too much out of our way to try and see her."

He sobered. "Do you have the address?"

"Yes, Lydia has it."

He glanced toward the car, where Julia, Lydia, and Penny waited, and then back at Kate. "All right. I can take you there after the lecture, if Julia allows it."

"Must we tell her?"

"Yes. We must. I won't go sneaking around behind my sister's back, especially not with you and Lydia in tow."

She tried to remain serious, but her smile slipped through. "Very well, if you insist."

"I do." He offered her his arm, and she tucked her hand through, happy to be by his side as they stepped outside into the pleasant spring morning.

An hour later, they found seats near the stage in Farcourt Hall. Quiet conversation filled the auditorium as they waited for the lecture to begin.

Julia leaned toward Kate. "It's quite an interesting crowd, isn't it?"

"Yes, there are certainly more people than I expected." Kate guessed at least four hundred. About two-thirds of them were women. Some were fashionably dressed, but most wore plain clothing that spoke of a simple life. Sprinkled through the crowd were men and women wearing Salvation Army uniforms, black with a touch of red and silver from the emblems on their collars.

Kate had heard about the group's evangelistic work among the poor, and twice she'd seen a Salvation Army band marching down the street as she traveled through London during the past few weeks. On their way to the lecture, Jon told her several thousand people had gathered earlier that month to hear General William Booth, the elderly founder of the Salvation Army, speak.

A few years before, he had been given an honorary doctorate from Oxford and received other awards for his work among London's poor and for training and sending out teams around the world to help those in need. His health seemed to be failing, and Jon thought it might be the last time the General would make a public appearance.

A tall, dignified man in a black suit stepped up on the platform, and the crowd quieted. "Ladies and gentleman, it is my privilege to introduce our speaker today. She has been involved in evangelistic work for several years and has accompanied her grandfather, General William Booth, on many of his travels, most recently on his motorcades throughout the Kingdom, where he preached the gospel in many villages and towns. She continues to assist her father, Mr. Bramwell Booth, and her grandfather in their ministry. She is also involved in training women officers at the Salvation Army's International Training College here in Clapton. Please welcome Miss Catherine Bramwell-Booth."

The audience responded with lively applause as Miss Bramwell-Booth walked to the podium and faced the crowd. She wore the simple black Salvation Army uniform dress with a bonnet that had a large bow tied to the side, under her chin.

She looked out across the audience with a serene expression. "It's a great joy to speak to you today and spread the wonderful news that God loves all people, those who live in great houses and wear fine clothes, and those who have nowhere to call home and barely enough clothing to keep themselves warm. Yes, my friends, He cares about them all, and not one must miss hearing this important message of God's love and salvation, for their eternal destiny depends upon it."

Miss Bramwell-Booth continued her speech, weaving in Scripture with inspiring examples of how peoples' lives had been touched through the ministry of the Salvation Army. The stories of her work among orphaned and abandoned children struck the greatest chord with Kate. A powerful longing like none she had ever felt before flowed through her.

"Some have questioned our methods. Some have even accused us of watering down the teachings of Christ and focusing too much on caring for the poor and destitute. On this point, let me quote my grandfather, General William Booth, 'My only hope for the permanent deliverance of mankind from misery, either in this world or the next, is the regeneration or remaking of the individual by the power of the Holy Ghost through Jesus Christ. But in providing relief of temporal misery, I believe I am only making it easy where it is now difficult, and possible where it is now all but impossible, for men and women to find their way to the Cross of our Lord Jesus Christ.'"

Those stirring words echoed through Kate's mind. How rewarding it must be to bring help and healing to those in such desperate need!

Then a pang pierced her heart. How had *she* spent her time and energy the last few months? Focusing on dress fittings, dancing lessons, and presentation practice. Since coming to London, her thoughts had been consumed with dinners, balls, parties…and finding the right man to marry.

But she had to do those things, didn't she? How else would she find a suitable husband? She couldn't be dependent on William for the rest of her life. Kate pushed her uncomfortable questions aside and focused on Miss Bramwell-Booth's next point.

The lecture continued for almost an hour, but the time flew by for Kate. When Miss Bramwell-Booth drew her message to a close with a moving challenge, the crowd burst into applause.

Kate jumped to her feet and joined in.

• • •

Jon glanced down the row, checking the ladies' responses to Miss Bramwell-Booth's final challenge. Penny wore a vibrant smile and clapped vigorously. Unshed tears glistened in Julia's eyes, and Lydia swiped moisture from her cheek. But Kate's response was the most surprising. She rose to her feet and clapped, her eyes sparkling with life.

Jon's chest swelled as he stood beside her. Kate sent him a radiant smile, and he felt as though he would burst. She had obviously been deeply moved by the message, and he longed to discuss it with her and hear her thoughts.

The applause died down. The crowd flowed into the aisles. Jon shepherded the ladies toward the rear doors of the auditorium and outside.

After they broke free from the crowd, Kate stopped and turned to him. "My, that was wonderful!" She clutched the program to her chest, her eyes still glowing. "I've never heard anyone speak with such strength and conviction."

"I couldn't agree more." Julia turned to Penny. "What did you think?"

"I enjoyed it. Her travels sound so exciting. Wouldn't it be thrilling to go so many places and speak to hundreds and hundreds of people?"

Julia took Penny's arm. "Sharing the gospel and seeing God at work is very rewarding." She glanced down the street to where the Ramseys' chauffeur waited beside their motorcar. "Shall we go?"

Jon glanced at Kate.

She gave a slight nod and turned to Julia. "If it's all right with you, I'd like to go with Lydia to visit her sister."

Julia hesitated. "Her sister?"

"Yes." Kate glanced at Lydia and back at Julia.

"Where does she live?"

Lydia took a letter from her purse. "This is her address, miss. It's the first time I've heard from Helen in several months. I'd like to see her if we can."

Julia glanced at the return address. "Jon, do you know where this is?" She held it out to him.

He scanned the envelope. "I've not heard of Bartlett Court, but I suppose if we asked a taxi driver, he could take us there."

Julia frowned slightly. "I'm sure our chauffeur could find the address."

Lydia's eyes widened. "Oh, no, miss. Helen's not expecting us. If we all showed up at her door, I'm not sure what she would think."

Jon stepped forward. "Why don't I escort Kate and Lydia, and you can take Penny home." If they took a taxi and had the man wait, it should be safe enough. He handed the letter back to Lydia.

"I wish you would've asked at home, Kate." Julia's brow creased as she glanced at the letter again. "I'm not sure how William would feel about you traveling around the city on your own."

"What harm could come to me with Lydia as my chaperone and Jon as my protector?"

Julia looked up and her expression eased. "I suppose it's all right to send the three of you together." She focused on Jon. "Please be cautious. I'm trusting you to bring them safely home after the visit."

"Of course. We'll return as soon as we finish."

Julia and Penny bid them good-bye and walked off toward the car.

Kate stepped closer and squeezed his arm. "Thank you, Jon. I knew you would handle that well."

Her praise sent a warm wave through him, but reality quickly broke through as he thought of their destination. He must be on his guard and make sure no harm came to Lydia or Kate.

• • •

"Shoes and Boots Repaired." Lydia stared at the peeling sign hanging over the doorway of the small, dingy shop. Peering through the grimy window, she spotted a faint light flickering inside.

"Are you sure this is the right address?" Katherine sent her a doubtful glance.

Lydia pulled out the envelope and checked once more. "The address is 413 Bartlett Court."

"Let's inquire inside." Jon pulled open the door. A bell jingled, and they walked into the dimly lit shop.

Lydia glanced around. The smell of leather and oil hung in the air, along with the scent of a fire burning in a stove in the corner.

A wizened old man with flyaway white hair sat at the workbench in the center of the shop. He looked up and squinted in their direction. "Can I help you?"

Jon stepped forward. "Good day, sir. We're looking for Helen Chambers."

The old man's forehead wrinkled. "Don't know anyone by that name."

"But I have a letter from her." Lydia held out the envelope to the old man. "She gave this as her address."

He pushed his spectacles up his nose and squinted at the writing. "That's the right address." He scratched his chin and thought for a moment. "I suppose she must be that woman staying with Charlie Gibbons."

Warmth rose in Lydia's cheeks. "Yes sir. I believe she is."

He lifted his thumb and pointed over his shoulder. "He rents a room behind the shop."

Lydia looked at the far wall, but there was only one door. It stood open and looked out on a shadowy courtyard.

The old man shook his head. "You can't get there through that door. You have to go outside, down the alley, and 'round back."

"Thank you, sir." Jon nodded to the shopkeeper and motioned toward the front door. They filed out, and Jon led them into the narrow alley at the side of the building.

The smell of the overflowing trash bins filled the air. A straggly, orange-and-white-striped cat ran out from between a pile of crates and dashed across their path. Lydia hurried to keep pace with Katherine.

Thank goodness she hadn't come on her own.

They reached the end of the alley, turned right, and walked into a stone-paved courtyard. A small woman in a faded green dress stood with her back to them, hanging a wet shirt on a sagging clothesline.

Lydia's steps stalled. "Helen?"

Her sister turned. Her eyes widened and she gasped. "Lydia!"

She rushed toward Helen and wrapped her in a tight hug, relief flowing through her.

After a few seconds, Helen stepped back. "What are you doing here?" She pushed a loose strand of hair from her cheek and tucked it into her untidy bun.

"I've come to see you, of course." Lydia smiled. "I got your letter, and I had to be sure you're all right."

Helen's chin trembled, and tears flooded her eyes. She lifted her shaking hands and covered her face.

Lydia pulled her close again. "Oh, Helen, I'm so glad we've found you."

Katherine looked on with misty eyes, while Jon waited at her side.

"I'm sorry." Helen sniffed and stepped back, wiping her face. "I'm such a mess."

"It's all right." Lydia turned to Katherine. "Helen, I want you to meet Miss Katherine Ramsey. I'm her lady's maid. And this is Mr. Foster. He's studying to be a doctor, and he was very kind to help us find our way here today."

Helen blotted her cheek with the edge of her apron. "Thank you. Please, come inside." She slipped her arm through Lydia's and slowly walked across the courtyard toward a faded, wooden door. She pushed it open, and they walked inside.

Lydia glanced around, and her heart sank. The flat was no bigger than her bedroom at Ramsey House. An iron bedstead that looked barely wide enough for two people filled one corner of the room. A straight-back chair and small wooden table sat by the lone window. Three crates stacked in one corner seemed to hold Helen's few clothes. An unlit oil lamp sat in the center of the table.

Jon watched Helen as she crossed the room. "It looks as though you're having a bit of trouble walking."

Helen ran a protective hand over her round middle. "I have some swellin' in my feet and ankles. Makes it hard to get around." She lifted her right hand, showing them her puffy fingers. "My hands too."

Lydia bit her lip. That couldn't be good. She glanced at Katherine, who shot an apprehensive glance at Jon.

Concern filled his eyes too. "Have you seen a midwife or a doctor?"

Helen shook her head. "Charlie's still lookin' for work. We don't have money for a doctor."

"Daystar Clinic is not too far away. I volunteer there a few afternoons each week. Patients only pay what they can. No one is turned away."

Helen gave her head a slight shake. "I don't think Charlie would like that."

Jon stepped closer. "May I look at your hands?"

Helen hesitated and glanced at Lydia.

She nodded and smiled, hoping to ease her sister's mind.

Helen looked at Jon again. "All right."

"Why don't you have a seat?" Jon motioned toward the chair.

Helen slowly lowered herself onto the wooden chair in front of the window. Jon took her hands and examined them both, front and back. "May I look at your ankles?"

Helen lifted her hands to her flushed cheeks.

"It's all right," Lydia said. "Let him have a look."

She lowered her hands and nodded to Jon. He knelt in front of her, and she raised her skirt a few inches.

Jon gently removed her worn slippers and examined her swollen feet and ankles, testing the skin with a gentle touch. "How long have you had this redness and swelling?"

"Two weeks, maybe three." Helen's chin trembled. "Is it serious? Will the baby be all right?"

"When is your baby due?"

"In July, I think, but I'm not sure."

He looked up at her. "Some swelling is to be expected in the third tri-mester, but it could indicate a more serious problem. Have you had any headaches or visual problems?"

Her lips parted, and her face paled. "I've had a headache off and on for a few days."

His mouth firmed, and he glanced at her hands once more. "I think it would be wise for you to be under a midwife's care or to see a doctor as soon as possible." He reached in his jacket pocket and took out a small card. "This is the address of Daystar Clinic. Dr. Alfred Pittsford is the physician in charge, but you can see any of the doctors."

Helen glanced at the card. "Charlie is out looking for work most days. He doesn't like me to go out without him."

Lydia laid her hand on Helen's shoulder. "You must take care of yourself, for your own sake and for the baby's."

Helen looked up at Lydia, tears filling her eyes again. "But I don't know what Charlie would say. Being out of work is hard on him. Most days he just goes to the pub and tries to drink away his—"

The door swung open, and a large man in a faded brown jacket and a red-plaid cap strode in. His eyes flashed, and he scowled at Jon. "What's going on here?"

Helen jumped up, her eyes wide. "Charlie! I thought you were working for Mr. Peterson today."

"I thought I told you not to let anyone in." His glare moved from Helen to Jon, then swung around to take in Kate and Lydia. "What's your sister doing here?"

"She came for a visit." Helen's voice trembled. "Isn't that nice?"

"How'd she know you were here? Did you write to her?"

Lydia stepped closer to her sister. "I've been searching for Helen for quite some time, and I'm glad to finally find her."

He huffed and stared at Lydia with a hateful glare. "So what are you going to do about it?"

"One thing is for certain," Lydia lifted her chin, "I won't let you keep her locked up here like some kind of prisoner."

Charlie's eyes blazed. "She's no prisoner!" He turned on Helen. "Is that what you told your sister—I'm keeping you under lock and key?"

Panic filled Helen's eyes. "Oh no, Charlie, I never said that."

"Then what did you tell her?"

"Nothing! I didn't tell her anything."

Jon lifted his hand. "Please, we mean no harm to you or Helen."

Charlie turned his scowled on Jon. "Who are you?"

"Jonathan Foster. I'm a medical student at St. George's Hospital. I don't want to alarm you, but I believe Helen may have complications with her pregnancy."

"What kinda complications?"

"Her headaches and the swelling in her hands and feet could indicate a serious condition that may be dangerous for her and the baby."

"There's nothin' wrong with Helen," he scoffed. "You're just tryin' to scare us."

"No sir, that's not my intention. Helen should receive medical attention as soon as possible."

"She'll be fine." Charlie's face flushed red under his scraggly beard and moustache. "I've heard enough of your lies. Go on! Get out of here!"

Jon's expression hardened to an icy glare.

Charlie took a step toward Jon. "I mean it! Get moving before I forget who you are and toss you out on your ear!" He swung around toward Lydia and Kate. "That goes for you two as well. Get out!"

Fire blazed in Katherine's eyes. "You're a foolish, stubborn man, Charlie Gibbons!"

Lydia gasped, and Helen's hand flew up to cover her mouth.

Charlie leaned toward Katherine. "No one talks to me like that, especially a rich little chit like you!" His liquor-laced breath filled the air.

Katherine grimaced and pulled back.

"That's *enough*!" Jon stepped between Katherine and Charlie, his fists clenched. He turned to Katherine. "We're leaving."

Her mouth dropped open. "You're just going to let him have his way?"

Jon took Katherine by the arm. "For now, yes."

Lydia grabbed her sister's hand and pulled her close. "Come with us," she whispered.

Helen trembled, then shook her head and pulled her hand away.

Charlie's scowl darkened as he jerked open the door.

Jon led Katherine outside. Lydia followed them, her heart in her throat. The door slammed, and Charlie's shouts followed them into the courtyard.

Katherine pulled away from Jon. "We can't just walk away and leave Helen in there with that brute."

His gaze darted from the door to Katherine, and the muscles in his jaw flickered. "I don't see any other option right now." He started across the courtyard.

Katherine strode after him. "Don't you care about Helen and the baby?"

Jon spun around. "Of *course* I care, but we can't force Helen to come with us. She has to make that decision herself. And I have to think of you and Lydia."

"But Helen needs medical care. Surely we can convince him to see—"

"Charlie Gibbons is a blind fool! He won't listen to us, and we won't help Helen by starting a brawl and endangering her and the baby!"

Katherine drew herself up. "I can't believe you would let someone like Charlie Gibbons get the best of you!"

Jon pulled back as if she'd slapped him, and anger flashed in his eyes.

Lydia reached for Katherine's arm. "Please, Miss Katherine, Mr. Foster is right. I asked Helen to come with us, but she won't leave Charlie."

"Thank you, Lydia." Jon tugged his jacket back in place. "At least someone is thinking clearly."

Katherine turned away and brushed off her sleeve, obviously trying to calm down.

Lydia glanced from Katherine to Jon. She hated to see them at odds over this.

Jon blew out a breath and stepped around in front of Katherine. "This is a complicated situation. Today we reached out and let Helen know she's not alone. And hopefully, next time, she'll be ready to get the help she needs."

"And leave that dreadful man," Katherine muttered.

Jon lifted one eyebrow. "If she did leave him, where would she go?"

"I'm sure Julia and William wouldn't turn her away."

Lydia shook her head. "She can't come to Ramsey House. Your aunt would put up a terrible fuss, and no one would be happy."

"Lydia's right. We've got to have a plan in place before I come back and try to convince her to leave."

Lydia swallowed and clasped her hands tight. "What if Charlie takes her away before that?"

"I'll speak to Dr. Pittsford tonight. I'm sure he'll have an idea for us."

Katherine's expression brightened. "That's an excellent plan. Why don't we go see him now?"

"No." Jon's voice was firm. "I'm taking you home."

"But I don't see why we—"

"Kate!" The fire burned in Jon's eyes again. "Don't ask me to bring you back here. I won't do it."

Lydia took Katherine's arm, and they followed Jon across the courtyard. As they rounded the corner into the alley, Lydia took a last look at her sister's door. *Lord, have mercy on my sister and watch over her.*

FOURTEEN

William pushed open the heavy front door of the police station and walked outside. Tilting his head from side to side, he tried to release the tension in his neck and shoulders. He had spent the last hour waiting in the hallway, pacing and praying, while three detectives questioned his brother. Only Mr. Bixby, their solicitor, had been allowed to go into the interrogation room with David. The look on his brother's face when he walked out told William it had been a grueling experience.

David and Mr. Bixby followed William outside and down the steps.

Mr. Bixby stopped and turned to David. "I'm sorry they were hard on you, but you handled it well."

David placed his hat on his head, glanced down the street, and then back at Mr. Bixby. "I told them the truth, though they don't seem inclined to believe me."

"They must have been convinced, or they wouldn't have let you leave."

William clasped his hands behind his back and turned to the solicitor. "What happens now?"

"We wait while the investigation continues."

David's brow creased. "Will Dorothea be called in for more questioning?"

"I would expect so."

A muscle in David's jaw flickered, and he looked away. "She is the one who is suffering the most, yet they treat her like a criminal."

"Everyone is a suspect until the crime is solved." Mr. Bixby ran his hand over his silver moustache. "If they question her again, will her story corroborate yours?"

"Yes, of course. We were the only ones there the night of the murder, except for the servants, but they didn't come in until after Reginald was shot."

"You'd be surprised. Two people may see the same incident, yet report it in entirely different ways."

"Well, I'll speak to her, and make sure—"

Mr. Bixby shook his head. "I wouldn't do that. In fact, my advice would be to stay clear of Mrs. Martindale until this whole matter is settled."

"I can't do that. Dorothea needs me now more than ever."

William reached for his brother's arm. "Listen to him, David. This is for your own good."

Hurt glittered in David's eyes. "You'd be happy to see Dorothea and me torn apart over this, wouldn't you?"

William tensed. "That's not what I said, nor what I meant."

"I know what you think of my relationship with her."

"I'm only trying to help you see what's best."

"Best for you, or for me?"

Two men passing by exchanged glances and hurried past.

Mr. Bixby placed his hand on William's shoulder. "Perhaps we should continue this conversation at my office or somewhere more private."

David waved him off. "There's no need. I understand what you're saying. You don't want me to see Dorothea."

"I'm sorry, but I believe that's best for you *and* Mrs. Martindale. If we can suppress the gossip about your relationship, it may help the outcome of the investigation. But if you persist in seeing her now, while everything is unsettled, then I fear the police will get wind of it and not look on you with any favor."

David's shoulders sagged. "All right. I'll go home and stay there."

Mr. Bixby sent him a serious look, but a hint of sympathy flickered in his eyes. "You may conduct your business and see your family. Carry on as usual—just be circumspect about your actions."

David nodded and glanced at William, a pained, hollow look in his eyes. "Would I be welcome at Ramsey House?"

"Of course. Come this evening."

David sighed and shook his head. "I don't think I want to go anywhere tonight."

"Then come tomorrow after you finish at the office, and plan to stay for dinner."

David lifted one eyebrow. "Do you mean that?"

"Yes. You're always welcome."

David studied him, as though trying to discern William's true intentions. "All right. I'll see you tomorrow." He shifted his gaze to their solicitor. "Thank you for your counsel. Good day." David turned and strode away.

The solicitor looked at William and kept his voice low. "I hope your brother takes our advice."

William gave a slight nod. "So do I."

"As it stands now, he has a slim chance of staying free, but if he is seen with Mrs. Martindale, I expect he will be behind bars before the week is through."

William's spirit sank as he watched David turn at the corner and disappear from sight.

Help him, Father. He's in a dark place, and he needs You.

• • •

Kate led the middle-aged woman in the shabby, gray coat into the examining room at Daystar Clinic. The woman's strained expression and sagging posture made her look worn and tired. She carried one little girl and held the hand of another who walked beside her.

Kate handed the chart to Jon. "This is Mrs. Martino and her daughters."

This was Kate's second time volunteering at the clinic, and she hoped to make it a regular commitment. Convincing her aunt would be a challenge, but Kate had not received one invitation since David's connection with the Martindale case had been reported in the newspaper.

How could her aunt object to her helping at Daystar, especially since Julia and Penny had agreed to come along?

She glanced at Jon, appreciation warming her heart. His kind and caring ways gave him a strong bond with his patients, and he seemed well liked by everyone at Daystar.

Jon greeted Mrs. Martino, looked through the chart, then smiled at the toddler seated on her mother's lap. "And who do we have here?" The little girl buried her face in her mother's shoulder.

"This is Angela." Mrs. Martino ran her hand over her daughter's wavy, brown hair. "She hasn't been able to keep any food down for the last few days, and I think she's running a fever."

Jon's serious gaze focused on the child. "How old is she?"

"She turned two last week." Mrs. Martino shifted her daughter a bit. "Come now, Angela, let the doctor see your face."

Angela slowly turned and looked at Jon. Her cheeks were flushed and damp hair matted her forehead.

Mrs. Martino's other daughter looked up at Kate with big brown eyes, and then glanced around the room. Her hair was darker than her sister's, and it fell in long curls over her shoulders. Kate guessed she might be five or six. As Jon and Mrs. Martino continued their conversation, the little girl twirled her hair around her finger and rocked back and forth on her feet. She bent down and reached in a bag at her mother's feet.

Mrs. Martino cast a stern glance at her daughter. "Leave that alone."

The little girl pulled her hand out of the bag, but soon she was fiddling with the handle on the lower cabinet and pulled it open.

"Maria, stop that! I'm tryin' to talk to the doctor."

Kate glanced at Jon and then Mrs. Martino. "Why don't I take Maria for a walk around the clinic?"

Mrs. Martino shook her head. "I don't want her to be a bother."

"She's not." Kate held her hand out to Maria, and the little girl glanced at her mother.

"It's all right. Go on."

Maria slipped her little hand into Kate's, and they headed down the hall toward the reception area.

Dr. Pittsford's wife, Martha, looked up and smiled as they approached the desk. "Hello there. What's your name?"

Maria smiled, but she didn't answer.

"This is Maria Martino. Her mother and sister are with Mr. Foster."

"That's right." Mrs. Pittsford stood up. "Would you like a sweet?"

The little girl's dark eyes lit up, and she nodded.

Mrs. Pittsford lifted a small wooden bowl from the shelf behind the desk and held it out. "Here you go."

Maria reached in and took a wrapped candy, then smiled at Mrs. Pittsford. "Thank you."

"You're welcome, dear." Mrs. Pittsford gave her a pat on the head.

Maria unwrapped the candy and popped it into her mouth. Then Kate took her hand, and they started down the hall again. The door to the supply room stood open, and Kate heard Julia and Penny working inside. They had taken on the task of organizing all the medical supplies.

Kate looked in and found Julia writing in a small notebook, while Penny stood on a stool, straightening a row of small bottles on the top shelf. Penny's auburn hair was tied back with a ribbon that matched her dark green dress, and both women wore aprons over their clothes.

Julia looked up and smiled at Kate and Maria. "It looks like you've found a new friend."

"I have." Kate introduced Maria, and Julia and Penny greeted her.

Kate glanced around the supply closet. "You seem to be making good progress."

"I think we are." Penny climbed down and brushed off her hands.

Theo looked in the doorway. "How is it coming along?"

Penny's cheeks flushed. "Come in and see for yourself."

He stepped through the doorway and looked around. "I'd say it's quite an improvement." He turned to Penny. "We certainly appreciate your help."

She sent him a smile. "We're glad to lend a hand."

Theo scanned the shelves. "I'm looking for a splint for a broken finger."

"I know just where they are." Penny pulled a small basket from a lower shelf and held it out to Theo. "Here you go." She gazed up at him, admiration shining in her eyes.

"Thank you, Penny."

"You're welcome."

Kate watched them closely. Penny was too young to have a serious suitor, but she obviously liked Theo. What did he think of her? He had danced with Penny at Kate's ball and greeted her warmly when they arrived this morning.

Dr. Pittsford stopped in the doorway. "It looks like we're having a convention in here." His eyes widened as he glanced around the small room. "My goodness. It's a miracle. I can actually see what's on the shelves."

Julia's face brightened. "We've rearranged things a bit, but we plan to add labels to help you find what you need."

"That's an excellent idea." Dr. Pittsford turned to Julia. "Do you think you could come on a regular basis and keep us organized?"

"We'll only be in town until early August, but I'll speak to William about it."

Dr. Pittsford nodded. "Very good."

Jon looked in from the hall and focused on Kate. "Mrs. Martino is ready to leave. Can you bring Maria out?"

"Yes, of course." Kate led Maria into the hallway to rejoin her mother. Mrs. Martino thanked her, then set off with her two daughters.

Dr. Pittsford joined them in the hallway. "Jon, do you have a moment?"

"Yes sir."

"I'd like to speak to you as well, Katherine. Why don't we step into my office?"

Kate's hopes rose as they followed Dr. Pittsford. It had been three days since they had visited Lydia's sister and had the upsetting encounter with Charlie Gibbons. Jon had told Dr. Pittsford about Helen that evening, and the doctor had promised to make some inquiries. But they hadn't heard anything since. Had he found a place for Helen?

Dr. Pittsford closed his office door and turned to face them. "I've spoken to several people about Helen Chambers's situation."

"Has someone stepped forward to help her?" Jon asked.

Dr. Pittsford shook his head. "I'm sorry to say they haven't. I'm very concerned about her condition as well as her living arrangements. I've given it a great deal of thought and prayer, and I've decided to invite her to stay in our home."

Kate's heart lifted. "Oh, that's very kind of you."

"Yes, it is," Jon added. "I hope it won't be too much of an inconvenience."

Dr. Pittsford had purchased a house near the clinic seven months earlier. He'd told Jon and Kate that he hoped living on the East End would earn the trust and respect of his patients, allowing him to share the gospel more easily. It was certainly a bold move on his part.

"We've had a few other young women stay with us for short periods of time, until a more permanent situation could be sorted out. My wife and daughters are agreeable; in fact, they're looking forward to meeting Helen."

It was reassuring to hear his whole family was in favor of the doctor's decision.

"Thank you," Jon said. "I'll pay Helen a visit as soon as I'm finished here today, and see if we can make the arrangements."

Dr. Pittsford's brow creased. "I don't think it's wise for you to go alone, not after what happened on your last visit."

Kate wished she could go, but she knew Jon wouldn't take her, no matter what she said.

Jon rubbed his chin. "I suppose I could ask Theo to come along."

"That's a good idea," Dr. Pittsford said. "Why don't you speak to Theo and leave at four if he is agreeable."

"Very good, sir. Thank you."

• • •

Kate lifted her hands, and Lydia slipped the pale-blue nightgown over her head. The silky softness of the material was a wonderful relief after the tight corset and stiff fabric of her dress. "Thank you, Lydia."

"Shall I unpin your hair, miss?"

"Yes, please." She sat at her dressing table and glanced in the mirror as Lydia pulled out the pins. Lydia moved at a slow pace, and there were pale gray shadows beneath her eyes. It was past ten, and Kate suspected Lydia had been up since six that morning.

Kate lifted her hand and laid it over Lydia's. "I'll finish. Why don't you go on to bed?"

Lydia's anxious gaze connected with Kate's in the mirror. "I was hoping Mr. Foster would come back and bring us some news about Helen."

Kate glanced at the clock on her bedroom mantel. "Yes, I thought he would've returned by now."

Lydia bit her lip. "I hope nothing has happened to him."

Kate's stomach tensed, but she pushed away her concern. "I'm sure he's all right. It just must have taken longer than we expected to help Helen settle in at Dr. Pittsford's."

"Yes, of course, miss." But Lydia didn't look as certain as she sounded.

Kate forced a smile. "I'm sure he'll give us a full report in the morning."

A knock sounded at the door, and Penny slipped through wearing a pink dressing gown and a bright smile. "Mind if I come in?"

Kate looked over her shoulder. "Not at all." Spending some time with Penny might be just what she needed to ease her thoughts.

Lydia stepped back. "Is there anything else you need, miss?"

"No, thank you. Good night, Lydia."

"Good night, miss." She nodded to Kate and Penny and left the room.

"I was hoping you were still awake." Penny pulled a chair up beside Kate's dressing table. "Today was lovely, wasn't it?"

"You mean helping at the clinic?"

"Yes. I thought I might be uncomfortable working there, but everyone was so kind and welcoming." Penny leaned closer, her eyes bright. "What do you think of Theo Anderson?"

"Why do you ask?" Kate laid the last hairpin on her dressing table and picked up her brush.

"Well…I was just wondering what you knew about him."

"Only that he is Jon's friend and a fellow medical student."

"Nothing about his family?"

Kate ran the brush through her hair as she studied Penny's reflection in the mirror. "You spent a good deal of time talking to him at the ball. I'm surprised you didn't ask him then."

"I should have, but he is a wonderful listener, and he kept asking me questions. I was so pleased with the conversation, I didn't even notice I hadn't learned much about him."

"Since he's Jon's friend, I'm sure he's a fine fellow, but you're too young to be thinking about romance."

"I'm almost seventeen, and Aunt Louisa said she is going to speak to William about me coming out next season."

"I wouldn't get your hopes up."

"Why not?"

"You know William is very traditional. I can't imagine him allowing you to make your debut at seventeen."

Penny rose and paced across the room. "But Aunt Louisa promised to sponsor me and pay all my expenses."

Kate shook her head. "I'm sorry, Penny. I doubt William will agree to it. His thoughts will be on his marriage to Julia and getting everything settled at Highland."

"Oh bother!" Penny flopped down on the bed. "Do you think Theo will still be interested in two years?"

Kate sat on the bed beside her. "If he is the right man and he truly cares for you, then he'll wait."

Penny rolled to her side and faced Kate, propping her chin up with her hand. "Do you think Edward will wait for you?"

Penny's question took her by surprise. "I don't know. I haven't heard anything from him since the news about David came out."

"I'm sorry, Kate. I know you must be terribly upset about it."

Kate looked away. She should be…but was she, really? When she first met Edward, she thought he might be the perfect match, the one who could give her all she hoped to gain from an advantageous marriage. When he'd spoken to her at the ball, it seemed like the answer to her prayer. But if one incident in her family could so easily cool his affection, maybe he was not the right man after all.

"Kate, what are you thinking?"

"Edward's silence is…disappointing, but I'm not heartbroken, if that's what you're asking."

Penny sat up. "But I thought you liked Edward."

"I do. He's handsome and charming and has many fine qualities, but…"

Penny tipped her head. "Has someone else caught your eye?"

Jon's face rose in her mind, but she banished the thought.

"Aha! I knew it. There *is* someone else, isn't there?" Excitement filled Penny's voice. "Who is it? Oh, please tell me, Kate. I promise I won't say a word to anyone."

"There's nothing to tell."

Penny stuck out her lower lip. "Oh Kate, how can you keep a secret from me? I've told you who I have my eye on."

"And I promise to keep your secret, but I have nothing to report." Kate stood and held her hand out to Penny. "Now it's time we both went to bed."

Penny took her hand and rose from the bed. "Oh, all right. I'll go…but I'm not giving up."

Kate held open the door. "Good night, Penny."

"Good night." Penny kissed Kate's cheek. "Sweet dreams." She sent Kate one more teasing grin before she walked out.

Kate closed her door and leaned back against it. Jon's image rose in her mind again, and this time she didn't dismiss it. Conversations they'd shared on their morning rides came flooding back. She loved hearing about his life in India and how those experiences had shaped him into the man he was today. She admired all he had accomplished, and she was inspired by all he hoped to do.

Her thoughts shifted to their times at Daystar. Working with him there and seeing the difference he made in people's lives touched her deeply. Sharing that with him made it even more meaningful.

Should she consider something more than friendship with Jon? Her aunt seemed to think he might be interested in her, but he'd never said as much to Kate.

And what about Edward? He'd seemed so sincere at the ball. But why hadn't he tried to see her or at least written? Would he really allow her family troubles to end their romance before it had even begun?

FIFTEEN

Jon glared at his face in the mirror, then turned away with a disgusted huff. His left eye was practically swollen shut, and red bruises spread across his cheek and jaw. There was no way he would be able to hide the events of last night from anyone.

He had planned to rise early and slip out before breakfast, hoping the evidence of his injuries would lessen by evening. But he'd overslept, and it took him longer than usual to wash and dress. And judging by his image in the mirror, it would take several days for the bruises to fade even a little.

He stifled a groan, closed his bedroom door, and set off down the hall. But each step was a painful reminder of the beating he had taken last night. He dreaded going downstairs. No doubt everyone would question him, and he'd have to repeat the story several times.

Kate stepped out of her bedroom as he crossed the upper landing. He tensed and looked her way. "Good morning, Kate."

"Good morn—" Her warm greeting turned into a startled gasp. "Jon, what happened?"

He lifted his hand to his jaw. "I ran into a bit of trouble last night."

"Was it Charlie Gibbons?" She hurried to join him at the top of the stairs.

"No. It wasn't Charlie."

"My goodness, it looks painful." She moved closer. "Your eye is so swollen. Can you see?"

Her scrutiny made him flush. "I'll be all right in a day or two."

"What about Helen? Were you able to take her to Dr. Pittsford's?"

He wished he had better news for her on that point, but perhaps he should tell her the whole story. "We arrived at Bartlett Court around five and knocked on Helen's door, but no one answered. So we waited by the entrance to the alley until after eight. We were both hungry by that time, so

Theo walked down to a pub to buy something to eat. He'd only been gone a minute when two men ran out of the alley and jumped me."

Kate's hand flew to her mouth. "Oh Jon, that's dreadful! Are you sure one of them wasn't Charlie?"

"Yes. The light was dim, but I saw them both clearly." He ran his hand over his bruised jaw. "One was about the same age as Charlie, but he was tall and thin. The other was older, maybe forty, but he was built like a prize-fighter. When I refused to hand over my wallet, the tall one held my arms, while the other man emptied my pockets. I put up a fight, but they knocked me out and made off with my money and the watch my father gave me before I left India."

Kate's eyes flashed. "That's dreadful!"

He clenched his jaw and looked away. "I never saw Helen." He steeled himself and glanced at Kate again, expecting to read disappointment in her expression.

But a warm light shone in her eyes. "You tried, Jon, and I'm grateful."

Kate's gentle words eased his frustration, but he was still bothered that he'd been careless and caught off guard.

"Did anyone try to help you when you were attacked?"

"No, but when I came to, a small crowd had gathered around." Jon frowned as he recalled the circle of faces looking down on him. "A man who owns a bakery across the street saw the men running away. He urged me to go to the police, but I didn't think that would do any good. Theo arrived and took me back to the clinic to clean up. Then we walked down to Dr. Pittsford's house. He insisted on examining me, and Mrs. Pittsford wouldn't let us leave until she fed us dinner."

"What did Dr. Pittsford say about your injuries?"

"He was concerned, but he says I'll heal in a few days."

"I'm glad to hear it."

He squared his shoulders. "This proves my point, Kate. The East End is no place for a young lady, especially at night. You can see why I didn't want to take you there."

She met his gaze. "Yes, and it also proves how important it is that we move Helen to a safer location as soon as possible."

"Yes, but how to do it, that's the question."

"Perhaps we should contact the police."

"I'm not sure they would help us. No law has been broken."

"I thought attacking a man and robbing him was a crime."

"It is, but I don't believe the attack was related to our efforts to help Helen."

"Well, we have to do something."

"Give me a day or two, then Theo and I will go again and search for Helen, but this time we'll stay together."

Kate stilled, watching him. Her anxiety was clear, but there seemed to be something more. Was it…tenderness? "You've already taken one beating. I wouldn't want that to happen again."

A rush of warmth flooded his chest, and though it was painful, he offered a half smile. "Thank you, Kate. Your concern is a great comfort."

Then he took her hand, lifted it to his lips, and kissed her soft and warm fingers.

Her eyes widened, and a pretty pink flush filled her cheeks.

Penny opened her bedroom door and hurried down the hall toward them. Kate slipped her hand from Jon's and turned toward her sister.

Jon glanced away, hoping to shield his injuries from Penny for a few more moments.

"Oh good. I thought I was the only one who was late this morning." Penny met them at the top of the stairs.

Jon steeled himself and turned to face Penny.

She gasped. "Oh, Jon, were you in an accident?"

"No, I was robbed last night."

"Oh my goodness! That's terrible! Where did it happen? Start at the beginning, and tell me everything."

Jon exchanged one more glance with Kate, then started down the steps with Penny, repeating the story once more.

• • •

Lydia sank onto her bed and finally let her tears flow down her cheeks. *Why Lord? How could You let this happen? We've made all the arrangements to help Helen, and now she's disappeared again.*

Miss Katherine had called Lydia into the bedroom after breakfast and told her what had happened the night before.

Ann walked through the doorway. "Oh, Lydia, what's wrong?"

"It's nothing." Lydia blotted her cheeks with a handkerchief.

Ann moved to Lydia's side. "I don't believe that. Come on, now. Tell me what's made you cry."

Lydia released a heavy sigh. "My sister is missing again."

"Oh no, really?

Lydia gave a defeated shrug. "It seems that way. Mr. Foster went to her flat last night and waited by her door for hours, but she never came back. We were hoping he could take her away from that terrible place, but while he was waiting, some men jumped him, then beat him up and stole his money."

"Oh, so that's why Mr. Foster is sporting a black eye this morning. I didn't think he was the kind to get into a tussle at a pub."

"No, he's a kind, God-fearing man."

Ann clicked her tongue. "What a shame."

"Yes, and all that for nothing. Helen's gone, and I'm afraid it's for good this time."

"But she sent you that letter. Maybe she'll write again."

Lydia shook her head. "That awful man she's with doesn't want her to write to anyone."

Ann's brow creased. "How could she get mixed up with someone like that?"

"She longed to leave the farm, and I'm afraid she listened to her heart and not her head."

"Do you think Mr. Foster will go back and search for her?"

"Miss Katherine says he will, but I'm afraid it's too late." Tears burned Lydia's eyes, and she clutched her handkerchief.

"You mustn't give up." Ann took hold of Lydia's hand and gave it a squeeze. "She knows where to find you, and there's always hope."

Lydia chin trembled. "I used to believe that, but I just don't know anymore."

The door squeaked open and Mrs. Adams looked in. Both girls sucked in a sharp breath and stood to face the housekeeper.

"I wondered where you two were." Kindness rather than a reprimand shone in her eyes. "What seems to be the problem?"

Lydia swallowed. "I was telling Ann about my sister, Helen." She shared a brief version of the story with the housekeeper.

Mrs. Adams listened patiently. "I can see why you're upset, and I'm sorry to hear it."

Lydia dabbed her nose with the handkerchief. "Thank you, ma'am."

"There's only one thing to do in a case like this."

"What's that?"

"Pray, of course. God knows the best way to help your sister. Let's ask Him to watch over her and help us to trust Him while we wait for His answer." Mrs. Adams smiled and tipped her head. "Shall I pray?"

"Yes, ma'am. I'd be ever so grateful." Lydia bowed her head and closed her eyes tight. As she listened to Mrs. Adams's prayer, her fears began to fade and courage began to build. All was not lost. She must hold on to hope and trust that the answer was on the way.

• • •

A light breeze blew up the Chelsea Embankment of the Thames and ruffled the netting on Kate's light-blue hat. She searched the faces of the crowd strolling across the grounds of the Royal Hospital. The number of people attending the Royal Horticultural Society Exhibit was much larger than Kate expected, still she didn't see anyone she knew, and no one had stopped to greet her or Aunt Louisa.

"Keep your eyes open." Her aunt tilted her parasol to gain a better view of those approaching them on the path. "The king and queen always attend the exhibition, and we don't want to miss an opportunity to see them." Two women walked toward them. Louisa nodded as they passed, but they both looked away.

Her aunt huffed and collapsed her parasol. "How rude! I've known Lillian Stevenson more than twenty years. She could at least acknowledge us."

Kate sighed. When was her aunt going to accept that most of their friends and acquaintances did not want to speak to them now that David's connection with the Martindales had been splashed across the front page of every newspaper in town?

She followed her aunt into the next large white tent, thankful to be in the shade. Floral arrangements of every size and color filled the tables spread out around the tent, and the scent of freshly cut flowers floated in the air.

Her aunt pursed her lips and inspected a large bouquet of roses, peonies, and lilacs in the center of the closest table. "I don't know why this arrangement won an award. The colors and scale are not nearly as pleasant as that one at the end." Barely stopping for a breath, her aunt continued giving her opinion about the other arrangements and the judges' decisions, interspersed with criticisms of the clothing and hairstyles of those they passed.

Kate silently scolded herself for folding to her aunt's insistence that she come along today. She would've much rather gone riding with Jon this morning and then volunteered at the clinic in the afternoon. That certainly would've been more enjoyable than walking through tents filled with floral exhibits and being ignored by everyone they passed.

Her conversations with Jon over the past few days flooded her mind, and the memory of his kiss on her hand stirred her heart. Their friendship seemed to be deepening and moving toward romance—if she would allow it.

But Jon's future was undecided. He might even return to India. If that was the route he chose, could she leave everything behind and go with him? Traveling halfway around the world sounded exciting, but she wasn't sure she was prepared for missionary life.

And what about Edward? Perhaps when the police discovered who had murdered Reginald Martindale, Edward would call on her again and want to resume their courtship. Should she hold on to that hope?

If only there was someone she could speak to in confidence. But her aunt would be furious with Kate for even entertaining the idea of encouraging Jon. She could talk to Penny, but her sister was a hopeless romantic and not mature enough to give her good advice. Perhaps she could talk to Julia without giving too many specifics. But it was difficult to hide anything from Julia. She seemed to be able to read between the lines of almost every conversation.

Oh, why did life have to be so complicated? Why couldn't the decisions about her future simply be made so she could get on with it?

Hoping to distract herself, she bent and sniffed a bouquet of peach and yellow roses, but her thoughts soon returned to Jon.

She'd been terribly upset when she'd seen his face so battered and bruised. The thought of him being outnumbered and attacked by those two robbers was dreadful. And how brave he was to promise he would return and continue the search for Helen.

How could she not want to encourage a man like that?

Louisa jerked on Kate's sleeve. "Look! The Wellingtons are here!"

Kate tensed and followed her aunt's gaze to the far side of the tent. It was difficult to see past all the people, but then the crowd thinned, and she spotted Edward speaking to his mother and sister.

"They're moving to the left." Louisa took Kate's arm. "Let's place ourselves in their path so they won't be able to avoid us."

"Oh no. Please, Aunt Louisa, I don't want to see them." She kept her voice low, hoping no one but her aunt would hear.

"Of course you do!" Louisa tugged Kate through the crowd. "This is our opportunity to clear the air and let them know we're not hiding at home simply because your cousin has made a fool of himself."

"But they never returned our call, and I haven't heard from Edward in over a week."

"Honestly, Katherine! We can't just sit back and do nothing. Sometimes you must take life by the reins and make things happen."

Kate swallowed a moan as her aunt moved them into position a few yards from the Wellingtons.

"Just act natural and pretend you're surprised to see them."

"Oh, it will be a surprise," Kate muttered, "a dreadfully uncomfortable surprise for all of us."

Louisa's eyes flashed. "That's enough! If you can't say something helpful, be silent!"

Kate glared at her aunt.

Her aunt plastered on a smile as the Wellingtons approached. "Eleanor, how lovely to see you."

Lady Wellington looked up, and her face blanched. "Louisa... Why, I didn't expect to see you today."

"I always attend the Royal Horticultural Society Exhibit." She turned to Kate. "We're enjoying all the lovely displays, aren't we, dear?"

Kate's face flamed. "Yes, of course."

"Katherine has always been extremely interested in flowers."

Kate lifted her eyes toward the roof of the tent. How could Louisa say such a thing? Kate had never been fond of gardening, and she couldn't imagine a less likable hobby.

Louisa's gaze moved from Kate to Edward. She smiled and lifted her eyebrows expectantly.

"I'm happy to hear it," he said. "I've enjoyed coming each year since I was a boy." He smiled. "It's good to see you, Kate."

Edward's warm expression eased Kate's discomfort, and she returned his smile. "It's a pleasure to see you as well." She shifted her gaze to his mother and sister. "Hello, Lady Wellington, MaryAnn."

His mother gave a slight nod. MaryAnn did the same, then she lifted her chin and looked away, making her feelings about the encounter painfully clear.

"We should be going." Lady Wellington looked toward the tent's front exit. "We need to meet Lord Wellington."

Edward turned to his mother. "Why don't you and MaryAnn go ahead? I'd like to speak to Kate." He shifted his gaze to Louisa. "If that's all right with you, Lady Gatewood."

Her aunt's eyes lit up. "Why, of course. That would be fine." She turned to Kate. "I'll be in the tea tent, dear. You and Edward take your time. No need to hurry." She smiled at Edward, then turned to Lady Wellington and MaryAnn. "So nice to see you again. I hope you enjoy the day."

Lady Wellington and MaryAnn bid them good day, but it was a very chilly farewell. They strode off toward the front exit, while Louisa walked in the opposite direction.

Edward offered Kate his arm. "I'm sorry about all that."

She slipped her hand through the crook of his elbow. "You don't need to apologize."

"But I do. It's terribly unfair of Mother and MaryAnn to treat you and your aunt poorly simply because of your cousin's...involvement with the Martindales."

Edward guided her out of the tent. "There's a spot in the shade." He motioned toward a wooden bench under a tall elm tree. "Would you like to sit down?"

"Oh yes, please. My feet are aching, and I'm dreadfully tired of walking out in this heat."

He grinned. "Kate, your honesty is always a pleasant surprise."

She sighed and sat down. "My aunt doesn't share your opinion, but I'm glad you don't mind."

"Not at all." He joined her on the bench. "I suppose this has been an upsetting time for you and the whole family."

"Yes, we're all quite concerned, for David and everyone involved. It's a terrible tragedy."

"I've kept my eye on the newspaper, watching for the latest developments, but I'm sure there must be more to the story than they're reporting."

"Yes, David has been in contact with William almost every day. He insists another man entered the house and killed Reginald Martindale, but he only saw his back as he was fleeing, so he's not able to identify him."

"How dreadful."

"William is committed to standing with David, no matter what the outcome."

"I hope he's not disappointed by that choice."

"William believes David is innocent, even though David and Dorothea have been..." Her face warmed, and she looked down, unable to finish the sentence.

Edward reached for her hand. "I understand. And I'm sorry your cousin's indiscretions have caused so much trouble for you and your family."

"It's certainly put a damper on my hopes for the season."

He wove his fingers through hers. "Well, I'm not giving up my hopes."

Kate stilled. She glanced at their hands, then looked up at him.

"I've spoken to my parents, but they're hesitant to make a decision until the case is resolved and your cousin's name is cleared."

"You've talked to them about us?"

"Of course. You've been a continual topic of conversation since the night of the ballet."

"Oh, I didn't realize..."

"Kate, I meant what I said the night of your ball. I'd like to resume our courtship, but it will take some time to convince my parents this scandal is going to blow over." He tightened his hold on her hand, his expression sincere. "Will you wait?"

Edward seemed to genuinely care for her, and he had many of the qualities she was looking for in her future husband, but she was beginning to realize there was much more she needed to consider before she could accept anyone's proposal.

Still, Edward was not proposing. He was simply asking her if she was willing to wait to resume their courtship—a courtship that seemed to be indefinitely on hold. Was she willing? What if she said yes, and then his parents never changed their mind? What would she do then?

She looked up at Edward. "I'm not sure it's wise for us to put our hopes on something that may never be possible."

"I'm sure if we're patient I can bring my parents around. I just need a little more time. Please, Kate. Don't give up on me yet."

The crowd suddenly stirred, and a wave of people stepped back from the walkway.

"The king is coming!" a young boy shouted as he ran past, then he wiggled through the crowd to claim a front-row view.

Edward stood and glanced over the heads of those gathered along the pathway. A smile broke over his face. "He's right. The king and queen are coming this way." He held out his hand to Kate. "Shall we find a spot with a better view?"

"All right." She took his hand and rose from the bench, and they made their way to the edge of the path.

King George and Queen Mary walked toward them, followed by several men in tall top hats and dignified suits and a few women in lovely dresses. Kate spotted Princess Mary among the entourage. She looked just as bored today as she had the day of Kate's presentation. Perhaps life as a princess wasn't as exciting as she'd always imagined. That thought brought a smile to her lips.

A wave of people bowed as the royal family reached Kate, and she lowered her head and dipped in a half curtsy, while Edward bowed beside her.

Several people fell in line behind the king and queen and followed them into the next tent.

Kate watched the royal family disappear in the crowd, then turned to Edward. Her stomach tensed. She was not ready to answer his question. "I should go. I don't want to keep my aunt waiting too long."

He searched her face. "I hope you'll think about what I said."

"I will." She couldn't promise him more than that. Even if she was willing, unless his parents changed their minds, there was no hope of them resuming a courtship.

"I'll walk with you to meet your aunt."

"There's no need. I know the way, and I'm sure you want to rejoin your family."

He smiled, but there was a hint of sadness in his eyes. "I'd much rather spend the afternoon with you."

"You're very kind. But we'll be going home soon." Would she see Edward again? She looked into his eyes. "Good-bye, Edward. I wish you the best." She pressed her lips together, turned away, and set off to meet her aunt.

• • •

Kate followed her aunt up the front steps, her frustration simmering. On the drive home, Louisa had insisted Kate tell her the details of the conversation with Edward. Kate reluctantly complied, but cautioned her aunt not to put too much hope in a positive outcome with Edward. Unfortunately, Louisa would not listen.

"This is such good news!" Louisa sailed through the front door and handed her parasol to the butler. "Good afternoon, Lawrence."

The butler's bushy dark eyebrows rose. "Good afternoon, m'lady." She rarely greeted him by name, and he was obviously as surprised as Kate.

"We had a wonderful time at the exhibition," her aunt continued.

"That's...very good, m'lady. Will you be joining the family for tea in the library?"

"Yes, I believe we will."

He turned and left through the doorway at the end of the hall.

Julia stepped out of the library. "You're just in time for tea. Come join us. How was the exhibition?"

"Excellent!" Louisa crossed to meet Julia. "We saw the king and queen, and Kate had a very favorable conversation with Edward Wellington."

Kate pulled off her glove. "I'm not sure I would put it that way."

"Nonsense! He is still interested in pursuing a courtship. That's exceptionally good news, and you should be grateful."

"But his parents are not in favor of it."

"Not yet, but in time, when things settle down, I'm sure he'll convince them."

Kate released a frustrated breath. Why wouldn't Louisa listen? Nothing was settled, and she did not want to give that impression to Julia or anyone else.

Mrs. Adams walked into the entrance hall. "Excuse me, Miss Foster, Mr. Lawrence said you wanted to see me?"

Julia turned to the housekeeper. "Yes, would you please tell Mrs.

Murdock there will be one more for dinner? And ask Lawrence to set an extra place at the table. Mr. David Ramsey will be joining us."

Surprise flashed in Mrs. Adams's eyes, then she lowered her gaze. "Yes ma'am." The housekeeper turned to go.

"Mrs. Adams, wait!" Louisa's voice rang out across the hall.

The housekeeper turned, her questioning glance moving from Louisa to Julia.

"You will stay here until this matter is settled." Louisa glared at Julia. "How could you invite that disgraceful man to have dinner with us?"

Julia's face blanched, but she straightened. "He is Sir William's brother, and I don't believe it is kind or respectful to speak of him in that manner."

"But his shameful actions have damaged the family's reputation and placed Katherine at a great disadvantage. How can you even consider including him at our dinner table?"

"Sir William invited him, and he has accepted."

"I certainly won't sit at the same table with a man who is involved in an affair with a married woman, especially one who may be responsible for her husband's murder!"

Julia stood very still for a moment, her gaze fixed on Louisa. "I'm sorry you feel that way." She turned to Mrs. Adams. "Lady Gatewood will be taking her dinner on a tray in her room."

Louisa gasped. *"What!"*

"Yes ma'am. I'll see to it." The housekeeper gave a quick nod and scurried out of the hall.

Louisa's face grew mottled. "This is outrageous! I have never been treated with such disrespect!" Spouting rage like steam from a boiling teakettle, she swung around and marched up the stairs.

Julia lifted her hand to her chest and closed her eyes. "My goodness."

"She's just horrid!" Kate glared toward the stairs and shook her head. "Having dinner with David might be uncomfortable, but it certainly isn't worth putting up such a fuss."

Julia moved to Kate's side. "William wants to show David we're sincere about supporting him through these troubles. We hope it will prompt him to have a change of heart."

"I understand. I'll greet him as I would any guest."

Julia's expression warmed. "Thank you, Kate. I appreciate it, and I know William will too."

• • •

Julia glanced in the mirror and adjusted her necklace to center the pearl pendant. In less than an hour David would join them for dinner. Her stomach quivered, and she ran her hand over her midsection.

She understood William's desire to encourage his brother, but it was hard to forget the way David had forced an unwanted kiss on her when he visited Highland last Christmas. He'd had too much to drink, but he knew what he was doing. She shuddered and pushed those thoughts away. She had learned her lesson. Never again would she drop her guard around David Ramsey.

A knock sounded at her door.

"Come in."

Kate looked in and hesitated in the doorway. "Are you ready to go down?"

"Almost. I just need to put on my earrings." Julia took out the pearl drop pair William had given her as an engagement gift.

Kate stepped in, folded her arms, and glanced around the room.

Julia studied Kate's reflection in the mirror as she fastened her earring. Was she feeling uneasy about David's visit, or was it something else?

"We weren't able to finish our conversation about your time at the exhibition. What did you think of it?"

Kate shifted her gaze to Julia. "It was hot and stuffy in the tents, and I'm not that fond of flowers. I would've much rather gone riding."

Julia turned. "Even though you saw the Wellingtons?"

"That was the only positive point of the day, but it was quite awkward at first. Lady Wellington and MaryAnn were clearly not happy to see us."

Julia gave a sympathetic nod. "How did Edward respond?"

"He was gracious as usual, and he apologized for his mother and sister when we were alone."

Julia raised her eyebrows.

"Not alone, alone. I just mean we took a short walk while Aunt Louisa visited the tea tent."

"I'm sure it was fine if your aunt agreed to it."

Kate lifted her gaze toward the ceiling. "You should've seen her. She was so happy she could barely contain herself."

Julia smiled, imagining Louisa's eager response.

"Edward and I found a bench where we could sit in the shade." Kate's brow creased, and she looked away.

"And how did the conversation go?"

"He's been following the Martindale case in the paper and was sympathetic, but his parents are quite upset about the whole thing. They don't want us to see each other until the case is settled."

"I'm sorry, Kate. That must have been upsetting news."

"Edward's not giving up the idea of a courtship. He thinks his parents will come around in time. He asked me to wait."

"What did you say?"

Kate hesitated. "Before I could answer, the king and queen came by, with a crowd following them. After everything settled down, Edward said he didn't need an answer right away, but he hoped I would think about it. I said I would…but I don't know what to think. I never imagined this would all be so complicated."

Kate leaned against the bedpost and looked at Julia. "How soon after you met William did you know he was the man you wanted to marry?"

Julia smile returned. "Well, it wasn't love at first sight, I can tell you that."

Kate's expression eased into a faint smile. "It wasn't?"

"No. The first day I came to Highland I saw him working on the broken-down motorcar about a quarter mile from the house. He had removed his jacket and rolled up his sleeves, and his fingers were covered with grease. We spoke briefly, and he seemed rather bold and arrogant." She smiled, her heart warming at the memory. "I thought he was the chauffeur."

Kate's eyes widened. "Really? Why haven't I heard that story before?"

She chuckled. "I suppose William is too kind to repeat it."

"So how did things change between you?"

"Over the next few weeks, I began to notice his positive traits, especially his love for Sarah and the children. I appreciated how he treated the staff and how diligent he was to manage the estate well, and my respect for him grew. The more I got to know him, the more I appreciated his character, and finally that appreciation grew into love."

Kate pondered that for a moment. "So even if a man and woman don't start out loving each other…those feelings could come later?"

Julia hesitated, weighing her words. "They could, but choosing whom you will marry should be based on more than just your feelings toward them."

Kate slowly nodded. "I know it has to be more than that."

"William and I share a bond of faith and a special friendship as well as romantic feelings. I hope weaving all those together will help us build a strong and lasting marriage." Julia wanted to say more, but a knock sounded at the door.

Penny looked in. "Oh, here you are, Kate. I've been searching for you."

"Well, you found me."

"Could you fasten this necklace?" She held out her hand, revealing the gold chain and beads.

"Of course." Kate took the necklace and placed it around her sister's neck.

Julia released a soft sigh. She was sorry Penny's arrival had ended her conversation with Kate. She had been praying for an opportunity to talk with her about Edward. He seemed like a fine young man from a good family, but she didn't know him well enough to judge his character. Did he have the qualities needed to be a good husband? Would he love and cherish Kate?

Kate's decision concerning whom she would marry could either bring her great blessing and happiness—or cause her regret for the rest of her life.

Julia committed herself to continue praying for Kate, asking that she be guided toward the right man and the best plans for her future.

SIXTEEN

J on placed his hat on the table in the entrance hall and followed the sound of conversation coming from the drawing room. He glanced at the hall clock as he passed. It was almost eight o'clock and time for dinner. He entered the drawing room, hoping William and Julia wouldn't mind if he didn't change this evening.

Julia, Kate, and Penny were seated near the center of the room, engaged in conversation, while William stood by the fireplace with his brother, David.

Jon's steps slowed and his eyebrows rose. No one had told him David would be joining them. He scanned the room. No doubt that was why Lady Gatewood was not present. Jon couldn't imagine her agreeing to have dinner with David Ramsey, not after all the terrible things she had said about him.

"Hello, Jon." Julia stood and greeted him with a smile, but the faint lines around her eyes testified to either tiredness or unease. "I'm glad you're home."

Jon kissed his sister's cheek. "Good evening, everyone. Sorry I was delayed." His gaze moved around the room until it reached Kate. She looked back at him with an unsettled expression. His chest tightened, and he wished he'd arrived earlier.

"Jon, you remember my brother, David, don't you?"

David glanced at Jon, his expression guarded.

Jon stepped forward and held out his hand. "Yes, David and I met at Sarah and Clark's wedding."

David resembled William, but was a few inches shorter, with darker hair and a trim moustache. He slowly reached out and shook Jon's hand. "That's right. It's good to see you again."

Jon nodded. "Thank you."

Lawrence entered and approached Julia. "Dinner is served, miss."

"Thank you, Lawrence." She stood and glanced at William. "Shall we all go in?"

Kate rose from her seat. Jon moved to her side and waited as the rest of the family walked out of the room, then offered her his arm. "Is everything all right?" He kept his voice low so only Kate would hear.

She gave him a furtive look and slipped her hand through at his elbow. "I suppose."

"I didn't realize David was joining us."

"It was only decided this afternoon. William and Julia want to show their support. I understand, but it's been more difficult than I expected."

"I'm sorry." He could see why William and Julia might want to encourage David, but inviting him to dinner didn't seem like the best way to do it.

They strolled into the entrance hall, and the front bell rang.

"Are you expecting anyone else?" Jon asked.

Kate looked toward the door. "I don't believe so."

Patrick, the footman, crossed the hall and opened the door. Two men in dark suits and bowler hats waited under the gas porch light.

"I am Detective Hammond, and this is Detective Peters. We understand Mr. David Ramsey is having dinner here this evening."

Jon straightened. What was happening now?

"One moment please, sir." Patrick turned toward Kate, his eyebrows slightly raised.

Kate's hand trembled on Jon's arm. "It's all right, Patrick. They may come in."

The footman stood back, and the detectives entered.

William stepped out of the dining room and surveyed the scene. "Gentlemen, what can I do for you?"

"Are you Mr. David Ramsey?"

William's eyes flickered, and his expression grew guarded. "No sir. I am not."

They repeated their names and their intention to see David.

Kate shot Jon an anxious glance, but before he could reassure her,

David stepped into the entrance hall. His searching gaze quickly took in the detectives.

Detective Hammond stepped forward. "Are you Mr. David Ramsey?"

David's face paled. He glanced at William, then back at the detectives. "Yes, I am."

The detective's expression hardened. "Mr. Ramsey, you are under arrest for the murder of Reginald Martindale."

Kate gasped and gripped Jon's arm.

Panic flashed in David's dark eyes. "But I don't understand. I went to police headquarters and explained what happened. Mrs. Martindale confirmed my story."

Detective Peters took metal handcuffs from his jacket pocket. "Things will go much easier for you, Mr. Ramsey, if you come along peaceably."

David shook his head and stepped back. "But I didn't shoot Reginald Martindale. Someone else killed him. I *swear* it."

William stepped up next to David.

"Mr. Ramsey?" Detective Peters approached with the handcuffs.

David's posture sagged, and he held out his hands.

The detective snapped on the cuffs, then took David by the arm. "Come along with us." He hustled David toward the front door.

William followed them. "I'll contact Mr. Bixby. You are not alone in this, David. I promise I'll do whatever I can."

But David hung his head and didn't answer.

Jon watched them in stunned silence. What a dreadful turn of events! If David was found guilty of Martindale's murder, he could hang. That would be a terrible price to pay for his illicit relationship with Dorothea Martindale...

Especially if he really was innocent.

• • •

Kate stared at the headline on the front page of the morning paper: "Arrest Made in Martindale Murder!" She folded the paper and looked across at Jon. "I've read the article twice, and I still can't believe they would arrest David."

"I'm sure there is more to the investigation than what we read in the paper."

"Yes, I suppose that's true."

She and Jon were the only ones still at the breakfast table. Julia, Penny, and the children had moved to the music room for their practice session. William had gone with Mr. Bixby to see David, then the two of them planned to meet with a private investigator who had been hired to search out the truth behind Reginald Martindale's murder.

Kate looked across at Jon. "Do you think William's efforts will help?"

"It's hard to say, but I doubt he'll rest until he's exhausted every option to free his brother."

Kate glanced down at her breakfast plate. The eggs had congealed, and the toast looked cold and unappealing. It didn't matter. Her appetite had vanished. She pushed the plate away and looked up at Jon again. "What are your plans for the day?"

"I'm going to pay my grandmother a visit this morning, then I'm going to Daystar after that."

Kate sighed. "That sounds lovely."

"Why don't you come with me? I'm sure my grandmother would enjoy meeting you."

"I'd like to, but it seems wrong for me to slip away and enjoy the day when Julia and William are so burdened about David."

"I don't think they'd mind." He glanced toward the newspaper lying next to her plate. "And it might be helpful to put all your concerns aside for a few hours."

Perhaps Jon was right. How was she helping anyone by sitting in the drawing room and worrying about the future? She might as well do something positive with her day. She looked up and met his gaze. "All right. I'll ask them and see what they say."

"Good." Jon placed his napkin next to his plate and scooted back from the table.

Before he could rise, Louisa marched into the dining room carrying

Kate's white hat, parasol, and gloves. "Come along, Kate. It's time we were going."

Kate frowned. "I didn't know we had any plans."

"Today is the Henley Regatta. We're meeting the Clarksons at ten."

Kate stared at her aunt. "How can you even *consider* going to the regatta?" She held up the newspaper. "*Look* at this headline."

Louisa scanned the words, and her expression hardened. "That's exactly why we must go."

"Aunt Louisa, please, it will only cause us more embarrassment."

"Nonsense! It will prove we have nothing to do with that…despicable man!" Louisa's mouth twisted into a sour line.

"*That man* and I share the same last name, and his brother is my guardian. He was arrested at our home. Everyone knows we're connected."

"I've made a commitment to the Clarksons, and I do not intend to disappoint them. Put on your hat and gloves. We must leave soon, or we'll be late."

Kate steeled herself. "I've made other plans."

"What *other plans*?"

"I'm going with Jon to visit his grandmother."

Louisa's eyes widened. "His grandmother?" She shook her head. "No, not today. We are going to the regatta." She waved the gloves toward Kate. "Come along. We've no time to waste."

A burning sensation rose in Kate's throat. She glanced at Jon. His jaw was set in a firm line, his eyes silently urging her to speak up. Her aunt continued to glare and hold out the gloves. She would disappoint one of them today. That much was certain. Which one had her best interest in mind?

The answer was obvious.

Kate rose from her chair and leveled her gaze at her aunt. "I'm sorry, but I am not going with you today."

Louisa's eyes bulged. "What!"

"I am tired of pretending nothing is wrong. My cousin has been arrested for murder, and that scandal is too fresh for me to be parading around at a public event."

Jon's tense expression eased, and he gave a nod of support, infusing her with courage.

Louisa huffed. "I've taken part in the season for more than thirty-five years. I know how to navigate troubled waters, but you must listen to me and do as I say!"

"I may not have been out in society long, but I know enough not to make myself the focus of needless gossip." Kate tossed her napkin on the table. "I'm not going."

Louisa clenched her hand. "Why you impudent, ungrateful girl!"

Jon rose from his chair. "Now see here. I won't allow you to speak to Kate like that."

Louisa turned her fiery glare on Jon. "Who are *you* to allow or disallow anything? You are an outsider. You have *nothing* to say about any of this."

"I am Kate's friend, and I believe that gives me a right to speak up for her."

"You are no friend. You're just a common pretender who has wormed his way into the good graces of a respected family, thinking you will take a step up in society—"

William strode into the dining room with Julia close on his heels. "What in the world is going on?"

Louisa pointed to Jon. "That young man has been rude and insulting."

Kate gasped. "That is not true. Jon was only trying to stop you from bullying me."

"Bullying you? Is that what you call it…after all I've done for you?"

"Yes, that's exactly what you're doing, and I'm tired of it."

"This is his fault." Louisa pointed at Jon again. "He has turned Katherine against me."

Kate glared at Louisa. "No, he hasn't. And I won't let you blame him."

William held up his hand. "Please, ladies, calm down, and one at a time, tell me what this is about."

Louisa narrowed her eyes at William. "There's no need to speak to me like a child in a schoolyard quarrel."

"I am not speaking to you like a child." William's tone grew more intense. "I am simply trying to understand what has happened so I can bring some order to this household."

"Very well." Louisa clasped her hands. "I promised my sister on her deathbed that I would make sure Katherine married well and that her future was secure, and I have made every effort to do that."

"Every effort?" Kate questioned. "You've dragged me from one event to the next and embarrassed me by—"

Aunt Louisa's hand rose to her throat. "Do you see what I mean? This is the way I am treated by your ward and her *friend.*"

William lifted his hand. "All right. I believe we all need some time to cool our emotions and consider our words before we continue this conversation."

"Well!" Louisa lifted her chin. "I know when my presence and opinion are not appreciated." She spun away and marched out of the dining room with a swish of her brown silk skirt.

Silence reigned for a few seconds as they all stared after her.

William turned to Kate. "Now, will you please tell us what started all this?"

"I simply refused to go with her to the Henley Regatta."

William's brow creased. "That's why she was so upset?"

"Yes. You know Aunt Louisa can't tolerate anyone disagreeing with her decisions."

Julia sighed. "It's no secret she tries to control everyone with her harsh words and scorching temper."

William closed his eyes and rubbed the bridge of his nose. "I've had about as much of her as I can tolerate. I'm prepared to send her back to Berkshire."

Julia rested her hand on William's arm. "Let's give her some time to settle down. We're all under a great deal of strain right now."

"All right." William shifted his gaze to Jon. "I apologize for Lady Gatewood's remarks. I'm sure they were uncalled for."

Jon nodded.

Kate clasped her hands behind her back and turned to William. "I'm sorry for my part in it. I know I need to learn how to speak my mind without losing my temper."

William's eyes widened for a moment, then he and Julia exchanged a smile. Clearly her apology had surprised—and pleased—them.

Kate glanced toward the stairs. "Perhaps it would be best if I stayed out of Aunt Louisa's way for a few hours."

William looked at Kate. "Did you have something in mind?"

"Jon invited me to go with him to visit his grandmother, and then he's going on to Daystar Clinic."

William lifted his eyebrows. "Julia, what do you think?"

"I'm sure our grandmother would enjoy a visit, if that's agreeable with you."

"As long as the chauffeur drives them." William sent Jon a serious look. "You'll make sure Kate is home in time for dinner?"

"Of course."

"Very well, then. You may go."

"Thank you!" Kate turned to Jon. "I'll go up and get my things."

"I'll call for the car and meet you in the hall in a few minutes." Jon's eyes shone as he turned and walked out of the dining room.

Kate started to do the same, but William called her back.

"Be wise and sensible, Kate."

She couldn't help it. She grinned. "Of course. Always." Then she hurried up the stairs.

• • •

Kate took Jon's hand as she stepped out of the motorcar. She lifted her gaze to the large brick house, and her eyes widened. "This is your grandmother's home?"

"Yes." He smiled as he scanned the house. "It's quite nice, isn't it?"

"Yes, it's lovely." The chauffeur closed the car door, and Jon and Kate started up the front walk.

"I'm looking forward to meeting your grandmother."

Jon opened the front gate and allowed Kate to pass through. "She can be a bit outspoken, but I suppose at her age she has earned the right."

"Julia said you only met her a few months ago."

"Yes, there was a rift between my parents and grandparents for many years."

"What caused the rift, if you don't mind me asking?"

"Julia didn't tell you?"

"She said your grandparents didn't approve of your parents' marriage, but there must be more to the story."

He nodded. "My father was from a middle-class family, and he'd just started his medical practice here in London when he and my mother met at a Keswick Convention and fell in love. Her parents wanted her to marry a wealthy, young aristocrat, the son of one of their close friends. Of course neither of my parents liked that idea.

"They waited more than a year, hoping my grandfather would change his mind, but he didn't, so they went ahead with their plans. My grandfather refused to attend the wedding, and he forbade my grandmother to go. When Julia and I were born, my grandmother pleaded with him to reunite the family, but he wouldn't allow it. In the end, he cut my parents off completely."

"My goodness, he sounds quite hardhearted."

"Well, he certainly wasn't one to change his mind once he made a decision." Jon looked as though he wanted to say more about that, then decided against it.

"And all those years your parents had no contact with them?"

"My mother and her sister, Beatrice, exchanged letters, and those were passed on to my grandmother without my grandfather's knowledge. When he died last December, my aunt arranged for us to see my grandmother. It was a touching reunion, especially for my mother."

They mounted the front steps, and Jon rang the bell.

Kate glanced over and studied his profile. Despite the fading bruises, he was a handsome man. But it was more than his appearance that impressed her. Jon was a gentleman, and he always treated her with kindness and respect. He wanted what was best for everyone he met. It didn't matter if the person was a wealthy member of society or a poor urchin on the street—he gave each one the same respect and thoughtful attention.

How could she not be attracted to such a wonderful man?

The door opened, and an elderly butler greeted them with a slight bow.

"Good morning, Higgins. We've come to see my grandmother."

"Yes sir. She is expecting you." He motioned them inside and led them to the drawing room.

Kate glanced around as she kept pace with Jon. The hall was filled with beautiful furnishings. Potted palms, heavy drapes, and a rich color scheme gave it an atmosphere reminiscent of the early Victorian era. They followed the butler to the drawing room.

"Your guests have arrived, m'lady." The butler stood back as Jon and Kate entered.

Jon's grandmother rested on a chaise near the fireplace. Several pillows supported her back, and a soft gold blanket lay over her feet and legs. A ruffled lace cap covered most of her hair, except for a few white curls in front.

Jon crossed toward her. "Good morning, Grandmother. How are you today?"

She looked up at them through watery gray eyes and held out her hand. "Jonathan, it's so nice to see you."

He bent forward and kissed her fingers. "Thank you, Grandmother."

She glanced at Kate. "And who is this lovely young lady?"

"This is Miss Katherine Ramsey. She is the cousin of Sir William Ramsey, Baronet of Highland Hall. He is her guardian, and Julia was her governess until recently." He turned to Kate. "This is my grandmother, Lady Henrietta Shelburne."

His grandmother squinted at Kate. "Ah yes, Julia told me about you."

Kate smiled. "It's very nice to meet you, Lady Shelburne."

She looked Kate over more closely. "You have a pleasing appearance. I like the color of your hair."

Kate hesitated. "Thank you."

Lady Shelburne looked back at Jon. "It's been too long since your last visit."

"Yes. I'm sorry about that. My summer schedule is much lighter. I hope to visit more often."

She adjusted her glasses and studied his face. "Are those bruises around your eyes?"

Jon's face took on a ruddy tint. "Yes ma'am, I'm afraid they are."

"What happened?"

A muscle in Jon's jaw flickered before he answered. "Two men jumped me the other night and stole my wallet and watch. I tried to fight them off, but the odds were not in my favor."

Lady Shelburne raised her hand to her chest. "Heavens! You should've just given them what they wanted rather than risk a beating."

Jon gave a humorless chuckled and rubbed his jaw. "Yes, I suppose so."

"What is the world coming to when a respectable young man can't walk down the street without being attacked and robbed. I'm glad I don't go out often. It doesn't sound safe or sensible to leave the house."

Jon and Kate exchanged brief smiles.

His grandmother shifted her gaze to Kate. "My daughter Beatrice tells me this is your first season. When were you presented?"

"At the first drawing room on April 26."

Jon's grandmother's gaze drifted toward the windows. "I remember my presentation in '59. Months before, we traveled to Paris to buy my wardrobe. There were eighty-two debutantes that year, and each young lady had to be personally approved by Queen Victoria. She only accepted those who were from the oldest and best families. When the day finally came, I wore a lovely white silk gown designed by the House of Worth. Everyone said I was the toast of the season."

Jon grinned. "I'm sure you were."

"I met your grandfather that May. He proposed in July, and we were married in December." Her faint smile faded, and she turned back to Kate. "But that was ages ago, and we were talking about you. What do you think of the London season so far? Has it met all your expectations?"

Images of all the dinners, balls, and parties she had attended rose in her mind, but they were quickly eclipsed by the memory of David's arrest in their front hall just a few days earlier. "It's certainly a change from country life in Berkshire."

"Yes, I imagine so. Have you met anyone special?"

Heat flushed Kate's cheeks. "Well...I've met a great number of people."

Lady Shelburne looked back and forth between them. "Perhaps you've already met that special someone, and you just don't want to tell us."

Kate looked away. How should she answer that?

Jon shifted in his chair. "Grandmother, please. That's not a fair question."

"I'm just trying to find out if Katherine is interested in a particular young man."

Jon's brow creased, and he shook his head.

"I'm sorry. I don't mean to embarrass you, Katherine." She turned to Jon. "How are your studies coming along at the hospital?"

Jon's posture relaxed. "Very well. I have only one more term at St. George's."

"And then?"

He paused. "Then I must choose where I will practice."

"And have you made your decision?"

Jon glanced at Kate and then at his grandmother. "It seems I have three options."

His grandmother cocked her head. "And they are...?"

Kate stilled, her attention fixed on Jon. He had mentioned two choices to her, but that was several weeks ago.

"I could apply to the London Missionary Society and return to India to continue my father's work at Kanakapura. Or I could accept a position Dr. Gleason has offered me at St. George's."

His grandmother's expression became more intent. "Yes, Beatrice told me about that."

Jon's eyebrows rose. "She did? I didn't realize anyone else knew about it."

"Your aunt Beatrice has connections all over town. I believe she and Mrs. Gleason are involved in the Ladies' Aid Society at her church. But go on, what is the third option?"

"I've been volunteering at Daystar Clinic on the East End with Dr. Alfred Pittsford for the past few weeks. There's a great need for medical care in the area. Dr. Pittsford has asked me to come on staff with him, but I haven't given him an answer yet."

Hope stirred within Kate. Working with Doctor Pittsford at Daystar wouldn't be as prestigious as taking the position at St. George's, but oh, what a difference he could make. Either way, if he did stay in London, the end of the season might not need to be the end of their friendship.

His grandmother watched him closely. "Tell me more about this Daystar Clinic."

Jon's expression grew more animated as he described the patients he'd met and the way they had been helped by visiting the clinic.

Kate remembered meeting some of the people he mentioned, and she smiled listening to their stories again. When she'd first come to the East End, she'd been shocked by the poverty and depressing conditions, but after she began volunteering at the clinic, her focus shifted to the individual people she met…and that made all the difference.

Lady Shelburne nodded. "It seems the third option is the one that has truly captured your interest."

"I believe it is the one I'd like to pursue."

"Well, you know I'd much rather have you stay in London than travel halfway around the world to India. You've sacrificed enough of your life to missionary service. You're needed here, now. I hope you'll keep that in mind as you make your decision."

"I don't consider our time in India a sacrifice. It was a wonderful experience that enriched our lives."

His grandmother lifted her hand and extended a shaky finger. "It was a sacrifice for me to miss your childhood and have you so far away."

Jon sent his grandmother an understanding look, but from the story he had told Kate, it didn't sound like he would have seen much of his grandmother even if his family had remained in England.

"My work at Daystar has helped me learn more about the conditions on the East End. Providing medical care is a good beginning, but there's much more that needs to be done."

"What are you thinking?" his grandmother asked.

"My greatest concern is for the children. Some don't have adequate food and clothing or opportunities for schooling and religious training."

"What about their families?"

"Many of their parents are too poor—and sadly, some children have no family at all. They live on the street or in abandoned buildings, wherever they can find a place out of the weather."

"My goodness, what a dreadful thought."

Kate remembered the three children they'd seen on the street the first time they'd searched for Helen. They'd helped them find their way to Daystar, but what had happened to them after that?

"Yes, just a few miles from your door, there are many who are suffering and in great need."

His grandmother released a sigh. "Of course, you read about the poor and the troubles in the East End, but I hadn't really thought about the children."

Jon leaned forward and clasped his hands. "Dr. Pittsford and I have been discussing opening a children's center. We want to provide a safe haven where children could come and receive a warm meal and clothing. We hope to recruit volunteers who could offer Bible classes and collect books for a library. We could offer vocational training for the older children to help them develop skills that could take them out of poverty and provide hope for their future."

A smile broke across Kate's face. "What a wonderful idea! So many children could be helped at a center like that."

His grandmother chuckled. "You both sound quite enthusiastic about it."

Jon sent Kate a warm smile, then looked at his grandmother again. "I think we could provide practical help to many children who feel abandoned and hopeless."

"Are you prepared to follow through with your plans?"

Jon straightened. "There is a vacant building just a few doors down from Dr. Pittsford's home. It's only a short distance from the clinic. It would be the ideal location."

"Have you started raising funds for the project?"

Jon's eyes widened. "Not yet."

"How much would it take to open this children's center?"

"I'm not sure, but I can discuss it with Dr. Pittsford."

"Please do, and report back to me. This sounds like the kind of project I want to support, especially if my grandson is going to be involved with it."

"Thank you, Grandmother. We would be very pleased to have your support."

"Helping children in need is a worthy goal, and if you were committed to it, then I'd be more than willing to become a sponsor."

Jon's eyes shone as he glanced at Kate. With his grandmother's support, the project might be a real possibility.

Excitement bubbled up in her heart. Coming to the aid of poor, homeless children and giving them hope for the future—what could be more rewarding? Perhaps she might be able to volunteer at the center as well. She could organize the library, read aloud to the children, or do any number of things to help Jon.

But a sudden thought struck Kate. Her dream of receiving a proposal this season had faded to a distant possibility. In a few weeks she would pack her trunks, say good-bye to Jon, and go home to Highland.

His dream of opening the children's center would come to pass, but she would not be here to see it or play any part in his life… And that thought pierced her heart.

SEVENTEEN

William slowly climbed the main stairs and walked down the hall toward the nursery. Late afternoon sunlight streamed through the upper hallway windows, brightening his path, but it did little to lift his spirit. Perhaps some time with Julia and the children would lighten the weight that was pressing down on him.

He'd spent a good part of the day with his solicitor, Mr. Bixby, coordinating his efforts to help his brother. First they'd met with David for almost two hours, then they conferred with Mr. Jeffers, the private investigator who was conducting his own inquiry into the Martindale murder. There had been little new information exchanged, and that had been frustrating for everyone.

Julia's voice drifted out of the nursery, and his steps slowed. It sounded as though she was reading aloud to the children. He stopped in the doorway and leaned against the doorjamb, taking in the scene.

Millie sat in her small rocking chair, her doll on her lap and her pensive gaze fixed on Julia. Andrew lay on the rug, his hands propping up his chin. For once, his son seemed as still as a statue. Penny sat beside the children in the overstuffed chair, her embroidery project abandoned in her lap as she gazed toward the window and listened to the story. Julia sat in the center with the book open in her lap and her back to William.

"'Peter Pan got by the window, which had no bars,'" Julia read. "'Standing on the ledge he could see trees far away, which were doubtless the Kensington Gardens, and the moment he saw them he entirely forgot that he was a little boy in a nightgown, and away he flew, right over the houses to the Gardens. It was wonderful that he could fly without wings…and, perhaps we could all fly if we were as dead-confident-sure of our capacity to do it as was bold Peter Pan that evening.'"

William waited, hesitant to break the spell the story had cast over them all, but Julia looked over her shoulder, as though she sensed his presence.

He held up his hand. "Don't stop on my account."

She smiled and glanced down at the book. "It's all right. We're near the end of the chapter, and we should go down for tea soon."

Andrew groaned. "Must we stop? We've finally come to the part where Peter is flying."

"Yes, I want to hear more of the story," Millie said.

"We'll read another chapter before bed," Julia closed the book and turned to Penny. "Will you stay with the children for a few minutes?"

"Of course." Penny picked up her sewing, while Andrew rolled over and then sprang up to his feet.

Julia rose and joined William in the hall. "How was your time with David?" She studied his face, and her brow creased. "You look tired."

"I am rather weary. Seeing David in such a depressing place was difficult, and not knowing what the future holds makes it more so."

"How did Mr. Bixby handle things?"

"He questioned David again about several aspects of the case and explained the process and what's to be expected."

"How is David taking it?"

"His spirits are quite low. He had hoped to hear from Dorothea, but she hasn't written, and I doubt she'll visit. I certainly wouldn't recommend it. The place is ghastly."

Julia nodded, concern reflected in her eyes.

"David is anxious about keeping things going at Ramsey Imports."

"Does he have someone there who can step in for him?"

William shook his head. "He had a disagreement with Charles Claxton a few weeks ago, and he let him go. He hasn't replaced him, and now there's no one who really knows all that needs to be done there…except me."

"You?"

He took her hand. "I offered to run things until David returns."

"Oh, William, that's quite a heavy commitment."

"Yes, but a necessary one. David could lose everything if someone doesn't take it on."

Julia looked up at him. "I hope he appreciates all you're doing for him."

"He does. When I offered to help at the office, he was so relieved he broke down. Then he thanked me quite sincerely. You could see how much it meant to him."

"I'm glad to hear it."

"It will mean several hours a day away from you and the children, but it will give me a chance to show I sincerely want to help him."

"You are a kind and forgiving brother."

"I'm trying."

She squeezed his hand. "And you're succeeding."

"I hope it will heal the wounds from the past and close the distance between us."

Julia nodded. "And the meeting with the investigator...how did that go?"

"It went well. Mr. Jeffers is very thorough and eager to get to the bottom of things."

"That's good. It seems our prayers are having an impact."

William nodded, and the weight he'd felt earlier eased a bit. Julia was right. They did not carry this burden alone. How blessed he was that he could share his concerns and know Julia would listen and respond with wisdom and compassion. How had he managed so long without her?

He took her hand again. "And how was your day, my dear?"

Her expression brightened. "I had the best news."

"What was that?"

"My father's health has improved enough for my parents to come to town for the annual meeting of the London Missionary Society. They asked if they might stay with us."

"Of course. They're always welcome in our home. When are they coming?"

"They arrive midday on Wednesday and will stay through Sunday."

"This week?"

"Yes. I know it's short notice. I hope you don't mind."

"Not at all. I look forward to seeing them."

Julia looked up at him. "I can't wait to tell Jon. He'll be so pleased, and now we can all attend the society's meetings together."

William smiled. It was wonderful to see her so happy. "You think I should attend as well?"

She tipped her head, and her expression held a hint of teasing. "Of course. I'm expecting you to come."

"Is that right?" He couldn't hold back a small chuckle.

"Yes, I may not be a full-time missionary any more, but I'm still very interested in the work of the London Missionary Society, and I hope you will be too."

How could he resist when her smile was so persuasive? "If it's important to you, my dear, then I'll plan to come."

"Thank you, William." Before they started down the stairs, she leaned over and gave him a quick kiss on the cheek. "I can't wait to introduce you to all our friends. And I'm sure Father will be invited to give a report about our work in India. It should be quite inspiring."

"I'm sure it will be." He paused when he reached the entry hall. "I'll attend as many meetings as I can, but I'll have to carry on with my duties at Ramsey Imports."

"Of course. I understand. I'll be happy to have you with us whenever you can come."

The sweetness of her smile drew him closer, and he leaned down and gave her a tender kiss.

• • •

Raindrops splattered on the side window of the motorcar, blurring Kate's view of the street, but adding to the cozy atmosphere of the ride home with Jon. They had finished their work at Daystar twenty minutes earlier and hurried to meet the chauffeur, who came to pick them up at six.

The traffic slowed to a stop, and raindrops drummed on the roof of the car. They usually took the omnibus home, but with this rain, it was a blessing Julia had sent the chauffeur to meet them.

Jon leaned forward. "What seems to be the holdup, Hardy?"

The chauffeur looked over his shoulder. "I'm not sure, sir. It could be the weather or an accident."

Jon glanced at his watch, then sat back and looked across at Kate. "I'm sorry for the delay."

How thoughtful he was. "It's all right. It's not your fault."

"But I promised Julia and William that I'd have you home in time for dinner."

"I'm sure they'll understand, and I don't mind…not at all." It had been a lovely day, in spite of the rain and the full schedule at Daystar.

His gaze warmed. "Thank you for helping at the clinic. I appreciate all the time you've given these last few weeks."

"I enjoy it…very much." She wanted to say spending that time with him and sharing in his work was what made it truly meaningful, but she didn't quite have the courage.

He reached for her hand. "Having you there with me is very special."

A sense of wonder flowed through Kate. She tightened her fingers around his, hoping her response would say what she could not…how much she admired him and how much she wanted to see all his dreams for the children's center come true. But the car lurched ahead, their hands slipped apart, and the moment was lost.

Even so, hope and new possibilities stirred in her heart.

• • •

Julia read through the list of preparations for her parents' visit. With such short notice, she was especially thankful for the help of her staff.

Mrs. Adams walked into the drawing room. "You sent for me, miss?"

"Yes, please sit down." Julia motioned toward the chair across from her. Mrs. Adams took a seat. "My parents are coming to town tomorrow, and I'd like to discuss the arrangements for their visit."

"Yes, miss." The housekeeper took a small notebook and pencil from her pocket.

"Their train comes in at twelve-thirty, and they should arrive at the house about one."

"Would you like to wait and serve luncheon after that?" Mrs. Adams asked.

"Yes. We'll give them a few minutes to settle in, then we should be ready to gather in the dining room by one-thirty. They'll be staying with us through luncheon on Sunday, and then take the three-thirty train back to Berkshire."

Mrs. Adams looked down and made a note of it. "Did you want to send the car to the station to pick them up tomorrow?"

"Yes, please ask Mr. Lawrence to make those arrangements. Jon and I will go and meet them."

"Very good, miss."

"I'd like my parents to stay in the Devonshire guest room. Would you air it out and make sure it's ready? And roses are my mother's favorite flowers. Please cut a nice bouquet for her."

"Yes, miss. I'll see to their room and the flowers."

"We'll be attending the London Missionary Society meetings while they're here, so I expect we'll have luncheon out on Thursday, Friday, and Saturday. And we'll attend the closing dinner on Saturday evening. But we'll have luncheon here on Sunday after church."

"Will Miss Penelope and Miss Katherine be attending the meetings with you?"

"Yes, the girls are coming, and Jon as well." She hesitated a moment, wondering if she ought to confirm that with him. He hadn't been as enthusiastic about his parents' arrival as she had expected, but then, he had been a bit distracted lately. Was it because of the robbery and his concern about finding Lydia's missing sister, or was it something else?

"And the children, miss?"

Julia looked back at Mrs. Adams. "They'll be here under Ann's care while we attend the meetings."

"Very good, miss. I'll let Mrs. Murdock know they'll be eating in the nursery for those meals."

"Yes, thank you." Julia glanced at her list, then sat back. "That's everything…unless you can think of anything else?'

"Did you want to speak to Mrs. Murdock about the menus?"

"I don't want to make any changes at this late date. My parents will be happy with whatever we have planned."

Mrs. Adams's expression warmed. "I'm sure it will be a lovely visit."

Julia smiled. "Thank you, Mrs. Adams. I'm very grateful for the efficient way you've run the house and taken care of us these past two months."

"I'm glad to know you're pleased, miss."

"I'm very pleased, and I'll be sorry to say good-bye when we return to Highland."

"That's kind of you, miss. I've enjoyed my time here at Ramsey House."

They had hired Mrs. Dalton, Clark's mother, to fill the position of housekeeper at Highland Hall. Julia hoped that would not be a difficult adjustment for them all, especially with the wedding scheduled for early September, just one month after they returned to Highland. "I'll be happy to write a good reference for you when the time comes."

"I'd be grateful, miss. Is there anything else I can do for you?"

Julia thought for a moment. "Yes, there is one thing. Come with me." They walked out to the far end of the entrance hall. "It's about this painting." She touched the gilded frame around one of the Ramsey family portraits. "It looks as though the canvas is coming loose from the frame."

Mrs. Adams gently moved the frame away from the wall and looked behind. "Yes, I see what you mean. I'll speak to Mr. Lawrence about it. I'm sure we can find someone to make the repair."

"Thank you. I'd appreciate it." Julia looked up at the painting of William's family, remembering the longstanding rivalry between him and David. But the brothers stood side by side in this painting, William's arm draped around David's shoulder. His sister, Sarah, stood on the other side of William, with their parents and the elder brother Nathaniel behind them.

The front door opened. Jon stepped forward and held the door for Kate with a playful flourish. "After you, m'lady."

"Thank you, kind sir." Kate looked up at him with a teasing smile as she passed through. Neither of them seemed to realize anyone else was in the entrance hall.

Kate waited for Jon at the bottom of the stairs, while he closed the front door and then joined her. "I should go up and change."

Julia tensed. Kate sounded a bit breathless.

Jon cocked his head and took a step closer. "If you must."

Her cheeks flushed. "Yes, I must." She started up the stairs, then stopped when she reached the lower landing. "I'll see you at dinner."

The look of affection in Kate's eyes left no doubt in Julia's mind.

It was time she had a talk with Jon.

• • •

Jon watched Kate climb the stairs while happy memories of the day replayed through his mind. What a pleasure to spend so many hours together, working side by side, sharing the same goals, and enjoying the same rewards for their service—

"Jon, may I have a word with you?"

Jon blinked and turned. Julia stood at the far end of the hall, a questioning look in her eyes. Mrs. Adams stood next to her.

He had been so caught up with thoughts of Kate that he hadn't even noticed them when he'd entered the house. "Yes, of course."

Mrs. Adams gave a brief nod to Julia, then left the hall through the doorway to the servants' stairs.

Julia motioned toward the open doorway. "Shall we go in the library?"

"As you wish." Jon straightened his jacket and followed his sister, feeling a bit like a young man who had been called into the headmaster's office. He cast off that thought. There was no need for him to feel apprehensive about a conversation with his sister.

She did not suggest they sit, but turned and faced him. "Have you spoken to Kate about your feelings for her?"

A shock wave jolted him. "What?"

"I know it's difficult to speak about such things, but I feel we must."

Jon looked away, searching for an answer. He didn't like to keep secrets from his sister, and now that she had asked him directly there was no way around an honest reply. "I'm very fond of Kate."

"Does she know how you feel?"

"We haven't spoken openly about it, but she has given me reason to hope."

Julia hesitated. "I'm sorry, Jon, but I'm not sure this is wise."

Heat rushed into his face. "Why do you say that? Because I'm not in line to inherit a title and an estate?" He shook his head. "I didn't think you were so tied to the conventions of society."

Hurt flashed in her eyes. "You know I'm not. What concerns me is that she may not be the best partner for you." She lifted her hand and glanced around the room. "Can you really see Kate leaving all this behind to travel with you to India?"

Jon straightened and steeled himself. "I won't be going back to India."

Julia pulled back. "What?"

"Dr. Pittsford has asked me to join him at Daystar as soon as I've finish my training. I've made my decision. I'm staying in London."

"Oh Jon, are you sure?"

He gave a somber nod. "I've prayed about it for quite some time, and I believe this is where God is leading me. I intend to tell Mother and Father when they arrive tomorrow."

"Are you doing this for Kate, because if you are—"

"No. I'm quite certain this is the next step the Lord wants me to take. And to be honest, working at Daystar and living on the East End makes it less likely Kate will accept a proposal from me."

A shadow seemed to pass over Julia's face, and she looked down. "Even if she were to agree to it, I have another concern."

"What is it?"

"I'm not sure Kate would be a good match for you spiritually. I see a flicker of interest in matters of faith, but no clear evidence she has made a true commitment to Christ."

"But you saw her response to Catherine Bramwell-Booth's speech."

"Yes, but enthusiasm for good work is not the same as genuine faith."

Jon wanted to argue that point, but he couldn't. Julia was right. There were many generous and caring people who sought to meet the needs of others, yet had no true saving faith.

"Have you talked to her about your commitment to Christ and your plans for the future?"

"We spoke of it one night a few weeks ago, but she simply referenced her baptism and church attendance...nothing more." Jon paced toward the window, his spirit sinking lower. Why hadn't he discussed spiritual matters with Kate more often? Not only to discover what she truly thought, but also to help her see the value of a close, vital relationship with Christ?

What kind of friend was he? A self-serving one, at best. His heart ached with the realization. He had to do more. No matter what the future held for him and Kate, he had a responsibility to encourage her spiritually and see that she understood God's love and free gift of salvation.

"You know Scripture says we must not be 'unequally yoked.' It's not a suggestion, but a command given for our benefit and the continuance of the faith among our children."

He clenched his jaw. "Of course. I know the verse well."

"I can't encourage you to move ahead unless you're certain Kate has given her heart to Christ."

"I understand."

She moved to his side and took his hand. "Please don't lose hope. Since the first day I came to Highland, I've prayed for Kate and Penny. I'm sure He's working in their lives and drawing them closer to Himself. We must continue to pray and wait on Him for an answer."

"Of course I'll pray, but waiting will be much more difficult."

"Receiving His answer will be worth the wait."

Would Kate open her heart to the Lord? Would her desire to help others be matched by genuine faith in Christ? Would she grow to love Christ as He loved her? Jon swallowed against the tightness in his throat and gripped his sister's fingers. "Pray for me as well, that I'll find the right words and not waste another opportunity."

Julia tightened her hold on his hand. "I will. Just do your part, and trust the Spirit to do His."

Wise words, he knew. If only he could heed them.

EIGHTEEN

Kate carried the tray bearing three steaming cups of tea and a plate of biscuits into the small back room at Daystar Clinic. "Here we are." She set the tray on the table by the window.

Young Rose Hartman sent her a bashful smile and eagerly eyed the plate of biscuits. Her little sister, Susan, reached out, but Rose stopped her. "Wait till she gives you one."

Rose pulled her hand back and looked up at Kate, her blue eyes wide.

"It's all right." Kate sent her a gentle smile. "Go ahead and help yourself." Kate sat in the third chair at the small table and added a good amount of milk to each of the girl's teacups while they nibbled on their treats.

Rose, Susan, and their brother, Jack, had been waiting by the clinic door that morning when Kate and Jon arrived. As soon as she saw the siblings, she remembered meeting them on the street the first day they'd come to the East End looking for Lydia's sister, Helen.

They had sent the children to the clinic that day, and Dr. Pittsford had treated the younger sister, Susan. This morning Jack was the one in need of the doctor's attention. He'd cut his hand on a broken bottle, and a few stitches would be required.

Dr. Pittsford suggested Kate take the girls out of the room and keep them occupied until the worst was over. So she had settled them in the back room and hoped to cheer them by offering some tea. Kate gave a half-filled cup to Rose.

The older girl carefully passed it to her little sister. "It's hot. Blow on it, Susan."

The younger girl blew across the top of the teacup, then took a small sip. She smiled at Kate. "It's good."

Kate returned a smile, then handed the second cup to Rose.

"I'm glad you came to the clinic today." Kate glanced at the girls. Rose's sweater had a rip near the shoulder, and her green dress was stained and spotted, but her face and hands were clean. Little Susan looked much healthier than she had at their first meeting, but her hair and clothes were in a sorry state. Kate's heart ached for them. If only she could do more than give them tea and biscuits.

The children's center Jon and Dr. Pittsford hoped to open would be a great help to them and so many others. How wonderful it would be to offer Rose and her siblings food, clothing, and the practical help they so desperately needed.

Kate's thoughts shifted to Jon, and a prayer for his safety rose from her mind. After he had escorted her to Daystar that morning, he and Theo had set off together, hoping to find Helen and convince her to come to the clinic. They had agreed it would be best for Dr. and Mrs. Pittsford to speak to her and hopefully convince her to move into their home.

"Can I have another?" Rose pointed to the plate of biscuits.

"Yes, please do." Kate took a sip of tea, savoring the warm, creamy mixture. "Did you have a long walk to get here today?"

The older girl shook her head. "Not too far."

Kate pondered that for a moment. Perhaps if she knew more about the children she could find some practical way to help them. "Tell me about your family."

Rose's hand stilled, and she lowered her cup to the table. "Mum got sick after Christmas. They took her to the hospital." She looked toward the window. "Our neighbor, Mrs. Green, told us she's gone to live in heaven."

"I'm so sorry," Kate whispered. She knew how painful it was to lose a parent, but she had servants to care for her and relatives to help her through those difficult days. These little ones seemed to have only each other. "And your father?"

Rose hesitated. "He delivers ice."

Something about the girl's reply raised questions in Kate's mind.

A wistful look filled Rose's eyes. "He used to live with us, but he went off to work one morning and he never came back."

Kate stifled a gasp.

"We waited for him more than a week, but Mr. Sawyer, the man who lives downstairs, he made us leave."

Had their father been injured or killed, or had he abandoned the children? Kate swallowed hard. "Where do you live now?"

Rose bit her lip, then looked across at Kate. "We been staying in a building not too far from here."

"Someone has taken you in?"

Rose shook her head. "Jack an' me, we watch over Susan."

Kate tried to hide her surprise, but she wasn't successful. "Just the three of you…alone in that building?"

Rose nodded.

"But how do you find enough to eat?"

"Jack makes deliveries for Mr. Tate. He gives us some food. And sometimes people give Jack a shilling or two when he makes a delivery."

This was not right. The Hartman children were too young to be on their own. How could they fend for themselves? The memory of Jon's attack flashed through her mind, and she swallowed hard. She must find a safe place for the children to live, and someone to watch out for them.

She set her teacup aside. Mrs. Pittsford would know what to do. She and Dr. Pittsford were well acquainted with the charities and ministries in the area. Surely one of them provided homes for orphaned and abandoned children.

Kate rose from her chair. "Enjoy your tea, girls. I'll be back in a few minutes."

Rose nodded, and little Susan took another biscuit from the plate.

Kate strode down the hall toward the front office, where she quickly shared the children's story with Mrs. Pittsford. The kindhearted woman listened with a concerned expression.

"We can't let them go back to that run-down building. It's not safe," Kate insisted.

"No, I'm sure it isn't." Mrs. Pittsford tapped her fingers on the desk for a few seconds, then looked up at Kate. "I'll speak to Dr. Pittsford as soon as he finishes with this patient. I know of a children's home not too far from here, but he may have another idea."

Kate reached for Mrs. Pittsford hand. "Thank you."

"I'll come back and speak to the children." She hesitated and looked Kate in the eyes. "It will be up to them, you know. They must be willing to go."

"I understand." As she turned to leave Mrs. Pittsford, the front door opened. From the corner of her eye she saw a short woman wearing a brown shawl walk into the reception area.

"Morning, ma'am." The woman's soft voice carried a slight tremor. "I'd like to see a doctor."

Recognition flashed through Kate, and she turned. "Helen?"

Helen looked up and blinked. "Miss Ramsey?"

"Yes!" Kate hurried to greet her. "Oh, my goodness, I'm so glad you're here." She turned to Mrs. Pittsford. "This is Helen Chambers, Lydia's sister, the one we've been searching for."

Mrs. Pittsford's smile spread wider as she rose from her chair behind the desk. "My, this *is* a day of unexpected miracles." She stepped forward and held out her hand. "Miss Chambers, we're so glad you've come."

Helen looked back and forth between them, then reached out and took Mrs. Pittsford's hand—but apprehension shadowed her soft brown eyes. "I don't want to be a bother, but Mr. Foster said I should come if the swelling and headaches didn't go away."

"Yes, of course." Mrs. Pittsford put her arm around Helen's shoulders. "Come with me. You can sit down and rest, and I'll have the doctor come and speak to you right away."

The tense lines around Helen's eyes eased. "Thank you, ma'am." With slow, swaying steps, she started down the hall with Mrs. Pittsford.

Kate's joy bubbled up from deep within as she followed them. Lydia would be so relieved. Jon and Theo would be delighted as well. She couldn't wait to see their faces when they returned from their search and she told them about Helen's arrival.

• • •

Jon walked into the drawing room to join the family who had gathered there before dinner. He glanced at Kate, and they exchanged a private smile.

What an amazing day it had been. Helen's safe arrival at Daystar and her willingness to stay with the Pittsfords had lifted a great burden from his shoulders. Her symptoms still raised concern, but Dr. Pittsford believed bed rest, healthy meals, and good care would see her through the last few weeks until her baby was born. She was safe with the Pittsfords now, and that was what mattered most.

Dr. and Mrs. Pittsford had also arranged for the Hartman children to stay with a family from their church until a more permanent situation could be found for them. Listening to Kate recount their sad tale made him even more determined to move ahead with plans to open the children's center, no matter what obstacles might stand in the way.

His parents had arrived that afternoon, but he hadn't had an opportunity to speak to them about his decision to stay in London and work at Daystar. He glanced across at them, and tried to push away his concern. Everything would be fine. They would understand. They might even be pleased he was staying in the country and would live only a train ride away.

"Come on, everyone." Julia rose and crossed to the piano. "Andrew has learned a new song, and he'd like to play it for us before dinner.

Andrew slowly followed her. "Do I have to play?"

"No, but I'm sure everyone would enjoy it."

"We would love to hear your song, Andrew." Jon's mother joined them.

"Yes, what a fine idea," Jon's father added as he rose from his chair.

Andrew sat on the piano bench and swung his feet back and forth. "Shouldn't we wait for Papa?"

Julia glanced toward the entrance hall, then back at Andrew. "You can play it again for him when he comes. I'm sure he'll be home soon."

"All right." Andrew opened his sheet music and placed his hands on the keys.

Everyone had circled around the piano except Lady Gatewood. She remained seated, tapping her fingers on the arm of her chair and glancing at the clock.

Andrew launched into the song with enthusiasm, but he soon hit a wrong note. Jon winced, and his appreciation for his sister's patience grew by a mile. Then his gaze drifted toward Kate.

She looked lovely this evening. Her white lace blouse was a fine contrast to her dark-blue skirt. The only jewelry she wore was a small cameo pinned at her neck, but with the light of the chandelier sparkling in her eyes and her face glowing with life, she didn't need any other jewels.

When he'd first come to Ramsey House, he had been impressed by her beauty but disappointed that her only goals seemed to be making an impression on society and receiving a marriage proposal before the end of the season.

But since David's misdeeds came to light and her social calendar cleared, Kate's interests had shifted. Her work at Daystar and her efforts to help Lydia's sister seemed to have awakened her to the needs of those around her. He hoped they had also softened her heart to the Lord...and to him.

Andrew hit another wrong note, and it drew Jon's attention back to the piano. The boy tried to find his place, but he made a series of mistakes.

Millie giggled and covered her mouth.

Andrew banged out the next chord, then scowled at Millie. "You don't even know how to play, so you've no cause to laugh at me!"

Millie's smile melted away, and her chin quivered.

"That's not kind, Andrew." Julia shifted her gaze to Millie. "Your brother has worked hard to learn this song. I'm sure you want to encourage him."

"Sorry, Andrew. Please play some more."

His scowl eased. He turned back and pounded on the keys again.

"Gently, Andrew." Julia laid her hand on his shoulder. "Gently."

Andrew lightened up as he finished the song. They all applauded, and he hopped up and bowed. Twice.

"Good work, Andrew." Jon clapped the boy on the shoulder.

The clock struck eight, and Lady Gatewood glared toward the empty doorway. "How long are we going to wait for William?"

Julia looked from Lady Gatewood to her parents. "I'm sorry. He must have been delayed at the office, but I'm sure he'll—"

William strode through the doorway. "I have wonderful news!"

Julia hurried to meet him. "What is it?"

"A man has confessed to Reginald Martindale's murder!"

Kate's mouth dropped open. Penny squealed and grabbed Kate in a tight hug.

Lady Gatewood lifted her hand to her chest. "Thank heaven!"

"Come and tell us everything," Julia said.

He took Julia's arm and walked to the center of the room. Everyone gathered around. "Our private investigator, Mr. Jeffers, discovered Reginald was behind an investment scheme that defrauded some of the wealthiest and most influential men in London."

Lady Gatewood gasped. "Good heavens. How dreadful."

"A man named Ernest Leifstrom, the owner of a ship-building company, had given Reginald huge sums of money to invest. Leifstrom introduced him to other businessmen, who were taken in on the scheme as well. But later Leifstrom's suspicions were roused, and he decided to go to the Martindales' home and search for evidence of wrongdoing. That was the night Reginald returned unexpectedly from Spain and found David and Dorothea together."

Penny lifted her hand. "Wait, you mean Mr. Leifstrom was in the study when Reginald ran in looking for his gun?"

"Yes. Apparently Leifstrom tried to run out, but he and Reginald wrestled their way into the entrance hall. Reginald tried to shoot Leifstrom, but Leifstrom turned the gun away, and it went off. He says he didn't mean to kill Reginald. He was only trying to defend himself."

Jon's mind spun as he took in the story. "Has Leifstrom been arrested?"

"Yes, Mr. Jeffers took the information about the investment scheme to the police this morning. They brought Leifstrom in for questioning, and he confessed."

"Has David been released?" Julia asked.

"Not yet, but Mr. Bixby has appealed to the judge, and he hopes David will be free very soon."

Lady Gatewood clasped her hands. "This is such a relief! As soon as this new spreads, Katherine will be welcomed back into society and invitations will begin arriving again."

Kate stared at her aunt. "But...do you really think the tide can turn that quickly?"

"Of course! Your cousin has been wrongfully accused of murder, and that will rouse everyone's sympathy."

Kate shook her head, still looking stunned by the news. "But his involvement with Dorothea is common knowledge now."

Lady Gatewood waved Kate's comment away as though it were an irritating fly. "Reginald Martindale's schemes and this other man's confession will overshadow all of that. And I will speak to a few people who will circulate our version of the story. I'm sure that will be all we need."

Penny took Kate's hand. "Isn't it wonderful?"

Kate hesitated. "Yes, I'm happy...for David."

"And when Edward and his parents hear the news, I think you'll be seeing much more of him." Lady Gatewood practically sang the words.

Jon watched Kate, his spirit deflating. Would she resume attending a stream of parties, balls, and dinners with Edward Wellington at her side? If she did, what hope was there for him to win her heart?

• • •

Kate's bedroom door opened, and the sound roused her from a disturbing dream. She had been chasing the Hartman children down a dark alley, but she could not reach them. She blinked a few times, pushed the hazy images away, and rolled over.

Lydia slipped in. "Good morning, miss." She crossed to open the drapes.

Kate started to reply, but her throat felt dry and painful. "Morning, Lydia." Her voice came out raspy.

"Are you all right, miss?"

Kate tried to swallow. "My throat feels dreadful."

Lydia crossed to the bed and scanned Kate's face. "You look flushed."

"I do feel rather hot, and my head is pounding." She sat up, but that only made her headache worse. "I won't be going down, at least not right now."

"Shall I bring up a breakfast tray, miss?"

Kate lay back on her pillows, then draped her arm over her eyes to block the light from the windows. The thought of facing eggs and sausages made her queasy stomach contract. "No, I don't think I can I eat anything."

"Perhaps some warm tea with honey and lemon might help your throat."

"Yes, thank you." Kate rubbed her temple. "Would you ask Miss Foster to come up?" She'd much rather ask Julia for advice than Louisa. Her aunt had no sympathy for anyone who was ill.

"Right away, miss." Lydia hurried out the door.

Kate sighed and closed her eyes. What a disappointment. She had been so looking forward to going with Jon and his family to the meetings of the London Missionary Society. Even if she could stir up the energy, she was most likely contagious, and it would be inconsiderate to expose everyone to this illness.

She would have to rely on Penny to give her a secondhand report about the meetings. Unfortunately, her sister was not known for paying attention to details.

A knock sounded at the door, and Julia looked in. "Lydia said you're not feeling well."

"Yes, please come in." Kate could do little more than whisper.

Julia crossed to the bed, and Kate explained her symptoms. Julia laid her cool, soft hand on Kate's forehead. "I'm afraid you have a fever." She frowned and studied Kate's face. "Perhaps I should ask my father to come up and see you."

"Oh no, I don't want to bother him."

"I'm sure he wouldn't mind."

"But I wouldn't want him to catch something from me, not when he's just regaining his strength after being ill for so long."

"Yes, that's true." Julia thought for a moment. "I'll ask Jon then."

Kate closed her eyes and suppressed a moan. "But I look dreadful, and I feel worse."

"Don't fret. Lydia can help you put on a dressing gown and brush your hair. Then I'll come up with him."

"But don't you have to leave for the meetings soon?"

"We're not going anywhere until I'm sure you're well taken care of." Julia tipped her head. "I'm sure Jon will insist on seeing you when he learns you're ill."

Kate's face warmed. "All right."

Julia straightened Kate's blanket. "May I pray for you before I go?"

"Yes, thank you." A few months ago that request might have made her uncomfortable. But the more time she spent with Jon and Julia, the more natural it felt to pray and take her concerns to the Lord.

Julia took Kate's hand and bowed her head. "Father, I lift up Kate to You. I ask You to comfort and strengthen her and bring her back to good health. While she rests and waits on You for healing, please speak to her and draw her even closer to You. In the name of Christ our Lord, amen." She leaned down and kissed Kate's forehead.

Hot tears rushed to Kate's eyes, but she quickly blinked them away. So few people in her life had expressed such genuine kindness and care that it was difficult to know what to say.

Julia patted her hand. "Rest easy, my dear. I'll send Lydia up."

"Thank you," Kate whispered, and this time it wasn't only her sore throat that made her words hushed and strained.

• • •

Jon clenched his jaw and hustled upstairs, guilt snapping at his heels each step of the way. Kate was most likely sick today because she had been exposed to some illness at the clinic earlier this week.

Why hadn't he been more careful and thought past his own desire to have her by his side? He should have made her safety a priority and kept her away from patients who might be contagious.

He knocked on her door, determined to do what he could for her now. "It's Jon. May I come in?"

Lydia opened the door and ushered him inside. Kate lay on her bed, her face flushed and her eyes glassy.

He clenched his jaw, surprised by his response. He dealt with patients every day, some who were gravely ill, and he had learned to hold his emotions in check, but seeing someone he cared about sick and in pain was a different experience altogether.

"Morning, Jon." Her voice came out as a hoarse whisper.

"I'm so sorry you're ill." He crossed to her bedside and asked about her symptoms.

She quietly listed them in as few words as possible. Her sore throat seemed to be what bothered her the most, though her fever and flushed appearance were a greater concern to him.

He nodded as he did a visual assessment. "May I take your pulse?"

She slipped her hand from beneath the blankets, and he gently took hold of her wrist. He counted the beats and checked his watch. It was a bit fast, but not too abnormal. "I'd like to take your temperature." He took out the thermometer Mrs. Adams had given him and shook it down.

She opened her mouth, and what a pretty mouth it was. He slid the thermometer under her tongue and shifted his gaze away, scolding himself for that unprofessional thought. But this was Kate, and it was impossible for him to remain detached.

Lydia stepped up next to him. "Is there anything I can do to help?"

"In a few minutes we'll know a bit more." He looked up. "I was very glad to see your sister at the clinic yesterday."

"Yes sir. It's a great relief."

He glanced at his watch, checking the time.

"Thank you for helping Helen," Lydia said softly.

He glanced at Lydia again. "In the end, she didn't really need my help."

"Oh no, sir. If you hadn't taken us to the East End, we might never have found Helen. And you were the one who explained her condition and told her about the clinic. I'm very grateful."

"Well, I'm glad she's safe and settled at the Pittsfords."

"Yes sir. I hope to see her on Saturday." Lydia glanced at Kate. "That is, if Miss Katherine is well and doesn't need me."

Kate reached up and took hold of the thermometer. "I'm sure I'll be fine."

Jon sent her a serious look. "You must be still for us to get an accurate reading."

She pressed her lips closed and scowled at him, but he could see the touch of humor in her eyes.

She was so adorable he could not hold back a smile. "It will only take another minute. Be patient."

She lifted her eyes to the ceiling, looking frustrated that she must wait in silence.

Lydia turned to him. "Could I ask one more thing, Mr. Foster?"

"Of course."

"Do you think Helen's baby will be all right?"

Helen was not out of the woods yet, but he wanted to ease Lydia's mind. "Her ankle swelling and headaches are a concern, but Dr. Pittsford is giving her the best care possible. I think she and the baby are going to be all right."

Lydia's tense expression eased into a faint smile. "That's good."

He nodded. "Yes, it is." Then he checked his watch and removed the thermometer.

Kate studied his face. "What does it say?"

"One hundred and one point two." He frowned, pondering the diagnosis. This was probably more than a cold, but she didn't display any extreme symptoms, though he wished he had a stethoscope so he could listen to her lungs. Perhaps he should skip one of the meetings and go by the clinic to borrow one.

He shifted his gaze back to Kate. "You must stay in bed and rest, and drink plenty of liquids." He turned to Lydia. "We want to keep her fever under control, so she must dress lightly and use only a sheet and light blan-ket." He folded back Kate's heavy comforter. "Put this away for now."

Julia strode in. "I'm sorry. Millie is having a difficult morning, and she needed me." She looked back and forth between Kate and Jon. "How is she?"

Jon relayed his findings and suggestions for her care.

"Thank you, Jon. That sounds like a sensible plan." Julia turned to Lydia. "Will you stay with Miss Katherine today?" The maid nodded. "You may call for Mrs. Adams if there's a need. And I'll ask her to check in with you a few times as well."

"Yes, miss. I'll make sure she has everything she needs."

Julia glanced at Jon. "I should go back and spend a little more time with Millie before I go down to breakfast." She laid her hand on Kate's shoulder. "Take care, my dear. We'll see you this evening."

Kate whispered her thanks, and Julia left the room.

Jon turned to Lydia. "Could you bring up another pitcher of water and a washcloth?"

Lydia bobbed her head and hurried out the door.

Jon pulled up a chair and sat down next to Kate's bed. "I'm sorry you won't be going with us today."

"Not as sorry as I am." Kate sighed and looked up at the ceiling. "But I'm glad you have this time with your parents."

"Yes." Jon's smile faded. "Although it may be a bit awkward."

Kate looked his way. "Why do you say that?"

"I've made my decision. I'm going to stay in London and join Dr. Pitts-ford at Daystar, and I'm not sure how my parents are going to take that news."

"Will you tell them today?"

"Yes. I hope they won't be too disappointed."

The slightest smile formed on her lips. "Well, I think it's wonderful, and I'm quite proud of you."

He straightened. "You are?"

"Yes. It's very brave to choose your own path rather than the one that everyone expects you to take."

"I don't know how brave it is. Some people have told me it's quite foolish."

Kate's eyes widened. "Who would say such a thing?"

"Dr. Gleason, for one. He said I was a fool to even consider teaming up with Dr. Pittsford."

"Well, don't listen to him. He's just upset you won't be joining him at St. George's." The most important thing is to follow your heart."

Jon frowned slightly. Was that what he was doing, making a decision based on desires and emotions? No, it was more than that, and he wanted to help Kate understand. "I believe the Lord is calling me to the East End, specifically to Daystar and the children's center. So I wouldn't say I'm following my heart."

Kate tipped her head, looking uncertain of his meaning.

"Your heart can sometimes lead you in the wrong direction if you're not careful."

"But doesn't the Bible say something about God giving us the desires of our hearts?"

"Yes, it does. But if we want to know God's will and make decisions that please the Lord, then we must do more than follow our hearts. We also need to seek godly counsel, spend time in prayer, and wait on Him for peace and confirmation."

She studied his face, questions shimmering in her eyes. "I wish I could be so sure of His leading for my future."

Jon stilled. This was his opportunity to speak to her, to tell her he loved her and wanted to share the future with her...but another voice broke through, reminding him of his sister's counsel and Kate's deepest needs.

He lowered his head as a wordless prayer rose from deep within.

"Jon, what is it?"

He looked up and met her gaze, and new strength flowed through him. "The Lord loves you, Kate. He wants to be your closest companion and guide. As you open your heart to Him, He will lead you toward the best path for your future.

Tenderness and tears glistened in her eyes. "Yes…I know He will."

His throat tightened, and hope rushed in like a flood.

Julia walked into the room. "Millie's settled. I'm going down." She hesitated, watching them both. "Are you coming, Jon? It's almost time to go."

"I'll be right there." Jon rose, but he wished he could stay with Kate. "I'll be praying for you." He offered her one more fleeting smile, then turned and walked out the door.

NINETEEN

Afternoon sunlight slanted through Kate's open bedroom window, warming the air around her. The sound of motorcars humming along the street and the rattle of passing carts stirred her frustration. She had missed attending the first two days of the London Missionary Society meetings, and if her throat didn't heal soon, she would miss the final day as well.

She crossed her arms and frowned at the ceiling.

Isolation and idleness were torture, and she'd had more than enough. Right now she would even welcome scrubbing pots and pans if they would only let her out of this bed.

Andrew and Millie had been kept away from her room in the hope that they would not catch whatever plagued Kate. Louisa had looked in once, but she would not come in the room. Perhaps that was not so much a burden as a blessing. Kate's only consolation had been Lydia's care and company, and the books Julia left for her to read.

She glanced at the stack on her bedside table—*Jane Eyre, Pride and Prejudice,* and the Bible.

Before Julia left, she'd laid her hand on the Bible with a wistful look in her eyes. "I think you'll find great comfort in these pages. This is my own personal copy. I hope you won't mind the notes and underlining."

That had stirred Kate's interest, and as soon as Julia left, she'd flipped through the pages, reading what Julia had inscribed beside several passages. Kate was surprised to see almost every page had at least one section underlined. Was it proper to write in the Bible? What did God think of Julia scratching notes on the pages of holy writ?

Kate lifted the Bible from the table and placed it on her lap. She flipped to Matthew 6 and continued reading in the middle of the chapter, where she'd left off earlier.

Julia had underlined verse 25: "Therefore I say unto you, take no thought for your life, what ye shall eat, or what ye shall drink; nor yet for your body, what ye shall put on. Is not the life more than meat, and the body than raiment?"

Kate gazed toward the window. She spent hours every day arranging her hair, dressing, and changing…getting ready for life. But how was she spending that life?

She glanced down and continued reading the rest of the chapter, which detailed God's care for every creature. Julia had underlined verse 33: "But seek ye first the kingdom of God, and His righteousness; and all these things shall be added unto you."

Kate lowered the Bible and pondered that thought. She had been seeking a place in society, an estate, and a life of her own…and most of all, a man who could give her all those things. But would that bring her love and sense of belonging? Would it soothe the aching heart that had plagued her for so long?

Lydia walked in the door carrying a tea tray. "A letter arrived for you, miss."

Kate closed the Bible and set it aside. Lydia settled the tray on her lap.

"Thank you." Kate glanced down at the tea, toast, and strawberries, and sensed a pleasant stirring of hunger rather than the awful churning she'd dealt with since Thursday morning.

"How are you feeling, miss?"

"A bit better this afternoon."

"I'm glad to hear it." Lydia glanced at the tray. "Can I get you anything else?"

"No, thank you, Lydia. I'm grateful for your kindness."

Lydia smiled, obviously pleased with the compliment. "You're welcome, miss. I'll be back in a few minutes." Lydia picked up the empty pitcher from the dressing table and left the room.

Kate glanced at the envelope. The handwriting didn't look familiar, and there was no return address. She slit it open, pulled out the stationery, and glanced at the bottom. Surprise rippled through her as she read Edward's signature.

Dear Kate,

I was so pleased to read the latest article in the newspaper about the Martindale case. I'm sure Mr. Leifstrom's confession is a relief to you and your family, and I hope it will open the door for us to continue seeing each other.

I have spoken to my parents, and they have softened their stance. But they are not comfortable with our being seen together in public, at least not yet. I thought they were being overly cautious, but I can see their point. It will take some time for your cousin's involvement with the Martindales to fade from people's minds. We don't want to rush ahead and stir up gossip that would hurt our reputation.

Kate paused. Whose reputation was he speaking of—his and hers, or his family's? Either way it made her uncomfortable that he valued the opinions of others more than he cared about her thoughts or feelings on the matter.

But I am eager to see you again, and I believe my parents will agree to it very soon.

With that hope in mind, I would like to invite you to accompany me to the Eaton versus Harrow cricket match on the seventh of July.

I also wanted you to know MaryAnn has accepted Charles Felton's proposal.

Kate gasped. That horrible Charles Felton—the one who had looked her up and down at her ball as if he were undressing her? He made her skin crawl! She'd heard rumors about his drinking and carousing, and his behavior at the ball seemed to confirm it. How could the Wellingtons encourage their daughter to marry someone with such poor character? She shook her head and looked at the letter again.

Their engagement should appear in the newspaper next week, and my parents have planned an engagement party on the fifteenth of July. I hope everything will be settled by then, and you will be able to join us that evening. Charles is from one of the finest families in London, and my parents are very pleased with the match. MaryAnn is not too keen on it yet, but I am sure she will see that my parents have her best interests in mind.

Kate shuddered. No wonder MaryAnn was not happy about her engagement to Charles Felton. How could she be?

Well, my dear Kate, it seems brighter days are ahead for us. I just knew everything would come out right if we were patient. I hope to hear from you soon.
    Sincerely, Edward

Kate lowered the letter and stared toward the windows. *Poor MaryAnn.* How dreadful to be forced to marry someone you didn't love. Didn't Lord and Lady Wellington realize how unhappy MaryAnn would be with a husband who lacked integrity?

Kate sighed and shook her head. There was nothing she could do about MaryAnn's situation.

She had her own issues to consider. She glanced at the letter, scanning the words once more. Edward said nothing about love or having any feelings for her. His letter seemed impersonal, almost like something he would've written to a friend from school. Should she respond and accept his invitation?

Her thoughts shifted to Jon. She laid the letter on her lap and looked toward the windows. Did he truly care for her? If he did, why didn't he tell her or speak to William about it? Maybe he thought she wouldn't want to marry a doctor who planned to practice at a free clinic on the East End.

She glanced around her room, questions stirring in her mind. Would he want to follow the Pittsfords' example and live close to the clinic and children's home? It made sense…but what kind of life would that be? Since she was a young girl, she'd always enjoyed comfort and ease. Could she leave that all behind and trade it for a very different kind of future with Jon?

• • •

Jon glanced down the pew at his father and mother while the speaker continued to describe his work in the Hunan Province of China. It was nearly four o'clock. The day was slipping away, and he still needed to speak to his parents about his decision. Why had he put it off so long?

The speaker finished his presentation, and the audience applauded.

As the applause died down, the crowd rose to their feet. Jon leaned toward his father. "Could we step outside and take a walk before the next session?"

His father stretched. "That's a good idea. I could use a bit of fresh air." He turned to Jon's mother. "Mary, will you join us?"

She smiled up at him. "Yes, it sounds lovely."

Jon led the way out the side door of the sanctuary. Clouds had moved in, but the day was still warm. A light breeze ruffled the leaves of the trees in the churchyard as they set off down the pathway.

"I've been thinking a great deal about what I ought to do when I finish my medical training." Jon glanced at his father.

Surprise flashed in his father's eyes. "Go on."

"I've been praying about it, of course."

"I'm glad to hear it."

Jon pulled in a deep breath. "I believe the Lord is calling me to stay in London and work at the Daystar Clinic with Dr. Pittsford."

His father's face fell. He cast a quick glance at Jon's mother, then looked back at Jon. "I thought you wanted to return to India and continue our work at Kanakapura."

"I did, for a long time, but over the last few months I've become aware of the needs on the East End. Dr. Pittsford has asked me to join him, and I would like to accept his offer."

His father's brow creased. "Are you sure about this, son?"

"As sure as anyone can be when they look ahead and try to choose the best path for their life."

His father looked down and clasped his hands behind his back. "I don't know what to say."

Jon's mother stepped closer to Jon. "What your father means is this is a surprise, and we need some time to consider it before we respond."

"I know if you saw the work, you'd be very impressed. It's just as challenging and rewarding as our ministry in India. But it's right here—in our own country."

His father's grim expression deepened to a scowl. "I didn't know you were so averse to working in India."

"I'm not averse to it. I have many wonderful memories of our years in India. I simply believe I have a different calling."

"So that's it? The decision is made without even consulting us? What am I supposed to say to Martin Van Cleave? I spent more than a half hour yesterday telling him what a splendid candidate you were going to be. I set the wheels in motion."

Regret burned in Jon's throat. "I'm sorry, Father. I should have spoken to you sooner."

"Yes. You should have." His father set his jaw and stared off toward the trees.

Jon's mother studied them both, lines creasing her face.

Finally, his father broke the silence. "Your mother is right. I need time to pray about this." With that, he turned and strode off down the path.

Jon's spirit sank.

His mother reached for his arm. "It will be all right, Jon. Just give him a little time."

"I'm sorry, Mother. I knew he might be disappointed, but I didn't think he would take it this hard."

She looked down the path with misty eyes. "He so much wanted to return to India and work with you there."

Jon swallowed. They'd talked about it for years, and he'd wanted it too. But it was no longer a possibility.

"Your father is struggling to accept all the changes brought about by his illness. I think he feels a bit guilty that he can't go back, and he thought sending you in his place might relieve those feelings." She sighed and shook her head. "Now he must face those issues and resolve them."

Jon glanced across the churchyard as his father passed under a stone archway and disappeared from view. He was a good man, and he had faithfully served the Lord for many years. He loved his wife and children, and he had brought hundreds into the kingdom through his sacrifice and service. Hurting him was the last thing Jon ever wanted to do.

His mother tucked her arm through his. "Tell me more about this Daystar Clinic."

He looked down at her, the ache inside easing a bit. "It's not just a medical clinic. It's the beginning of a larger ministry that will reach out and offer practical help to hundreds of people on the East End, especially the children."

Warmth and affection filled his mother's eyes. "What do you hope to accomplish?"

They strolled through the churchyard, and as Jon told her about their plans for the children's center and expanding the clinic, the burden grew lighter.

• • •

Kate lay back against her pillow, fighting off her disappointment. "But this is the last day of the conference. Are you sure I must stay home?"

"I think it's best." Jon expression was serious, but kindness shone in his eyes. "Even though your lungs are clear and you no longer have a fever, your throat is still a bit red."

Kate folded her arms across her chest. Her throat only hurt a little when she swallowed. Other than that, she felt fine. Why did she have to stay in bed while everyone else went off to enjoy the day? Even Lydia had left to visit her sister, Helen, at the Pittsfords'.

"If you rest today," Jon continued, "perhaps you'll be able to attend church tomorrow and enjoy some time with my parents."

Kate sighed. "Oh, all right, I'll stay home. But I confess I'm growing very tired of it."

"I understand, and I wish you could come with us, but I don't think it's wise."

His gentle tone tugged at her conscience. "I'm sorry. I don't mean to be such a terrible patient… It's just that I'm not used to being ill and confined to my room."

"Well, hopefully it won't be much longer. So chin up, and follow the doctor's orders." He nodded to her with a teasing grin.

"Yes sir." She gave him a mock salute. "I will rest and read and order my stubborn heart to get back in line."

"Now that's the Kate I know and admire."

Pleasant warmth spread through her as she returned his smile. Jon's kindness and care were such a gift. She didn't want to be a burden to him or anyone else. She smoothed her hand across the blanket on her lap, determined to shift the conversation to a more pleasant topic. "Have you enjoyed the conference?"

"Yes, the speakers have been excellent. The directors and everyone have been very kind to my parents. I know that means a great deal to them." His expression dimmed, and he glanced away.

"But…?"

He looked at her again. "I told my parents about my decision to practice at Daystar."

"And?"

"It didn't go as well as I'd hoped. In fact, my father is quite upset."

No wonder Jon looked discouraged. He loved his parents and especially looked up to his father. "I'm sorry," she said softly.

"Yes. So am I. I'd hoped he would take it in stride and perhaps even be pleased I'll be staying in England."

"Oh, I'm sure he's not disappointed about that."

"You didn't see how he responded." Jon glanced toward the windows. "He was certain I would return to India and take his place."

"Surely he understands your desire to take a different path."

"My mother says he's grieving the loss of his ministry and trying to come to terms with all the changes in his life."

"Yes, I'm sure that's been very difficult."

"I didn't realize how much it all meant to him, until this week."

"Now that he has recovered, perhaps he could find some way to use his medical skills again."

"Yes, I suppose." Jon stared toward the fireplace, looking lost in thought.

Penny walked through the doorway carrying her shawl and gloves. "How are you feeling, Kate?"

"Much better."

"That's wonderful. I'm so glad. I'm sorry you can't come with us today. The speakers have told the most amazing stories. Missionary life sounds so very exciting. It makes me want to sign up to go to China or somewhere else exotic like that."

Kate smiled. Penny's enthusiasm was admirable, but she doubted her sister was serious about going overseas. "Enjoy it for me, and take notes, then you can tell me the best stories when you come home."

"I will. I promise." Penny's eyes lit up. "And did you hear David is being released this morning?"

"No, I hadn't heard."

"Cousin William and Mr. Bixby are picking him up at ten o'clock." She grinned and leaned closer. "I'm so glad we won't have to listen to Aunt Louisa going on and on about it anymore."

"Yes, that will be a relief." Kate forced a smile, but she wasn't looking forward to resuming the whirl of social events with her aunt when she was well.

"Take care, Kate. We'll see you this evening." Penny waved good-bye and walked out the door.

Jon turned to Kate. "I suppose I should head downstairs as well. Is there anything I can get you before I go?"

"No, I'm fine. I feel very well looked after." She smiled, trying to have a good attitude, but her spirit slipped lower as Jon walked out and left her alone.

• • •

Jon followed his parents, Julia, and Penny toward the front entrance of St. Paul's Church in Knightsbridge. This special session for those involved in the work in India would be bittersweet for him and his family. He glanced at his father and hoped it wouldn't cause him greater pain.

Just before they reached the front door, his father slowed and looked his way. "May I speak to you for a moment before we go in?"

Jon's shoulders tensed. "Of course."

Jon's mother glanced back at them. "We'll go ahead and save you some seats."

"Yes, thank you, Mary." His father stepped closer, his expression sober. "I've thought a great deal about our conversation yesterday."

"I have as well."

"I believe I owe you an apology."

"No. Please, Father, that's not necessary."

His father lifted his hand. "Yes, it is. I reacted poorly to your news, and I regret it. I hope you will forgive me."

"Of course. I should have given you more warning."

"Perhaps, but your letters were filled with your experiences at Daystar. It was obvious your focus had shifted from India to London. I should have realized that."

"There is a great need on the East End."

"I trust what you said about praying and waiting on the Lord for direction is true." His father cocked one eyebrow, making the statement sound like a question.

Jon gave a swift nod. "Yes sir, it is."

His father considered that for a moment, then looked back at Jon again. "If that's the case, then I have no cause to be upset with you or your decision."

Jon released a deep breath. "Thank you, Father."

"Your mother and I raised you to seek the Lord's guidance in every decision, whether great or small."

Jon nodded, the truth of that statement filling him with confidence. Along with it came the firm conviction that God was guiding him on the right path.

"Then it would be foolish for me to discourage you from doing that very thing." His father extended his hand toward Jon. "I affirm your decision, I give you my blessing, and I promise to faithfully pray for your work here."

Jon reached out and gripped his father's hand. "Thank you. That means a great deal to me."

"There's one more thing I must ask."

"Yes sir?"

"Are you staying in London with the hope of winning Katherine Ramsey's heart?"

Jon stared at his father. "Did Julia tell you that?"

"No. You mentioned her often in your letters, and I observed you together that first evening we were at Ramsey House. You've also spoken of her several times in the last few days, even though she hasn't been with us."

Jon glanced away, then looked back at his father. "I do care for Kate, a great deal. But I'm not sure anything will come of it."

"Why do you say that?"

"Well, there are obvious differences in our background."

"That's true, but with the inheritance you'll receive and the connections your grandmother is eager to offer, the gap between you is not so great."

"I'm not an aristocrat, and when I receive my inheritance, I'll probably use it to provide for my needs until Daystar has a broader support base."

Father rubbed his chin, his expression thoughtful.

"I'm not sure Kate would want to join me in my work on the East End. It's certainly not the kind of life she planned to lead."

His father's gaze softened. "There aren't many women as strong as your mother. She gave up a tremendous amount to marry me and serve the Lord by my side in India."

Jon's throat tightened. His parents had faced a great deal together. Their loving commitment provided an excellent example that he hoped to emulate in his own marriage and family.

"Your mother and I are praying you'll find a wife who loves the Lord and is eager to serve Him." His father clamped his hand on Jon's shoulder. "That kind of wife is worth waiting for."

Jon nodded and swallowed past the tightness in his throat. A vision of Kate dressed in her finest gown dancing at Sheffield House flashed across his mind. It was quickly replaced by a second image of her wearing a simple dress and holding the hand of one of his young patients at Daystar.

Kate's interests and ambitions seemed to be changing. Were those changes motivated by genuine faith, or were they simply a response to the challenges the family had been facing? He hoped they signaled a true change of heart...one that would sustain her and continue to grow...and one that might open the door for them to enjoy a future together.

TWENTY

Lydia carried the tray of tea and sandwiches into the Pittsfords' cozy parlor and set it down on the table next to Helen. "Here we are."

Lydia was thankful she and Helen had the house to themselves. Dr. and Mrs. Pittsford had greeted Lydia when she arrived, but they'd left for the clinic soon after, and their two daughters had gone to visit a sick friend.

Helen rested on the couch, her feet up and a light blanket over her legs. "I should be the one serving you tea."

"I don't mind." Lydia placed the tea strainer on top of Helen's cup. "It makes me happy to see you resting." She poured the tea, added sugar and milk, and then passed the steaming cup to her sister.

Helen took a sip. "Ah, that's good. Thank you."

Lydia prepared her own tea and sat across from Helen. "How has it been, stayin' with the Pittsfords?"

"They been kind and ask nothin' in return."

"I'm glad." Lydia passed Helen a plate with two small sandwiches. "That's an answer to prayer."

Helen's hands stilled, and she looked down at her teacup.

"Helen, what is it?"

She bit her lip, then glanced at Lydia. "I feel like a fool for running away with Charlie. I don't know how the good Lord can stomach hearing my name in a prayer."

"Well, thank goodness He doesn't see things like that."

Helen's brow creased. "What do you mean?"

"He knows the mistakes we're going to make before we even make them, and He loves us anyway."

"But I ran away from home and turned my back on all we were taught. I lived with Charlie even though we weren't married. How could He overlook something like that?"

Lydia wanted to comfort Helen, but she didn't want to pretend what she had done was right. She sent off a silent plea for the right words. "He knows what happened, and it breaks His heart. But all you need to do is confess it to Him and ask forgiveness. That wipes the slate clean."

"But I'll still be having a baby in a few days, and there won't be any husband to care for us."

"You're right. That won't change. But you don't have to carry the guilt or shame. Jesus carried those for us when He died on the cross. And He did it all for love."

Tears filled Helen's eyes. "How can you be sure?"

"Because it says so in the Bible." She glanced around the parlor. Surely, a godly family like the Pittsfords had a Bible somewhere nearby. Lydia headed for the bookshelf in the corner. As she passed the window, her steps stalled. A large man in a brown coat crossed the street and walked toward the house. Lydia gasped.

Helen followed her gaze. "What is it?"

Lydia ran to the front door, jerked down the shade, and slid the chain lock into place.

Helen sat forward. "Lydia? What's wrong?"

"Shh!" Lydia lifted her finger to her lips as footsteps clomped up the front steps and a loud knock sounded at the door.

Helen froze and stared at Lydia.

The knock came again, harder this time. "Helen! I know you're in there!"

Helen's hands flew to cover her mouth and stifle her cry.

"Open this door and let me in!" Charlie pounded so hard the door rattled on its hinges.

Lydia jumped back. *Please, Lord, help us!*

"I'm not leaving till I talk to you! Now, open up!"

"Oh, Lydia, he sounds so angry." Helen's voice trembled.

Lydia waved her hand to quiet her sister, then she crept across the room and leaned close to Helen's ear. "Is there a back door?"

"Yes, through the kitchen," Helen whispered.

"Stay here, and don't answer the door, no matter what he says." On light feet, Lydia raced down the hall and into the large kitchen. The back door stood open to a small rear courtyard. She rushed forward, pushed the door closed, and turned the lock.

Charlie's angry shouts echoed through the house as she ran back to the parlor. Standing to the side of the parlor windows, she quickly lowered one shade and then the other.

"You can't run away from me!" Charlie yelled. "I won't let it rest!"

Helen's chin trembled. "What are we going to do?"

Lydia crossed to her sister's side. "Stay quiet and pray."

Helen clasped her hands and squeezed her eyes tight. Her lips moved silently as the pounding and yelling continued. Lydia barely had time to form her thoughts into a prayer before another voice rang out.

"What's going on out here?"

Helen's eyes flew open, and she stared at Lydia.

"It's none of your business," Charlie shouted back.

"Surely 'tis! You're disturbin' the whole street!"

"I'll be doing more than that if you don't go back in your house and leave me alone!"

"Don't be telling me what to do! This is my street, and you're the one makin' trouble where it's not wanted! Now be off with you, or I'll go for the police!"

Charlie growled and banged on the door. "I'm not finished, Helen. I'm coming back for you." He stomped down the stairs, and his footsteps faded away.

Lydia laid her hand on her chest, trying to still her racing heart.

Tears overflowed down Helen's cheeks. "Oh, Lydia, what am I going to do?"

"I don't know, but you can't stay here."

"Where can I go?" Helen's panicked gaze darted around the room.

Lydia laid her hand on Helen's shoulder. "We must find somewhere safe, and we must do it today."

Helen sniffed and swiped a tear from her cheeks. "But if we try to leave, he might be out there waiting."

Lydia swallowed and tried to focus her thoughts. Helen was right. Charlie might be watching the house. She could run to the clinic for help, but Dr. Pittsford was a peaceful man with a slight build—no match for Charlie Gibbons. She needed someone stronger. Two or three men would be a better idea. Mr. Foster and his friend Mr. Anderson might come. But could she find them and bring them back before Charlie returned?

She had no other idea and no time to waste.

She knelt in front of Helen and took her hand. "I'm going to get help. Stay here and keep the doors locked."

"Don't leave me here alone!" Helen tightened her grip on Lydia's hand. "What if he comes back?"

"Don't answer him or unlock that door. I promise I'll return as soon as I can." Lydia squeezed Helen's hand. "Gather your things, and keep on praying."

"All right."

Lydia kissed her sister's cheek, then hurried out the back door and slipped through the neighbor's property behind the Pittsfords'. If Charlie Gibbons waited on Conover Street, Lydia didn't want to be seen by him.

She scrambled down the street, repeating her prayer as she ran: *Please, God, help us!*

• • •

Kate walked across her bedroom, opened the window, and looked out at the lovely day. Only a few wispy clouds drifted across the bright blue sky. A chorus of birds sent up a song from the trees in the front garden.

She glanced over her shoulder. Did she really have to go back to bed? Her throat felt much better, and if she hurried there was still time to dress and attend the afternoon sessions of the conference and the final dinner. Jon might be surprised, but when she explained—

The door flew open. Lydia rushed in, her face flushed and her hat askew.

"Goodness, Lydia, are you all right?"

"Oh, Miss Katherine, Helen's in trouble!"

Kate met Lydia in the middle of the room. "What happened?"

"Charlie found out she's at the Pittsfords'."

Kate gasped.

"He came to the house and pounded on the door like a madman."

"Oh my goodness."

"We locked him out and pulled the shades, but I was afraid he was going to break down the door and drag Helen away." Lydia laid her hands on her cheeks. "He wouldn't stop yelling until a neighbor came out and told him he was going for the police."

"That stopped him?"

"Yes, he stomped off, but he said he's coming back for Helen. She's terrified!"

"We've got to get her away from there." Kate strode to her wardrobe and pulled open the door. "Help me dress, and I'll go with you."

"Oh no, miss! We can't go back alone. It wouldn't be safe." Lydia hurried to her side. "Do you think Mr. Foster would help us?"

Kate's mind raced. "I'm sure he would, but he's at the mission conference at Saint Paul's Church in Knightsbridge."

Lydia's face fell. "That's so far away." She wrung her hands, then looked up. "What about Sir William?"

Kate shook her head. "David is being released today. They've gone to pick him up. I have no idea where that is or when he's coming back."

"Should we go to the police?"

Kate clenched her hands. "I don't know that they would help us unless Charlie attacks Helen, and we can't let that happen."

"Oh no, miss!"

Kate paced across the room, trying to think of another idea, but there was no time. She turned back to Lydia. "You must go to St. Paul's, and tell Mr. Foster what's happened. I'm sure he'll go with you to the Pittsfords'. Then you must bring Helen here."

"Will Sir William allow it?"

"When I explain the circumstances, I'm sure he'll understand." She crossed to her dressing table and took two five-pound notes from the top drawer. She pressed them into Lydia's hand. "Take a cab. Have the driver wait for you in Knightsbridge, and then at the Pittsfords'."

Lydia took the notes and then clutched Kate's hand. "Thank you, miss. I'm ever so grateful."

Kate pulled Lydia in for a quick embrace.

Lydia slipped away and rushed out the door.

Kate closed her eyes. *Father, please go with Lydia. Help her find Jon, and guide them quickly back to the Pittsfords'. And please watch over Helen and keep her and the baby safe until they arrive.*

Kate lifted her head, and an unsettled feeling washed over her. She crossed to the nightstand, picked up the conference program, and scanned the schedule. Today's morning session at Saint Paul's in Knightsbridge concluded at twelve. She glanced at the clock, and pulled in a sharp breath.

The meeting had ended forty minutes ago. She scanned the rest of the schedule: there was a break for luncheon and then three more sessions that afternoon, starting at one o'clock, one at All Saints' and the other two at St. Matthew's.

Where was Jon? How would Lydia ever find him?

Kate sank down on the bed and stared across the room.

Who would help Helen now?

• • •

Jon shifted in the pew and glanced at his watch. The early afternoon hours were a difficult time to listen to a speaker, especially a soft-spoken one who seemed to be droning on and on. If he didn't get up and take a break, he would probably fall asleep and embarrass himself and his parents.

He leaned toward his mother. "I'm going to slip out for a bit."

"Is everything all right?"

"Yes. I just need to stretch my legs." He excused himself past the two elderly women at the end of the pew and walked out of the sanctuary. With a sigh of relief, he pushed open the back door and stepped outside.

A woman rushed up the steps. She lifted her head, looked up at him, and her eyes widened. "Mr. Foster!"

"Lydia, what are you doing here?"

"I need your help."

Alarm shot through him. "Is it Miss Katherine?"

"No, it's Helen." Lydia poured out the story in frightening detail.

"Does Dr. Pittsford know?"

Lydia shook her head, looking dazed. "I should've gone there first, but I went back to Ramsey House to find you. Then Miss Katherine told me to go to Saint Paul's. I couldn't find you there, but a kind priest saw me crying and sent me here." Lydia gulped in a breath.

Jon laid his hand on her shoulder. "It's all right. I'll go with you. We'll make sure Helen is safe."

Lydia sniffed. "Thank you, sir."

He slipped back inside and told his parents he needed to leave and would explain later, then he guided Lydia down the steps and into the waiting cab.

• • •

Kate clenched her hands in her lap as the cab turned the corner and started down Conover Street. "It's just a few houses down, on the right."

The gray-haired driver glanced in the rear view mirror.

She leaned forward. "There it is—number 322."

The cab rolled to a stop in front of Dr. Pittsford's home. The elderly driver climbed out, circled the cab, and opened Kate's door.

Kate stepped up to the curb. "Please wait for me. I should only be a few minutes."

"All right, miss." He touched his black cap and closed the door.

Kate looked down the street. Two little girls squatted in front of the house next door, petting a gray-striped cat. A few houses down on the left, an old man sat on his front step smoking a pipe. But there was no sign of Charlie Gibbons.

Kate lifted her skirt and climbed the front steps. The curtains were all closed, and the house stood silent. She knocked on the front door and waited, but no one answered. She knocked again, harder. "Helen, it's Katherine Ramsey."

Two seconds passed. She heard the chain slide and the lock turn. The door opened a few inches, and Helen peeked out, her eyes wide.

"May I come in?" Kate kept her voice calm, hoping to ease Helen's fears.

Helen's gaze darted around, then she opened the door a little wider. Kate slipped through. Helen quickly closed the door and slid the chain lock back in place.

"Where's Lydia?" Helen whispered.

"She went to find Mr. Foster, but I'm afraid I gave her the wrong address."

Helen bit her lip, a frantic look filling her eyes. "What are we going do?"

Kate laid her hand on Helen's arm. "Everything's going to be all right. I have a cab waiting right outside the door. The driver will take us to Ramsey House."

Tears flooded Helen's eyes. "Oh miss, are you sure? What about your family?"

"I'm sure they'll agree this is the best plan."

Helen nodded. "All right. Thank you."

"Let's pack your things, and we can be on our way."

Helen motioned toward the satchel and small suitcase by the door. "Lydia told me to get ready to go." She started to reach for them.

Kate held out her hand. "I'll take them."

"Thank you, miss." She glanced around the parlor. "I wish I could thank the doctor and his wife. They've been kind."

"We can send them a note when you're settled at Ramsey House. I'm sure they'll understand why you needed to leave."

Helen unlocked the door and stepped outside. She shot a wary glance around before she lumbered down the steps, one hand lifting her skirt and the other resting over the babe within. Kate followed her down, carrying the bags.

The cab driver opened his door and stepped out. "Can I take those bags for you, miss?"

"Yes, thank you." Before the driver was halfway there, a man strode around the back of the cab. Kate looked up and pulled in a sharp breath.

Charlie lunged for Helen and grabbed her arm. "Where do you think you're goin'?"

Helen cried out.

"Hey now!" The cab driver spun toward Helen.

Charlie tugged Helen out of the driver's reach.

"No, Charlie, please! You're hurting me!"

"Let *go* of her!" Kate dropped the suitcase and swung the satchel at Charlie, smashing it into his arm.

He growled and released Helen, then turned on Kate, curses flying from his mouth. He ripped the satchel from her hand and threw it aside.

Fear clawed at Kate's throat, stealing her breath. Charlie's face contorted. He lunged and grabbed her by both shoulders. Kate gasped and tried to pull away, but he tightened his grip, and slid one hand toward her neck.

His fingers closed around her throat.

God! Save me!

TWENTY-ONE

J on leaned forward in the back seat of the cab. "Can you hurry, please?"
The driver looked over his shoulder. "We're almost there, sir."

Lydia glanced out her window as they rounded the corner at Conover Street, her expression taut.

The driver slowed. "What's the number again?"

"Three twenty-two." Jon scanned the street. Up ahead, Dr. Pittsford and two men stood in front of the building they planned to open as the children's center. Jon gripped the door handle. "Stop the car! We'll get out here."

Lydia looked at Jon. "Why are we stopping?"

"We may need Dr. Pittsford's help." Jon thrust some money at the driver and hopped out of the cab. Lydia slid out behind him.

Dr. Pittsford lifted his hand and smiled. "Jon, you're just in time to meet Mr. Yardley and Mr. Pennington. They're writing an article for the *Daily Mail* about our fund-raising program for the children's center."

Jon glanced at the two men. One man carried a camera attached to a wooden tripod, and the other held a small pad and pencil, apparently taking notes for the article. "I'm sorry to interrupt, Doctor, but something has happened. You're needed at home."

Dr. Pittsford straightened. "What is it?"

A scream pierced the air.

Jon's heart jerked, and he spun around.

Down the street, in front of the Pittsford's house, Charlie Gibbons grabbed Helen. Another woman swung a satchel at Charlie, knocking his hand away from Helen—

It was Kate!

Energy surged through Jon, and he took off running toward them.

Charlie lunged for Kate. Helen screamed and tugged on his coat. A whistle pierced the air. Across the street, two policemen ran toward the scene.

Charlie's head jerked up, his eyes wide. He shoved Kate hard. She crashed on the steps in a crumpled heap.

The shrill whistle blasted again. Charlie dashed away. The policemen crossed the street, one chasing Charlie and the other heading toward the Pittsfords'.

Jon ran toward Kate. Charlie passed him, running in the opposite direction, with the policeman close behind. Footsteps pounded the pavement behind Jon, but he didn't look back to see who followed.

He dropped to the ground next to Kate. She lay still, her eyes closed, her face deathly pale. Icy panic pulsed through him. "Kate!" His voice came out a raspy whisper.

She didn't move.

Dr. Pittsford rushed toward them and knelt next to Jon. He leaned over Kate, reached for her hand, and began assessing her condition.

Helen's hysterical cries filled the air, making it difficult for Jon to focus or hear the doctor.

Lydia hurried to Helen's side. "It's all right. He's gone now. He won't hurt you."

"But he hurt Miss Katherine." Heaving sobs shook Helen as she turned into her sister's embrace. Lydia wrapped her arms around Helen and held her close.

"What happened here? Who is she?" The panting journalist squatted on the other side of Jon, his pencil poised above his pad.

"Not now!" Jon leaned toward Dr. Pittsford, trying to block the journalist's view of Kate.

Dr. Pittsford lifted Kate's eyelids. "The blow to her head has knocked her unconscious."

Jon swallowed and stared at Kate. He should do something to help, but he could barely pull in the next breath.

The doctor looked up. "Let's take her inside."

Jon bent and carefully slipped his hand under her head. A warm, sticky substance slicked across his fingers. He gulped in a breath and pulled out his hand. Kate's blood smeared his palm.

Dr. Pittsford's gaze riveted Jon. "We've got to stop the bleeding. Pick her up carefully."

Jon scooped Kate up as gently as he could and moved toward the steps.

A light flashed, and a small puff of smoke rose in the air.

Jon scowled at the photographer. "That's enough!"

The man raised his head from behind his camera and averted his eyes.

Jon clenched his jaw and turned away. If he hadn't been carrying Kate, he would've knocked that scoundrel to the ground and sent his camera flying after him.

"What's your name, sir, and the young lady's?" The journalist stepped in front of Jon, blocking his path.

"Get out of my way!" Jon shouldered past the journalist and carried Kate up the steps and into the Pittsfords' house. He carefully laid Kate on the couch.

Kate stirred and looked up at him. "Jon…"

Relief poured through him, and he took her hand. "Yes."

Confusion filled her eyes. "What happened?"

Dr. Pittsford knelt next to her. "You've fallen and hit your head." He looked up at Jon. "Let's help her turn on her side." They positioned Kate so they could see the wound. "Get my bag by the door."

Jon hustled over and returned with the bag.

Dr. Pittsford laid his hand on Kate's shoulder. "There's a cut on the back of your head we must attend to." He pressed a clean bandage to the wound. "Hold this here, Jon."

Jon took over, applying gentle pressure. Dr. Pittsford gathered what he needed to clean the wound and prepared the needle.

Helen, Lydia, and one of the policemen walked in the front door. Dr. Pittsford directed them to the kitchen to give Kate some privacy,

While the doctor stitched the wound, Jon held Kate's hand. Silent tears rolled down her cheeks, tearing at his heart. He tightened his hold on her hand, wishing there was some way he could trade places and carry that pain for her.

A few minutes later the policeman finished questioning Helen and Lydia, then left by the front door.

When the stitching ordeal was finally over, Dr. Pittsford called Jon and Lydia aside. "Kate may have a concussion. She must be watched carefully for the next few days, and she'll have to be awakened every two hours through the night to be sure she can regain consciousness."

Lydia gave a firm nod. "I'll stay with her, Doctor."

"I'll be sure she has everything she needs," Jon added.

He glanced back at Kate, a dreadful band of anxiety tightening around his chest. They'd stopped the bleeding and stitched the wound, but how long would it take for her to recover… And what would William and Julia say when he brought her home?

• • •

Jon paced the hallway outside Kate's bedroom door. The events of the last two hours replayed through his mind for the hundredth time, washing over him with another wave of mind-numbing regret.

He could hear Kate's aunt now, her shrill tone rising and falling behind the bedroom door. The words were not clear, but the message behind them was. He clenched his fists, barely able to keep from bursting through the door and demanding she leave Kate in peace. How could she recover when her aunt was going on and on like that?

The bedroom door opened, and Lady Gatewood stalked out. William stepped out after her and quietly closed the door.

"I don't understand!" Lady Gatewood huffed. "What was she thinking—running off on her own to that area of town!"

William's dark eyebrows lowered. "Please, keep your voice down. The doctor said Katherine needs to rest, but that's not possible when you're creating such a stir."

Louisa lifted her chin. "I am concerned about my niece, and I will not rest until we get to the bottom of this!"

"I understand, but there are better ways to show your concern."

Lady Gatewood started to reply, but William held up his hand. "If you want to discuss this further, we can do that later. I'm going downstairs." He turned and strode off without waiting for her answer.

"Well!" Lady Gatewood glared at William's back.

Jon shook his head and turned to follow William.

"Wait just a minute, young man!"

Jon slowly turned and faced her. "If you have something to say to me, kindly step away from Kate's door so we don't disturb her any further."

"Very well." She marched a few steps down the hall.

Jon followed, trying to rein in his temper.

She turned and glared at him. "I hope you are satisfied."

He squinted at her. "What?"

"I hold you one-hundred-percent responsible for her injuries!"

Her words singed, but he set his jaw and remained silent.

"She never would have gone to the East End on her own if you hadn't taken her to that awful clinic full of criminals and prostitutes!" Lady Gatewood shuddered.

A sharp reply rose in Jon's throat, but the hammer of conviction slammed down against it. He *had* involved Kate in his work there, and that ended up costing much more than either of them ever expected. It would be a long time before he forgave himself for what happened to her today.

"Well, don't you have anything to say?"

He squared his shoulders. "I'm sorry Kate was injured. But I admire her courage and willingness to help someone in need, even at the risk of her own life."

"Courage?" Lady Gatewood gave an unladylike snort. "What she did was reckless and foolhardy!"

"Call it what you wish. Kate saved a young woman's life today, and most likely the life of her baby. Rather than shouting and carrying on, you ought to look for ways to comfort her."

"Julia will comfort Katherine. *I* must find a way to clean up this mess and make sure Katherine's hopes for the future are not destroyed."

Jon looked down and stifled a groan.

"I suppose I'll have to make up some sort of story to explain her injuries to Edward and his family."

Jon's head jerked up. "Why would you tell them anything? Kate hasn't seen Edward for weeks."

Lady Gatewood sniffed. "Well, that shows how little you know."

Jon tensed.

"Now that the issues with David Ramsey have been resolved, I'm confident Katherine and Edward will resume their courtship."

"Courtship! How could you encourage Kate to be involved with a man who turned his back on her at the first sign of trouble in her family? Doesn't character—or lack of it—mean anything to you?"

"Edward is an outstanding young man from a fine family. There's nothing lacking in his character!"

Jon shook his head. "He's not the right man for Kate."

"You have nothing to say about that decision."

Heat surged into Jon's face.

"I know you fancied yourself in line to become one of Katherine's suitors, but that will never happen. Edward spoke to Katherine the night of her ball. They have an understanding."

"I don't believe it." But even as the words left his mouth, the memory of Kate and Edward together on the balcony at Sheffield House flooded his mind. Edward had kissed her hand, and Kate had allowed it.

"It's true. Ask her yourself." Lady Gatewood motioned toward Kate's bedroom door, a hint of challenge in her eyes.

A cold wave washed over Jon.

"Their engagement will be announced as soon as the details and timing have been agreed to by both families."

How could it be true? Why hadn't Kate said anything to him?

"The Wellingtons are respected members of society, and someday Edward will inherit his father's title and everything he owns. That will make Katherine a countess."

"And you think that's what she wants?"

"Of course! We've discussed it at length. Edward can give Katherine the kind of life she deserves." She took a step closer and narrowed her eyes. "It's time you faced the truth and got on with your life."

Her words sliced through Jon.

"Now, step aside. I have important matters to attend to." Lady Gatewood swung away and strode down the hall.

Jon stared after her, his heart a stone in his chest.

• • •

Lydia carried Miss Katherine's breakfast tray into the kitchen and set it down by the sink. Mrs. Murdock, the cook, and her two young kitchen maids stood around the large table in the middle of the room. Ruth peeled potatoes, while Jean rolled out a batch of pastry.

Mrs. Murdock cracked an egg into a large bowl and looked up at Lydia. "How's Miss Katherine this morning?"

"She still has a headache, and she's feeling a bit woozy, but Dr. Foster looked in on her. He says she's coming along fine." Lydia stifled a yawn and leaned against the sink.

Mrs. Murdock cocked her head. "Did you get any sleep last night?"

"Not much. I had to wake Miss Katherine every two hours to make sure she was still all right."

"Well, I'm sure you were glad to see the sunrise."

Lydia nodded. "I was."

"What a load of trouble." Mrs. Murdock clicked her tongue. "That Gibbons fellow sounds like a scoundrel. Can you imagine someone trying to kidnap a pregnant woman, then pushing a young lady down so hard she's knocked out?"

"It was frightening. I hope they find Charlie and lock him up for good." Lydia shuddered and rubbed her arms.

"How is your sister?" Mrs. Murdock pulled a whisk from the drawer and began beating the eggs.

Lydia had just looked in on Helen. "She's resting in my room. She said she had trouble sleeping last night, but I think she'll be all right."

"I'm sorry Lady Gatewood put up such a fuss about her staying here."

Lydia's stomach tensed as she recalled Lady Gatewood's stormy reaction. She'd wanted to send Helen back to the Pittsfords', but Julia and Sir William had stood up to Lady Gatewood and allowed Helen to stay, at least for now.

Patrick rushed through the doorway carrying the newspaper. "Where's Mr. Lawrence?"

Mrs. Murdock wrinkled her nose. "I'm sure I don't know."

"I have to find him. He'll want to see this." Patrick held out the newspaper.

"What is it?" Lydia crossed the kitchen and met Patrick by the doorway.

The footman pointed to a photograph on the lower half of the front page.

Lydia gasped and stared at the grainy image of Mr. Foster carrying Miss Katherine toward the Pittsfords' front steps. "Oh no!"

Mrs. Murdock wiped her hand on her apron and scurried to Patrick's side. "Let me see." The cook scanned the photo and lifted her hand to her mouth. "Oh my stars!"

Lydia read the headline: "Debutante Attacked in Whitechapel." The caption under the photo read: "Miss Katherine Ramsey is carried to safety by Mr. Jonathan Foster following the attack on Conover Street Saturday afternoon."

Mrs. Murdock shook her head. "I wouldn't want to be in the room when Lady Gatewood sees this. She's gonna have a fit."

A sick, dizzy feeling flooded Lydia. Would the family blame her for the story being in the paper? She'd answered the policeman's questions and named Miss Katherine and Mr. Foster while that reporter stood by and wrote everything down. She was also the one who had asked Miss Katherine to help Helen.

Would they sack her, or insist Helen leave…or both?

Patrick glanced at Lydia. "How did they get this photo?"

Tremors traveled down Lydia's back. She explained how she and

Mr. Foster had stopped to speak to Dr. Pittsford and then heard Helen's screams. "The reporters followed us, and one of them set up his camera and took the picture."

"What a shame." Mrs. Murdock shook her head. "Just when this awful business with Sir William's brother ends, now the family has this new load o' trouble."

Mr. Lawrence walked in. "Dr. and Mrs. Foster will be staying one more day. You'll want to add them for meals through luncheon on Monday."

Mrs. Murdock looked up, and everyone waited in silence.

"Well, what is it? Why are you all staring at me?"

"We've just seen this, sir." Patrick held out the newspaper.

Mr. Lawrence frowned and took the newspaper. He glanced at the photo, and his dark bushy eyebrows lowered. "How could this happen?"

They all looked at Lydia. She cringed and wished she could sink under the table, but she quietly repeated her explanation to Mr. Lawrence.

"You'd better come with me." Mr. Lawrence folded the newspaper. "The family is preparing to leave for church. They need to be apprised of the situation before they step out the door."

Lydia swallowed. "Yes sir." She followed him up the stairs, whispering a prayer for mercy.

• • •

Jon leaned forward in his chair, clasped his hands, and rested his forearms on his thighs, the weight of the situation bearing down on him. William had called them all into the drawing room and showed them the article and photograph in the *Daily Mail*. With that disheartening news echoing through his mind, he tried to think of some kind of explanation that might satisfy William.

There was none.

William stood by the fireplace, a brooding frown lining his face. Jon's parents and Julia sat across from Jon. Penny and Lady Gatewood shared the settee on Jon's right. Kate rested in her room, and the children had been sent upstairs with Ann.

"I don't see how we can go to church this morning." Lady Gatewood glared at Jon. "The whole congregation will be talking about the incident."

Julia turned to Lady Gatewood. "But it's times like these when we need the comfort and support of our friends."

"I doubt that's what we would receive at St. Matthew's this morning." Lady Gatewood waved her hand toward the newspaper on the low table in front of the settee. "This is disgraceful!"

Julia's face flushed. "The article may cause a stir, but I'd hardly call it disgraceful."

Lady Gatewood continued as though she had not heard Julia. "It would not be so damaging if we weren't already dealing with the aftermath of David's connection with the Martindales. His behavior has permanently stained the Ramsey family name and put us all in a very difficult situation."

William cleared his throat and sent an apprehensive glance at Julia's parents. "We all know David's choices reflect poorly on the family, but the problem we're facing today is not David's fault." He shifted his gaze to the newspaper on the table. "I should never have allowed Katherine to go to the East End or volunteer at Daystar Clinic. That was a mistake on my part."

Those words hit Jon like a blow to the chest.

Lady Gatewood sniffed. "I'm glad you've finally come to your senses."

Julia looked from Louisa to William. "I don't see how volunteering at the clinic has anything to do with what happened to Katherine yesterday."

"It has everything to do with it!" Lady Gatewood shifted her heated glare to Julia. "Her familiarity with that area gave her the foolish idea it was safe to travel there on her own, when that's the farthest thing from the truth. Her lack of judgment is deplorable!"

Jon had kept silent out of respect for William and Julia, but he could do so no longer. "Kate is an intelligent young woman. She was well aware of the danger, but she believed the need to help Helen outweighed it."

Julia glanced at Jon, her gaze reflecting her agreement.

"Nevertheless," William continued, "I can't allow Katherine to return to Daystar or spend time on the East End with the Pittsfords."

Julia's eyes clouded as she looked up at William. "Surely you don't blame them for what's happened?"

"No, I don't blame the Pittsfords." His somber gaze shifted, then settled on Jon. "I am Katherine's guardian, and I must do what's needed to protect her."

Jon's gaze locked with William's.

"This is *not* Jon's fault," Julia insisted. "He never purposely put Katherine in danger."

William set his jaw, but he did not reply.

The uncomfortable silence stretched several seconds. Finally, Jon rose to his feet. "I'm sorry Kate was injured—more sorry than I can say." He straightened and looked at William. "I take full responsibility, and I agree with you. Kate should not return to Daystar or travel to the East End for any reason."

Pain flashed in Julia's eyes, and she lowered her gaze. Lady Gatewood glared at him, while Jon's parents exchanged concerned glances.

William silently stared toward the fireplace, his posture rigid.

There was nothing else Jon could say. He turned and walked from the room.

"William, please, this is not how we should end this conversation…"

Julia's pleading voice faded as Jon crossed the entrance hall.

He did not slow to hear William's reply, if he gave one. Instead, Jon climbed the stairs with determined steps. Kate's safety was more important than his desire to involve her in his work. He was willing to risk his own safety to serve those in need, but he could not ask that of Kate. More to the point…

He would not.

TWENTY-TWO

K ate sat at her dressing table and slowly pulled the brush through her hair, carefully avoiding the painful stitches on the back of her head. The medicine Dr. Foster had given her helped reduce her headache, but it still throbbed a bit.

Lydia walked in carrying the blue dress Kate had worn yesterday. "Here we are, miss. All clean and pressed."

"Were you able to remove the bloodstains?"

"Yes, Mrs. Adams showed me how."

"Thank you, Lydia. I'm sorry to cause you extra work." Kate paused and looked at Lydia's reflection in the mirror. "I appreciate everything you've done."

"I'm glad to do it, miss." Lydia hung Kate's dress in the wardrobe. "Can I help you with your hair?"

"No, it's all right." But after a few more strokes, Kate sighed and held out the brush to Lydia. "I suppose I would like some help."

"Of course, miss." Lydia took the brush and eased it through Kate's hair.

"It's strange how the least bit of effort seems to drain my energy."

"You've had a serious blow to your head. The doctor said it would take time to recover."

"Yes, I have to remember that." Kate glanced at Lydia again. "How is Helen?"

"Dr. Foster checked on her after luncheon. He says the swelling has gone down since she's been off her feet, and the baby's heartbeat is strong."

"That's good. I'm so relieved. Did he agree with Dr. Pittsford about the baby's due date?"

"Yes, he thinks only one week or two."

Kate smiled. Though the circumstances surrounding Helen's pregnancy were not the best, every baby was a gift. And Kate intended to do all she could to help Helen and her child build a new life. She wasn't exactly sure how she would do it, but Jon and the Pittsfords would know how to help her, she was sure of it.

Julia slipped in the door. "Kate, I'm surprised to see you out of bed."

"I've only been up for a bit." She turned toward Julia. "I'm feeling more steady this afternoon. The headache is practically gone."

"Good." Julia glanced at Lydia. "Would you leave us for a few minutes?"

"Yes, miss." She laid the brush aside and walked out the door.

Kate leaned back in her chair. "How was church?"

Julia glanced away, a faint line appearing between her eyebrows. "Interesting."

"Why do you say that?"

Julia took a folded piece of newspaper from her skirt pocket and held it out to Kate. "I thought you should see this."

Kate unfolded the clipping, and her gaze dropped to the photograph at the bottom. She blinked and looked up at Julia. "How did they get this picture?"

Julia sighed and relayed the story they had pieced together from Jon and Lydia.

"So everyone in the entire city of London knows I was in a street brawl with Charlie Gibbons?"

Julia sighed. "Only those who read the newspaper."

Kate handed the article back to Julia, then lifted her hand and gently rubbed her temple. "I'm not supposed to read for a few days. What does the article say?"

"They describe you as a brave young woman who was intent on saving her maid's pregnant sister. They also praised Jon and Dr. Pittsford for rescuing you after you were injured." Julia's smile looked a bit forced.

"What else does it say?"

"It mentions you're a debutante who was recently presented...and that you're David Ramsey's cousin."

"Did it explain why my relationship to David is newsworthy?"

"Yes, I'm afraid so." Julia sent her a sympathetic glance. "This morning at church, several people asked us about it. I'm afraid some of their comments were not very kind."

Kate sighed. "I suppose Aunt Louisa is upset."

"That would be putting it mildly."

"And William?"

"He's...very concerned." Julia glanced away.

Apprehension rippled through Kate. "What did he say?"

"He's your guardian, the one who is responsible to protect you, so I'm afraid he considers it a failure on his part."

"But Jon explained what happened, didn't he?"

"Yes, William questioned Jon and Lydia. Jon stood up for you, and so did I, but in the end we must accept William's decision."

Kate tensed. "What decision?"

Julia slowly shifted her gaze to meet Kate's. "He says you're not allowed to return to Daystar or travel to the East End for any reason."

"What!" Tremors raced down Kate's arms.

"I'm sorry, Kate."

"That is so unfair. Why should I have to stop volunteering at Daystar?" Kate strode across the room and sank down on the side of the bed.

"William feels it's for the best."

"Is there any chance he might change his mind?"

"I don't know. We can pray that he does."

There had to be some way to convince William to relax his rule. She glanced at Julia, replaying what she'd just said, and an idea rose in her mind. "Let's pray about it now."

Surprise flashed in Julia's eyes, then her expression warmed. "All right." She walked over and slipped her hand in Kate's.

Kate held tight to Julia and bowed her head. Surely God would hear their prayer and make William change his mind.

"Father, You know Kate's desire is to continue her work at Daystar, so we ask You to open that door for her at the right time. Please show us how we ought to respond as we wait, and help us to have willing hearts, ready to do Your will, whatever that may be."

Kate's throat tightened as she listened.

"May we handle all of this with grace, and may everything we say and do honor You. In Jesus's name, amen."

Kate's eyes burned as she whispered amen. She'd expected the prayer to be about William, including a plea that he would change his mind and let Kate return to Daystar. Instead, Julia's gentle words had convicted her of her own need to yield to the Father's will and trust Him to do what was best.

Could she trust Him with something that was so important to her?

Please, Lord, help me be willing.

• • •

Kate settled back on the settee Monday afternoon, thankful she finally felt strong enough to come downstairs and join the rest of the family. Everyone, except William and Jon, had gathered in the drawing room to spend time with Dr. and Mrs. Foster before they took the train home to Berkshire.

Andrew walked forward and stood in front of the fireplace, ready to recite the verses he had memorized.

Julia smiled at him. "Go ahead, Andrew."

The boy stood up straight. "The Twenty-Third Psalm, a psalm of David." He took a deep breath. "'The LORD is my shepherd; I shall not want. He maketh me to lie down in green pastures: he leadeth me beside the still waters.'" Andrew glanced toward the ceiling and bit his lip, then relief filled his eyes. "'He restoreth my soul.'"

Kate's gaze drifted to the empty chair next to Dr. Foster, and her spirit sank a little lower. Where was Jon? Why hadn't he checked on her? It didn't make sense.

When he didn't look in on Sunday morning, she thought it must be because the family was preparing to leave for church. But when he didn't come that afternoon, she grew concerned. Was he upset with her about what had happened? He'd warned her about the dangers on the East End, and she had disregarded those warnings and gone off on her own to help Helen.

She considered asking Julia or Penny why he hadn't come to see her, but that would only lead to more questions… She didn't want to admit she missed Jon terribly.

Goodness, what was wrong with her?

She was the one who was uncertain about encouraging Jon. Now he ignored her for one day, and she was flustered by it. Well, it had actually been almost forty-eight hours since she'd seen him…and that was much too long.

Andrew's recitation slowed to silence, and it brought Kate back to the moment.

"'Surely goodness…'" Julia prompted softly.

Andrew nodded and hurried on. "'Surely goodness and mercy shall follow me all the days of my life: and I will dwell in the house of the LORD for ever.'"

"Bravo, Andrew!" Dr. Foster clapped, and everyone joined him.

"Yes, very nicely done," Mrs. Foster added.

Andrew grinned, his face glowing pink beneath his freckles, and he gave a little bow.

Millie sprang up from the settee, jostling Kate in the process. "May I say my verses?"

Kate winced and lifted her hand to her head. Her headache was only a faint throb, but sudden movements made her head swim.

Julia glanced her way. "Are you all right, Kate?"

"Yes, I'm fine." She rubbed her temple.

Dr. Foster regarded her with a concerned look. He took his watch from the pocket of his vest. "We don't have to leave for the station until three. Why don't we take the children for a walk to the park?"

Andrew's eyes lit up. "That's a fine idea."

"Oh yes!" Millie looked up at Julia. "May we please go?"

Julia smiled. "All right. Go up and get your hats, then meet us in the front hall."

Andrew and Millie rushed out of the room, and their feet pounded up the stairs. Louisa excused herself, saying she needed to write some letters.

Dr. Foster approached and looked down at Kate. "Hopefully, a little peace and quiet will allow you to rest."

She sent him a faint smile. "Thank you."

Penny crossed to Kate's side. "Would you like me to stay with you? I wouldn't mind."

"No, it's a beautiful day. Go enjoy the sunshine."

"All right, if you're sure."

"I am."

Julia laid her hand on Kate's shoulder. "Why don't you put your feet up and relax?"

Kate lay back and closed her eyes. Footsteps faded and the room grew quiet. She pulled in a deep breath and tried to quiet her muddled thoughts.

Dr. Foster told her the concussion might make it difficult to remember Saturday's events clearly, and it was true. She recalled carrying Helen's bags down the Pittsfords' front steps, but she had no memory of Charlie Gibbons grabbing her and throwing her down, though Lydia told her that was what happened.

Her first clear memory was waking up in Dr. Pittsford's parlor with Jon hovering over her. His face had been fuzzy and his voice distorted, but she would never forget the look of relief that filled his eyes when she whispered his name.

At least that was what she thought she remembered.

But Jon was a compassionate man. Perhaps he would've responded the same way when any of his patients regained consciousness.

Still…he'd held her hand while Dr. Pittsford stitched her head wound and wiped her tears with his handkerchief. At the time it had seemed wonderfully caring and romantic, but perhaps she was attaching romantic feelings to his actions when that was the farthest thing from Jon's mind.

Was he simply her friend, or had he grown to care for her in a deeper way…the way she cared for him? Surely he knew she couldn't be the first one to speak about her feelings. That had to come from him.

Kate sighed. It was all so confusing. Maybe her head injury was making her imagine the whole thing. If that was the case, she must stop pining for Jon, or she would be headed for heartbreak.

After all, if he had deeper feelings for her, he would make them known. If not…

A painful, hollow feeling tightened Kate's stomach, but it wasn't caused by hunger. At least…not physical hunger.

Someone walked into the drawing room, and Kate opened her eyes.

"Look what just arrived!" Louisa waved two envelopes at Kate.

Kate's brow creased. "What is it?"

"Invitations! One is for a ball at the Taylor-Mumfords' on the twenty-first, and the other is a garden party at the Hildebrants' on the twenty-third."

Kate sat up. "You opened them?"

Louisa averted her eyes. "Well…I didn't want to take a chance they might be upsetting notes about the article in the paper."

Kate pursed her lips. "Really, Aunt Louisa, there's no need to treat me like a china doll. I've had a concussion, but I'm going to be fine."

Louisa handed Kate the invitations. "I called on Sylvia Ralston this morning. It seems the damage from the newspaper article may not be as bad as we'd first feared. In fact, Sylvia says it has stirred up a great deal of sympathy for you."

Kate slid the Taylor-Mumfords' invitation out of the envelope. July twenty-first was almost three weeks away. Would she be well by then? Did she want to spend her last few weeks in London resuming the maddening round of social events? She sighed and looked up at her aunt. "I'm not sure I—"

Nelson stepped through the doorway. "Mr. Edward Wellington is here to see you, miss."

Kate stared at Nelson. She hadn't expected to see Edward, especially not today.

A triumphant smile spread across Louisa's face. "Show him in."

The footman exited, and Edward entered the drawing room a few seconds later, carrying a large bouquet of bright summer flowers.

"Edward." Louisa hurried to greet him. "How kind of you to come, and what beautiful flowers." She turned to Kate. "Isn't it wonderful of Edward to bring you such a lovely bouquet?"

Kate forced a smile, barely able to cover her surprise. "Hello, Edward. How are you?" She laid the invitations on the table.

"I'm well." He stepped forward and presented the flowers to her.

"Thank you." The large, expensive bouquet included lilies. Their powerful fragrance flooded the air and made her head hurt. "Aunt Louisa, could you take these for me?"

"Oh yes, of course. I'll just go and ask someone to put them in water." She smiled at Edward again. "I'm sure you two have things you'd like to discuss." She strolled out, leaving the drawing room door open.

"May I sit down?"

"Oh yes, please." She should've suggested that, but her brain seemed to be processing every thought in slow motion.

He sat in the chair closest to the settee. "I saw the article on Sunday. I've been worried about you. I had to come."

"That's kind of you."

"I would've come yesterday afternoon, but my parents were not convinced it was wise."

Kate studied his face trying to understand his meaning.

"My father initially agreed to the visit, but when my mother heard about my plans, she confronted my father. MaryAnn sided with mother, as she always does. Of course I supported my father, but it didn't end well." Edward sighed. "I'm afraid it caused quite a fuss."

Heat flooded Kate's face. "I'm so sorry." How embarrassing to be the cause of an argument between Edward and his parents.

"But this morning, for some reason, my mother changed her mind and gave me permission, so here I am." He smiled as though he had won a great victory.

Kate looked away, questions stirring in her mind. Was Edward so dependent on his parents that he couldn't pay a call on anyone without their permission?

"So how are you feeling?" He waited, a slow smile forming on his lips. "You look lovely."

"I'm fine, or I will be very soon."

"That's good." His brow creased. "The photograph in the paper was quite disturbing. I thought your injuries might be much worse."

"I have a headache from a concussion, and it's a bit of a bother. I'm not allowed to read or do anything taxing for a few days. The doctor says I must rest my brain."

Edward grinned. "You'll just have to enjoy being a lady of leisure."

"Yes, I suppose so."

He glanced at the invitations lying on the table, and surprise flashed across his expression. "Forgive me, but is that an invitation from the Taylor-Mumfords?"

"Yes, they're hosting a ball on the twenty-first."

"What a stroke of luck. We've been invited as well." He smiled again. "At least now we know we'll be able to see each other that day."

Kate pondered that for a moment, her unease growing.

"I know in my letter I invited you to the cricket match on the seventh, but I'm not sure I'll be able to escort you that day. I'll have to check with my parents."

"What about your sister's engagement party on the fifteenth?"

Edward's face colored. "Oh…yes. I mentioned that too, didn't I?"

"Yes, you did."

"Well, I hoped my parents would send you an invitation, but…"

She looked down. What was she supposed to say to all of this? She wasn't at all sure she wanted to go to Charles and MaryAnn's engagement party…still it was disheartening to know she had been excluded.

"I'm sorry. I can see you're disappointed."

Kate looked up. "No, no. It's all right."

He reached for her hand. "I promise I'll speak to my parents about it. I'm sure when I tell Mother you've been invited to the Taylor-Mumfords', she'll be more open to the idea."

She shook her head. "You don't need to do that."

He tightened his hold on her hand. "Please, Kate, I know it's been difficult to wait for my parents to soften their stance against us, but you must admit it's not entirely their fault."

She stiffened. "Are you saying it's *my* fault?"

He tipped his head. "Well, I'm not sure I would put it that way, but your decision to go to the East End was...disappointing."

Kate's throat burned. "I went there to help a woman who was in great danger."

"I understand, but couldn't you have sent someone else?"

Before she could reply, Jon walked through the doorway. He shot a glance at Edward and Kate. "Forgive me, I didn't mean to interrupt."

Kate slipped her hand from Edward's. "You're not interrupting. Please come in."

Edward frowned, but nodded to Jon. "Foster."

Jon returned a nod, his expression unreadable. "Wellington."

Seconds ticked by. Kate searched Jon's face and struggled to find something to say.

Jon broke the silence. "I was hoping to see my parents before they left for the station."

Kate swallowed. "They've gone to the park with the children."

He studied her and Edward a moment more, then nodded. "Thank you." He turned to go.

"Jon, wait, please," Kate called, her head pounding again.

He looked back, his jaw firm, his eyes unwavering.

"They...should be back soon."

"I'll go look for them." He strode out of the room.

Kate's heart plunged.

TWENTY-THREE

Jon poked at the potatoes on his dinner plate, then laid his fork aside. The words he needed to say had lodged in his throat, and it was impossible to finish the meal. He warned himself not to look at Kate, but this was the last time he would sit across the table from her, and he wanted to have a clear memory to carry with him.

She looked beautiful tonight in an ivory gown with golden threads woven through the lace. Fluttery short sleeves covered her shoulders like a filmy cape. She wore a jeweled comb in her hair, and her diamond earrings and diamond-pendant necklace sparkled in the light from the chandelier.

Pain sliced through him at the thought of leaving and not seeing her every day, but he had no choice. He could not ask her to marry him. The dangers of life on the East End were too great. He would not put her life at risk, nor could he turn his back on his calling.

For Kate's sake and his own, he had to leave.

Lawrence, Nelson, and Patrick stepped forward and cleared away the dishes from the final course. Julia looked around the table and started to rise. "Ladies, shall we pass through?"

"Wait." Jon looked up and met his sister's gaze. "Before you go, I have something I'd like to say."

"All right." Julia sat down again.

He forced his gaze to remain on his sister rather than on Kate. "I want to thank you for your hospitality. It's been a pleasure becoming better acquainted with…everyone."

Kate looked up then, questions flickering in her blue eyes.

"We've been very happy to have you with us." Julia smiled, obviously unaware of what was coming.

"I know you'll be returning to Highland Hall in a few weeks," Jon continued, "so I've spoken to Theo, and we've found a flat near St. George's. I'll be moving there tomorrow."

The color drained from Kate's face.

"Oh Jon, there's no need for you to go yet," Julia said. "Can't you stay with us a little longer? We won't return to Highland until early August."

He hesitated, wishing he could, but that would only make matters more difficult for everyone. "Thank you, but I think this is best."

Julia's gaze darted to William, her eyes urging him to speak.

William placed his napkin on the table. "We'll be sorry to see you go, Jon. I hope you're not leaving because of our conversation yesterday. If I offended you, I apologize."

"No, I'm not offended." Jon met William's gaze. "Everything you said was true."

Kate looked back and forth between Jon and William, confusion in her eyes, but Jon couldn't speak to Kate about it here in front of everyone. Or, for that matter, in private. His heart was too sore, and he might say more than he intended. That would only add to her hurt and confusion.

"I don't think you should go." Andrew looked across the table at Jon. "Who will play draughts with me?"

Jon forced a smile for the boy's sake. "Perhaps you could teach Millie how to play."

Andrew scowled. "That wouldn't be any fun."

Millie stuck out her lip. "I could learn."

"Girls are not good at draughts. Everyone knows that."

"Andrew." Julia sent the boy a warning with her eyes, then shifted her gaze back to Jon. "If you must go, then promise you'll return to have dinner with us as often as you can."

Jon glanced at Kate, then quickly looked away. "Thank you, Julia." But he wouldn't make a promise he didn't intend to keep. After he left Ramsey House tomorrow morning…

He did not plan to return.

● ● ●

Kate paced across her bedroom and stopped at the window to check the street once more. The family's motorcar pulled into the front drive, and the chauffeur hopped out. She heard the front door open downstairs. She watched Jon descend the steps and walk toward the motorcar, carrying a small suitcase. The chauffeur loaded two boxes onto the back and strapped them down.

How could Jon leave without saying a word to her?

Obviously, she'd been wrong to think he had any romantic feelings toward her. Apparently, he didn't even consider their friendship important enough to warrant a good-bye.

Last night after dinner she'd waited for him to join them in the library as he often did. But he'd stayed in his room the rest of the evening. This morning she'd risen early and gone down well before nine, hoping to see him before everyone gathered for Scripture reading and prayer, but he joined them at the last minute and hadn't even looked her way. Afterward, he said he would not be joining them for breakfast and retreated up the stairs without a backward glance.

The whole painful series of events made her sore head pound. Why was he leaving? Was it because he'd seen her holding hands with Edward? Or was he still upset that she'd ignored his advice about the dangers of the East End?

She glanced out the window again. Jon passed his suitcase to the chauffeur. He looked back at the house and lifted his gaze to her window.

Kate's breath caught in her throat.

Their gazes connected and held.

She should step back and pretend she didn't care he was leaving, but she couldn't miss this last chance to see him. She watched him until tears blurred her vision and his image became a swirl of beige and brown against the green of the garden. He turned away and climbed into the backseat of the car. The chauffeur closed Jon's door, then slid in behind the wheel and started the engine.

Kate gripped the windowsill and leaned her forehead against the cool glass.

As if she'd called to him, he looked up at her once more. The sorrow in his expression was clear this time, but he did not lift his hand to wave. The car pulled away, and Jon disappeared from sight as it rounded the corner.

Kate let the curtain fall back in place. Tears slipped down her cheeks, but she didn't wipe them. Jon was gone, out of her life, but she would treasure his memory forever.

● ● ●

Julia slipped her arm through William's and strolled down the lakeside path at Wiltshire Park. Kate and Penny walked several paces in front of them. Andrew and Millie had raced even farther ahead.

"I'm worried about Kate."

William glanced at her. "Why do you say that?"

"She hasn't been herself the past two weeks."

"She has been rather quiet, but I thought that was due to the headaches and her recovery from the concussion."

"It's more than that." Julia looked away, sorry now that she hadn't told William the reason for Kate's sagging spirits and Jon's departure.

William studied her. "What's troubling her?"

"If I tell you, you must promise to weigh your response very carefully."

"Now you *must* tell me."

Julia looked up at him. "I think she's suffering from a broken heart... and so is Jon."

William's steps slowed. "Jon...and Kate?"

"Yes. You didn't see it?"

"I had no idea." He shook his head, looking a bit stunned. "How could a romance develop between them right under my nose without my knowledge?"

Julia smiled. "The clues have been very subtle, so don't take it too hard. Men aren't often in tune to that sort of thing."

"You're right about that. And I've been distracted by the plans for our marriage and David's problems."

"You have had a lot to deal with these last few months."

William looked at her again. "If Jon cares for Kate, why didn't he come and speak to me?"

"I noticed his interest in Kate, but I encouraged him to wait and pray about it before he talked to you or to her."

"And why is that?"

"I was concerned Kate might not be the best match for him spiritually."

William considered that for a moment. "Jon is a very dedicated young man with a strong faith. I would not have said the same about Kate before we came to London, but she has changed a great deal these last few months."

"Yes, I've seen it as well."

"Her attitude and actions have certainly improved. Remember how difficult she was when you first arrived at Highland?"

Julia smiled at the memory, though it had been a trial at the time. "I believe Kate's faith is coming into full bloom, and that's made all the difference." She looked up at William. "If Jon were to come to me today, I would give him very different advice."

William nodded. "And you think they would be happy together?"

"Yes, very happy…though I doubt Louisa would agree."

William's expression hardened. "I put very little stock in Louisa's opinion. Her constant criticism and dramatics have worn my patience thin."

"She has been difficult, though she probably has good intentions."

"I want more than good intentions for Kate."

Julia smiled. "Well said. Kate needs an upstanding young man, with good character and spiritual strength. Those are the qualities that will build a lasting marriage."

William gazed at her, and his expression warmed. "How did I ever convince such a wise woman to accept my proposal?"

Julia laughed softly. "We do make a good team."

"Yes, we do—I'm sure of that." They walked on a few more steps. "So, what shall we do about Jon and Kate?"

"I thought he might come for dinner or at least pay us a visit, but he may not feel welcome."

"You mean because of our conversation the day that article came out in the newspaper?"

"Yes. I think he needs to be reassured that we hold nothing against him."

"I'll write to him."

"Don't say anything about Kate. Not yet."

"Why not?"

"I just think it's best if we wait and give the Lord time to work in both their hearts."

• • •

Kate's shoulders tensed as she walked through the entrance to the Taylor-Mumfords' elaborate mansion. Music drifted from the open double doorway at the end of the hall. She stopped and handed her shawl to a waiting footman, and her aunt did the same.

"Come along, Katherine." Her aunt sauntered down the hallway, trailing after a large group of guests who had entered before them.

Kate followed, though she was not looking forward to making conversation with strangers or dancing with a host of men she did not know. But they had accepted the invitation, and her aunt insisted if she was well enough to go to church, then she would attend tonight's ball.

They stepped in line behind the other guests waiting to be announced, and Kate's thoughts drifted to all that had happened in the last few weeks.

Her symptoms from the concussion had slowly faded, and she could finally resume her normal routine, but William had not changed his mind about allowing her to return to Daystar. Helen remained at Ramsey House, resting in Lydia's room and waiting for the arrival of her baby, but she was growing more anxious and uncomfortable every day. Dr. Pittsford had stopped by to check on her yesterday, and he assured them the baby was fine and would make an appearance any day.

She had not seen Jon since he'd left Ramsey House. She hoped he might write, but he had not. And the pain of missing him had increased with each passing day.

She loved Jon. She was sure of that now, and she was very sorry she had not done more to let him know how she felt before he left.

Her aunt leaned closer. "Now remember, some very important people will be here tonight. You must do all you can to rebuild your reputation."

Kate sighed and looked away. Did it really matter anymore?

"For heaven's sake, stop looking so glum. You could at least pretend you're happy to be here."

"That's a bit difficult when it's the farthest thing from the truth."

"You had better change your attitude, young lady. Men are not attracted to a woman who is somber and moody."

"My attitude reflects how I feel, and nothing you say is going to change that."

Her aunt took her arm and pulled her closer. "Now listen to me, Katherine, I have used every ounce of my influence to help you rejoin society, and I will not allow you to throw it all away simply because you are not in a happy mood. Now stand up straight and greet everyone you meet with a smile."

Heat surged through Kate, and she clenched her jaw. This was not the life she wanted, and her aunt's scorching criticism made her more certain of it. She was tired of pretending to be someone she was not.

They stopped at the entrance to the ballroom, and her aunt turned to the butler waiting at the door. "Lady Louisa Gatewood of Wellsbury and Miss Katherine Ramsey of Highland Hall."

The butler announced them, and they walked into the ballroom. The music had stopped just before they entered, and several guests paused their conversations and looked their way. A ripple of whispers traveled around the room.

Kate's face flamed, but she lifted her chin and returned the bold stares of the guests.

"Smile, Katherine." Louisa forced the strained words past her clenched teeth.

But Kate could not, so she looked away.

A woman wearing a royal-blue gown and beautiful diamond tiara approached. "Lady Gatewood, I'm so glad you could join us this evening."

"Lady Taylor-Mumford, we're so pleased to be here." Louisa turned to Kate with a lift of her eyebrows.

Kate dipped a brief curtsy. "Thank you for inviting us."

"Of course, my dear. When I read how you risked your life to help that poor woman escape from that ruffian, I wanted to do all I could to offer my support." She took Kate's hand. "I was sorry to hear you suffered a concussion. How are you feeling now?" Her words were sweet, but there was a hint of something false in her expression.

"Much better, thank you."

"I'm glad to hear it. Now, I want you to meet some of the other young people who are here this evening." Lady Taylor-Mumford took Kate's arm and guided her away from Louisa.

Kate glanced over her shoulder, feeling a bit confused by the hostess's warm welcome, but Louisa motioned Kate to go ahead.

Lady Taylor-Mumford took Kate a quarter of the way around the room and introduced her to at least a dozen people. As they moved toward the next group of guests, Kate tensed. Edward stood off to the side, speaking to a beautiful young woman with dark-brown hair and a porcelain complexion. As they came closer, the woman looked their way. She appeared to be a few years older than Kate and had exquisite hazel-green eyes.

"Florence, I'd like you to meet Miss Katherine Ramsey." Lady Taylor-Mumford smiled at Kate. "This is Miss Florence Piedmont."

Florence's eyes widened, and her face flushed as she stared at Kate. "Miss Ramsey."

Kate returned the greeting, uncertain why Florence seemed uncomfortable. She didn't think they'd met before, but her name sounded familiar.

Lady Taylor-Mumford looked Kate's way again. "And of course you know Mr. Edward Wellington."

He cast an embarrassed glance at Kate, then looked back at Florence. "Yes. Hello, Edward."

He nodded to her, his face ruddy. "Miss Ramsey."

Sudden clarity flashed through Kate. Florence Piedmont was the woman

Edward had pursued for two years, but his parents disapproved of the match.

"Now that I can leave you with friends, I'll go and see to my other guests." Lady Taylor-Mumford offered a smile that looked anything but genuine and glided away.

Did Lady Taylor-Mumford know about Edward's past with Florence and his present interest in Kate? Whatever her reason for making this introduction, it was quite awkward. Kate smoothed her hand down her skirt. "I'm sorry to interrupt your conversation."

Florence pressed her lips together and sent Edward a pained glance.

"No, we're glad you joined us." But Edward wiped a trickle of perspiration from the side of his forehead.

Kate leaned toward them and lowered her voice. "I truly don't want to push my way in between you."

Tears flooded Florence's eyes, and she blinked several times. "I'm so sorry."

Edward shook his head. "Please, ladies, I am the one who should apologize."

"There's no need." Kate looked toward the other end of the ballroom. The musicians began to play the next waltz. Several couples moved onto the dance floor. She glanced at Edward and Florence again, a wave of sympathy bolstered by courage spurred her on. "Edward, weren't you just about to ask Florence to dance?"

He stared at Kate for a moment, then understanding dawned in his eyes. "Yes, I was."

"Please, go ahead." Kate motioned toward the dance floor.

Florence's face brightened, and hope shone in her eyes. Edward held out his hand. Florence slipped her fingers into his, and they swung away in time to the music. Florence's loving gaze rested on Edward as if he were the only person in the room. Edward's gaze was equally warm.

A bittersweet pang shot through Kate as she watched them. If only Jon were here to take her in his arms for the next dance. She let that dream fade as she watched Florence and Edward circle the dance floor once more.

Resolve stirred within Kate. They obviously loved each other, and she would not stand in the way of them being together. It wouldn't be right.

Someone grasped her sleeve and she turned.

"What are you *doing*?" Aunt Louisa tugged her toward the wall.

Kate stifled a gasp.

"How could you encourage Edward to dance with that woman?"

Kate pulled her arm out of her aunt's grip. "Please stop. I'm sure you don't want to create a scene."

"I will do whatever it takes to make you wake up! That is Florence Piedmont. Edward has had a fixation on her for years, but she is totally unsuitable."

"I know who she is, and I know what she means to Edward."

"Then what are you thinking!"

"I was thinking they are very fond of each other, and they would enjoy dancing together. Is that so hard to understand?"

"You foolish girl! How could you push Edward into her arms?"

"Please, stop lecturing me. I know what I'm doing."

"If that were true, you would have an engagement ring on your finger, and we would be planning your wedding!"

Fire flashed through Kate. "That's *enough*! You will stop this tirade, or I'll leave at once."

"Don't speak to me in that tone!"

Kate leaned toward her aunt. "I want to make myself perfectly clear. If you say one more harsh word, I will summon a cab and go home on my own."

"Katherine Ramsey, you will apologize this instant! I will not put up with this nonsense any longer. You will listen to me and do as I say, or I—"

Kate spun away. The rest of her aunt's comments faded into the music as Kate crossed the ballroom and strode out the door.

TWENTY-FOUR

Kate slowly climbed the main staircase toward her bedroom, relief and regret battling within her. Releasing Edward and confronting her aunt had sealed her fate. She doubted she would receive any more invitations, and even if she did, she had no desire to accept them.

She was done with the season. Tomorrow she would speak to William and Julia, explain what had happened, and ask how soon she could return to Highland.

Just before she reached her bedroom, hurried footsteps pounded down the servants' stairs at the end of the hall. Kate looked up.

Lydia ran toward her. "Miss Katherine! The baby's coming, and Helen is in terrible pain. We have to send for the doctor."

Energy pulsed through Kate, and her mind shifted into action. "Wake Julia. I'll fetch Mrs. Adams. I'm sure between the four of us we can do what's needed for Helen."

"Please hurry, miss!" Lydia turned and ran back up the steps.

Kate opened her bedroom door and tossed her bag and shawl on the bed. There was no time to change. She hurried downstairs and found Mrs. Adams resting in her small parlor next to the servants' hall, with her feet up and damp cloth on her forehead. Kate quickly relayed the news about Helen.

Mrs. Adams plucked the cloth from her forehead and sat up. "I'm afraid I'm not well."

Panic shot through Kate. "What's wrong?"

"I'm not sure. It might be the flu. Whatever it is, I don't want to give it to Helen or the baby."

"No, of course not. I understand. Lydia and Julia are with Helen. I'll go up and see what I can do."

"Birthing a baby is a natural process. Just watch over her. She should be fine."

Kate hurried up the three flights of stairs to the servants' rooms. As she started down the hallway, Helen's pain-filled scream rent the air. A tremor raced down Kate's back.

Jean and Ruth, the two kitchen maids, stood huddled together in the hallway. "Is she going to be all right?" Jean whispered.

"Yes. I'm sure she'll be fine. Please go back to bed and get some rest."

The girls exchanged worried glances, but they turned away and walked across the hall.

Kate paused and tried to focus her thoughts. *Dear God, please give me courage.* She opened Lydia's door and entered. A lantern on the bedside table illuminated the small, simply furnished room. Helen lay on the narrow bed, her eyes closed, face flushed, and her hair a tangled mess. She moaned and tossed her head. Julia stood on one side of the bed, and Lydia on the other.

Lydia looked up at Kate, her eyes wide and anxious. "Is Mrs. Adams coming?"

Kate shook her head. "She's ill."

Concern flashed in Julia's eyes. She rinsed a cloth in water and wiped Helen's face. "There now. Just rest between the contractions as much as you can." She passed the cloth to Lydia and whispered something Kate couldn't hear. Julia met Kate by the door.

"How is she?" Kate whispered.

"Let's step out for a moment." Julia opened the door and slipped into the hallway with Kate. "Lydia says she's been in labor for several hours, but she's no closer to delivering the baby. I think we should send for Dr. Pittsford."

Relief coursed through Kate. "Yes. I'm sure he'll come."

"I'll let William know, then I'll go down and speak to Lawrence. We'll send the chauffeur to Dr. Pittsford's with the message." Julia glanced toward the bedroom door, then at Kate. "Do you have any experience helping a woman in childbirth?"

"No." Kate swallowed, hoping she could find the strength to face this challenge.

"It's not an easy experience for the mother or those watching, even when everything goes well. Are you ready for that?"

Kate straightened, determination flowing through her. "Yes, I am."

Julia touched her arm. "When the baby arrives, it will be a blessed relief. For now, do what you can to calm Lydia and comfort Helen. I'll be back in a few minutes."

"All right."

Julia turned to go, then looked back. "Pray for Helen, and do what you can."

Kate's throat tightened. "I will."

• • •

Jon sank back in the comfortable chair and stared at the quivering flames in the Pittsfords' fireplace. The quiet crackle and hiss soothed his weary mind. He needed some relief after the extra hours he'd put in at the hospital and clinic these last few weeks. He'd filled his schedule, hoping it would ease the ache in his chest, but it had only drained him physically and barely dulled the pain of missing Kate.

Dr. Pittsford lit his pipe and settled back in his chair. Mrs. Pittsford sat beside her husband, her knitting needles clicking in her nimble fingers. Their daughters, Beth and Lucy, had excused themselves to wash the dinner dishes and clean up the kitchen.

"Two more donations came in today. Along with your grandmother's gift, that gives us enough to start the renovations."

Jon looked up and met Dr. Pittsford's gaze, replaying his words and trying to focus on the conversation. "So...we've received enough donations to start the renovations on the children's center?"

Dr. Pittsford nodded.

Mrs. Pittsford lifted her gaze. "Are you all right, Jon? You seem distracted this evening."

"I'm sorry. I just…have some things on my mind."

Dr. Pittsford puffed on his pipe and studied Jon. "What's bothering you?"

Jon hesitated, uncertain if he wanted to explain his personal troubles.

Mrs. Pittsford's knitting needles stilled. "Perhaps if you tell us what's weighing you down, it will lighten your load."

Jon shifted his gaze away. It would be humbling to admit he'd hurt his sister, damaged his relationship with his future brother-in-law, and ruined his chances with Kate. But as he looked back and met the doctor's gaze, he had a feeling that was exactly what he needed to do. "If you don't mind listening, I could use some wisdom."

"Have at it, my boy, and we'll do our best."

Jon poured out the story, explaining William and Julia's reactions to Kate's injuries and his reasons for leaving Ramsey House. After he had finished, he sagged back in the chair, feeling spent.

Dr. Pittsford took his pipe from his mouth. "So you love Kate, but you've decided not to propose… Why is that again?"

"Well…I believe the Lord has called me to Daystar, and William has forbidden Kate to set foot in the East End. I can't just disregard his decision and pursue her against his wishes. He's going to marry my sister in a few weeks."

"That does make it a bit more complicated." Dr. Pittsford drummed his fingers on the arm of his chair. "I understand why William is hesitant to let Kate come here after what happened, but—"

"I'm afraid he's right. I can't marry Kate and bring her to the East End. I'd be constantly worried about her safety. And even if I didn't have those concerns, Kate was raised in the country surrounded by wealth and privilege. I doubt she'd even consider a proposal from a medical student who wants to serve the poor."

Dr. Pittsford frowned. "How do you know? You haven't even asked her."

Mrs. Pittsford laid her needles in her lap. "Are you afraid of what she might say?"

"No, I'm not afraid! I love Kate, and I think she may feel the same way about me. But that doesn't mean we should marry. There's much more to be considered."

Mrs. Pittsford studied him, compassion in her eyes. "That's true, but to find someone you love and who loves you, that's a precious gift."

Jon's throat tightened and burned. "Yes, it is, and that's why I have to think of what's best for Kate, and I'm not convinced that includes a life on the East End."

Dr. Pittsford sat back and gazed into the fire. "When Martha and I considered moving here and opening Daystar, we had some very long discussions. One of our main concerns was our daughters' safety. We didn't want them to be fearful of our neighbors or those we serve at the clinic. But we also had to be realistic about the dangers they might face.

"We prayed together and wrestled it through for a few months," the doctor continued. "Finally the Lord confirmed His will to both of us, and He gave us His peace."

Mrs. Pittsford's gaze softened as she looked at her husband. "We believe we're called here, and we've entrusted ourselves into His care."

Dr. Pittsford pointed his pipe stem at Jon. "That doesn't mean we're careless or we take unnecessary risks. He expects us to be wise and responsible. We must do our part, then trust Him to do the rest."

Mrs. Pittsford looked at Jon, her expression confident and peaceful. "The Lord doesn't promise us we'll never face difficult or dangerous circumstances, but when we do, He promises to walk with us through them. Remember that, Jon."

He pondered Mrs. Pittsford's words, letting them sink in deep. They rang true and reminded him of comments his parents had made about their decision to serve in India. Could he trust God like that, not only with his own life, but also with Kate's?

Dr. Pittsford studied Jon. "Your concern for Kate's safety—that's the main reason you haven't proposed?"

"That, and the fact that she's almost engaged to a man named Edward Wellington. He's the oldest son of a wealthy earl with a large country estate."

Mrs. Pittsford tipped her head. "What does Kate think about him?"

"I don't know. I've hardly seen them together, but her aunt says the engagement is going to be announced as soon as the families agree on the details of the marriage settlement."

The doctor's expression lightened. "So she's not officially engaged?"

Jon shook his head. "Not yet."

"Well then, don't you think she's worth fighting for?"

"Yes, of course…but I'm not sure William would allow it, or if Kate even wants to marry me."

Dr. Pittsford grinned. "Don't you think it's time you found out?"

A knock sounded at the front door.

Mrs. Pittsford glanced at her husband. "Goodness, I wonder who that could be at this hour."

Dr. Pittsford rose from his chair, crossed to the door, and pulled it open.

James Hardy, the Ramseys' chauffeur, touched his cap. "Good evening, Doctor. I have an urgent message from Miss Foster." He handed the note to the doctor.

The doctor invited Hardy in and read the note. He looked up. "Helen is in labor. Julia is concerned she's not progressing as she should. She wants me to come."

Mrs. Pittsford rose from her chair. "Would you like me to go with you?"

"No, my dear, you've had a long day. Why don't you stay here with the girls?" He turned to Jon. "Would you like to come along?"

Jon stood. "Yes sir."

"All right, then." The doctor took his bag and hat from the bench by the door.

Jon followed him out, his thoughts rushing ahead to Ramsey House. Surely with Dr. Pittsford's skill and experience they could help Helen bring her baby safely into the world…and, Lord willing, he might even see Kate.

That thought spurred him on, and he hurried after the doctor.

● ● ●

Kate poured water into the bowl on the nightstand next to Helen's bed and glanced at the small clock. Eleven fifteen. Where was Dr. Pittsford? Surely Hardy had delivered the message by now.

Helen's pitiful cries had grown weaker, and Julia's tense actions conveyed her growing concern. Lydia scurried from one task to the next, trying to find some way to comfort her sister.

Kate approached Julia. "Shall I go down and get some more water?"

Before Julia could answer, the door opened. Dr. Pittsford strode in, with Jon close behind him.

Relief poured through Kate. "Thank goodness you've come."

Jon shot a quick glance her way, then he followed the doctor to Helen's beside. Julia explained Helen's condition and what they'd done for her.

The doctor listened carefully as he observed Helen. He took out his watch and lifted Helen's hand to check her pulse. "Ladies, I'd like to examine Helen. Would you step out for a moment please?"

Julia guided Lydia toward the door. Kate followed them, but before she crossed the threshold, she glanced back at Jon.

He looked up and met her gaze. Affection flowed from his eyes, and her throat tightened. She returned a look she hoped he could read as easily, then she slipped out the door and pulled it closed.

Julia laid her hand on Kate's arm. "I want to give William an update."

Kate nodded. "We'll be fine. Go ahead."

Julia hurried off down the hall. Beyond the closed bedroom door, Helen issued a pitiful, moaning cry.

Lydia shook her head. "I don't understand it. Our mother had seven babies, and she never had trouble like this."

Kate clasped her hands and focused her thoughts. "Dr. Pittsford and Jon will know what to do."

"But she's so weak." Lydia's eyes flooded. "I'm so afraid for her, miss."

A tremor passed through Kate, and she reached for Lydia's hand. "Let's pray for Helen."

"Yes." A flicker of hope lit Lydia's expression. She tightened her grip and lowered her head.

Kate closed her eyes tight. Fearful thoughts rushed in, threatening to steal her words, but she pushed them away. "Dear God, please take care of Helen and help her deliver her baby. Be with the doctors, and show them exactly what to do. Help us trust You to take care of everything. Thank You for hearing our prayer. In Jesus's name. Amen."

"Amen," Lydia whispered.

Kate looked up, then blinked in surprise. Jon stood beside her. She hadn't heard him join them, but she could tell from the look in his eyes that her prayer had touched him in a special way.

"Thank you," he said softly.

Lydia turned to Jon. "How's Helen?"

His expression grew sober. "Dr. Pittsford wants to take her to St. George's. The baby is breech. Helen may need surgery."

Lydia bit her lip and glanced at Kate.

"I'm sure the doctor knows what's best. What can we do to help?"

Before Jon could answer, William and Julia hurried down the hall toward them. Jon explained the situation, and within minutes, Dr. Pittsford, Jon, and the two footmen carefully carried Helen down the main staircase on a stretcher they had made from a sturdy blanket. The men eased Helen into the backseat of the waiting motorcar.

Dr. Pittsford turned to William. "Jon and I should go with Helen. Perhaps the chauffeur could return and bring Lydia after?"

"Yes, of course." William gave instructions to Hardy. The chauffeur touched his cap. Dr. Pittsford checked on Helen once more.

Kate looked up at William. "I'd like to go with Lydia when Hardy returns."

William hesitated. "I'm not sure that's wise."

Julia laid her hand on William's arm. "I could go along as well. I'm sure we'd be a comfort to Lydia."

His expression eased. "All right."

Kate's gaze followed Jon as he circled the motorcar. He looked back at her one last time before he climbed in next to Dr. Pittsford. She lifted her hand, and the motorcar sped off into the night.

But unlike the last time she'd watched a car carry him way, Kate's heart overflowed with hope.

• • •

Kate glanced up at the clock on the waiting room wall and leaned back in the hard chair. They'd been here almost two hours, but still no news of Helen and the baby.

Lydia sat beside Kate, staring toward the dark windows. Julia walked across the room and picked up a newspaper sitting on an end table. Two anxious, expectant fathers waited in chairs at the opposite side of the room.

Lydia fiddled with a loose thread on the sleeve of her sweater. "Why is it taking so long?"

Kate looked her way. "I'm sure we'll hear something soon."

"But isn't there someone who could tell us something?"

Julia laid the newspaper aside. "I suppose I could go and see if—"

The door swung open, and Jon walked in wearing a surgical gown over his clothes.

Kate held her breath.

A smile broke over Jon's face. "Helen delivered a beautiful girl. They're both going to be fine."

"Oh, thank heaven!" Lydia lifted her hand and covered her mouth.

Kate's throat felt so clogged she couldn't speak.

Jon approached and lowered his voice. "She didn't have to have surgery. Dr. Pittsford was able to turn the baby."

"That's remarkable." Julia's gaze fastened on Jon. "She seemed too weak to manage the delivery."

He nodded. "I'd say it's a miracle."

"And the baby is all right?" Lydia's voice trembled slightly.

Jon smiled again. "Yes, she weighs six pounds, twelve ounces, and has a very strong cry. She looks perfect in every way."

Lydia stood and embraced Julia.

Kate blinked away her tears and looked up at Jon.

He sat down beside her, weary lines creasing his forehead. "I'm glad you were here, Kate. I know it meant a lot to Lydia."

"I'm so very thankful there's a happy outcome."

"I meant what I said about it being a miracle." He looked into her eyes. "I believe God heard your prayer for Helen and the baby."

A wave of awe washed over Kate. "You really think so?"

Warmth and sincerity flowed from his eyes. "Yes, and I'm very grateful for those prayers…and for you."

Joy flooded her heart. "As I am for you," she whispered.

Jon stilled, a look of awe filling his eyes. Then a smile overtook his mouth.

A wave of relief surged through Kate. Whatever had caused their separation was no longer important. The gap between them had been bridged. A new connection drew them closer…and Kate couldn't be more thrilled.

TWENTY-FIVE

Just before sunrise Kate yawned and climbed the main stairs at Ramsey House. Her shoulders ached, and a headache throbbed at the base of her neck, but she was very glad she'd stayed at the hospital long enough to see Helen and the baby. Jon was right. Little Emily was precious and perfect in every way. With that happy thought in mind, Kate climbed into bed and drifted off to sleep.

She awoke a few hours later in the middle of a vivid dream. She lay still, trying to recapture the poignant scene before it faded. Jon had arrived at the front door of Ramsey House carrying a newborn baby and bringing several children with him. She couldn't see all their faces, but the first three looked like Rose, Susan, and Jack, the children they'd met on the East End and treated at Daystar. She had been surprised to see them, but she welcomed them all inside.

The dream seemed so real that Kate had a hard time dismissing it from her mind. It was probably the result of her conversation with Jon at the hospital and the powerful emotions she'd felt as she waited for Helen to deliver her baby. Maybe it was a combination of everything she'd experienced in the last few weeks.

Rather than ringing for Lydia's help, she chose to wear a simple skirt and blouse, and then tied back her hair. The clock in the entrance hall struck eleven as she came downstairs and entered the library. William sat at his desk, and Julia sat beside him, reading a book.

"May I go see Helen at the hospital this afternoon?"

William turned and looked her way. "Good morning, Kate. How are you today?" He raised his eyebrows, reminding her of her manners.

"I'm sorry. Good morning. I hope you're both well."

Julia laid aside her book. "I'm a bit tired, but very happy we were able to help Helen."

Kate smiled. "It was wonderful, wasn't it?"

William's serious expression softened into a slight smile. "Yes, I understand we have much to be grateful for today."

Kate nodded. "Would it be all right if Hardy drives Lydia and me to St. George's at three o'clock? That's when visiting hours begin."

William glanced at Julia. "I suppose Hardy could take them, but David and Dorothea are coming for tea at four."

Julia pondered that for a moment. "I don't think Kate needs to be here for their visit. In fact, it might be best if it was just the four of us."

"Yes." William turned back to Kate. "I have some news regarding David. He has proposed to Dorothea, and she has accepted. They're planning a private ceremony in a few weeks. They're coming today to discuss their plans for selling Ramsey Imports and their London properties in preparation for their move to New York."

"They're going to America?"

"Yes. They want to make a fresh start, and they feel it would be easier in the States than here. I tend to agree, although it will put a great distance between us."

Lawrence stepped through the library doorway. "Mr. Edward Wellington is here to see Miss Katherine."

Kate swung around. "What?"

"Mr. Edward Wellington is waiting in the entrance hall. Shall I show him in?"

What on earth was Edward doing here? Whatever the reason, she didn't want to prolong his visit by inviting him in. "No, I'll come out." Kate strode into the entrance hall, questions thrumming through her head.

Edward waited there, his hat in his hand. "Good morning, Kate."

She returned his greeting. "I…wasn't expecting you."

He glanced at Lawrence, who stood by the library door. "May I speak to you in private?"

She glanced around, uncertain where they might go.

"Perhaps we could step outside, into the garden." He motioned toward the front door.

Goose bumps rose on Kate's arms. "All right."

Lawrence opened the door for them. They walked outside and down the steps.

Edward led the way into the small rose garden to the left of the front walk. He continued down the path and stepped into the shade under the trees, then turned to face her. "First, I want to apologize for the uncomfortable situation at the ball last night."

"Oh, there's no need." With all that had happened during the night, the ball seemed ages ago.

"Yes, there is a need. Lady Taylor-Mumford is my mother's friend, and I believe she invited you and Miss Piedmont, hoping it would create a… confrontation."

Kate stared at Edward. What did Lady Taylor-Mumford hope to gain from such an act? Did Edward's mother know about it? Was she the one behind it?

"I understand you had a disagreement with your aunt. I could see you were upset when you left. I hope I was not the cause."

"No, please don't worry about it. My aunt tends to be critical and controlling, and it's only gotten worse since we've come to London. Last night I finally told her I'd had enough."

"Well, I'm glad you're not upset with me."

"Actually I'm grateful. Last night's events helped me clarify some important things in my mind."

He nodded, looking pleased. "Then I have some good news for you— at least I hope you'll consider it good news."

"What do you mean?"

"My parents met with your uncle—"

"My uncle? You mean Lord Gatewood?"

"Yes, he and your aunt called on my parents yesterday, and they came to an agreement about the terms of our marriage settlement."

Kate's mouth dropped open. "Our *marriage* settlement?"

"Yes…you weren't aware of their visit?"

"No. I was not." Irritation pulsed through her. How could they make such an important visit without consulting her?

"I think you'll find the terms very agreeable. And now that nothing stands in our way, I want to ask you to become my wife."

Kate stared at him, stunned by his words. How could he propose to her now, after everything that had happened? How could he imagine she would want to marry him when he was in love with someone else? "Edward…I'm sorry, but I can't marry you."

His confident expression melted away. "But…we have so much in common, and your family is obviously in favor of it."

"Perhaps, but you love Florence Piedmont. Anyone who came within a mile of you last night could see that."

His face flushed, and he looked away. "It's true I'm very fond of Florence, but there's no future for us. My parents won't allow us to marry."

"And why is that?"

"They believe she is…unsuitable."

"Do you agree?"

"No, Florence is a wonderful woman with many fine qualities, but—"

"Then why don't you marry her?"

He pulled back. "I can't go against my parents' wishes… They would cut off my income."

"Couldn't you take up an occupation so you can support a wife and family?"

He stared at her, clearly shocked by the suggestion. "But I'm a gentleman."

"Surely, with all your schooling and connections, you could find a position that would enable you to provide for yourself and Florence."

"So you think I should just give up everything—the inheritance, title, and estate—to marry for love?"

"Yes! That's exactly what I think. If you love Florence and she is a worthy young woman who loves you, then you should make any sacrifice that's needed."

He shook his head, confusion clouding his eyes. "So you're saying you won't marry me?"

She released an exasperated breath. "I can't, Edward. It wouldn't be right. Neither of us would be happy."

"But you would please your family, and someday you would share everything that's going to be mine."

Within a second the decision was made. "When I first came to London, that was what I wanted, but I've changed. Now I know I was meant to lead a different kind of life." Jon's image rose in her mind, along with the hope that she might share that life with him, but she had no guarantee. He had not made her any promises.

But her course was set. With or without Jon, she would find a way to build a meaningful life with less focus on meeting society's expectations and more on love and service to God and others.

Edward took her hand. "Are you sure, Kate?"

"Yes, I'm positive."

He shook his head, but admiration flowed from his eyes. "You know your own mind, Kate, and you're honest to a fault…but the man who captures your heart will win a fine prize."

Sisterly affection warmed her heart as she looked at him. "So, will you take my advice and look for a way to support yourself and marry Florence?"

Doubt shadowed his eyes, but he held tightly to her hand, as though gaining strength from her. "I will consider it."

She was about to tell him good-bye, when a movement caught her attention and she turned.

• • •

Jon crossed the street toward Ramsey House, all the while rehearsing what he would say to William, then hopefully to Kate. He lifted the latch on the front gate and looked across the garden.

Kate and Edward stood facing each other, their hands clasped.

Pain shot through him, and his hand froze on the gate latch.

He couldn't see Kate's face, but strong emotion filled Edward's face. As if Kate sensed his presence, she turned. Her gaze locked with his, and some undefined emotion flashed in her eyes.

Jon stepped back and swung away.

What a fool he was! How many times did he have to see them together to realize Kate loved Edward Wellington? The engagement would be announced before the end of the season, and their wedding would be planned to follow Julia and William's.

Last night at the hospital, he'd felt certain he'd seen affection in her eyes. But it must only have been relief and gratitude for the way he had helped Helen. He should never have mistaken it for love or believed Kate would give up all she had hoped and dreamed of for so long to marry him.

He set off down the street, not sure where he was going. It didn't matter, as long as it was far away from Kate.

"Jon, wait!" Kate's voice rang out behind him.

He clenched his jaw and kept walking. He did not want to face her right now. Heaven knew what he might say if he did.

"Please, Jon, I must speak to you!"

He could hear her footsteps, running to catch up with him. He stifled a groan. Should he tell her the truth or pretend he didn't care? He shook his head, disgusted with himself. She might not love him, but he still loved her, and she shouldn't have to chase him down the street to speak to him. He steeled himself and turned to face her.

She ran the last few steps. Her cheeks were flushed and sunlight glinted on the golden strands in her hair. She looked more beautiful than ever, and that only made the pain cut deeper.

"Where are you going?" She lifted her hand to her chest as she tried to catch her breath.

He glanced back toward the house. "I'm sorry to intrude on your time with Edward." He had a difficult time even speaking the man's name.

"You're not intruding. We're finished with our conversation." She glanced back at the house, then looked at Jon again. "Is everything all right?"

He frowned and glanced away. Nothing was all right, and it wouldn't be for a very long time, but he couldn't say that.

"I mean with Helen and the baby." She looked up at him, her blue-eyed gaze wide and achingly sweet. "I thought you might've come to bring us some news from the hospital."

"The hospital? No. I haven't been back there yet."

She studied his face. "Oh…then why did you come?"

He swallowed, knowing he ought to at least be honest. He owed her that much. "I came to see you, Kate."

Her expression brightened as though the sun had risen and shone on her face. "Truly? You came to see me?"

He stared at her, trying to process her response. Was it possible? Did he hold a special place in her heart after all? A wave of hope flooded through him. "Yes, I came because last night at the hospital I sensed that you might care for me as I care for you. And if that's true, then I ought to…"

She sent him such a loving look that everything he wanted to say faded from his mind. Her smile warmed, inviting him closer. "You ought to…?"

A rush of energy surged through him. "I ought to make my feelings plain and see if there was any possibility you feel the same."

The hopeful light in her eyes glowed brighter, filling him with courage.

He reached out and took both her hands in his. "I love you, Kate, so very much. I have from the first day I came to Ramsey House. And every experience we've shared has made me more certain of it. I can't imagine living my life without you."

"Oh Jon." Her eyes glistened as she looked up at him. "I love you too."

His heart pounded out a joyful beat, and he tightened his hold on her hands. "Kate Ramsey, will you do me the honor of becoming my wife?"

Her eyes widened, and a smile burst across her face. "Yes! Oh yes!" She flung her arms around his neck.

He wrapped her in a tight embrace, thanks and praise rising from deep

within. She loved him. What an unbelievable, amazing gift. He closed his
eyes, holding her close and soaking in the joy of the moment.

• • •

With her heart overflowing, Kate took Jon's hand, and they hurried back to
the house to see William and Julia. They walked into the library together,
and Jon asked William if they could talk privately. William agreed, and
Julia and Kate stepped out into the entrance hall, leaving the men alone.

Julia closed the door and turned to Kate. "What's that about?"

Kate grasped Julia's hand. "Jon has proposed!"

Julia gasped, and a happy smile flooded her face. "Oh, Kate, that's
wonderful!"

"Do you think William will give his consent?"

Julia nodded. "We've already discussed it."

Surprise and wonder flooded Kate. "I've admired Jon since we first met,
but I didn't realize how much he meant to me until he left, and then I
thought it was too late."

"Well, I'm very glad he had the good sense to come back and speak to
you."

Kate smiled. "Yes, so am I."

Nelson walked down the main staircase carrying two large suitcases.
Louisa followed him, dressed in a navy-blue traveling suit and a large hat
covered with ostrich feathers and netting. When she saw Kate and Julia, she
stopped and narrowed her eyes. "I've done all I can for Katherine this season. I've decided to return to Berkshire."

Surprise rippled through Kate. Was her aunt leaving because of their
confrontation at the ball last night, or was it because she believed she and
her uncle had finalized the arrangements for Kate's engagement to Edward?
Either way, Kate needed to make things clear.

Louisa stepped down into the entrance hall.

Kate met her there. "Before you go, I have something to say."

Louisa pursed her lips and tugged on her gloves. "If you are going to apologize and ask me to stay in London, it won't do any good. I've made up my mind."

"I understand, but that's not what I was going to say."

"Well then, what is it?"

"Jon has proposed, and I have accepted." She shouldn't have felt so gleeful to see Louisa's shocked expression, but she couldn't help herself.

"You *can't* marry that man! He has no place in society, no future."

"Jon loves me. He has admirable character, excellent training, and wonderful potential. And I am going to marry him."

"But we've spoken to Edward's family. Everything is arranged."

Kate shook her head. "Edward proposed this morning, but I turned him down. I'm going to marry Jon."

"But that's ridiculous! What kind of life can he offer you?"

"Exactly the kind of life I want—one filled with love and meaningful service to God and others."

Julia clasped her hands in front of her mouth, barely able to hide her smile.

William strode into the entrance hall, with Jon close behind. "Is there a problem?"

Louisa glared at William. "You have mishandled your responsibility toward Katherine all season, and now look what's happened! She wants to marry this…man who has no connections and no future."

A muscle jumped in William's jaw. "Louisa, that's quite enough."

Her aunt's eyes bulged. "Yes, for once we agree! I've had more than enough. I'm leaving."

William motioned toward the front door. "I think that would be best."

"Very well!" Louisa looked at each one, and when no one stopped her, she huffed and flounced out the front door.

The door swung closed, and Julia lowered her hands to her chest. "Thank goodness, I thought she would never go."

William crossed to stand with Julia. "Perhaps we'll finally have some peace in this house."

Jon shifted his gaze to Kate, and a smile tugged at the corner of his mouth.

She pressed her lips together, but soon her laughter bubbled up and overflowed, and Jon joined her. After she caught her breath, she turned to William. "I'm sorry."

"It's all right. I'm glad you haven't let your aunt spoil your happy day."

Jon took Kate's hand, his eyes bright. "Nothing could ruin our happiness today, not even Lady Gatewood."

Kate tightened her hold on Jon's hand. He was right. Louisa's departure would allow them to enjoy these last few weeks in London.

William motioned toward the library. "I believe we have a very important conversation to finish."

They all returned to the library. Kate and Jon sat together, across from William and Julia.

William looked at Kate. "Jon has asked for your hand, and I've given him my consent. Julia and I believe you are well matched, and we look forward to helping you prepare for marriage, but I would ask two things." He paused and sent them both a serious look. "I'd like Jon to finish his medical training before the wedding, and I'd like to be sure you have a safe and proper place to live."

That meant she and Jon would have to spend at least four months apart, but it wouldn't seem so long once they set a wedding date and could start making plans. Finding a suitable place to live would be a greater challenge, but she was eager to start a new life with Jon, no matter where they lived.

Jon looked her way, and she nodded. He faced William again. "We're grateful for your counsel and ready to do as you've ask."

William smiled and nodded. "Very well, then I give you my blessing."

• • •

During those next few weeks, Kate felt as though she floated on a cloud of happiness. She and Jon had found a way to see each other almost every day. Jon became a regular dinner guest at Ramsey House, and after a serious discussion, William relaxed his rule and allowed Kate to return to Daystar.

The Pittsfords invited them for dinner one evening, and Kate enjoyed discussing plans for the children's center. Knowing she would partner with Jon to see the project completed brought her great joy.

Two days before the family was scheduled to return to Highland, Jon and Kate enjoyed a leisurely stroll through Wiltshire Park. It was a perfect afternoon, with warm sunshine and fresh, clear skies.

When they returned to the house, Lawrence greeted them at the front door. "Sir William asked that you join him in the drawing room."

"Thank you, Lawrence." Kate sent Jon a questioning glance, and he returned the same. They crossed the entrance hall and entered the drawing room. William stood by the fireplace, and Julia sat in a chair nearby.

Kate searched their faces. "You wanted to see us?"

"Yes, please sit down." William motioned to the settee. "We have something important to discuss."

Kate took a seat, and Jon sat next to her.

"My brother, David, and Dorothea came for a visit today and gave us a wedding gift."

Julia's smile hinted at some secret. "It's quite a surprising gift...and as William and I talked about it, we realized it needs to be put to good use."

Kate looked back and forth between them. "What is it?"

William's expression brightened. "David has given us his half interest in this house. And now that it's ours to do with as we please, we would like to give it to you and Jon."

Kate's mouth dropped open. "You want to give us this house?"

"Yes, we do."

Kate quickly tempered her response and looked at Jon. What did he think? Would he want to live in a large house like this?

Jon's brow creased. "That's kind of you, but..."

William held up his hand. "I understand your hesitation, and I want to assure you Julia and I will continue covering the expenses until your inheritance becomes available."

Jon's expression eased. "That's very generous, but with just the two of us, I'm not sure it would be wise to take on the responsibility for such a large home."

Kate released a deep breath. Of course, Jon was right. She must be sensible. As much as she would enjoy living here, it might not be the best home for them after they married.

Julia's eyes twinkled. "We thought you might feel that way, so we had another idea to propose." She glanced at Jon and Kate. "What if you used the house in connection with your ministry?"

Kate's hope rose, and she looked at Jon.

Interest sparked in his eyes. "What were you thinking?"

"Perhaps you could extend the work of Daystar and the children's center by opening a home for orphaned and abandoned children."

The vivid dream that had awakened Kate the morning Jon proposed flashed through her mind. Had God given her that dream to encourage her to consider this new idea?

Jon's expression brightened, and he turned toward Kate. "It sounds intriguing. What do you think?"

Her smile spread wider. "It's a wonderful idea."

"We'd need to find some others to help us, but we have time to make those plans."

Julia nodded. "I wondered if Helen might want to stay on and help you care for the children, and perhaps Lydia would want to work with you as well."

"That's an excellent suggestion." Kate couldn't wait to ask them to consider staying on at Ramsey House…or would they call it the Daystar Children's Home?

Jon rose and extended his hand to William. "Thank you."

"You're welcome." William shook Jon's hand.

Kate stood. "Yes, we're very grateful." She embraced William and then Julia.

Jon took Kate's hand again, confidence and expectation flowing from his hand to hers. Her heart felt so full it nearly burst with joy. Her prayer had been answered. The path toward her future was clear now, and the man she loved would walk with her on that journey. They would fill this house with love, faith, and family, and the Lord's blessing would cover them all.

TWENTY-SIX

On a frosty morning, three days before Christmas, feathery snow-flakes floated down, dusting the countryside around Highland Hall. Kate gazed out the side window of the motorcar as they traveled into the village of Fulton, along narrow streets, and past shops and lampposts decorated with evergreen boughs and holly.

"Isn't the snow pretty?" Penny looked out the opposite window. "It's like God is sending down His blessing on your wedding day."

"Yes, it's beautiful." Kate smiled, her heart feeling as light as one of those dancing snowflakes. Today she and Jon would take their vows before family and friends and begin their new life together. And though they had spent five months planning for this day, it didn't quite seem real.

William looked over his shoulder from the front seat. "I'm just glad the snow didn't start earlier. We wouldn't want it to keep anyone away from the ceremony."

"I'm sure it won't." Penny smiled at Kate. "I'm so excited. I can't wait to see everyone." Kate guessed she was thinking especially of Theo Anderson, who would stand with Jon as his best man.

Kate gazed out the window again, happy memories and hopeful dreams filling her heart. They had kept their promise to William. Jon had finished his training at St. George's, and there were now two Dr. Fosters in the family. His parents had been so proud when he received his medical degree, and they were thrilled with Jon and Kate's plans to open the Daystar Children's Home.

The motorcar pulled up to the front of Saint John's Church. Hardy opened William's door, and then Penny and Kate's. Her sister climbed out first and helped Kate lift her train off the snowy walkway. She felt like a princess in her white silk gown, decorated with pearl beading and Belgian lace. They passed under the stone archway, then stepped inside. Soft organ music greeted them, along with the scent of lemon oil and fresh-cut flowers.

Julia met Kate in the narthex and took her hand. She had come in the other car with the children, Sarah, and Clark. "You look lovely, Kate." Tears shimmered in her eyes as she leaned in and kissed Kate's cheek. "God bless you," she whispered, then she slipped away and entered the side door to take her place in the family's pew up front.

Sarah and Clark approached, carrying two bouquets. Sarah handed one to Penny, and Clark offered the other to Kate.

"Thank you, so much. They're beautiful." Kate knew the red and white roses, ferns, and ivy had been grown in Highland's greenhouse and carefully tended by Clark himself.

"We're very happy for you, Kate." Sarah kissed Kate's cheek. "We wish you and Jon all the best." Kate thanked them. Sarah took Clark's arm, and they entered the sanctuary.

Andrew shifted his weight from one foot to the other and looked up at William. "Is it almost time, Papa?"

William rested his hand on Andrew's shoulder. "Yes, we'll be going in soon."

Millie stood beside Andrew, wearing a white dress with a red sash that matched Penny's. She grinned up at Kate and then took her place next to Penny.

Mrs. Fields, the minister's wife, touched Kate's arm. "Are you ready, my dear?"

Kate's stomach fluttered, and she glanced at William. "Yes, we are."

William offered her his arm, along with a misty smile.

Mrs. Fields opened the center door, and a happy shiver of anticipation traveled through Kate. Friends, family, and Highland staff filled the pews. Jon stood up front, facing the altar with Theo at his side. The organ music changed to Wagner's Bridal Chorus, and the guests rose to their feet.

Kate tightened her hold on William's arm, and they started down the aisle. Penny, Millie, and Andrew followed, helping Kate with her train.

Jon turned and faced Kate. Surprise and delight filled his eyes as he gazed at her. He looked wonderfully handsome, dressed in his morning coat with a white rose pinned to his lapel. Theo stood next to him, dressed in a similar fashion.

Kate fixed her eyes on Jon, and everyone else seemed to fade from view. She met him at the altar, and as he took her hand, William stepped away. Relief flowed through Kate. With Jon at her side, she could catch her breath and enjoy the ceremony.

Hymns, Scripture, and sacred prayers and promises were woven together over the next hour. Jon placed the ring on her finger, his voice husky as he repeated his vows. Kate's hand shook slightly as she gave Jon his ring and repeated the promises that would forever change her life.

Reverend Fields lifted his hand and prayed a final blessing over them. Joyful organ music filled the sanctuary, and they followed Reverend Fields into the vestry to sign the wedding documents, with Penny and Theo as their witnesses.

"It's official." The reverend looked up. "You're now Mr. and Mrs. Jonathan Foster."

"Congratulations!" Theo pumped Jon's hand and grinned at Kate.

"Thank you, Theo." The men clapped each other on the shoulder, looking relieved.

Penny kissed Kate's cheek. "I wish you every happiness." She handed Kate her bridal bouquet.

Happy tears sprang to Kate's eyes. "Thank you, Penny. I'm so glad you're here with me today."

Then Jon took her hand again. They walked back into the sanctuary and started up the aisle together, the guests smiling as they passed.

When they reached the narthex, Mrs. Fields closed the main door and turned to them with twinkling eyes. "Would you like a moment alone before the guests come flooding back?"

Jon tightened his hold on Kate's hand. "Yes, thank you." He led Kate to the corner by the arched window. The snow had stopped, and sunshine broke through the clouds.

He looked down at her with a tender smile. "Well, Mrs. Foster, we've made our promises and signed our names. There's no turning back now."

"I wouldn't want to." She felt a bit breathless as she met his gaze. "You've made me the happiest girl in the world today."

His smile warmed, and he drew her closer. "Is that right?

"Yes," she whispered. "So very happy."

He leaned down and brushed his lips softly over hers. Her eyes drifted closed, and her heart seemed to beat with his as they shared their first tender kiss as man and wife.

"The guests are coming," Mrs. Fields called.

Jon reluctantly released her, and Kate stepped back. His loving look told her this was just the beginning of all they would enjoy together in the days to come. She clasped his hand, and they took their places by the open front door.

The guests poured out of the sanctuary, and a chorus of "Congratulations" and "Best wishes" filled the air around them. From the church tower, bells rang out, adding their joyful song to the celebration.

Kate lifted her face to the sunshine streaming down from an opening in the clouds, and her heart overflowed with thankfulness. How blessed they were to have family and friends who loved them and who shared their happiness today. In a few weeks she and Jon would open the Daystar Children's Home and begin investing in the lives of needy children. She knew the road ahead might not be easy, but with God's help and guidance, she was confident they would build meaningful lives for themselves and the children…and no title, estate, or life of privilege could ever compare to the future she and Jon would share.

READERS GUIDE

1. Before Kate came to London for the season, she and her aunt created a list of qualifications for Kate's future husband. She hoped for a proposal from a man who was from a wealthy family and in line to inherit a title and estate. How do her views change over the course of the story? What do you think are the most important qualities in a mate?

2. Lady Louisa Gatewood wanted Kate to make a good match and be assured of a place in London society. Why was she so intent on this? What did you think of her methods of achieving this goal? What role do friends and family take today in helping someone move toward marriage?

3. Kate and Julia's relationship has changed a great deal since they first met each other. How did those changes happen, and what are the results of those changes for them? Have you ever struggled in a relationship and seen it change for the better?

4. Jon is torn about where he should practice when he finishes his medical training. Why does he struggle with this decision? What factors were important to Jon as he made the decision? What do you think of his choice?

5. Dr. Pittsford decided to move his family to the East End, which is a dangerous area known for poverty and crime. Why did he do this? How do you think it impacted his family and his ministry? Have you ever been involved in an inner-city ministry, and how did it impact you?

6. William struggled to have a good relationship with his brother, David. When David is called in for questioning and then arrested, how does William show he is committed to helping him? What were the results of those efforts? Have you ever had a difficult

relationship with a sibling or other family member, and what has helped you draw closer to them?

7. Edward Wellington seems sincere in his pursuit of Kate, but he is strongly influenced by his parents. What do you think of Edward? What are his good points? What are his weaknesses?

8. Kate is very inspired by Catherine Bramwell-Booth's message about helping those in need balanced with clearly presenting of the gospel. Do you know of any ministries today that have a similar emphasis?

9. Helen was afraid to tell her parents she was pregnant, so she ran away with Charlie. Her situation went from bad to worse as she spent more time with Charlie. How was she able to find the courage to get the help she needed for herself and her baby? Discuss what you would do if you were called upon to help someone in a similar crisis.

10. Jon and Kate's desire to help orphaned and abandoned children leads them to open the Daystar Children's Center and the Daystar Children's Home. Do you think they will do well in this type of ministry? What qualities do you think they will need to be successful in helping the children?

ACKNOWLEDGMENTS

I am very grateful for all those who gave their support and encouragement and provided information in the process of writing this book. Without your help it would never make it into readers' hands!

I'd like to say thank you to:

- My husband Scott, who provides great feedback and constant encouragement, and who never seems to tire of listening to me talk about my characters and their dilemmas. Your love and support allows me to follow my dreams and write the books of my heart.

- Cathy Gohlke, fellow author and friend, who helped me brainstorm ideas for this series, talked me through difficult days, and then traveled with me to visit Highland Hall–Tyntesfield. It's great to share this journey with you!

- Terri Gillespie, Vickie McDonough, Claudia Gentile, Caty Dovgala-Carr, and Ella Furlong, my fellow authors and dear friends, for providing help with brainstorming and thoughtful critiques. You have helped me so much. I appreciate you!

- Steve Laube, my literary agent, for his patience, guidance, and wise counsel. He has been a great advocate who has represented me well. I feel blessed to be your client.

- Shannon Marchese, Karen Ball, Laura Wright, and Rose Decaen, my gifted editors, who helped me shape the story and then polish it so readers will truly enjoy it.

- Kristopher Orr, the multitalented designer at WaterBrook Multnomah, and Mike Heath, of Magnus Creative, for the lovely cover design. Thanks for inviting me to have input in the process. You did an awesome job, again capturing the mood of the story and my heroine.

- Heather Brown, Amy Haddock, Ashley Boyer, and the entire WaterBrook Multnomah team, for their great work with marketing, publicity, production, and sales. You all are the best!

- My children, Josh, Melinda, Melissa, Peter, Ben, Galan, Megan and Lizzy; and my mother-in-law, Shirley, for the ways you cheer me on. It's great to have a family who love and appreciate each other—and you do!
- Most of all, I thank my Lord and Savior, Jesus Christ, for His grace and provision in my life. I am thankful for the gifts and talents He has given me, and I hope to always use those in ways that bless Him and bring Him the glory and honor.

ABOUT THE AUTHOR

CARRIE TURANSKY has loved reading since she first visited the library as a young child and checked out a tall stack of picture books. Her love for writing began when she penned her first novel at age twelve. She is now the award-winning author of thirteen inspirational romance novels and novellas.

Carrie and her husband, Scott, who is a pastor, author, and speaker, have been married for more than thirty-six years and make their home in New Jersey. They often travel together on ministry trips and to visit their five adult children and four grandchildren. Carrie also leads women's ministry at her church, and when she's not writing she enjoys spending time working in her flower gardens and cooking healthy meals for friends and family.

She loves to connect with reading friends through her website, www.carrieturansky.com, and through Facebook, Pinterest, and Twitter.

Coming soon!

Look for

A REFUGE *at* HIGHLAND HALL

in October 2015.

———•—•————————•—•———